> *"I go where I please.*
> *And no mere duke or one ...*
> *amateurish kiss*
> *can convince me otherwise."*

"Amateurish?" Sebastian echoed, moving up behind her. "You knew it would happen. That's why you came here in person instead of sending a note."

Reaching past her, intentionally brushing her bare arm with his hand, he pulled open the door. "You've been attempting to seduce me since the moment we met."

"*Mentiroso,*" Josefina snapped. "Liar."

"Mm hm. You wanted me to kiss you," he murmured into her ear. "You want me to do so again."

SUZANNE ENOCH

Sins
OF A
Duke

AVON BOOKS
An Imprint of HarperCollins*Publishers*

This is a work of fiction. Names, characters, places, and incidents are products of the author's imagination or are used fictitiously and are not to be construed as real. Any resemblance to actual events, locales, organizations, or persons, living or dead, is entirely coincidental.

AVON BOOKS
An Imprint of HarperCollins*Publishers*
10 East 53rd Street
New York, New York 10022-5299

Copyright © 2007 by Suzanne Enoch
Not Quite A Lady copyright © 2007 by Loretta Chekani; *Sins of a Duke* copyright © 2007 by Suzanne Enoch; *Sleepless at Midnight* copyright © 2007 by Jacquie D'Alessandro; *Twice the Temptation* copyright © 2007 by Suzanne Enoch
ISBN: 978-0-06-084307-6
ISBN-10: 0-06-084307-1
www.avonromance.com

First Avon Books paperback printing: June 2007

Avon Trademark Reg. U.S. Pat. Off. and in Other Countries, Marca Registrada, Hecho en U.S.A
HarperCollins® is a registered trademark of HarperCollins Publishers.

Printed in the U.S.A.

10   9   8   7   6

For everyone who's been waiting,
some patiently and some not,
for Sebastian's story.
You know who you are.
Enjoy.

Chapter 1

June 1813

From the expressions on the faces of the soldiers who marched up from the Horse Guards, someone was in for a bloodbath. With a silent curse Sebastian Griffin, the Duke of Melbourne, galloped past them, reaching his destination a half mile in front of the soldiers. Not much distance, and not much time.

He pulled his bay stallion to a halt and swung to the ground. "Who's in charge here?" he yelled into the wall of noise before him, scarcely noting his two younger brothers and his brother-in-law riding up behind him.

"That would be me," a guttural voice came from the front of the angry crowd. A stout man dressed as most of his fellows were in the worn clothing of farmers and other members of the working class pushed his way through to Sebastian on one side of the crowd. "What d'you want, boy?"

Boy. No one had called him a boy in seventeen years, since he'd inherited the dukedom at the age of seventeen.

He lifted an eyebrow. "I want to know why you think that battering down the gates of Carlton House will gain any of you either food or sympathy for your cause."

"And who the bloody hell are you, to ride up on your fancy horse with your fancy friends?" the fellow demanded.

Sebastian ignored the question, instead turning to face the second group of riders just arriving. "Buy every food item in the market at Picadilly," he instructed his secretary. "Have it delivered to Westminster Abbey."

Rivers nodded, turning his gelding. "Right away, Your Grace."

"Jennings, go with him. I want blankets and a selection of clothing for any who might need them."

"Fast as the wind, Your Grace."

When he faced the large fellow again, a portion of his belligerent expression had been replaced by confusion. "So you think you can give us some bread and a shirt and we'll go away? That is not—"

"There are what, three hundred of you?" Sebastian broke in, taking a moment to look at the dirty, hungry, desperate faces in the crowd and resisting the urge to check over his shoulder for the soldiers. "Go to Westminster, and I'll meet you there. We will sit down like gentlemen and discuss how to keep your people well and fed until your fields can be replanted and the irrigation situation improved."

"I don't—"

"If you persist in attacking the Prince Regent's residence, he will be forced to summon soldiers for his own protection." He held the man's gaze for a moment. "You have children here, sir. Do not make this worse. Not when I give you my word to help you make it better."

"I still don't have your name, sir . . . Your Grace. Don't know that I trust a nobleman."

"I am the Duke of Melbourne. If you know anything

about me, you know that when I give my word, I do not break it."

The fellow took an abrupt step forward. Both Shay and Zachary moved in, but Sebastian motioned his brothers back. These people were desperate, and looking for someone on whom to take out a season's worth of frustrations. Damn Kesling for ignoring the plight of people whose farms bordered his estate. With a measured breath he held out his hand.

The muscles of his jaw jumping, the farmer shook it. "I'm Brown, Your Grace. Nathan Brown. And I have heard of you."

"I will meet you in the Abbey in two hours, Mr. Brown."

Brown nodded. "I'll be there."

At Mr. Brown's encouragement, the crowd began to move east, in the direction of Westminster Abbey. Several of them grabbed his hands, and he smiled and nodded at them as they passed. As the last of them left the Carlton House gates, he took a deep breath.

"Well done, Seb," his youngest brother, Lord Zachary Griffin, commented. "Considering that I only had one pistol with me, that might have been a bit sticky."

"Mm-hm. Shay, go tell the Rector of St. Margaret's that the Abbey will have guests for a day or two."

His middle brother turned for the Abbey. "On my way."

Sebastian swung back up onto Merlin. "So am I. I have a meeting in two hours."

His brother-in-law, Valentine Corbett, Lord Deverill, flashed him a grin. "What do you do on mornings when you're not rescuing the monarchy and feeding the poor and the destitute?"

"I feed Zachary, which can be nearly as perilous," he returned, trotting over to have a word with a shaken-looking secretary of Prinny's as the man appeared on the far side of the gate, flanked by a half dozen equally unnerved royal guards. "The rest of you go back to whatever you were doing. Green will stay with me."

His groomsman nodded, and the rest of his group departed, Zach and Valentine last. Though he pretended not to, he could hear their muttering about the chances he took and what might have happened if Mr. Brown had been armed with more than righteous indignation. As far as he was concerned, though, as a duke, and in particular as the Duke of Melbourne, he was doing no more and no less than his duty to the Crown, and to the people of England. And that was how he spent every morning. And afternoon. And evening.

Once he left Carlton House, passing the soldiers less than a street away from the Regent's residence, he slowed the bay to a civilized trot more suitable for navigating Mayfair. Three streets down they turned onto Grosvenor Square and then up the gated drive of Griffin House. Sliding out of the saddle, Sebastian flipped the reins to Green and strode up the front steps as the groom took Merlin around the house to the stable.

As he reached the front door it opened. "I trust you were successful, Your Grace?" the butler asked, stepping back to allow Sebastian entry.

"Thankfully, Stanton. Is my daughter awake yet?"

"I don't believe so, Your Grace. Shall I send for her?"

"Yes. I want to see her before I leave for Parliament. When Rivers returns, please inform him that we'll have to reschedule our luncheon meeting for tomorrow. I'll need to be at Westminster Abbey for a good part of the day."

"Very good, Your Grace."

Handing over his hat, gloves, and caped greatcoat, Sebastian strolled into the breakfast room. On the sideboard generous piles of bread, fruit, and sliced meats awaited his selection, while the *London Times* had already been ironed flat and set by his place at the head of the table. He chose his meal and then seated himself to read about the latest tariff agreements reached between Britain and the United States, averting any possible renewal of hostilities between the two countries. According to the news writers, apparently His Grace, the Duke of Melbourne, had pressed the government until it came to its senses.

"For the moment, at least," he murmured to himself, gesturing for coffee. One of the pair of footmen hurried forward to pour a steaming cup. Sebastian inhaled deeply before he took a sip. Thank God for the Americas.

"I was awake, Papa," a lilting young voice came from the doorway, and he looked up.

"Good morning, Peep," he said, grinning. "You look very pretty."

At nearly eight years of age, Lady Penelope Griffin had begun to develop her own sense of fashion, and this morning she wore a bright yellow muslin dress dotted with white flowers, and a matching yellow hat covered with a profusion of white daisies. She curtsied to him before she pranced up for a kiss. "I am very fetching, aren't I?" she returned, adjusting her hat.

"I take it you and Mrs. Beacham are attending Mary Haley's birthday party, then?"

"Yes. I'm giving Mary a matching white hat with yellow daffodils."

"You will be the loveliest young ladies in London, then."

She took a peach and two toasted slices of bread from the sideboard, then sat at his elbow. "I think we will be. Might I invite Mary over to tea tomorrow?"

"I thought you were having luncheon with your aunties tomorrow," he said, covering his slight frown.

"Oh, yes. I forgot. My schedule is frightfully busy these days, you know."

For a moment Sebastian gazed at his dark-haired, gray-eyed daughter. It physically hurt to think that in ten years or so her schedule would include outings with beaux and evenings at soirees where he would watch her dance with eager young men.

"Vauxhall has acrobats tomorrow evening," he said a little abruptly. "Why not ask Mary and Lord and Lady Bernard if they'd care to join us there?"

Peep bounced in her chair. "Acrobats? And jugglers?"

"I believe so."

"Yes, please!" She took a large bite of peach, then looked at him sideways. "But you know that Mary's aunt is visiting, and she'll want to join us, and then she'll want to marry you."

Wonderful. "Well, in that case, perhaps we—"

The breakfast room door opened. "Good morning, all," his youngest brother, Zachary, said, sauntering into the room and heading directly for the sideboard.

"When I said you should go home, I meant *your* home," Sebastian observed, smiling at his brother's back. Obviously Zach had been designated to make certain the family patriarch had returned home in one piece.

"Caroline has a morning sitting with the Duke of York. She said my presence would remind him of you, which would remind him that he's not very well liked in the House of Lords."

"Is that because he had favors from that chit, and she made him promote all those soldiers?"

Good God. "What do you know of that, Peep?" Sebastian asked his daughter, sending an annoyed glance at Zachary as his brother took the seat opposite her.

"Uncle Shay said that the Duke should learn to keep his trousers buttoned, and he wouldn't owe women favors. Did she sew up his trousers for him?"

"Exactly," Zach put in, chuckling. "The end result of all

this being that I get to come to Griffin House and have breakfast with my favorite niece."

She shook her dark curls. "You shouldn't say that. What if Aunt Nell and Uncle Valentine heard you? They would be hurt that you don't like Rose as much as you like me."

"Yes, Zachary, how would you ever explain to your sister that her daughter is inferior to mine?" Sebastian prompted, lifting an eyebrow and for the moment pretending that he wasn't supremely grateful to have a bit of adult company about for other than preventing riots. Since Shay had married and left Griffin House last summer, things had been . . . He shook himself. *None of that, now.*

"Well, Rose is lovely, of course, but she's only five months old. You have to admit that her conversation isn't terribly sparkling."

Penelope laughed. "That's because she doesn't have any teeth yet." She reached across the table and patted her uncle's hand. "Don't worry. I'm sure you'll like her better when she gets a bit older."

Zachary smiled back at her. "I'm sure I will. And I appreciate your discretion."

"Of course. I don't want Uncle Valentine to punch you in the head."

"Thank you. Neither do I."

They chatted about nonsense until Sebastian pushed away from the table. "Do you have a moment, Zach?" he asked.

His brother stood. "Certainly. Peep, I'll give you a shilling if you put marmalade on that slice of bread for me."

"Two shillings," she said, reaching for the jar.

"Done."

Sebastian stepped across the hallway to the morning room and half-closed the door as Zachary joined him. "Peep wishes to ask Mary Haley to Vauxhall tomorrow night. Her aunt, Lady Margaret Trent, will likely be joining us."

Zach made a face. "I thought you were going to ask me to help you with Mr. Brown and his very annoyed friends. Of course Caro and I will join you at Vauxhall."

Sighing in relief, Sebastian clapped his brother on the shoulder. "Mr. Brown is simple. Lady Margaret I want to keep my distance from."

"As if any of us want old pinch face added to the family."

"Hm." He lifted an eyebrow. "Not likely to happen regardless of your chaperoning services."

His brother reached back to close the door the rest of the way. "Are you well, Seb? I mean . . . aside from your occasional morning acts of heroics, with just you and Peep living here now, it's—"

"I am not having this conversation." Sebastian clenched his jaw. "So whatever you're implying, don't trouble yourself."

"I see. My apologies. Are you still bringing Caro and me to the Elkins soiree, then, or shall we fend for ourselves?"

"I'll be by with the carriage at eight." Sebastian studied the view out the front window. "And I'm well. I'm adjusting to a smaller household. Again." To anyone outside of his family, he never would have admitted that much.

Zachary cleared his throat. "It's just . . . Don't bite my head off, but within the past two years Nell, Shay, and I have all married. You . . . I don't wish to see you sad when we've all found such happiness." He shrugged. "I know I'm not saying it well, but I do remember, you know. I remember you four years ago when Charlotte died. Just because we've moved out doesn't mean we've abandoned you. The—"

"For God's sake, Zachary," Sebastian retorted, using

every ounce of his infamous self-control to keep his voice cool and level, "I'm not an invalid. And don't try to put yourself in my boots. I've been the head of this family for the past seventeen years. Once you've held that responsibility for even a day, then you can empathize. Until then, you'll have to take me at my word." He took a step closer. "Now, if you'll excuse me, I have to leave for Parliament, then take luncheon with three hundred angry farmers and their families."

Without another word he brushed past his brother, pulled open the door, and returned to the breakfast room. "Peep, my love," he drawled, putting a smile back on his face, "promise me that you'll tell me all about the party today when I return."

She stood up, and he squatted down to hug her. "I promise. You'll be home for dinner?"

"I should be home well before that."

"And then you're going to that ball with Uncle Zachary and everyone."

"I have to, Penelope." He hugged her tighter. "When I give my word to be somewhere and then don't make an appearance, it hurts peoples' feelings." That didn't even begin to explain it, but his daughter still had plenty of time to learn the nuances of being a Griffin and a duke's daughter.

"Very well," she said with a deep sigh, releasing him. "I love you, Papa."

"And I love you, sweetling. Be good."

"I will try."

"Bloody, short-sighted, penny-pinching—"

"Melbourne!"

Drawing his frayed temper back under hard control, Sebastian slowed his exit from the hallway outside the House of Lords. In all the years he'd been attending

Parliamentary sessions, he could only recall a handful of times he'd escaped the building without being hounded for some reason or other. After the way he'd spent the luncheon break, though, he was almost eager for this encounter. "Yes, Kesling?"

The viscount trundled up the hallway, stopping two feet in front of Sebastian and reeking of some kind of French cologne that did little to disguise his overripe body odor. He tightened his control further to keep from taking a step backward.

"Melbourne, I thought you were more progressive-minded than that."

"Than what?"

"You claim to care about the welfare of the common people, and yet every time Prinny asks for funds for one of his follies, you vote to support him. I don't underst—"

This conversation again. "Perhaps you could explain to me, Kesling, why it is that every time a vote arises which places a tax on property, the resulting government income to be used for public relief, *you* vote it down. And that doesn't even begin to explain the callousness with which you treat the people who live on your own land."

"Why should the burden be placed on us, simply because of an accident of birth? It's hardly—"

"Ah, that's the problem, then," Sebastian cut in. "*My* birth wasn't an accident. I'll explain it to you—once. In order for the United Kingdom to remain a power in this growing world, we must be able to progress. For that we need citizens who are educated and content. And in order for the rest of the world to see us as a power, our government must appear to be healthy. This government, therefore, supports its monarch and its people. Or it will, for as long as a Griffin remains in the House of Lords. Good day, Kesling." He turned on his heel.

The front door of Griffin House opened the moment his coach stopped on the drive. "Stanton," he said, stepping to the ground, "has Lady Peep returned yet?"

"Not yet, Your Grace. But you have a note from Carlton House."

The duke lifted it off the silver salver and opened it in the doorway. "When did this arrive?"

"Twenty minutes ago, Your Grace."

He turned around again. "Tollins, wait there," he called, stopping the coach before it could head around to the stables. Sticking the note in his pocket, he reclaimed his hat and gloves. "Please let my daughter know where I've gone, and that I'll return as soon as I can."

The butler inclined his head. "Of course, Your Grace."

With a sigh Sebastian headed back into the streets of Mayfair. He had a good idea what Prinny wanted; whatever the events of the morning, the Regent continued to be obsessed with finishing his pavilion at Brighton regardless of how empty his coffer might be. And today had been the preliminary vote in the House of Lords.

Somewhere along the way Sebastian had moved from being a staunch supporter of the monarchy to being Prince George's confidante and advisor. Despite the occasional inconvenience, it did give him some additional control over the course of the country. And it let him into what seemed to have become a secret: If one could overlook his occasional tantrums and frequent, theatrical dramatics, Prinny was a bright fellow with exquisite taste.

As soon as he arrived at Carlton House one of the attendants ushered him into the formal white room, which was odd. The white room was for guests, and he'd long since ceased being anything that formal. Obviously Prinny had something in mind, though, so Sebastian walked to the window that overlooked the garden and waited.

He was still standing there five minutes later when the door opened again. "Melbourne!" Prinny's familiar voice came, "I hadn't realized you were here. No doubt you have some pressing matters to discuss with me."

Sebastian faced the Regent, masking his confusion with a smile as he realized Prinny had a dozen people following him into the room. Ah, so now he was an ornament for tourists. "I do, Your Highness," he agreed, bowing.

"I'll be with you in just a moment, then," Prinny returned. "First, I would like to present His Majesty Stephen Embry, Rey of Costa Habichuela. Also his wife, Queen Maria. Your Majesties, His Grace, the Duke of Melbourne, one of my closest advisors."

The man standing at the forefront of the entourage stepped forward and offered his hand. "Very pleased, Your Grace," he said, in an accent that sounded distinctly Cornish.

Hm. As far as Sebastian knew, Cornwall had not seceded from England and altered its name. "Your Majesty," he returned, shaking hands.

In addition to his accent, the rey was tall with yellow hair, a golden moustache, and decidedly English features despite his Hispanic title. He wore a striking black military-looking uniform, as did the four men who surrounded the group. His was differentiated by a narrow white sash over his left shoulder and tassled at his right hip. Several obvious military decorations adorned the sash, all of them dominated by a simple green cross at his breast.

Unlike her escort, the lady with her hand on the rey's arm was clearly of Spanish decent—tall, black-haired, olive-skinned, and brown-eyed. Queen Maria, undoubtedly.

"May I ask where Costa Habichuela is located?" he asked after a moment, focusing on the rey.

"Ah, glad you asked," Embry returned, smiling. "We're on the eastern coast of Central America. A wondrous place, really. I was greatly honored when the Mosquito King deeded it to me and my heirs."

This was the third country to be formed in South or Central America over the past year and a half, then. "The Mosquito King," he repeated. "That would put your territory along the Mosquito Coast."

"Yes, very good, Your Grace. You know your geography."

"It's a much less well-known fact, however," a soft, feminine voice slid in from the left of the rey, "that the area is named after a group of small islands known as the Mosquitos rather than after the insect."

Sebastian turned his head. Brown eyes gazed into his. Deep brown, like rich, newly turned soil in the springtime, set into a face the color of fresh cream, smooth and flawless. And her hair, long and loose with a hint of curl, the flowing mass as black as a raven's wings.

"Your Grace," the rey's voice broke in, "my daughter, Princess Josefina Katarina Embry."

Blinking, Sebastian mentally pulled himself back. He felt distant, off balance, as though he'd been staring for an hour—but it must have been less than a minute. "Your Highness," he intoned, bowing.

She returned a shallow curtsy, her eyes glittering as though she knew precisely the effect she'd had on him. "Your Grace."

"The rey and his family are here to secure some loans," Prinny put in. He clapped his beefy hands together. "You know, Melbourne, you would be the perfect contact for that. I'm appointing you British liaison to Costa Habichuela. How do you like that?"

Not much at all. "I'm honored, Your Highness," Sebastian said aloud, setting a cool smile on his face. "I'm not certain how much actual assistance I'll be able to provide, but I'm happy to lend my advice—such as it is."

"Splendid. You're attending the Elkins soiree tonight, are you not?"

"I had planned to."

"Then you'll escort our new friends there. Unfortunately, I have a previous engagement, or I would do so, myself."

For a moment Sebastian wondered whether Prinny considered just how much legitimacy he was granting this new country by involving the Duke of Melbourne in the rey's introduction to London Society, but in almost the same instant he knew the answer. What Prince George saw was an opportunity to impress a few foreigners with his generosity and influence.

"It would be my pleasure," he said, because at the moment he didn't have any alternative.

"I'm afraid Queen Maria and I also have a previous obligation," the rey said with an apologetic look.

Thank God. "I'm sorry to hear th—"

"Princess Josefina, however, will do a fine job of representing Costa Habichuela in our stead."

"Yes, it would be my pleasure," the rich voice came again.

A responding shiver ran down Sebastian's spine. "Then tell me where you're staying, and I shall be by at eight o'clock."

"Josefina, please see to it," the rey said, turning to ask Prinny about one of the many white marble figures lining the room.

"We're presently lodging at the home of Colonel Winston Branbury, until we find a suitable consulate," the princess said, taking Sebastian's arm.

"Branbury. I know it." He didn't want to stand still, so he walked them away from the others, toward the nearest window.

"Good. I would be incapable of providing directions,"

she continued with a smile, "being a stranger to London, myself."

He found himself staring at her mouth, at her full lips with their slight Spanish pout. "Don't worry yourself," he forced out. "My coach will arrive at Branbury House promptly at eight."

Her smile deepened. "I do like a prompt gentleman. Rumor has it, Your Grace, that you performed some heroics this morning."

Sebastian shook his head. "I performed my duty. That's all."

"Ah. Gallant and modest."

Attractive—mesmerizing—as she was, Princess Josefina conversed in the same way, and seemed impressed by the same things, as any other woman of his acquaintance. But those eyes . . . "My gallantry has yet to be proven," he said, freeing his arm from her fingers and glad she wore gloves. He had the distinct feeling that her flesh would burn his. He backed to the door. "Until this evening."

Out in the corridor, Sebastian leaned back against the wall to catch his breath. He felt abruptly as though he'd run all the way from Marathon. What the devil was wrong with him?

Firstly, he should have realized what Prinny's intentions were and excused himself from participating. Secondly, he was not some fresh-faced schoolboy. He was four-and-thirty, for God's sake. And he'd set eyes on pretty chits before. He'd married one. And he hadn't felt as . . . off-kilter since then. Even ordinary conversation with her felt unique.

Shaking himself, he pushed upright and headed for the front entrance of Carlton House. He'd been put in an unfortunate position, but he would deal with it in the same way he did everything else in his life—swiftly and efficiently. As for the rest, he'd turned ignoring anything other than family and business into an art form. Putting Josefina Katarina Embry aside would be no challenge at all. He wouldn't allow it to be.

Chapter 2

Sebastian climbed into the coach opposite his brother and sister-in-law. "Shall we?"

Zachary rapped on the ceiling, and the coach jolted into motion. "Are you going to tell us?" he prodded after a moment of silence.

"Tell you what?"

"Why we're in my coach tonight. Peep's not eloping in yours, is she?"

"I sent it to bring someone to the soiree."

"Who?"

"Zachary," his wife, Lady Caroline, chastised.

As far as Sebastian was concerned, the less said about any of this, the better. His brother, however, was more curious than a cat, and possessed the tenacity of a bulldog. He would have to tell them something. "I'm doing a favor for Prinny."

"I thought you already did one of those this morning."

Sebastian ignored the comment. "He asked me to escort a foreign dignitary to the party."

"And again, why are you in *my* coach?"

"Because it wouldn't be seemly for me to be in mine." And because he didn't care for a repeat of the oddness that had come over him earlier, the feeling of being supremely focused and completely scattered all at the same time, heat burrowing into his skin.

"It's a female someone, then."

Sebastian yanked himself back to the conversation in time to lift an eyebrow. "Your mental acuity continues to amaze me."

"Doesn't the chit have a maid or something? That would remove any appearance of impro—"

"I'm sure she does," the duke countered. "I opted to share a ride with the two of you, though now I'm beginning to think your wife and I might have done very well without you."

Zach scowled. "I only asked a question."

Caroline patted him on the knee. "You were prying."

"You can't pry when it's family." He shifted on the leather seat. "So how ugly is this chit?"

"Zachary!"

Flashing a quick grin at his wife, Zachary sat back again. "That's it, isn't it? A foreign dignitary that Prinny pawned off on you for the evening. She must be an absolute rotten sack of potatoes. You don't have to dance with her, do you? Or is she gouty? Probably. The—"

"Caroline, how goes your portrait of the Duke of York?" Sebastian broke in.

"Quite well, thank you. As long as no one reminds him that I'm now part of the Griffin family, we get on famously."

"I don't know why you're avoiding the subject, Seb," Zachary attempted again. "We're going to see her at the party. And I am going to stick to you like spots on a leopard until you introduce me."

A shiver ran down Sebastian's spine. Reluctance? Dread? Anticipation? He didn't know. But the sensation wasn't a pleasant one, regardless. "Do as you will," he said coolly. "Just know that Willits and Fennerton will be dogging me as well, so you'll all have to stand there together."

Zachary wrinkled his nose. "Fennerton?"

"Fennerton."

As they disembarked from the coach, Sebastian put the dark-eyed image of Princess Josefina away from his thoughts again. Hopefully being the liaison to Costa Habichuela would involve nothing more than introducing the rey to Sir Henry Sparks at the Bank of England. For tonight, as a matter of courtesy he was providing transportation and an arm to hang on. Nothing more. And the unsettled feeling in his gut was purely due to something he'd eaten. Most likely it had been the fricandos of veal Cook had served up at dinner.

"Shay and Sarala are here," Zachary noted, raising an arm as the middle Griffin brother and his wife approached.

"Did you hear," Charlemagne said without preamble, "that Prinny's been named something called an honorary Knight of the Green Cross? He's apparently over the moon about the royals from some new South American country—Costa something. Even appointed one of his minions their translator or some such nonsense."

Damnation. "Liaison," Sebastian corrected stiffly. Of course the more politically active Shay would have a better idea of what was going on than Zach. "To Costa Habichuela."

"You?" Zachary choked.

"Yes, me. I don't expect it will entail much, and Prinny requested it of me."

"Still, Seb," Shay countered, his expression a combination of amusement and surprise, "appointing the Duke of Melbourne any kind of liaison to . . . what? I've never even heard of it." He stepped closer, lowering his voice. "Is Prinny angry with you for stepping in this morning?"

Usually Sebastian would never have tolerated anyone speculating about his duties and motives. Tonight, though, Shay was probably only echoing what the rest of his peers were or would be saying once they heard the news. If he wanted to stop any unflattering comments, he needed to know what they were likely to be.

"No, Prinny's not angry with me," he returned. "A new, apparently stable regime in the southern Americas is a rarity, and especially one that favors England. I don't know all that much about it yet, but I do know that if England doesn't provide what they need, they may go elsewhere— France, for example. Besides, if the rey gets his loan here, it could be a potentially lucrative opportunity for trade and even settlement."

"Lucrative?" Shay repeated, his light gray eyes beginning to gleam.

Beside him, Sarala grinned. " 'Potentially lucrative,' " she corrected. "I believe that means wait and see, does it not, Sebastian?"

He nodded. "I am glad you two have married ladies with sense, as you clearly have none on your own." A ripple of movement by the ballroom doors drew his attention, and he caught a glimpse of raven-black hair.

"That's hardly fair, when y—"

"Excuse me," he said, cutting Zachary off.

Princess Josefina, a maid and one of the black-uniformed men flanking her, faced him as he approached. Tonight she wore a rich yellow gown, low cut enough that the creamy mounds of her breasts heaved as she drew a breath. God, she was spectacular. Of course that didn't signify anyth—

She slapped him.

Sebastian blinked, clenching his rising hands against the immediate instinct to retaliate. The blow stung, but of more concern was the responding roar from the onlookers in the Elkins ballroom. He looked directly into her dark brown eyes. "Never do that again," he murmured, curving his lips in a smile that felt more like a snarl.

"My father and your Regent made a very simple request of you," she snapped, no trace of the soft-spoken flirt of this afternoon in either her voice or her expression. "If you are incapable of meeting even such low expectations, I will see you relieved of your duties to Costa Habichuela immediately, before you can do any harm with your incompetence."

It took every ounce of his hard-earned self-control to remain standing there, unmoving. No one—*no one*—had ever spoken to him like that. As for hitting him . . . He clenched his jaw. "If you would care to accompany me off the dance floor," he said in a low voice, unable to stop the slight shake of his words, "I believe I can correct your misapprehension."

"*My* misapprehension? I, sir, am a royal princess. You are only a duke. And I am most displeased."

The circle of the audience that surrounded them drew closer, the ranks swelling until it seemed that now people were coming in off the streets to gawk. Sebastian drew a deep breath in through his nose. "Come with me," he repeated, no longer requesting, "and we will resolve our differences in a civilized manner."

"First you will apologize to me," the princess retorted, her chin lifting further.

All he needed to do was turn his back and walk away. The crowd would speculate, rumors would spread, but in the end his reputation and power would win the argument for him. As far as he was concerned, though, that would be cheating. And he wanted the victory here. He wanted *her* apology, *her* surrender, *her* mouth, *her* body. Slowly he straightened his fingers. "I apologize for upsetting you,

Your Highness. Please join me in the library so we may converse." He reached for her wrist.

The princess drew back, turning her shoulder to him. "I did not give you permission to touch me."

At the moment he wanted to do so much more than touch her wrist. God. It was as though when she hit him, she'd seared his flesh down to the bone. "Then we are at an impasse," he returned, still keeping his voice low and even, not letting anyone see what coursed beneath his skin, "because I am not going to continue this conversation in the middle of a ballroom."

She looked directly into his eyes. Despite his anger, the analytical part of him noted that very few people ever met him straight on. Whatever she saw there, her expression eased a little. "Perhaps then instead of conversing, we should dance."

Dance. He wanted to strangle her, and she wanted to dance. It did admittedly provide the best way out of this with the fewest rumors flying. The rumors it *would* begin, though, he didn't like. Was she aware that she was making this look like some sort of lover's quarrel? He couldn't very well ask her. Instead he turned his head to find Lord Elkins. "Could you manage us a waltz, Thomas?" he asked, giving an indulgent smile. "Princess Josefina would like to dance."

"Of course, Your Grace." The viscount waved at the orchestra hanging over the balcony to gawk at the scene below. "Play a waltz!"

Stumbling over one another, the players sat and after one false start, struck up a waltz. That would solve the yelling, but not the spectacle. "May I?" Sebastian intoned, holding out his hand again.

After a deliberate hesitation, the princess reached out and placed her gloved fingers into his bare ones. "For this dance only."

With her now in his grasp, the urge to show her just who was in command nearly overpowered him. Mentally steeling himself, he slid a hand around her waist, in the same moment sending a glance over his shoulder at Shay. "Dance," he mouthed. Not for all of heaven and earth would he prance about the floor alone.

"Are you going to explain to me why you sent a carriage without bothering to attend me yourself?" Princess Josefina asked.

"Your English is surprisingly good for a foreigner," he said deliberately. "As a native, allow me to give you a little advice. No matter who—"

"I will not—"

"—you may be elsewhere," he continued in a low voice, tightening his grip on her as she tried to pull away, "you should consider that in England you do not strike a nobleman in public."

"For *your* information," she returned in the same tone, "my English is perfect because until two years ago I *was* English, raised mostly in Jamaica. And I will strike anyone who insults me."

That settled it. She was a lunatic. "You're mad," he said aloud. "I can conceive of no other explanation as to why you would speak to me in such a manner."

She lifted an elegant eyebrow. "If I am the only one who tells you the truth, that does not make me mad. It makes everyone else around you cowards."

The muscles of his jaw were clenched so tightly they ached. "I should—"

"You should what, Melbourne?" she cut in, her gaze unexpectedly lowering to his mouth. "Arguing with me excites you, doesn't it?" She drew a breath closer in his arms. "And there is nothing you can do about it, is there?" she whispered, lifting her eyes to his again. Abruptly the smooth-voiced seductress of earlier swayed gracefully in his arms.

She felt the attraction between them as strongly as he did. That realization should have made the dance, the conversation, the looking at her easier, but it didn't. Just the opposite. As Sebastian spun her about the polished dance floor, his focus narrowed until all he could think of, all he could imagine, was Princess Josefina naked and spread beneath him, begging for him, begging for mercy, begging for release. He'd never felt so close to the edge of his famous control as he did at that moment.

"Come now, duke," she cajoled, "do you have nothing to say at all?"

"I prefer action to words," he ground out.

"Do you, now? What sort of action?"

Princess Josefina Embry just barely kept herself from wetting her lips. Only the look in Melbourne's eyes, and the suspicion that he would jump on her right there in the middle of the ballroom kept her from doing so. The stays on her gown felt so confining that she could barely breathe. All afternoon she'd anticipated . . . him. The touch of his fingers as he handed her into his coach, the witty banter they would exchange on the way to the ball—the kind of banter she'd missed and longed for while spending the last three weeks crossing the Atlantic Ocean in a very cramped ship with only sailors and her father's people for company.

And then his carriage had arrived—without him inside.

"I don't wish to further offend Your Highness by describing the action I'm imagining," Melbourne returned in a low, sensual growl.

A tremor ran down her spine. Did he have any idea how his mere presence must affect women? Dark brown hair just curling where it brushed his collar, that tall, lean, hard figure, those high cheekbones and that Roman aristocrat's chiseled nose and jaw, and especially those glittering, storm-gray eyes—how could he not know? He could have any female he wanted. He probably did, whenever he chose.

"You've already offended me," she goaded, trying to keep her voice steady. "Answering my question couldn't possibly make matters worse. What action would you take against me?"

He lowered his head toward her, so she could feel his breath warm against her skin, their mouths only inches apart. "You're panting for it, aren't you, Princess?" he murmured.

The music crashed to a crescendo and stopped. Everyone began applauding.

"You'll have to imagine," he whispered, brushing her ear with his mouth as he released her. "Because next time, you'll have to ask *my* permission for a touch." Straightening and stepping back in the same motion, he gestured her toward the side of the room where Conchita and Lieutenant May stood waiting.

Blast him, the devil. "You are still my escort for this evening, Melbourne," she countered before he could vanish somewhere. "Pray do try to remember that."

The duke sketched a bow, just deep enough to avoid insult, and shallow enough to make clear that he was doing no more and no less than custom dictated. "Of course." He gestured to someone out of her line of sight. "Allow me to introduce you to our host and hostess for the evening, Lord and Lady Elkins. Thomas, Mary, Princess Josefina of Costa Habichuela."

"You do us great honor, Your Highness," the viscountess gushed, sinking into a deep, reverential curtsy.

That was more like it. "I'm very pleased to meet you," she said, putting into her tone all of the graciousness she refused to grant Melbourne. Every fiber of her seemed aware of him, and the angrier and less controlled he became, the more she liked it. Not quite the course of action her mother had recomended, but she couldn't deny that the results excited and aroused her. *He* aroused her.

"You must meet everyone," Lady Elkins continued, reaching out as if to take Josefina's arm and then obviously reconsidering. "If you'll join me, Your Highness?"

"Yes, of course," Josefina replied, and snapped her fingers at Melbourne. "Don't wander too far, Duke."

He favored her with a hard smile. "I wouldn't dream of it, Princess."

Good. Deliberately holding himself in check or not, at least the Duke of Melbourne understood his place. As for who would ask permission to touch whom, she would see about that.

Chapter 3

As Lady Elkins led Princess Josefina into the admiring crowd, Sebastian turned his back and headed for the nearest floor-length window that opened onto the grounds. It was closed, but he shoved it open and stepped outside onto the stone terrace. Shaking, he clenched the granite balustrade in front of him so hard his knuckles showed white.

"Seb?"

He closed his eyes, trying to slow his breathing and the beat of his heart. "Go away," he grunted.

Instead he heard the crunch of boots on old leaves as Charlemagne walked closer. "Apologies. People are talking, and I'm having a bit of trouble coming up with an explanation as to why Her Highness would hit you. Any suggestions?"

"Let it be."

Shay cleared his throat. "Are you certain about that? The look you gave her when you were dan—"

Sebastian whipped around to face his younger brother.

"What look?" he snapped. If he couldn't rid himself of this frustration, he was going to burst.

"Christ, Melbourne. Nothing."

"What look, Shay?" he pressed. Angry, frustrated, aroused—whatever the devil she'd done to him, he couldn't think straight. He advanced on his brother. "What?"

"Fine. Lust. You—you looked like you wanted to throw her on the floor and . . . I know that's not you, but half a hundred people saw—"

"Lust," Sebastian interrupted again. Heat burned just beneath his skin. Lust made sense. "Let them say what they will. My reputation can withstand the charge that I had a lustful look on my face."

With a nod, Shay stepped backward. "Don't kill me, but are you well? How about a whiskey? I'll fetch you one."

The duke looked at his brother for a long moment. "It may surprise you, but on rare occasion I do have baser thoughts."

"You're human, Seb. I know you'd like us all to forget that sometimes, but you are."

If this chaos was being human, he didn't like it. "Whatever thoughts I might entertain, I have no intention of acting on them. So go back inside with me, and laugh."

"Laugh?"

"Yes. We're highly amused by the eccentricities of Princess Josefina." Putting his usual calm expression back on his face, he threw an arm across Charlemagne's shoulders and steered him back in the direction of the ballroom. "So laugh, dammit."

Whatever the devil the princess thought to accomplish by attacking and baiting him, she would learn that she'd just engaged in battle with a master. If she knew what was best, she would immediately surrender. Of course, considering how close he'd been to physical embarrassment earlier, the wisest course of action for himself would be to call the meeting a draw and stay as far away from her as possible.

However strong his resolve to be untouched by any of this, the rest of the Griffin clan remained annoyingly attentive. The moment he convinced Shay to go away, Zachary and Caroline appeared. At least they served to distract him from the damned princess.

"It's as bloody hot as Hades in here," Zachary complained, tugging on his elegant white cravat and clearly doing his damnedest to avoid talking about anything significant.

"Of course it is," Sebastian returned, keeping his back to the dance floor and whomever Princess Josefina might be dancing with. "You know how Lady Elkins feels about air from out-of-doors."

"At least you could have the good grace to sweat, Seb."

It was his internal temperature that troubled him tonight. "I'm a duke; I don't sweat," he offered. "Go dance with your wife."

"I'm keeping you company."

"You're keeping an eye on me, you mean."

"All I'm saying is that Shay and I wrestled for it, and I lost."

Beyond Zachary's shoulder a pair of cabinet ministers hovered, red-faced and sweating. Sebastian swiftly hid a frown of his own before it could alter his expression. Truthfully, after that slap he'd thought he would be mobbed with members of Parliament, all of them convinced that he must be weakening and that the Elkins ball was the time and place to attack. He only hoped one of them *would* anger him—he had a great deal of ire bottled up and waiting to explode.

"Your Grace," a sweet, feminine voice cooed behind him, "surely you might take pity on a poor miss without a partner for the quadrille."

Setting an amiable expression on his face, he turned around. "Lady Frederica. You look lovely this evening."

The young lady curtsied, all burgundy gown and coiled blonde hair and impossibly long eyelashes. "Thank you, Your Grace. That's very kind of you."

"I would be pleased to escort you to the refreshment table, my lady, but I won't be dancing again this evening."

He knew the rules, and he knew how to use them to his advantage. He'd danced with the princess, but that could be seen as a clear exception. If he danced with Lady Frederica, however, every other lady present would with good reason assume he would be just as willing to partner with them. By refusing the first request he received, they should likewise all understand that he wished to be left alone.

He knew why they pursued him, but for God's sake, after four years they should realize he had no intention of remarrying. The only way he could make it more clear was to hang a sign around his neck, and that would ruin his cravat.

Lady Frederica reddened. "Of course, Your Grace. An escort would be welcome."

Very well, so now he would have to chat with a few of the other stubborn, marriage-hunting females prowling about tonight. It was still better than having to dance with them—and far easier to conclude.

And that was a good thing. He had enough on his plate this evening. As he looked up, he caught Princess Josefina gazing at him. Their eyes mét, and she swiftly turned away. If she knew what was good for her, she wouldn't protest when he sent her home all by herself. Because calm as he might look now on the outside, inside he felt just short of a predatory lion. And this lion intended to keep his pride intact.

* * *

"How was your evening, daughter?"

Josefina handed her cloak to her maid, Conchita, and made her way into the room her father had commandeered for his office. "It was abysmal," she said, sinking into the chair across the desk from him. "I don't know where you heard that the Duke of Melbourne would be able to help you forward the development of Costa Habichuela, but I found him to be aloof, rude, and arrogant." Well, not aloof, perhaps, but definitely the other two.

She still fairly shook with unreleased tension, but except for blasted Melbourne, she'd done Costa Habichuela proud this evening, if she did say so herself. And she'd meant to be nicer to him. If he hadn't surprised her by not appearing in person to escort her and then by simply walking up as though he owned the world, she would have reacted differently.

Or she thought she would have. Something about him just . . . sent her off-kilter. Insulting as his parting words were, perhaps it would be for the best if they simply avoided one another from now on. She certainly had enough to do without battling dastards.

"His assistance could mean the difference between success and failure," the rey replied on the tail of her thoughts. "And I doubt we'll find a more worthy spouse for you anywhere in England."

"That may be a bit much to expect. He makes me uncomfortable."

He looked up from the map that covered the desk between them. "That's good. It will keep you on your toes. Complacency never led to anything but failure." The rey smiled. "And just remember, though our royal ascension may be recent, we *are* royalty. And however arrogant he may be or how uncomfortable he makes you, your blood is bluer than his."

"I think ice runs in his veins and not blood at all, but yes, I remember."

Her father nodded. "That's all I ask. Now get some sleep. We have a very full day planned for tomorrow."

Rising, Josefina stepped around the table to kiss her father on the cheek. After three weeks on a ship from Jamaica, two days in a bumpy coach from Brighton, and one very long day in London, she could use some sleep. And she hoped that whatever her father had planned for tomorrow *did* include Melbourne. Perhaps they didn't like one another, but she would not be the one to concede defeat. That would be for him to do.

"No. I won't pay a penny more than four shillings a sack," Sebastian said, reaching for a paper at his elbow.

"It's rumored to be a very high-quality crop." Shay made a note in the ledger book in front of him. "We paid three shillings eight last year."

"It's coffee beans, Shay. Not gold dust. Four shillings. I doubt they'll find a better price elsewhere. Let them look."

The middle Griffin brother nodded. "That's all I have for now, then." Slowly he closed the ledger. "So are we ever going to discuss last night?"

Sebastian cleared his throat. "No, we are not. I was forced by duty to dance with a lunatic, and I did so. The end."

"But you were attracted to her; that was obvious."

"Was it?" he asked sharply.

"To me. To the family, I mean. Caro nearly slapped Zachary, his jaw was hanging open so far. No one else noticed a thing, I'm certain."

"She's pretty." He stood, practically shoving Charlemagne out of the opposite chair and into the hallway. "And a lunatic. I find the combination at first glance intriguing, and at second glance horrific."

"All the same, Seb, it's been a long—"

"Stop it," Sebastian interrupted. "I loved Charlotte. I still love her. With you and Zach and Eleanor married and procreating, and with Peep nearly eight, the Griffin bloodline is secure. That would be my only reason for pursuing anyone, and I'm grateful to all three of you for saving me from being placed in that position."

"Still, even if you aren't interested in remarrying, there is still the fact that sex is fun." Charlemagne made a face. "Not with the lunatic, I mean, but there are any number of—"

"Have I *ever* given the impression that I require your advice or assistance with anything regarding women?" For God's sake, one slap from that . . . female and his own family thought he'd lost his ability to reason. He could only imagine what the rest of his peers must be thinking. And that, unfortunately, could be a problem.

"Of course not. But the thing is, you haven't shown the slightest interest since Charlotte died."

"I believe that to be my affair. To you I'll admit that Princess Josefina surprised me last night. From now on I'll stay out of slapping range." Sebastian forced a smile. "And I won't be sorry to see her gone, something which will hopefully come about sooner rather than later."

Shay spent another moment gazing at him. Sebastian didn't know what he might be looking to see—regret? Evidence of prevarication?—but he wouldn't see anything his older brother didn't wish him to.

"Fine," Charlemagne finally said, walking down the hallway. "You're the one who can read minds, not me. You can hardly blame us for wanting to see you happy, though."

"I am content," Sebastian returned diplomatically. "And at any rate, bedding a mad woman would not be conducive to my continued peace of mind."

"I'll write Prask with our offer. I imagine he'll accept it, since you're right about the price."

"I'm always right."

As he walked Shay out the front door, he could feel the relative emptiness of Griffin House pushing against his shoulders. Peep was there, and servants aplenty, but it was a bloody large house for just Penelope and him to rattle around in.

"Melbourne?"

He started. "Apologies, Shay. What were you saying?"

"I just asked if you were still going to Almack's tonight."

"Prinny sent a note asking me to escort the Costa Habichuela contingent there, so yes, I suppose I am. I had to cancel my visit to Vauxhall with Peep. Lord and Lady Bernard are taking her and Mary Haley."

"I wager it was a close choice, though, Lady Margaret Trent or Her Highness." Shay shot him a brief grin. "You might want to put on Great-grandfather Harold's suit of armor before you go."

"I'll consider it."

Chuckling, Shay clapped him on the shoulder and made his way down the front steps to his horse. A moment later he was gone down the street. Sebastian watched for a moment, then turned back inside.

"Any letters, Stanton?" he asked, as the butler closed the door behind him.

"Yes, Your Grace." Stanton lifted the salver off the foyer table. A pile of hand-delivered missives and invitations and calling cards awaited his attention. His secretary, Rivers, would have taken the business correspondence, which meant all of these here were social.

He scooped up the lot of them. "Thank you."

"Very good. And Your Grace? I was instructed to inform you that Lady Penelope requests an audience at your earliest convenience."

Sebastian grinned. "Where is she?"

"In the music room with Mrs. Beacham—and an unnamed friend."

"Unnamed?"

"At Lady Penelope's request, Your Grace."

Dropping his correspondence off in his office, Sebastian climbed the stairs to the first floor. Even from the far end of the house and through the closed door he could hear the pianoforte. Either Peep's playing had vastly improved since yesterday, or the unnamed friend was playing—and quite well.

"Please don't let it be Lady Margaret Trent," he muttered, and pushed open the door. "You wanted to see me, P—" he began, and clamped his mouth shut.

His daughter danced a jig across the floor, but she wasn't what caught his immediate, startled, attention. Sitting at the pianoforte, an easy smile on her face as her fingers flew nimbly across the keys, was *her.* The lunatic. Princess Josefina Embry. The low tug began again in his gut.

"Papa, look!" Peep gestured toward the instrument. "She's a princess."

"Yes, I know. We've met." Belatedly he sketched a bow. "Your Highness."

Still playing, she inclined her head. "Melbourne."

"If I might ask," he said, sending an annoyed glance at Mrs. Beacham, "what are you doing in my music room?"

"I came to see you, actually."

"I saw her at the door," Peep took up, "and told her you were closeted with Uncle Shay. And then she said she was Princess Josefina, so I invited her to come listen while I took my music lesson. She grew up in Jamaica, and she knows pirate music."

"That's not pirate music," Sebastian corrected. "It's a sailor's jig." He returned his gaze to the princess, aware that he didn't like having her in his house—which was odd, considering the number of parliamentary members whom he personally detested but had welcomed in over a brandy simply to gain their support on some matter or another. "Where did a royal princess learn a jig, if I might ask?"

She finished with a flourish. "I wasn't always a princess. My father was only granted Costa Habichuela and proclaimed rey by its people two years ago."

He took a step closer as she stood. She'd worn a white sprig muslin dotted with a rainbow of spring flowers, a green cross sewn onto the left sleeve. "And what were you before you became a princess?"

"The daughter of a much-decorated and well-beloved army colonel, and the granddaughter of a Venezuelan viceroy," she returned, lifting her chin. "What were you before you became a duke?"

"A duke's son." And the Marquis of Halpern, but that didn't signify at the moment. He knew the point she was attempting to make.

"Hm. So my father earned his royalty by acclaim, and you inherited your title."

"And what did you do to gain yours, Your Highness?"

She sniffed. "And to think, I came here with the idea of asking for peace between us, and you only continue to insult me."

"Did you insult her, Papa?" Peep asked from beside Mrs. Beacham, where both had been watching the exchange, wide-eyed.

"Not until she slapped me."

"You hit my papa?" Peep exclaimed, her gray eyes narrowing. "He's the Duke of Melbourne—the greatest man in England!"

Princess Josefina's gaze hadn't left his face. "England is a very small country, my dear."

"You—"

"Mrs. Beacham," Sebastian interrupted, "please remove Lady Penelope and yourself immediately."

The governess gave a hurried curtsy and pulled Peep to the door. "At once, Your Grace." As the door swung to behind them, he heard her continue. "And that is why we do not invite strangers into the house, young lady."

"But she said she was a prin—" The door clicked shut.

Sebastian took a deep, hopefully steadying breath. "Since you are unchaperoned, Your Highness, allow me to escort you outside. I will provide my coach for you if you wish, and then I will send a note to Prinny explaining that for personal reasons I must decline his offer of a position aiding your country's government."

Considering that as head of the Griffin family he could probably buy and sell her little country, he expected a swift apology and a hasty retreat. Instead the princess stalked up to him, hands on her hips. "Good! I'm certain your Regent could find someone more qualified than you by looking in the nearest brothel!"

"Enough," he snarled, striding forward. She would stop insulting him.

Sebastian grabbed her by the shoulders. He yanked her forward. And then he kissed her.

He wasn't delicate about it, either. The princess shoved against his chest, then groaned and swept her arms up behind his neck, tangling her fingers into his hair. God, her lips were soft and warm, melting against his. Heated arousal swirled down his spine. Holding her hard against his body, he nudged her mouth open with his tongue, tasting and plundering.

With another shuddering moan from her that had his cock straining at his trousers, Princess Josefina abruptly pushed him away so hard that he stumbled. *"Maldita sea!"* she exclaimed, her gaze focused on his mouth. "What the devil do you think you're doing?"

Christ, what was wrong with him? "It seemed the most effective way to shut you up," he panted, wiping the back of his hand across his mouth.

"You—for my father's sake, I will say nothing of this," she managed, straightening the front of her gown and belatedly backing away from him. "You had best do the same."

"Don't fret about that," he returned feelingly.

"But you now owe me a good turn," she stated.

"How is that?"

"You assaulted me!"

"I did no such thing."

"Bah! My father has set an appointment to see Sir Henry Sparks today, and he asks that you join him at the Bank of England at three o'clock. I do not wish to have to tell him why you chose to decline, so I will expect you to be there, Duke." She retrieved her reticule from the seat of the pianoforte. "Is that clear?"

Ruthlessly he squelched his flaring desire. If he grabbed her again, he wouldn't stop at a kiss. "Abundantly clear. I can only hope, however, that you will be elsewhere."

She stopped halfway to the music room door. "I go where I please. And no mere duke or one . . . amateurish kiss can convince me otherwise."

"'Amateurish'?" he echoed, moving up behind her. "You knew it would happen. That's why you came here in person instead of sending a note." Reaching past her, intentionally brushing her bare arm with his hand, he pulled open the door. "You've been attempting to seduce me since the moment we met."

"Mentiroso," she snapped. "Liar."

"Mm-hm. You wanted me to kiss you," he murmured

into her ear, blocking her way with his shoulder. "You want me to do so again."

"I cannot be responsible for your flights of imagination, Melbourne. Now move aside."

He stepped sideways, letting her pass. Sebastian watched her hips sway as she descended the stairs. "Stanton, hire Her Highness a hack," he instructed. Whatever she was up to, it seemed to have something to do with connecting herself to him. He would therefore take steps to minimize that.

"Right away, Your Grace."

For a second she turned to stare back up at him, her brown eyes glinting. "Bah," she finally muttered, and stomped out the door behind the butler.

As he turned around he caught sight of another of the footmen, taking firewood into the drawing room. "John, when Stanton returns to his post, please inform him that I am not to be disturbed," he grunted, and clomped down the stairs to his office without waiting for an answer.

He'd thought that—well, he hadn't thought at all, in the music room—once he kissed Josefina he would understand her nature, seductive and demure one moment, and a direct, confrontational force of nature the next, and be able to set her aside. After kissing her, though, the foremost thought in his mind was that he wanted to do so again. Badly.

Chapter 4

Josefina lowered the magnifier and looked up at her father. "Are you certain Mr. Halloway hasn't done this all his life?" she asked with a smile in the clerk's direction. "Father always said you were a fine army clerk, but I believe legal documents are your forté."

The clerk blushed. "Thank you, Your Highness. I've been studying English property law."

"It shows."

"We'll have nearly a hundred of the bonds for our meeting this afternoon."

The clerk made a quick calculation on a piece of scrap paper. "One hundred thirty-seven, by three o'clock, Your Majesty."

"Splendid."

Josefina took her father's arm as they left the back rooms of Colonel Branbury's house. "Who would have thought that making a country would require so much ink?"

He chuckled. "I never would have, if I hadn't watched so

many other movements rise and fall. It's all well and good to declare independence from Spain and set up a government based on strong principles. But Spain has principles, as well, and even more importantly, they have an army."

"An army you've fought on numerous occasions."

"Under Diego Rivera and Simon Bolivar—who both have failed with nothing but principles and conviction to back them up. This is now *my* great project. And at the moment I have a personal guard and some poorly armed volunteers. It's logical that we raise capital. I think the Bank of England will see that. Once Sir Henry Sparks accepts our proposal, his own people can take over the printing of the bonds, and *our* people can concentrate on stirring interest in buying them."

"What if Spain steps in before you have your capital? Or what if England refuses to invest?"

"You worry too much. King Qental gave me the land, and Spain is presently much more concerned with Bonaparte than with the Rey of Costa Habichuela. And I did a great deal of research before I requested that we be introduced to the Duke of Melbourne. He knows if we aren't successful here we'll have to go to Prussia or to France. England wants another toehold in Central America, and even more than that it doesn't want France to have one. We are a very low-risk proposition, Josefina, with a very great opportunity for reward and profit."

"You are brilliant, Father, if I haven't told you so recently," she returned. It made a great deal of sense. Her father was a master strategist, and even without his abundance of wit and charm, Sir Henry, the Bank of England, Melbourne, and anyone with a few extra pounds to invest would be foolish to pass the opportunity by.

"Thank you. And of course if the daughter of the rey were to marry the head of one of the oldest, most respected, and wealthiest families in England, that would help the cause of Costa Habichuela more than any words possibly could. As I said, I did my research."

And that very person had kissed her only an hour ago. Melbourne kissed like the devil himself—all heat and no quarter given. He'd practically devoured her. Her pulse sped at just the thought of it. "A good fit for our needs or not, Melbourne isn't a fool. He will know the two of us are being thrown together, if he hasn't realized it already."

"And what's wrong with that? He's a duke, and you're a princess."

"Two years ago I wasn't a princess. A Griffin has been a duke practically since before Caesar."

"And yet he is a man, and you, my dear, are a very attractive young lady of two-and-twenty."

"Five-and-twenty."

"Previously married dukes, I've found, prefer their brides to be young and virginal. For Costa Habichuela you can lose three years." He smiled at her again, his blond moustache curving. "Even when I was Captain Embry in George the Third's army, even when I was Colonel Embry under General Bolivar, you were a princess. Wherever we went, do you think your mother and I provided you with the best education, the best tutors, so you could marry a farmer or a shopkeeper? I've always said that everything happens—"

"—for a reason," she finished, smiling back at him. "So you were meant to be the Rey of Costa Habichuela."

"Yes, I was. It's the second greatest achievement of my life, after you." He kissed her forehead again. "And you were meant to marry a man so great that in my youth I wouldn't have dared look him in the eye."

A shiver ran through her, though she wasn't certain whether it was one of anticipation or of dread. Melbourne kissed well, but if he ever blinked and realized that he'd been led somewhere he didn't want to go, the consequences could be disastrous. "Before his wife died she gave him a daughter, you know."

"I know. And you'll give him a son. And a country to rule." He pulled out his pocket watch as Captain Milton appeared at the foot of the stairs. "Ah, it's time. Let's go meet a banker, shall we?"

The impression they made this afternoon with Sir Henry Sparks would be the most important of their trip to England. Josefina knew her father had rehearsed his arguments for weeks, though he hoped they wouldn't be necessary. As for her, she was ready to be regal and confident, whatever insults Melbourne might throw at her. She had a good head for figures, and she'd done her own research, as well.

As the coach stopped at the foot of the wide steps leading up to the Bank of England building, she leaned past Mr. Orrin, her father's business advisor, to look through the window. A short, portly man with a sparse peppering of gray hair stood there. Beside him and wearing dark blue and gray, stood the much taller and leaner figure of Melbourne.

"Right on time," her father muttered, stepping to the ground and offering his hand. "A very good sign."

She hoped so. As Melbourne faced their approach, she could practically feel his dark gray gaze on her skin, even through the elegant emerald-colored gown she'd worn for the occasion. Josefina resisted the urge to touch the small silver tiara woven into her hair—she'd only worn it once before and considered it a bit much, but as her father had said, this was the meeting that would dictate the course of their future.

"Your Majesty, Your Highness," the duke said, inclining his head, "may I present Sir Henry Sparks, director of the Bank of England? Sir Henry, Stephen, Rey of Costa Habichuela and his daughter, Princess Josefina."

The bank director bowed low, much more respectfully than Melbourne had. "I'm very pleased to meet you, Your Majesty, Your Highness. His Grace tells me that you have some business you wish to discuss."

"Indeed we do," her father said with an easy smile.

"Then let's go inside to my office."

As they followed Sir Henry into the large building, employees and clients alike stopped to watched them pass. They probably recognized Melbourne, but she and her father and their advisor and two bodyguards must have made an impression, as well.

They sat in front of a large mahogany desk set in the middle of the small but well-appointed office. Sir Henry offered the seat behind the desk to Melbourne, but the duke declined, instead leaning a haunch against a low credenza. Orrin stood directly behind her father.

"Now, Your Majesty," the banker began, "what may I—and the Bank of England—do for you?"

"Before I answer that," her father returned, "perhaps I might give you a little information about myself and Costa Habichuela."

"Of course."

"I was born in Cornwall, and thanks to my family's influence, bought a lieutenant's commission in the army when I turned seventeen. After ten years I found myself growing restless, sold what had become a captaincy, and decided to travel."

"That's very admirable," Sir Henry commented. Josefina didn't think he meant it as a compliment. He would.

"Thank you. It was when I reached the northeast coast of South America, however, that my true adventure began. I hadn't been there long when I began hearing of the oppressive Spanish rule, and of a growing move to force Spain to give up her American territories. At this same time I gained an introduction to General Simon Bolivar, a champion of the people. Apparently he was as impressed with me as I was with him, because he offered me a position as a major under his command.

"For years we fought together, driving the Spanish out of town after town, valley after valley. I gained a promotion to colonel under my own command, in the meantime meeting and marrying my wife, Maria Costanza-y-Veneza, and having a daughter, Josefina."

"This is all fascinating, Your Majesty, but—"

"Please allow me to finish, Sir Henry," her father broke in. "I assure you, this all has relevance."

"Go on," Melbourne said quietly. Much more than Sir Henry, Josefina guessed, he was assessing her father's words. After all, if the bank decided to issue bonds to aid the development of Costa Habichuela, it would be in part because of him. Even in Jamaica, everyone knew of the Griffin family and their impeccable reputation and unmatched power and influence. Yes, the investment was a sound, low-risk one, but Melbourne as much as Sir Henry needed to be convinced of that.

"My men and I were on a sweep of the eastern coast of Central America, on our way south to rendezvous with the main army. We came across a group of Spanish soldiers attacking a small, beautiful city located between a low range of mountains and a deep, secluded harbor. We drove them off, and the people thanked us with a three-day-long feast. As we were preparing to leave and meet up with the main forces, Qental, King of the Mosquito Coast, arrived. Seeing that I was English, he told me that without outside help even isolated parts of the Mosquito Coast such as this one would be lost to Spain. And then he gave it to me."

She'd heard the story a hundred times, but Josefina still enjoyed listening to it. Her gaze caught Melbourne, to find that he was looking straight back at her. She didn't know what he might be hoping to see, but to herself she could admit that she liked having him look.

"That same night the people of San Saturus—that's the name of the city we saved—declared me to be their ruler, their rey, as they call it. And their well-being and safety became my primary concern. There is so much potential for growth and expansion there—which is why I need your help."

"An English foothold other than Belize in Central and South America could be very beneficial," Sir Henry said absently, almost to himself. "Are the citizens Spanish? Once their gratitude at being saved from marauders wears thin, they may want to return to Spanish rule."

The rey sat forward. "That's the beauty of Costa Habichuela. The citizens never were Spanish. They are mostly natives, coupled with a great many English and Scots who've migrated there from other, Spanish-dominated territories. They are extremely happy to have even more distance between themselves and Spain. And to be honest, with the mountains at our back and an easily defensible bay at our front, we are in a perfect location to ensure a long and stable rule."

"How much land did the Mosquito King give you?" Sir Henry asked, practically rubbing his hands together.

"A million acres. I have a map," the rey returned. "Orrin? I can show you precisely."

As the former sergeant dug into his satchel and produced a large map of Costa Habichuela showing its position on the eastern coast of Central America, Melbourne straightened and moved closer.

"What happened to the men?" he asked.

The rey furrowed his brow. "Beg pardon?"

"You said that you and your men were supposed to rendezvous with the main part of the rebel army. What happened to them, and to the army?"

"Oh. I sent them on under my second-in-command. I tendered my resignation, as did several of my most loyal men—the ones who'd served with me through the years, like Orrin here. They now make up most of my personal guard and cabinet ministers."

"So you have a stable government, a stable population, and a beautiful capital city in an ideal location," Melbourne said, looking over the map.

"Precisely."

"What do you need a loan for, then?"

Josefina's father actually sent *her* a quick, annoyed glance. Was she supposed to have swayed Melbourne already? She'd only seen him four times, now. And kissed him once. She drew a breath. "Not even Eden could stand still in the midst of progress and hope to survive," she said. "Costa Habichuela needs to be able to thrive into the future. We must be able to govern effectively, and to protect ourselves. If England is unable to assist us," she continued for good measure, "we will have to find someone who can. We have no choice in this."

"What amount did you have in mind?" Sir Henry asked, running a finger along the generous borders of Costa Habichuela. "A loan to a newly formed country is a risky proposition at best."

"Actually," the rey returned, "this loan won't be much of a risk at all. I would like the opportunity to secure a permanent friendship between our two countries. I've taken the liberty of having several bonds drawn up. That way any loan you made to my government would immediately become an investment opportunity for every progress-minded Englishman."

"Hm," Sir Henry mused, pinching his chin between his thumb and forefinger. "I have to say, given the background of Costa Habichuela, purchasing bonds from you—or me, rather—certainly seems far more sound than a European investment right now. And as you said, a great portion of South America is fighting over who governs it." He looked up at Melbourne. "What's your opinion on this, Your Grace?"

Melbourne looked at the map for a long moment while Josefina held her breath. She and her father might both outrank the duke, but here in England he definitely had more power and influence.

"Costa Habichuela might very well be a safer investment than any other foreign one I can think of at the moment," he finally said, "but it's also very new and very far away. I think if you intend to garner sufficient interest to support a loan of any large amount, you'll have to offer some sort of incentive."

"A discounted bond perhaps?" Sir Henry continued. "That worked quite well for bolstering monetary support of Chile a few years ago."

The rey sat back, stroking his moustache with his fingers. "You know, gentlemen, that is a very fine idea. By offering to sell hundred-pound bonds for ninety pounds, say, we are both stating our confidence in the future and insuring a level of profit for investors."

"At ninety pounds to the hundred the interest rate can't be more than three percent—say over ten years?"

"That sounds fair and equitable." Stephen Embry gave a rueful smile. "We do, however, have one more point to discuss."

"The amount of the loan," Melbourne supplied. Josefina couldn't read his expression; if she didn't know better, they might well have been discussing the weather. "I assume you have a figure in mind, Your Majesty?"

"Yes, I do. To establish import and export, and even immigration, I will need to hire ships, purchase cargo, and of course establish a permanent consulate here in London. I think one hundred thousand pounds should cover that."

Sir Henry choked. "One hun . . . hundred thousand? Good God! I thought you would ask for twenty thousand or so."

"Twenty thousand would hardly be enough for us to approach anyone on equal footing," the rey replied calmly. "As His Grace said, we are very young. We need to begin from a position of strength or we will never find one." He blinked, as if suddenly remembering something. "I'm such a fool. Orrin, the prospectus, if you please."

Melbourne raised an eyebrow. "You have a prospectus?"

"I had a surveyor write one last year, as we prepared for our trip here." The minister pulled a fat manuscript from his satchel and handed it over. "It details everything," the rey continued, leaning forward to set it on the desk. "Agriculture, temperature, climate, trading routes, population and growth equations—and it's illustrated." He flipped open the leather cover to reveal a sketch of a three-masted rig sailing into a harbor, mountains behind it in the distance and a picturesque mixture of houses, huts, and paved roads flowing down to the dock at the water's edge below.

"San Saturus, I presume?" Melbourne drawled.

"Yes. And a very good likeness, if I say so myself."

"This is most impressive," the banker said, pulling the prospectus around to flip through several of the pages. "Rainfall, planting seasons, even figures for wood harvesting."

"As I said, Sir Henry, we are very serious about placing Costa Habichuela permanently on the map. I would like it to be listed there as an ally of England."

The banker stood and stuck out his hand. "One hundred thousand pounds."

The rey rocked to his feet and shook hands with Sir Henry. "My deepest and most humble thanks to you, sir."

"Congratulations," Melbourne put in, his gaze moving

once more to Josefina. "You don't happen to have another copy of that prospectus, do you?"

"We had a dozen printed," she said. "I'm afraid the rest are at Colonel Branbury's house, however."

"Come by at eight o'clock tonight," her father suggested. "We'll have a brandy before we venture to Almack's, and I'll give you one."

The duke nodded, turning for the door. "I will. If you'll excuse me, I have some business to take care of before tonight."

"Good day, Melbourne. And thank you."

"Until tonight." His parting glance was at Josefina, and she took a slow breath. She needed to secure his interest. Apparently she already had his attention.

Chapter 5

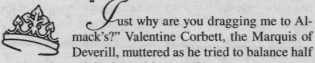"*Just* why are you dragging me to Almack's?" Valentine Corbett, the Marquis of Deverill, muttered as he tried to balance half a glass of scotch in the rocking coach.

"Because you married my sister and you're now part of the family." Sebastian snagged the glass from his closest friend and took a swallow. "And because you're incurably cynical."

"A character trait of which I've always been proud." Deverill recaptured the scotch and nearly had it jostled out of his grip. With an annoyed scowl he opened the coach door and tossed out the liquid, dropping the glass onto the seat beside him. Out of their sight on the street a male voice yelled a curse.

"Valentine. That's my crest emblazoned on the door, you know."

"And this is a new jacket. I didn't want to see it ruined. Though after wearing it to Almack's I may never want to see it again." He sat forward. "So I ask you once more, Melbourne. What am I doing here?"

"I want your opinion."

"Very well. On what?"

This time Sebastian frowned. "I'm not certain."

"That's helpful."

"Just keep your eyes and ears open tonight."

"Regarding your new royal friends, I suppose?" Valentine looked at him, then sat back again. "Very well."

It would have been so much easier if he'd known what it was that had been tickling at him all afternoon. For a former soldier, Stephen Embry definitely knew his way around matters of finance. With two years to formulate a plan, however, he *should* have been knowledgeable. The rey was also glib and charming—but again, if he hadn't been, King Qental wouldn't have been moved to grant him a substantial piece of the Mosquito Coast. Granting the loan made sense—even with a hundred thousand pounds at risk, the probability of a profit to investors was very high. And the benefit of having another friendly port in the New World couldn't be overstated.

"What do you know about Central and South American politics?" he asked, since he couldn't be more specific even if he wanted to be.

"Only the broad strokes. Spain governs most of it, but the independence movement seems to be filtering south from the Colonies. Bits and pieces are being chipped away, and Spain's not happy about it. With Bonaparte in their home territory, though, their focus isn't on undeveloped land an ocean away."

Sebastian cracked a brief smile. "I sometimes forget that you do pay attention."

"I'm a husband and a father, now. I've found that that circumstance both narrows and broadens one's perspective." He kicked Sebastian in the ankle. "If this is going to be another lunatic assignment from you of the keeping-an-eye-on-someone sort, I want more details. What's going on?"

"You heard about last night, I presume."

"The chit slapping you and then you dancing with her? No, didn't hear a bloody thing."

"Mm-hm. Prinny's gotten some sort of honor from them, and he thinks very highly of the rey and his entourage. For me, what's the saying? If something seems too good to be true, etcetera, etcetera." The explanation was as vague as he could make it; Valentine was as sharp as a knife blade, and no one needed to know that he'd blundered so far as to kiss Princess Josefina.

"I'm a damn chaperone."

"You—"

"Shay's the diplomatic one. Why isn't he here?"

Sebastian cleared his throat. *Because Shay already thinks I'm interested in the chit* wouldn't suffice; he wanted an unbiased opinion of the entire situation, not his . . . insanity where it came to Josefina. "I want eyes, not diplomacy."

"You're being obtuse, and I think it's deliberate. But since you've dragged me along, I shall do my utmost to fulfill my duty at whatever it is I'm doing."

The duke nodded. "That is all I ask."

Ten minutes later as they left the carriage, Colonel Branbury's butler opened the front door for them. "Your Grace, His Majesty awaits your pleasure in the drawing room. This way."

"Thank you."

With Valentine on his heels, Sebastian followed the butler upstairs. The house was well-kept, if small by his standards, and he guessed that Branbury had been a compatriot of the rey's when Embry had served in the British army. "Where is Colonel Branbury, if I might ask?"

"The colonel has given over his house to the Costa Habichuela delegation," the butler returned, "though he has been called back to the Peninsula. He hopes to return before the end of the Season."

Did Branbury's absence mean something? Bonaparte *had* been creating havoc on the Peninsula, so the timing of the colonel's trip might well have been mere coincidence.

Stopping before a set of double doors, the butler knocked and then pushed them both open. "His Grace the Duke of Melbourne and guest, Your Majesty, Your Highness."

Princess Josefina sat in one of the chairs beside the fire. Sebastian tried to steel his expression, the effort hampered by Valentine elbowing him in the back and muttering "'And guest'? Since when am I 'and guest'?"

Sebastian bowed, deliberately keeping his gaze on the seated rey rather than the princess. "Your Majesty, Your Highness, may I present my brother-in-law, the Marquis of Deverill? Valentine, this is Stephen Embry, the Rey of Costa Habichuela, and his daughter, Princess Josefina."

They both remained seated. Recently crowned or not, neither the rey nor his daughter seemed to require any schooling in social rankings. Sebastian rubbed his left eye to cover the jump of his muscles.

"I'm pleased to meet you, Lord Deverill."

"And I you, Your Majesty," Valentine returned with one of his charming smiles. "Sebastian mentioned something about brandy."

"Yes, indeed." Finally the rey rose, gesturing to the footman who stood beside the liquor cabinet. "Three brandies and a glass of red wine, if you please, lad."

"Very good, Your Majesty."

As Valentine wandered over to collect his drink, Sebastian finally turned his gaze to Princess Josefina. For the barest of moments his breath caught. Tonight her silk gown was violet, dotted with silver to look like starlight.

"Join me, Melbourne," she said, gesturing at the chair her father had vacated.

"Of course." She smelled like lilacs, he decided as he moved past her to sit, though the scent was more likely deadly nightshade.

"So, Your Grace," she continued in a lower voice, while behind them Valentine and the rey chatted about boots, "have you finally decided to mind your manners?"

"I'm searching for the most diplomatic way to offer you another piece of advice," he countered, focusing on the emeralds dangling from her ears, sparkling against the midnight of her hair. The ear bobs jangled as she shifted, and he blinked, refocusing in time to see her gaze on his mouth.

"I don't expect diplomacy from you. Say what you will."

Even if she wanted to begin an argument, he would not play along. He'd learned that strategy. "I only wanted to advise you that it is the custom here for young ladies making their first appearance at Almack's to wear white for their presentation to the patronesses."

Josefina looked down at her dress. "Don't you like my gown?"

He swallowed, his cock twitching. "It's very nice. But that's not the point."

"What would those patronesses say to a young lady who didn't bow to their dictates?"

Was that hesitation? Until this second he'd never seen her unsure of her footing. "I've seen them ask girls to leave, never to be invited back again," he answered truthfully.

"That's absurd."

"I agree. But it's also custom."

"I am not customary."

A smile tugged at his mouth. "No, you are not that."

"They wouldn't dare ask a princess to leave."

Wouldn't they? They counted a minor princess among their number. "Honestly, Josefina," he said in a low voice, "I think you should wear white. Your father is trying to find investors, and some of them will be in attendance tonight. You seem eager to cause a stir, but I do not recommend one of that sort."

She swept to her feet, the lilac scent intensifying. "Stuff and nonsense," she muttered. "Is there anything else I should know about this wretched assembly?"

"If you wish to waltz, you have to be presented to the patronesses and gain their permission."

"Very well. I will wear white, and you will present me." With that she stomped out of the room.

"A female presents you," he amended to her back as she vanished.

A snifter of brandy appeared over his shoulder. "As Zachary would say," Valentine murmured, "St. George's buttonholes. That chit is exquisite."

"She's mad," Sebastian returned feelingly, keeping his voice down as the rey approached them. "And irritating." He faced her father. "Do you have a copy of that prospectus for me, Your Majesty?"

"I do." The rey lifted the tome from a side table and handed it over. "And let me say again how much I respect your business acumen and how thankful I am that the Regent has appointed you to aide us."

Sebastian inclined his head. "Will Queen Maria be joining us tonight?"

"Yes, she will." The rey chuckled. "The one universal truth about females everywhere is that they take a very long time to dress." He turned his attention to Valentine. "I hope His Grace might encourage you to invest in Costa Habichuela as well, Lord Deverill."

"The—"

"Ah, there she is. Maria, you know Melbourne. And this is his brother-in-law, the Marquis of Deverill."

A more matronly version of her daughter, Queen Maria stopped inside the drawing room doorway to curtsy. Where her husband seemed friendly and agreeable, the queen fit the traditional view of royalty—elegant, quiet, and a little aloof. Her daughter had inherited all of those qualities except for the reserved tongue.

"Good evening, gentlemen," she said, straightening. "And thank you, Your Grace, for informing Josefina of the proper custom of dress for this evening. We were unaware."

"My pleasure, Your Majesty."

"I expected more retainers or guards or hangers-on running about the house here," Deverill commented. "Melbourne's got more than this, and he's considered spartan in the area of minions."

"We're in the process of recruiting more of them," the rey said, chuckling.

They talked about the weather and other insignificant topics for the next ten minutes. Sebastian was grateful that he'd brought Valentine along, because the marquis held up their end of the conversation while his mind wandered elsewhere. Mostly his fingers itched to open the prospectus and delve deeper into Costa Habichuela. At the back of his mind, though, he was waiting, listening for footfalls on the stairs just outside the door.

Did he like her? Did he hate her? Certainly no one in his thirty-four years had ever spoken to him as she did. All he knew was that in her presence he felt like a lion prowling for its next meal; dark, primal, and not the least bit civilized or even rational.

As long as he was aware of it, he supposed that he

would be able to carry on with his duty to Prinny and ignore it. God knew he'd set aside his personal needs and feelings before.

He heard her come back into the room as the others continued to chat. Blowing out his breath, he faced her.

She wasn't in white. Rather, a flowing, low-cut gown of ivory draped from her like cascades of shimmering water. With her pale skin, black hair, and dark eyes, she looked like a porcelain doll. A very sensual porcelain doll.

Her lips parted a little, and she smiled at him. "Better?"

He should never have opened his mouth and told her to change clothes. Good heavenly God. This was trouble. She was trouble. "Much more appropriate," he said stiffly. His mouth felt dry.

"You'll make me blush, giving me such compliments," she returned, eyes glittering.

"There you are, my dear. Shall we go, Your Grace?"

Grateful for the distraction, he turned his back on her. "As you wish, Your Majesty."

From the corner of his eye he caught Valentine glancing at him before the marquis walked over to offer his arm to the princess. Sebastian didn't like that, but he immediately buried the emotion. *Splendid.* Now even Deverill had better manners than he did. But if he touched Josefina now, without giving himself a moment to put some distance between her and the . . . turmoil she roused in him, he would kiss her again. Or worse.

"Thank you, Lord Deverill," Josefina said, taking the marquis's arm. Melbourne probably would have left her standing there in the drawing room and gone ahead without her if he could.

It didn't make sense. Men didn't walk away when they

were attracted to someone. Not when both parties were unmarried and of compatible social rank, anyway. For heaven's sake, if anyone turned away it should be she, because he was only a duke.

"Tell me about Costa Habichuela," Deverill suggested as he handed her into the coach.

With her parents seated on one side and Melbourne by himself on the other, at this moment the duke wasn't going anywhere. *Ha.* She sank onto the leather seat beside him, pressing closer as Deverill stuffed himself in next to her. "I haven't seen much of it, I'm afraid," she said, smiling at the marquis.

"You haven't?"

"Well, my mother and I were able to join Father for two days in San Saturus," she conceded, noting that there wasn't so much as an inch of give to Melbourne's side as she rocked against him. It was as though he was fashioned from granite. "That was when our ship anchored in the harbor to collect the rey on our way to England."

"Where did you reside, then?"

"Morant Bay, in Jamaica, most recently. With my father fighting against Spain in the Americas, he wanted Mother and me somewhere safe and stable. Once he received Costa Habichuela, he was so busy organizing a government and surveying the country that he requested we remain in Jamaica and do what we could to aid him from there."

"And a tremendous asset Josefina has been, believe you me," her father put in. "Sharp as a dagger point, the princess is."

"Father," she interrupted, more for effect than out of shyness.

"It's true. And Maria has been invaluable, as well," the rey continued. "She's the daughter of a viceroy, you know."

On her other side, Melbourne finally stirred. "Her

Highness mentioned that. When you married an English ex-patriot, Your Majesty, did you have any idea this would happen?"

Maria Embry smiled, sending her husband a fond glance. "Nothing surprises me where Stephen is concerned."

Melbourne continued to clutch the prospectus across his lap as if he thought a stiff breeze would whisk it away. "Still, to become a king—rey, excuse me," he pursued. "That's extraordinary."

"I felt humble and grateful, and determined to do my utmost for my people," the rey said. "That's why we're here. And when we leave, it will be to make Costa Habichuela our permanent home."

"Barring invasion from Spain," Deverill commented.

"The funds I'm raising and our close alliance with England will help to prevent that."

"Tell me, Melbourne," Josefina began, mostly to give her parents a few moments to prepare for their largest public outing as the leaders of a country, "how many waltzes will be played tonight?"

"Most likely two—one at the beginning of the evening and one near the end. We will have missed the first. You're permitted to join all the other dances. It's only the waltz that requires the patronesses' permission."

"It seems silly. Who are these women?"

"Old frumps, mostly," Deverill drawled. "Stiff and cranky. Their only amusement is looking down their noses at everyone else, and the only way they could manage that was to settle in as hostesses of the most boring soirees in London."

Josefina grinned. At least someone seemed willing to give straight answers. "Why does anyone attend, if it's so dull?"

"Because everyone worries that they'll be the only ones not attending if they don't appear. It's quite complex, and a very sad happenstance." He sighed. "And extremely prudish. No alcohol allowed."

She started to ask why *he* was attending, but changed her mind. He didn't seem to worry over anyone else's opinion, so obviously Melbourne had asked him along. Why, though? Did the duke dislike her? Not according to that kiss. Perhaps he was afraid of her, though given his standing and reputation that didn't seem likely, either. Hm. A puzzle. And the thing she liked best about puzzles was solving them.

Though she had several questions for Melbourne, answers weren't likely to be forthcoming with her parents and his brother-in-law present. She would save them for a dance. And he *would* dance with her; she would make certain of that.

They arrived at the assembly rooms, and once again it was Deverill who offered a hand to assist her. She wondered briefly whether the handsome marquis might be infatuated with her, but dismissed the notion just as quickly. He looked at her with nothing more than the same slightly amused curiosity as he did her parents and everyone else around them.

"Excuse me," she said, freeing her hand from his arm and stepping over to where Melbourne chatted with her father. At least the duke had left the prospectus behind in the coach. "If you will," she said, offering her hand to him.

"Of course." He took her fingers and placed them over his dark sleeve.

"That's good," she returned in a lower voice as he led their group to the entrance, "because otherwise I would think you were slighting me, and I would be insulted again."

"Ah," he breathed, keeping his profile to her. "If you slap me here tonight, I will reciprocate in kind." Finally he glanced down at her. "Consider that you've been warned."

"If you want to frighten me, why don't you threaten to kiss me again?" she returned.

"Because you want me to kiss you again," he murmured.

A slow smile curved his mouth, and heat spun through her. How could anyone who portrayed himself as so stern and aloof have a smile that . . . heart-stopping?

"I do not," she stated belatedly.

"Then stop arguing with everything I say."

"I do not argue with everything you say."

His smile deepening, he pulled out his pocket watch with his free hand. "Nine seconds," he said, snapping it closed again.

Her cheeks heated, and she dug her fingers into his sleeve to retaliate. "So you think you have me figured out, do you? I daresay you have no idea."

"Enlighten me then, Princess."

She sniffed. "First present me to these absurd women."

"Say that any louder, and you'll be asked to leave before I have time to check my watch again."

Blast it all. She wanted to slap the smug expression off his face. At the same time she absolutely believed that he hadn't been bluffing, that he would slap her right back, and in the middle of the room. She'd already seen how he reacted to her arguing, but there was a time and a place for making her annoyance known. This was neither. "Fine," she muttered. "Let's get on with it, then."

"Very well, but it won't be me presenting you." He lifted a hand and signaled at someone across the room.

"Why not?" she demanded.

"Two reasons. One, I will not put myself in the position of being turned away by anyone, much less those chits, and two, if—"

"But you'll have me put in that position?"

"You already are," he returned calmly. "As I was saying, two, if I present you, then rumors will fly that I'm courting you and that I'm trying to force Society to accept you. That will be the surest way to see that they don't."

It made sense. "So you're doing me a favor by abandoning me," she said anyway.

He snorted. "Princess Josefina, this is my aunt, Lady Gladys Tremaine. Auntie, may I present Princess Josefina Embry?"

Josefina turned to face a stout woman wearing a matronly blue silk gown and an easy, infectious smile. "Good evening, Your Highness," the woman said, sinking into a curtsy and then grabbing Melbourne's free arm to drag herself upright again.

Belatedly Josefina nodded back at her. "Lady Gladys."

"So you're the one half of London's been talking about," Melbourne's aunt continued.

"Indeed she is," Melbourne commented, slipping free of both of them. "I'll see you in a few minutes."

And just like that he vanished into the growing crowd. "Infuriating man," Josefina muttered.

"Oh, he is that," his aunt agreed. "Come along, there's quite a crowd tonight. I think everyone's here to see you and your parents."

With Melbourne out of sight, Josefina finally took a moment to look around. The assembly rooms seemed nearly stuffed to the rafters, and the part of the crowd that hadn't surrounded her parents closed in around her. No one chatted with her, of course; they only wanted to stare. She lifted her chin and squared her shoulders, sending up a quick thanks to Melbourne for suggesting that she wear white. All of the other young ladies were.

"When it's our turn," Melbourne's aunt was saying in

a quiet voice, "they'll ask you a few silly questions and then they'll all take turns nodding or welcoming you to the assembly." She grinned. "Melbourne escorted you in, so they won't have any choice."

"But he said he wouldn't risk them making him look foolish."

"Gentlemen don't make the presentation, so to his face one of them might have dared make a row over the break in tradition. With him looking on and having respectable old me do the honors, you'll have as easy a time as anyone ever did, except perhaps for his sister, Nell. That was quite an evening, with everyone falling all over themselves to be nice to Eleanor, and her just eighteen." Lady Gladys moved them closer to a group of a dozen or so women seated in chairs at one side of the room. "Oh, yes, they're all here. And if they ask whether you waltzed at the Elkins soiree, tell them you don't recall."

"You mean I can't waltz *anywhere* without their permission?"

"That's the tradition. Believe me, if anyone would ask *them* to waltz, they wouldn't care so much about what other girls are doing."

The crowd in front of them parted. How strange, that something she hadn't known about an hour ago had become of tantamount importance. Her parents wouldn't care whether she received permission to waltz or not, only that she made a good impression. No, this was about wanting to be able to waltz with Melbourne—not just tonight, but any night hereafter that she chose to do so.

"Ladies," Lady Gladys said, abruptly much more formidable than she'd been a moment before, "may I present Princess Josefina of Costa Habichuela? Her parents, as you've probably heard by now, are rey and queen of that country."

Josefina inclined her head, not knowing what was customary but refusing to curtsy before a group of social inferiors. One of them, Lady Jersey, was rumored to be a mistress of the Regent, but that did not make her royalty.

"How old are you, Your Highness?" one of them asked, her voice cool and condescending.

None of your blasted affair. "Two and twenty," she said aloud, remembering her father's advice. Lose three years, and gain a duke—it seemed a fair-enough trade, though it was still entirely likely that the duke was more trouble than he was worth.

"And how long do you plan to remain in London?"

"That depends on my father the rey's wishes," she returned.

One of them glanced beyond Josefina's shoulder, then gave a tight smile. "We are pleased to welcome you to Almack's, Your Highness. We do hope you enjoy your evening."

"Nod again, thank them, and we walk away," Melbourne's aunt whispered.

Josefina nodded. "Thank you," she said, and walked back into the crowd. *There*. She'd done it.

"Well done, Princess Josefina," a deep, masculine voice came from just off to one side.

Her breath stilled. "Thank you, Melbourne," she returned. "Is there somewhere I might get a breath of air?"

"Certainly," he said, moving up beside her and offering his arm again. "Don't tell me *that* overset you."

"I am not overset," she stated, wrapping her hand around his sleeve and allowing him to lead the way toward a doorway halfway down the length of the room. "It is stifling in here."

"It is that."

A large man blocked their path. "Melbourne, the—"

His arm jerked a little, and she looked up at his face. Had that been annoyance? Whatever the expression, it was gone so quickly that she couldn't be certain. "I'll be with you in a moment, Shipley," he said, moving around the obstruction.

"Business?" she asked, her general antagonism toward him drowned by curiosity.

"It's always business. I hope your father realizes what he's let himself in for."

They went through the crowded doorway, turned a corner, walked through another door, and ended up outside at what looked like a service entrance. A blank wall faced them across the alleyway, a narrow band of dark sky and dim stars above.

"Not much of a view," she said dryly.

"No, but it is air."

It was also relatively quiet, and at this time of evening, private. "I don't know about you," she said, looking into gray eyes turned black in the gloom.

"What don't you know about me?"

"You offer me good advice, then you practically cut me, then you gain me acceptance at Almack's, insulting me once or twice in the process, then find me a quiet place where I can catch my breath."

"Ah," he returned, humor in the brief word. "Let's talk about you for a moment. You attack from all angles, like a troop of marauding huns. A jab here, a smile there, an arrow to my pride, and a javelin to my sensibility."

"And what does all that mean?"

"You irritate me."

Josefina frowned. "Well, isn't that nice to kn—"

He tilted her chin up with his fingertips and closed his mouth over hers. Fire danced along her nerves. The Duke of Melbourne kissed with an intensity, a heat, almost a desperation, that she'd never encountered before. As stoic as he could be in conversation, his embrace overflowed, overwhelmed, with emotion.

Her back thudded against the wall. Thoughts tangling, overlapping, receding, Josefina clutched his lapels, pulling him still closer. The amount of desire he had—it felt like faith he placed in her, faith that she could provide what he wanted. That was a new sensation, and it frightened the devil out of her.

"Stop," she gasped, the word muffled against his mouth.

Slowly he pulled back, lifting his head. His expression—lust, need, arousal—burned into her. Just as swiftly, though, it was gone behind his mask of calm command. And it was a mask, she realized. With what roiled inside him, she was amazed he could fool anyone, much less everyone. What could he tell about her, from the way she clung to him?

"Apologies," he muttered, moving back another step.

"That's quite—"

He turned on his heel and strode off into the dark depths of the alley.

She felt cold. Bereft and insulted. "You owe me a waltz," she called in his general direction, though she couldn't see him in the gloom.

"You'll have it," his voice returned, clipped and toneless.

Josefina stood for a moment in the dark. As the night sounds of London crept closer around her like a not quite comfortable cloak, she pulled open the door and returned inside alone. Her father wanted to see her wed to Melbourne. For the first time she considered what making such a union would mean to Sebastian Griffin. He was not a man who *had* to marry. If he wed again, it would be because someone could answer the deep . . . need . . . in him. If that person was her, God forgive her if she betrayed it or proved herself false or unable to live up to it—because the Duke of Melbourne would have no mercy at all.

Chapter 6

 "How do you mean, 'odd'?" Eleanor, Lady Deverill asked, shading her eyes to look at her husband pacing beside the daffodils. With her other hand she scooped their five-month-old daughter, Rose, back onto the blanket and away from the butterfly she was attempting to eat.

"I'm not certain," Valentine returned, the unaccustomed hesitation in his voice as troubling as what he was attempting to say. "I would say he seemed . . . confused."

"Sit down here before you blind me," she said, patting the blanket beside her. "And tell me how my brother seemed confused. Last night was Almack's. I would equate that with boredom, rather than confusion."

Her husband sank onto the blanket beside her, absently lifting Rose onto his lap to twiddle his fingers at her. "I am painfully aware of that, believe you me." He drew a breath, as thoughtful and concerned as she'd ever seen him. "He asked me to join him so I could 'observe with my usual cynicism,' or so he said. The Costa Habichuela people were polite and eager to make a good impression, as anyone coming to London in search of funds and support would be. But the chit . . ."

"You're referring to Princess Josefina, I presume? The one who slapped my brother in public?"

"Put your knives away, my heart." Valentine leaned sideways and kissed her in that soft, sensual way that made her glad she was sitting down. "He looks at her when she's not looking at him, but to her face he either argues, or is so formal he's almost rude."

Her breath caught. "He likes her. Good heavens."

"That's what I thought, as soon as he admitted that she annoys him. But . . ." Valentine lifted Rose to look her in the eye. "You are staying away from men, my sugar cake. Men are evil, wicked, and devious. I know this, because I am one."

Rose laughed, grabbing her father's handsome nose.

"Oh, you think it's funny now. Just you wait."

"Valentine, you're changing the subject."

He stood, holding Rose in one arm and pulling Eleanor to her feet with the other. "You should go talk to him. You're a chit and his sister, so he might converse with you about things he won't with me."

Nell smiled, leaning up against his arm to kiss him again. "Look at you, caring about other people. *And* holding a baby."

"Yes, I'm doomed. Go. Rose and I will discuss the merits of celibacy."

With a fond look back at her husband and daughter, Eleanor went inside Corbett House to call for a coach and to change clothes. The odds were very small that her oldest brother would confide in her, but if Sebastian's behavior had cynical Valentine troubled, it was something she needed to look into.

Four years ago when Charlotte had wasted away and

died, Sebastian had asked her to stay on at Griffin House instead of moving in with their Aunt Tremaine for her debut London Season. He'd asked Charlemagne and Zachary to abandon their bachelor apartments and return home, as well. They'd all done so without hesitation, but now all of them had left again, married and happy and pursuing their own lives.

Was Sebastian considering moving forward as well? She hoped so with all her heart. On the other hand, he'd only known this Princess Josefina for what, four days? Three? She definitely needed to find out what the devil was going on. Immediately.

"Would you care for another biscuit, Your Grace?"

Sebastian looked up from the Costa Habichuela prospectus and recrossed his ankles to ease the ache in his hip. Sitting in the tiny chair in Peep's playroom was well and good for a petite seven-year-old girl, but he was two inches over six feet. "That would be splendid, Lady Penelope."

She set one of the treats onto his china plate. "You know, I am so glad you allowed me to go see the acrobats last night. I think I could be an acrobat. Or a juggler."

He nodded. "Juggling could be an asset to your piracy career."

"That was my thinking." She poured herself another cup of lemonade from the miniature teapot. "I had hoped to have more time to talk with that princess, you know."

Sebastian hid the shiver that ran through his muscles. "Did you like her?"

"Well, she played the pianoforte well, and she told a funny story about going shopping in Jamaica. But she did insult you. If I'd known that you didn't like her, I wouldn't have been so polite."

"Ah. It wasn't that I don't like her," he countered, wondering why he was defending Josefina. "It was just that her being here wasn't appropriate."

"I understand," Peep said, nodding. "But I hope you realize that even though you get to see Prinny and other royal people all the time, I don't."

"My apologies, then. I'll keep that in mind."

The playroom door swung open. "Good afternoon," Zachary said, sketching a deep, formal bow. "I heard that Lady Penelope was holding a tea. May I join you?"

Peep stood, curtsying. "Of course, Lord Zachary. Do take a seat."

Zachary headed toward one of the adult-sized chairs at the side of the room. "A seat at the table," Sebastian instructed, flipping a page of the prospectus.

"I was only taking off my jacket," his youngest brother said, removing his gray jacket to expose his black waistcoat. Returning to the middle of the room, he gingerly sank onto one of the four remaining children's chairs.

"You'll do anything for a biscuit, won't you?" Sebastian observed.

"Apparently."

Peep served more lemonade and biscuits while Sebastian resumed his perusal of the book. The detail amazed him—variations in climate according to elevation, with a huge portion of the text devoted to, basically, how a new arrival in the country might go about making a comfortable living. Both town occupations and farming were covered thoroughly. Parts of it sounded both familiar and deathly dull, but he couldn't count the number of the damned things he'd read over the years.

"You went to Almack's last night, I heard," Zachary said abruptly.

Looking up, Sebastian took a sip of lemonade. "I did."

"And Prinny made an appearance?"

"For about twenty minutes or so. I believe he and Lady Jersey are on the outs. Why do you ask?"

"Just making conversation." Zach devoured a biscuit. "You escorted the Costa Habiba people again."

"Costa Habichuela," Peep enunciated. "It's in Central America."

"Yes, I did," Sebastian answered again. "Are you taking a survey?"

"No." Zachary laughed, the sound strained. "Of course not."

"I wish you had brought Harold today," Peep said, sighing. "He likes biscuits."

Sebastian set the prospectus aside. "That dog is not welcome in this house."

"Just because I named him after Great-grandfather? That's a bit—"

"Because you named him after *me*, Zach. As in Sebastian *Harold* Griffin. When I suggested you prove your capacity for responsibility by getting a dog, that was a jest."

"But Harold's a good dog," his daughter chimed in again.

"He would be as good a dog if his name was Foxy or Royal or something."

Zach's grin was easier this time. "It actually does bother you that I named him Harold, doesn't it?"

"Yes, it does." As if he'd ever made any secret of that.

"Good. It was meant to."

"Gentlemen, please," Peep put in, placing a hand on each of their shoulders, "let's be civil."

The playroom door opened again. "What are we not being civil about?" Shay asked.

Penelope stood again. "Lord Charlemagne, how delightful! Please join us for tea."

With a glance between them and the full-sized chairs, Shay lowered himself into one of the miniatures. "When we did this with Nell, I don't remember the chairs being so small."

"That was fifteen years ago," Zachary pointed out. "*We* were smaller."

If anyone outside their circle ever spotted the three large Griffin males hunkered down at a miniature table for a tea party, no one would fear them any longer. Sebastian eyed the sibling closest in age and temperament to himself. "What brings you here?"

"Just visiting. I had no idea there would be tea—" he took a sip from the undersized cup Peep handed him and made a face "—lemonade, I mean, and biscuits."

As Sebastian watched, his brothers looked at each other, neither seeming terribly pleased at his sibling's presence. Hm. "Are you joining us at the Beardsley recital tonight, Shay?"

"No. Sarala's parents have invited us for dinner." He cleared his throat. "I think they're hoping to hear . . . news," he continued, glancing at his niece.

Startled, Sebastian sat forward, nearly dumping himself out of the tiny chair. "And is there . . . news?"

Shay's face reddened. "I am not prepared to confirm or deny anything at this moment. In another week or so, perhaps."

"Is Aunt Sarala going to have a baby?" Peep asked, giving a scowl and folding her arms across her chest. "You can tell me such things, you know. I'm not six."

"We should know in a few days," Shay said, taking Peep's hand. "You will be the first to hear, one way or the other."

"It seems as though you should have decided something that important already, but very well."

Sebastian looked down at his cup of lemonade. He'd made certain that Penelope would be extremely well-off for her entire life, but he couldn't do anything about his title. With no son of his own, upon his death it would go to his nearest male relation—Shay. If Sarala *was* with child, and if the babe was male, the Griffin name would continue with the Melbourne title for at least another generation. Thank God.

"Seb?"

Shaking himself, he looked up. "Yes?"

"How was Almack's last evening?" Shay asked, then winced as Zachary kicked him in the foot. The low table bounced. "Very subtle, nick ninny."

"What did you two hear?" Sebastian demanded.

"Nothing," Shay said hastily. "It was the first large public introduction of the rey and his party. I just wondered how it went."

"It went well. Perfectly uneventf—"

The door opened again, and Eleanor stepped into the room. "Hello, everyone," she said with an exasperated smile. "Don't you boys look . . . imposing. Did I miss an invitation to a family meeting?"

"No, it's a tea," Penelope corrected. "Are *you* having another baby?"

Her face went white. " 'Another'? Sebastian, is Princess Josefina pr—"

"*What?*" He shot to his feet, the little chair toppling over backward behind him.

Zachary and Shay were right behind him. "You mean Melbourne and the princess are—"

"*No!*" he interrupted before Zach could finish. "Is that what this little invasion is about? For God's sake, if that's the rumor, why the bloody hell didn't anyone say—"

"It's not," Nell said, hurrying forward to put a hand on his arm. "It's not. Not at all. But when Peep said—"

"She was talking about Charlemagne and Sarala."

"Oh. *Oh.*" She turned around and hugged Shay, who belatedly returned the embrace. "Congratulations, Shay."

"It's not certain yet. But why did you think Melbourne and the—"

"*Enough!*" Sebastian roared. "You two," he ordered, gesturing at his brothers, "sit down and have tea with your niece. You," he continued, taking Nell by the arm, "come with me."

"May I have a look at this prospectus?" Shay asked as they strode for the door.

"Yes. Stay put."

Ignoring the rest of the protests and commentary, he practically dragged Eleanor out of the playroom and shut the door behind them. He headed down the stairs and into his office, where he closed that door, as well.

"If you think you're going to lecture me about gossip or something, you are sadly mistaken," Nell said sharply, moving behind the desk and sitting in his chair. "And you certainly won't do it from here, the way you used to. I am a married woman, not a child."

Things had definitely changed over the past two years. "Will you be quiet for a moment?" he muttered. "I'm thinking."

From her expression, she hadn't expected that response. He didn't give it often. And he would never have admitted he was unsure about anything to anyone—until now, apparently. Until bloody Josefina Embry had appeared in his life.

"Why would you come to the conclusion that I am—or was—having an affair with Princess Josefina, with whom, I might add, I've only been acquainted for four days?"

She grimaced. "You have to admit, walking into the room to see you sitting there like overstuffed midgets and then hearing 'Are *you* having another baby'—it was a bit offputting. And you are the only other of us who has 'another' child."

He nodded. "Very well. I'll grant you that." Slowly he walked to the window and back again. Whatever else he was, he remained the head of this family. As such, he was unused to having his actions questioned, and he disliked the idea that his family in particular might be doing so. "Zach and Shay are here asking about last night at Almack's. Why?"

"Why don't you ask them?"

"I did." He moved forward again, taking one of the chairs on the opposite side of the desk from his sister. "What did Valentine say that has you over here, as well? And don't tell me to ask him, because you're the one who decided you should be here."

"He said that you appeared to be off-balance last night. And he thought that you might have an interest in Princess Josefina."

"That rat. I asked him to observe them, not me."

"Is it truc, then?"

"Honestly," he said, uneasy at even discussing it, "I don't know. I've been alone for four years, and yes, I find her interesting. Whether it's because of her or because of the four years, I'm not certain."

"But it is her specifically, and not any or every lady you encounter."

"I suppose so."

"Then you should see more of her."

He lifted an eyebrow. "Thank you. Advice from a chit twelve years my junior."

Nell smiled. "Now you sound like Melbourne again."

"That's the thing, Nell. I *am* Melbourne. I am not going to pursue the only offspring of a foreign king. If his country lasts past Michaelmas, if and when he dies, Josefina becomes rey or queen or whatever they decide the title should be. If it passes to her spouse, then that would make me the King of Costa Habichuela." He forced a smile. "I prefer being an Englishman, and I won't give up my title to be otherwise."

"But Sebastian, if you like her, then—"

"Then what? Firstly, I said she interests me. I'm not certain whether I like her or wish to wring her neck. Secondly, I've known of her existence for four days. Thirdly, I don't want to have an affair. I am not of a mind to pursue at all, especially when there's no future in it."

Slowly she stood. "Since you've thought it through from every angle, measured the logic and found it wanting, I suppose there's no more to say."

"I suppose not." He rose as well, and opened the door for her. "Tell the halfwits, if you please, so they'll stop pestering me, but do so away from Peep's hearing. She doesn't need to know any of this."

"As you wish." With a swish of her muslin skirts, she left the room.

Sebastian watched her up the stairs, then closed the door again and seated himself in the chair she'd vacated. Hopefully this nonsense would go no farther than his own family. And the best way to insure that would be to avoid Princess Josefina Embry at every opportunity, however much he looked forward to another argument—another kiss—with her. Sighing, he opened his desk and removed a sheet of paper. He needed to write a note to Prinny.

"Ready?" Lieutenant May asked, ducking his head back into the coach.

Josefina parted the curtains and peeked out. "Good heavens," she breathed. "I had no idea the enterprise would be this popular."

Beside her, Conchita reached over to fluff her sleeve. "Ready, Your Highness?"

"Even if I wasn't, since Mother and Father are on their way to Scotland to talk with the banking ministers there, I don't think I have much choice." She drew a breath. "But yes, I'm ready."

Lieutenant May hopped out to lower the coach steps and offered her a hand to the ground. As she emerged, the true size of the crowd struck her.

More than two hundred people lined the street in front of the Bank of England, and the doors hadn't even opened yet. They'd advertised the availability of the stocks in the newspaper only yesterday, but the well-heeled queue wrapped all the way around the building and into the alleyway.

As they approached, Sir Henry Sparks emerged from the group of employees standing at the entrance. "Good morning, Your Highness," he said, beaming. "Quite a turnout we have, isn't it?"

"This is amazing. Do you think they'll mind if I say something?"

"I think they would love it."

Lieutenant May turned a crate on its side and helped her onto it. "Good morning," she said in a carrying voice, and the noise around her died down. "I am Princess Josefina, and I want to be the first to welcome you to your new partnership with Costa Habichuela!"

The crowd roared. At Sir Henry's signal, the bankers opened the door and stepped through. Behind them, the queue moved forward. Costa Habichuela was officially open for business.

She stepped down and waded into the crowd, recognizing many of them from her excursions into their ballrooms and assembly halls. For over an hour she smiled and shook hands and answered questions. Originally Melbourne was to have been with her, but all her father had said that morning was that there had been a change of plans. In a way, though she could have used his presence to further bolster investor confidence, the day's goal was to sell bonds—not to think about kissing Melbourne.

Finally she thanked Sir Henry once more, and nodded

at May. The lieutenant helped part the crowd again for her to exit. Applause followed her as she stepped back into the carriage.

"My goodness, that went well," Conchita exclaimed, grinning. "Your father will be so pleased."

"I'll send him the news as soon as we return to Branbury House," she said, settling back and fanning her face. They had all worked so hard for this, and now, finally, they could begin to see the results.

At the moment, though, she looked forward to nothing so much as a quiet sit-down with a book. Her face felt stretched from smiling for so long.

"Are you still attending the Allendale soiree tonight?" Conchita asked. "I thought perhaps the mustard-colored silk would be appropriate."

"I assume I am. Melbourne was to escort me. If he hasn't sent over a note, I suppose I shall be forced to send one to him."

When they stopped on the front drive of the borrowed house, however, she thought that perhaps a note wouldn't be necessary. A curricle stood there, and though she'd never seen Melbourne in one, she supposed that he owned several.

"I trust your morning was successful, Your Highness?" Grimm the butler intoned as he pulled open the front door.

"Indeed it was. Who is calling?"

"Charles Stenway, the Duke of Harek, Your Highness. He awaits your pleasure in the morning room."

"Harek? I've never heard of him." She sighed as she pulled off her gloves. "Very well. Conchita?"

The two of them walked into the morning room. Halfway inside, she stopped. A well-built man of medium height stood by the fireplace, his blond hair edged with copper in the fire's glow. He faced her, then sketched a deep, reverential bow. "Your Highness," he said in a low, cultured voice.

Belatedly she inclined her head. "Your Grace. I'm pleased to meet you, but I have to admit, I'm somewhat at a loss as to the reason for your presence. You're aware that the rey my father is on his way to Scotland?"

"Yes, your butler informed me. Might we sit?" He gestured at the couch.

"Certainly." Rather than the couch, though, which would mean a more intimate conversation, she sank into one of the overstuffed chairs that bordered the fireplace. Conchita stood behind her. "What may I do for you, then?"

"The Prince Regent sent for me this morning, and requested that I serve as the British liaison to Costa Habichuela. I gratefully accepted the honor, of course. And so I came directly here to—"

"What happened to Melbourne?" she interrupted.

"His Highness said that his duties demanded his attention elsewhere." He flipped his fingers in a dismissive gesture. "Truth be told, Melbourne is always engaged in some enterprise or other. He would have made a fine merchant."

She swiftly reassessed her opinion of Harek. He seemed both ambitious and eager to please, and apparently was either very traditional or very jealous of Melbourne. "You don't approve of a nobleman engaging in business?"

"It's unseemly. Business is what solicitors and accountants and bankers are for." He gave her a warm smile. "Let us not talk of such things. I believe you are attending the Allendale ball tonight? It would be my pleasure to offer you escort."

Josefina smiled back at him. "If I might ask, are you married, Your Grace?"

"I am lamentably single," he returned. "I have spent the last few years abroad in Canada, and only recently returned."

"And what did you do in Canada, Your Grace, since you do not personally engage in business?"

"I hunted. Remarkable place, Canada. Deer, moose, bears, mountain lions, geese, wolves, beavers—an amazing variety of wildlife."

"And how thoughtful of them all to be located in one place for your pleasure."

"Ah, you jest." He chuckled.

"And now you've returned home."

His green eyes twinkled as they met hers. "And now I've returned home. A hopefully fortuitous event for both of us."

Well, he'd made his meaning clear enough. "We shall see." Gesturing at Conchita, she rose. "If you'll excuse me, I have some correspondence. May I expect you at eight o'clock tonight?"

He stood when she did. "I will be here. If you require anything before then, please send me word. I've given my address to your butler, and I am at your disposal."

"Thank you, Your Grace. I shall see you tonight."

Harek took a step forward. "With your permission," he said, and reached for her fingers. Silently he bowed over her hand, brushing his lips against her knuckles. "Until tonight, Your Highness," he said, bowing again.

"Good afternoon," she returned, watching as Conchita showed him out.

As the maid returned, Josefina made her way to the writing desk. "That was interesting," she said, pulling out a sheet of paper. "I'll have to let Father know that we have a new liaison."

"One who already wants to marry you, I think," Conchita added.

"At least he's polite. I can't see myself moved to slap him."

But could she see herself moved to kiss him? That, she supposed, was beside the point. Damn Melbourne anyway, the coward. She'd obviously been too much for him, and he'd fled. She only hoped he would attend the ball tonight, so she could show him how easily he'd been replaced.

Chapter 7

"illits, haven't we had this conversation already?" Sebastian asked over the noise of the country dance being played in the Allendale ballroom.

"I remain unconvinced that reducing a labor force is good for the economy," the viscount returned.

"Then vote against the measure. Personally, I believe that encouraging families to send their children to school rather than having them make bricks will better benefit England into the future. An ignorant population requires more monetary assistance from its government, rather than less."

"But—"

"No," Sebastian cut him off. "That is my argument. Agree with it, or don't. I'm not going to discuss it further." He inclined his head and turned away. "Good evening."

"That was a bit harsh," Zachary said, approaching from the doorway, his wife on his arm. "You'll make him weep."

"I've discovered there's only so much idiocy I can tolerate," the duke returned, drawing a breath and trying to cool his temper. Willits might have deserved a set-down, but the man could provide helpful votes on occasion.

"This should make you smile, then," Zach commented, already grinning. "You tell him, Caro. I don't want to get blamed for it."

Caroline delicately cleared her throat. "My mother has just written me. She and my father are coming to London. I'm not sure who else will be joining them."

Oh, good God. "That's good news," he said. "I know you've missed them."

"Look," Zachary chortled. "Now Seb's going to cry."

"Don't you think it's a bit cruel, brother, to vaunt your wife's family as a device of torture?"

"I . . . I meant no such thing. You know *I* like them." He faced his wife. "You know I do, Caroline."

She smiled. "He's bamming you, Zachary."

"That's nice, isn't it? I'm going to get a drink." With a half-amused glare, Zachary stomped off.

"I do love him, you know," Caroline said quietly, a look of happiness on her face as she gazed after her husband. "So much. He rarely takes people at their face value. He always sees more. Very painterlike of him, really."

"Which is why so many people like him." Leaning down, Sebastian kissed Caroline on the cheek. "I shall apologize every day if you like, for trying to discourage your union. You are very good for him."

"And he is very good for me." Her smile deepened. "Instead of a string of apologies, I will ask for the next dance."

"It's yours." He held out his hand, and she clasped it.

"Oh, I say," Zachary grumbled, a trio of glasses in his hands, as they joined the line forming for the country dance.

The music began, and the two rows of dancers bowed

to one another. As soon as Sebastian stepped onto the floor it seemed as though every unmarried female present grabbed a father or a brother or a slow-moving male by-stander to join in, but he was accustomed to that. And this time it was, in a sense, a relief. Whatever his family might reckon, no one else seemed to think that he'd formed an attachment to any one female in particular. Which was good, because he hadn't.

He circled Caroline, then the chit standing to her right, sidestepped, and touched hands with the next female over. Lightning coursed from his fingertips to his toes at the contact. *Christ.*

"Oh, good evening, Melbourne," Princess Josefina said, and moved back down the line again.

It took all of his control to keep from rubbing his fin-gertips. They felt burned. What the devil was she doing there? The Costa Habichuela contingent had journeyed to Scotland in search of further loans—or so he'd thought.

As he turned, he slid a glance down the line. Josefina stepped forward around the man opposite her and moved back to the line again. The Duke of Harek.

For the next ten minutes he kept the easy, mildly amused expression on his face. Inside, however, he didn't feel nearly as calm. It was one thing to see her when he hadn't ex-pected to, when he'd thought he would have another fort-night to resolve his . . . confusion before he saw her again. It was something else entirely to stumble across her in the company of another man.

They shifted, circling one another again. "I thought you too busy to attend a party," she said.

"It was the escorting duties that took too much of my time," he returned. "Not the soirees."

"Ah. I thought perhaps it was fear of me."

Before he could answer that, the dance swept her away again. *Damnation.* How could her mere presence set his world spinning? He practically governed England, and he couldn't speak to her without . . . without wanting more of her. Wanting her. Badly.

The music ended. He shook himself and joined in the applause, then escorted Caroline back to Zachary.

"Seb?" Zachary muttered, handing over a glass of port.

"I'm fine," he grumbled, taking a deep swallow.

"I meant that she's—"

"May I take one of your precious moments?" her melodious voice came from behind him.

Steeling himself, he turned around. "Of course, Your Highness," he said crisply. "Harek."

"Melbourne," Harek replied. "I wanted to come over and thank you. When you resigned from your liaison post, Prinny summoned me to take it over. I have never been more pleased to serve my country." He smiled at Josefina.

"Yes," she took up. "His Grace is a delightful gentleman. He's escorting me to the theater tomorrow night. I've always longed to see a London theatrical."

"Perhaps we can convince players to visit Costa Habichuela," Harek commented.

" 'We'?" Sebastian repeated. "Are you emigrating, then, Harek?"

The duke's smile deepened. "One never knows."

Sebastian wanted to hit the duke, wanted to wipe the confident, arrogant grin from his pleasant face. He curled his fingers into a fist.

Abruptly Zachary moved between them. "A word with you, Melbourne?" he said, gesturing toward the doorway and then glancing at Harek and the princess. "Excuse us for a moment. It's a family matter."

"Of course," Josefina said, her gaze still on Sebastian.

When Zachary nudged his shoulder he started, then turned and left the room. He kept walking, hearing Zach and Caroline on his heels, until he reached the Allendales' library. Once the three of them were inside, his brother closed the door.

"Apologies," Zachary said slowly, "but I wanted to avoid a scene."

Sebastian rounded on him. " 'A scene'? You didn't want me to cause a scene? How dare you take it on yourself to—"

"*I* nearly caused a scene," his brother said forcefully. "That ape. As if Harek is anything more than a poor replacement for you, because you were being noble."

He wasn't so sure there was anything noble about it. "Oh."

"Shall we leave? I'll have the coach brought around."

"Don't be ridiculous. I won't be chased away from a soiree because of a nitwit and a chit, royal or not."

"But I thought you were trying to distance yourself from her. That's why you resigned the position."

"I don't need you to protect me, Zachary. I am quite aware of who I am and what I am and what is at stake every time I open my mouth or put pen to paper. That is my responsibility and my duty and my position. Not yours."

"Fine. That's my fault, I suppose, for thinking you might have grown a new heart. Good evening, Melbourne." With that he stalked out of the room. Caroline offered a more sympathetic glance and then followed her husband.

As the door closed, Sebastian walked to one of the long windows. The moment he returned to the ballroom Willits would be there, trying to compliment his way back into the fold. A dozen other peers he'd greeted and avoided were still expecting a moment of conversation with him, as well. And since he'd danced with Caroline, all of the single chits would think they had a chance with him tonight.

Scowling, he wandered to the back of the room where

Allendale kept the majority of his ill-read library. A moment later one of the books caught his eye, and he shifted the step stool over so he could climb up and reach it high on its unread perch. *A History of the Southern Americas*. From the publication date it was six years old, but he paged through it, anyway.

Only a small portion of the text had been devoted to the Mosquito Coast, but he sat by the fire to read the section, anyway. The Spanish had taken most of Central and South America and all the riches therein, but they had conspicuously avoided the Mosquito Coast. The reason for this, according to the author, one John Rice-Able, was because the area had been deemed worthless, a miasma of flooded, malaria-ridden deltas, impenetrable jungles, and oppressive year-round heat and humidity.

The description couldn't have been farther from the one in Embry's prospectus. Here he found no mention of gentle sea breezes or easily cleared land, or of a thriving town filled with promise. Admittedly, this was two pages of generalizations versus the four hundred and twenty detailed ones of the prospectus, but it was enough to raise some questions.

Well, he knew of one way to get further information: Find Mr. John Rice-Able, who hopefully resided somewhere reachable. Slowly he closed the book and returned it to its place. Something about Costa Habichuela and its royalty had felt too good to be true, however nebulous his suspicions. This wasn't much, but enough pieces formed a complete puzzle.

As he stepped down from the stool, the library door opened again. "I thought to find you hiding here," Josefina's voice came from behind him.

He faced her. "Did you tire of your new liaison? Surely he can't have regaled you with all of his hunting stories already. Or did he run from you in terror?"

"Ha! The Duke of Harek is a very agreeable man. I may marry him."

It took all of his willpower to keep from surging forward and grabbing her. "I hadn't realized your standards were so low," he returned, just managing to keep his voice even. "He does share your affinity for nonsense, I suppose."

She stalked forward, her mustard-colored gown swishing with each step. "What the devil is that supposed to mean?"

He was not about to mention any of his nonsensical thoughts aloud. "Your absurd air of superiority that you over-reach because you have no real concept of how to behave like royalty," he said instead.

"I should have you hanged for that," she snapped, her fine cheeks darkening.

Apparently he'd made a hit. "Come and try," he taunted.

To his surprise, she kicked off her slippers. "Before I became a princess," she said, fury etched on her pretty face, "I was a soldier's daughter." She stalked over to the fireplace and removed a rapier from its display. "Defend yourself, Melbourne."

"You *are* a lunatic."

"And you will stop insulting me with every breath. Since words don't seem to have any effect on your highly inappropriate behavior, perhaps this will. Defend yourself. I won't warn you again."

For a long moment he looked at her, her bosom heaving and her chin held high. She was absolutely magnificent. "No."

"What?"

"You may have forgotten your station, Your Highness, but I haven't forgotten mine. I have no intention being discovered dueling in someone's library. Especially not with some chit twelve years my junior."

Abruptly she dropped the weapon and sat on the chair

he'd vacated earlier. "Then I surrender," she said, turning her gaze to the fire.

Perhaps he'd gone mad, hadn't realized it, and was now ensconced in Bedlam, talking to himself. "Beg pardon?"

"I know you like me, because you kissed me. Twice. But then you simply left our—my—presence without a word. So I thought I would try arguing with you, since that seems to pull you out of that haughtiness of yours. You walked away again. My next option was to provoke a fight. Not even that did more than cause you a moment of annoyance. So I surrender."

He clenched his jaw so his mouth wouldn't drop open. "You mean to say that this—all of this—was some sort of seduction?"

"My father's read all about you and your family, and he's quite an admirer of yours. A union between us was his dream, I suppose. He even asked me to pretend to be three years younger than I am, because he said that gentlemen who remarry prefer young wives. But then after you kissed me that second time, you've done nothing but avoid me."

Sebastian blinked several times as he tried to absorb what she was saying. He prided himself on knowing things, frequently before anyone else did. His siblings even credited him with the ability to read minds. On rare occasions he found himself surprised. Since he'd made Princess Josefina's acquaintance he'd been in that state almost constantly, but never more so than at that moment. "You're five-and-twenty, then," he began, considering mathematics the easiest bit to grasp.

Josefina sighed. "Yes, I am. I'm sorry I lied to you." She stood again, retrieving the rapier and replacing it on its wall bracket. "I'd best go; Harek's probably looking for me." She stepped back into her shoes.

"Will your father set you after Harek now?" he asked,

taking a step after her. When she entered a room, the lights brightened. Letting them dim again seemed criminal.

"Of course he will. He wants me to marry, and as a princess, even a new one who can't remember her station, I can't wed less than a duke."

He wasn't used to being considered on the bare cusp of acceptability, but for the moment he put that aside. It simply wasn't the point, and he needed to concentrate. "Do you like him?"

She reached the door and looked back over her shoulder at him. "I like *you*. Good evening, Your Grace."

Bloody hell. "Why don't you and Harek join me in my theater box tomorrow night?" he suggested. "Harek doesn't have a box, and mine is the best in the house."

Josefina faced him. "Why?"

Because I like you, as well. "Because an appearance of cooperation between your former and present liaisons will be more helpful than the appearance of a rift."

She studied his face for a moment, then nodded. "I shall inform him."

"Very good." He took a breath. "Just to satisfy my curiosity, Your Highness, what in the world made you think that being outrageous and argumentative would attract me?"

"Because everyone speaks your name with bated breath. You don't have enough people being argumentative or outrageous in your life," she answered. "That is still my opinion."

Then she left the room. He hadn't mauled her this time, at least, but that was more because of the rapier than because of any self-control on his part. This Josefina, the less arrogant, more sincere one, seemed closer to being a princess than the previous one. And she attracted him even more. Still more troubling, when he talked with her, argued with her, kissed her, for the first time in four years he didn't feel . . . lonely.

* * *

That had been close. Thank goodness she'd seen him reading that book. All her father needed was for a very influential duke to decide he didn't like the Central American coastline and discourage all of his peers from purchasing bonds, discounted or not.

As a consequence, though, she had to keep him closer now than she felt comfortable doing. Having someone like Harek escorting her and courting her was much easier—Harek wanted power and prestige and money, and she wanted an ally. Melbourne, on the other hand, seemed to want . . . her.

"There you are, Your Highness," the Duke of Harek said, approaching from the direction of the ballroom. "We can't have you getting lost; that would cause an international scandal."

Josefina smiled, taking his arm. "I'm pleased you're here to look after me."

"Not as pleased as I am, I'll wager."

Well, she could agree with that. "It might interest you to know that the Duke of Melbourne has offered to share his box at the theater with us. He wants you—and everyone else—to know that Costa Habichuela still has his support and endorsement."

Green eyes swept across hers. "Is that the only thing he wants me to know?"

She frowned. "What do you mean?"

"Come now, Your Highness. You have men falling at your feet. Melbourne, though, is considerably more serious competition than"—he looked across the room as they returned inside—"than him, for instance." The duke gestured at a rounded gentleman with red cheeks and a kindly expression.

The fellow saw their attention, and excused himself from a circle of his fellows to join them. "Your Grace," he said, bowing, "would you do me the great honor of introducing me to your companion?"

"Oh, please, Henning," Harek snorted. "What in God's name for? It's not as though you could have anything in the world to converse with her about."

"I—"

"There you are, Francis," a familiar deep voice came from behind her. The Duke of Melbourne moved around them to shake the round fellow's hand. "Have you been introduced to London's newest delight?"

"I say, Melbourne, no, I hav—"

"Allow me, then. Your Highness, Mr. Francis Henning. Francis, Her Highness, Princess Josefina of Costa Habichuela."

Henning bowed even lower than he had for Harek. "A very great honor," he said, as he straightened again. "You shine like a diamond, if I may be so bold."

"Why, thank you, Mr. Henning." She glanced at Melbourne, to find his gaze on her. This surprised her; she'd thought him incurably arrogant and high in the instep, and yet here he'd arrived to rescue a man much below his station from embarrassment. Her new escort's reaction had been high-handed and rude in the extreme. Was that how he saw her? She'd certainly been that way toward Melbourne, but that had been personal.

"What do you think, Henning," Melbourne continued, "should I ask Her Highness for the next dance?"

Oh, dear, she'd barely had time to collect herself since their last conversation. The Francis fellow, though, was grinning. Whether that was because of the question or because the Duke of Melbourne was treating him like a bosom friend, she didn't know.

"Most definitely, Your Grace," he chortled.

All three men looked at her expectantly. To escape a dance all she had to say was that she'd already promised it to her escort. Melbourne would go away, and she would have until tomorrow night to prepare for their next encounter. Still, if it kept his attention on her and away from meddling, she didn't have much of a choice. Truthfully, it wasn't a difficult decision, anyway. He was a very fine dancer.

She held out her hand. "If you think you can manage it," she said.

Taking her fingers, he lifted an eyebrow. "As long as you resist maiming me, I don't foresee any difficulty."

Josefina could dispute that, but his touch made her tremble a little. "I make no promises," she returned.

As Melbourne guided her onto the dance floor, he smiled. In response, her heart flip-flopped. Amazing, that a simple shifting of muscles could so alter a man's demeanor. "You should do that more often."

"Introduce you to untitled gentlemen?"

"Smile."

"Ah. I'll try to remember that in between slappings and attempted skewerings."

"You know I never meant to run you through."

Gray eyes assessed her. "What would you have done if I'd picked up the other rapier?"

The heat his presence caused began to spread. "You would never presume to prick me," she returned in a low voice.

Music began. A waltz, blast it all. With a country dance they wouldn't have been able to discuss anything . . . personal. His sensuous, capable lips curved again, as though he knew exactly what she was thinking.

His hand slid around her waist, drawing her closer. As they swayed and turned in time to the music, the fingers that held hers flexed. *Madre de dios*. She wanted to kiss him again, to feel his mouth on hers, to taste the desire she knew he had for her.

And still he said nothing.

"Is this the way you mean to refrain from arguing with me?" she finally interjected. "To have no conversation with me at all?"

"What do you wish me to say?" he returned in a low murmur. "That I've been thinking of pricking you since the first moment we met?"

She gulped a breath. "Have you, now?" she asked, heat spreading downward.

"Yes. You've been thinking the same thing, I'll wager." Slowly he pulled her a little closer to him.

"Then why is Harek your country's new liaison to mine?"

Her father should never have requested that Melbourne be involved with something as precarious as Costa Habichuela, she began to realize. Harek was a much more suitable presence. Now, though, she had two dukes to deal with. And this one, the man who saw her far more clearly than she wished, the one whose touch made her shiver and whose kiss melted her insides, this was the one from whom she needed to distance herself. When he'd given her the chance, though, she'd intentionally drawn him back in.

"Harek is your new liaison now because I won't be led down the garden path all unawares," he returned.

She shook herself. *Concentrate, blast it all.* "Which garden path is that?"

"Yours."

"I don't know what you're tal—"

"If I am seen in your company, it will be because I decided it should be so—not because someone else ordered or requested it." His dark gray gaze held hers. "And I won't be played for a fool."

"I hardly think that trying to arrange a marriage between a duke and a princess makes either one of us foolish."

For a moment he danced with her in silence. "You are a great deal of trouble," he finally whispered.

"Oh, yes, I am that." She smiled, trying not to shiver at the warm intimacy of his tone. "So what do we do next?"

"We attend the theater tomorrow night."

"Yes, but when will you kiss me next?"

She thought something flashed behind his eyes—surprise? Lust? It was gone so swiftly that she couldn't be certain.

"Tomorrow night, at the theater," he returned.

Oh, my.

Chapter 8

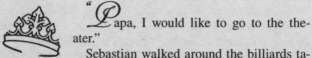"Papa, I would like to go to the theater."

Sebastian walked around the billiards table to make an intentionally poor shot. "I know you would. But the performance tonight is *Hamlet,* and I don't think you'd like the ending very much." Aside from that, he didn't want Peep to witness any more of his barely controlled behavior around Princess Josefina Embry.

"Is it a tragedy?"

A second later he realized that she was talking about the play. "It is. A very large tragedy." He stepped back as she made her own shot. It wasn't bad at all; in another two or three years she could probably challenge even Shay's mathematical precision. "I'll make you a bargain, Peep. The next play to open at Drury Lane is *A Midsummer Night's Dream.* If you'll forego *Hamlet*, I will take you to see the other."

His daughter leaned on her billiards cue. "Just you and me?"

"Just us."

She nodded, her smile bright enough to put the sun to shame. "Then yes, I agree. You and I don't get to spend as much time together as I would like."

Sebastian tilted his head at her. "You think not?"

"Well, no," she returned, lining up another shot. "Except for today, I feel like I've hardly seen you all week. I'm very busy, and you're very busy. We need to make time for one another."

"I apologize for that, then." He knew he'd been distracted since Prinny had assigned him to Costa Habichuela, but he hadn't been aware of neglecting Penelope. She was his world, after all.

"A very large birthday party with acrobats would make up for a great deal," she continued.

"I see." He stifled a grin. "I'll keep that in mind."

Abruptly she set her cue across the table and faced him. "When I said just you and me," she began, her small face serious, "I didn't mean that it always has to be that way."

Sebastian leaned his own cue against the table. "Beg pardon?"

"Well, my friend Mary Haley says that you have to remarry because I'm not a boy."

"That's not true," he said slowly, considering his answer. "You can't inherit my title, but your Uncle Shay can. I don't need to remarry, and I don't need a son. I have you."

"But do you want to? Get married again, I mean. Because sometimes I think it might be nice to have another female in the house besides me."

He walked around the table, crouching in front of his daughter. "You have three aunties, now."

"Yes. And Aunt Nell knows all about fashion, Aunt Caroline is teaching me to paint, and Aunt Sarala knows how to charm snakes."

"But?" he prompted after a moment, hearing the unspoken reservation in her statement.

Her face folded into a thoughtful scowl. "Nothing. They go home at night, and Aunt Nell has Rose, and nobody has me." Tears welled in her eyes.

Sebastian pulled his daughter into a tight hug. "I have you, sweetling." Christ. The thoughts of a seven-year-old humbled him. "Do you want me to get married again, then?" he asked, touching his forehead to hers.

"Not to Mary's aunt. She laughs like a donkey." Peep brayed in demonstration.

"So that was her?" he returned, forcing a grin. "I thought it was an actual donkey." He pulled out his pocket watch. "Shall we adjourn for some luncheon? I have a meeting this afternoon."

She kissed him on the forehead. "You're a very good Papa, you know."

"I do try."

Rising, he took her hand and they went downstairs to the breakfast room. Peep wanted a mother. It made sense; she probably had only a very vague memory of Charlotte, and though they talked about her often, he'd noticed lately that the tales had the same feel to them as any fairy story.

Did he want to remarry? A year ago he would have dismissed the question. Two years ago, it would have made him angry. Now, though, he simply didn't know.

What he did know, however, was that Mary Haley's aunt would make a better match for him than Josefina Embry. For one thing, Lady Margaret Trent wasn't heir to a Central American monarchy. For another, Margaret didn't spin his head around as Josefina seemed able to do. He didn't want his head spun. He liked being in control and having things go as they should.

He barely knew the damn princess, anyway. Josefina claimed to prefer him over Harek, but he doubted that would make any difference if Harek proposed and he didn't. And he wouldn't. Sebastian blew out his breath. If he had a quarter of the heartless, calculating resolve he was well-known for, none of this should be troubling him. Yet obviously it was.

Damn the chit. What he needed to do was take a mistress, someone on whom he could exercise the physical demons that after four years had abruptly made themselves known again. Someone discreet, compliant, and with a pretty enough face that he could forget the dark-eyed one that continued to haunt him. Peep looked up at him.

"What's wrong?"

Wonderful. Now he couldn't even conceal his emotions from an infant. "Nothing. Go ahead, will you? I need to make a note of something before I forget."

She nodded, walking into luncheon without him. "Stanton," he heard her say, "did Cook remember that I particularly like cheese toast and asparagus soup?"

"Indeed she did, my lady."

Sebastian returned upstairs, heading not to his office, but to the library. There, over the fire, hung a portrait of his lovely Charlotte. Her blue eyes twinkled, even on the flat, painted surface. Chestnut hair coiled atop her head and escaped from the pins that held it, as though it had been ruffled by a stray breeze while she'd paused in the garden to smile at him.

He could still recall her voice, her laugh, her touch, just as he remembered her last days, when her skin had been pale and drawn, her eyes dull, and her smile a mask that hadn't fooled either of them.

What he couldn't remember was the last time she'd been in his dreams. For months it had been every night, to the point that if not for Peep and his siblings he wouldn't have wanted to awaken again. Then she'd begun to visit a little less regularly, but still frequently—more days in a month than not. When, then, had it stopped? And why for the past five nights had he dreamed of someone else?

He knew Charlotte's painted expression wouldn't change, just as he knew without thinking that of course she would want him and their daughter to be happy. But he wasn't certain whether it was happiness he would find with Josefina, or disaster.

Gathering himself, he ducked into his office and wrote out a swift note to Lord Beltram, one of the ministers of public records. If anyone could determine the present whereabouts of one John Rice-Able, Beltram could. Before he allowed his heart to become tangled in anything, even pure impossibilities, his mind wanted some answers as to why one person's paradise was another's insect-infested swamp.

"I don't understand," Conchita said, as she fastened the pearl necklace around Josefina's neck. "You have two dukes courting you now?"

"No," Josefina returned, taking one last look into her dressing mirror before she stood, "officially, I am not being courted at all."

"But unofficially?"

She smiled. "Unofficially I think one of them wants to marry me, and the other one wants to bed me."

"Jo—Your Highness!"

"I would call that a very promising beginning, wouldn't you?"

"I wouldn't call it any such thing."

Halfway out her bedchamber door, Josefina turned around. "Are you, or are you not, my confidante, Conchita?"

The maid dipped a curtsy. "I am, of course."

"Then I will say such things to you, because you should know what's going on." She frowned briefly. "And because I certainly can't say those things to anyone else."

"I apologize, Your Highness."

Josefina didn't answer. After having Conchita with her for over ten years, she probably did tend to be a little over-familiar, but at the same time she wanted someone about whom she could trust.

None of that explained why she hadn't mentioned to her maid that Melbourne had kissed her, or that he meant to do so again tonight. If the cause of Costa Habichuela required that sacrifice of her, she would make it. Josefina touched her fingers to her lips, smiling as her heart accelerated. She would make that sacrifice gladly, and would do so several more times, if required.

The Duke of Harek waited in the foyer as she descended the stairs. "You are lovelier than any creature on this earth," he said reverently, bowing.

He'd probably hunted enough of those creatures to know. "Thank you, Your Grace. Shall we go? I'm eager to see the theater."

Outside he handed her and Conchita into his coach, then climbed in behind them. As soon as the door closed, they rumbled down the drive.

"Did you attend the theater in Jamaica?" the duke asked.

"Whenever I could. The last two years, though, we were simply too busy."

"I've been a bit starved for culture, myself. Theater in Quebec consisted mainly of natives dancing about in cured deerskins."

"I hope we shall both be pleased, then." Josefina was beginning to wonder whether he ever spoke a sentence that didn't have a dead animal in it.

"Tell me, when does your father return from Scotland, Your Highness? I confess that I'm anxious to meet the rey and begin my official duties as liaison to Costa Habichuela."

"You're fulfilling them already," she returned, "simply by allowing me to be seen. As for the rey, he meant for the trip to be a brief one, and he should be back in London by the end of next week."

"Splendid. Most excellent."

"Yes. I miss him and the queen, and we must begin purchasing supplies for our return voyage."

"I hope there may be room for additional passengers on that voyage," he said with a charming smile. "I'm sure there must be a few Britons who would like to start life anew, in the company of the right . . . well, companion."

"That will be up to my father," she returned just as smoothly. If he attempted to make his intentions any clearer, he would have to produce a pastor from his pocket.

"Of course." He turned the conversation to fox hunting there in England, and seemed to think it would be something she would enjoy watching, if not participating in.

Finally the coach stopped, and he disembarked first. "I know which duke wants to marry you," Conchita whispered as he handed them down to the ground.

"Hush."

A horde of vehicles crowded the street in front of the theater. Once they made their way inside, so many people filled the lobby and flowed up the central staircase that she couldn't even find her own feet. Princess, duke, knight, or wealthy merchant—in the lobby no one had room for a deep breath.

And then the path in front of her cleared. "This way, Your Highness," the Duke of Melbourne said, offering his arm.

She took it gratefully, belatedly noticing that his brother, Charlemagne, stood just beyond him. Melbourne rarely seemed to go anywhere alone, though at the same time even a complete stranger would know who commanded the group. He wore all black tonight but for his stark white cravat, and the result was ... mesmerizing. Given the other females devouring him with their eyes, she wasn't the only one to find him so.

"Is it always this crowded?" she asked, climbing the stairs beside him. Before them the crowd parted like a receding ocean wave. For one of the few times since this all had begun, she absolutely felt like a princess.

"You are the toast of the Town, Your Highness," he returned. "Everyone wants to see the Embrys, who seem to be bringing London so much good fortune."

" 'Seem to be'?" she returned, keeping the amused expression on her face.

"I know you slapped *me*," he pointed out, humor deepening his voice. "Who knows how many others you might have maimed."

"Only you, Melbourne."

"You may call me Sebastian, if you wish."

A breath shivered through her. "We'll see."

The upstairs crowd wasn't as dense, and it was there that she saw people whom she recognized from other *ton* gatherings. And she realized that what Melbourne had said was true—as many theater-goers gazed at her as stared at him.

As they continued along the ever-more empty hallway, she glanced behind her to see Harek and Lord Charlemagne in step and discussing something—probably hunting—with Conchita a few feet behind them. After the crowd below, she was somewhat surprised that their party remained intact.

"Almost there," Melbourne said in a low, intimate voice, sending her a brief sideways glance.

"This theater is far larger than the one at Morant Bay."

He nodded. "London is a larger city than Morant Bay."

"And I always had a chaperone with me," she continued. "Is that why your brother is here? To protect you?"

"From you, I suppose?"

"Who else are you afraid of?"

A heart-stopping smile touched his mouth. "My brother is here to keep Harek occupied, in case you should need me to show you to a private closet."

"And what if I don't require that?"

"I leave it up to you, Your Highness."

"You're that confident, are you?"

He moved a fraction closer to her. "I suppose we'll find out." Melbourne straightened again. "Here we are. After you." Pulling aside the rich red curtain, he gestured her to step inside his private box.

She felt as though she'd stepped into another world. This theater was easily triple the size of the one she'd frequented in Morant Bay. And the rows of theater-goers below looked like a glittering, multicolored ocean. And all of those people would see her sitting with two dukes and a lord. She smiled. Even her father couldn't have dreamed of loftier heights.

"Your Highness, you and Harek take the front chairs," Melbourne was saying. "Shay and I bow to your popularity."

But she'd wanted to sit beside him. Three chairs sat at the front of the box, another four behind. Conchita had already claimed the least visible one in the corner. She didn't suppose, though, that Lord Charlemagne would wish to sit in the second row by himself.

Melbourne held her chair for her. "You'll have to imagine me sitting behind you, gazing at you, at the soft curve of your ear," he murmured as she sat.

She twisted her neck to look up at him. "I daresay I'll scarcely remember that you're there," she whispered back.

He bowed, almost brushing her cheek with his lips, but not quite. "Liar," he breathed, and the hairs on the back of her neck stood up.

Whatever his doubts about Melbourne's motives, Harek was obviously pleased as a cat with a ball of twine to be seen sitting beside her in the front of the theater's best box. Behind her, Melbourne and Lord Charlemagne were quietly discussing something about a birthday party and acrobats, though she couldn't overhear all of the conversation in the midst of the chattering that surrounded them.

Harek leaned toward her. "As a word of warning, this play is so blasted long that we won't see intermission for nearly two hours. Luckily falling asleep's not a sin, as long as you don't fall out of your chair."

"I don't think I shall have to worry about that, but thank you."

As he leaned over the edge of the box to greet someone below, she distinctly heard Melbourne's brother mutter the word "buffoon." That troubled her; not that Harek seemed anything but a buffoon to her, either, but that the *haute ton* in general might think him one. She certainly didn't need that sentiment joined in any way to her family.

A moment later the curtain lifted and the play began. Though she'd read *Hamlet* in the course of her studies, she'd never seen it performed before. She sat forward.

Twenty minutes later she heard a soft snore beside her, and turned to look. Sunk down in his chair, arms crossed and his head tilted back, Harek had at least braced himself so that he wouldn't succumb to his own sin of falling out of his chair.

The box behind her was silent, but she knew without any doubt that Melbourne remained wide awake. He would be gazing at her, he'd said. Her skin prickled. Dammit, he'd said that she would be thinking about him, about how he wanted to kiss her again. It wasn't just that, though, that started warmth between her thighs.

He wanted to do more than kiss her, and it would be in the best interest of her father's plans to allow him to do so. As for her own best interest, she knew with an abrupt clarity that she wanted him to be her first. Every other man she knew would settle for a kingdom and seconds, but not Melbourne.

She had no wish to sit next to a snoring buffoon for four hours—not when she could spend at least a little of that time being kissed by a man whom her cause needed, a man who heated her from the inside out. She rose.

"Excuse me for a few moments," she whispered, moving to the back of the box as Conchita stood.

"I'll show you the way," Melbourne said easily, getting to his feet. "Shay, might I get you a port?"

"If you don't mind," his brother replied in the same low voice, rising halfway to his feet and then sitting again as she passed by him. "I'll make sure our guest doesn't lose his balance."

The candlelit hallway seemed bright after the dimness of the theater, and Josefina blinked as they emerged. "This way," Melbourne said, leading her a short distance to one of the curtained privacy alcoves. Then he slowed, drawing even with the maid. "What's your name?"

"Conchita, Your Grace."

"Conchita, you will wait exactly there," he said, indicating the wall several yards away. "You will ensure Her Highness's privacy, and you will not hear anything. Is that clear?"

The maid sent Josefina a nervous look. "Your Highness?"

"Do as you're told, Conchita."

With a curtsy the maid moved away to where Melbourne had indicated. The duke glanced up and down the empty hall, then held the half-open curtain aside. "After you."

Even if she'd wanted to refuse him, she wasn't certain

she would have been willing to argue with that tone. He stepped in behind her and pulled the curtain closed. Echoing dimly from inside she could hear the play continuing.

> *"He hath, my lord, of late made many tenders*
> *Of his affection to me."*

"I have to say," she whispered, facing him in the tiny alcove lit only by a single candle, "this is quite bold of you."

He continued to gaze at her, the sensation disconcerting. As he took a slow step closer her breathing deepened. For heaven's sake, she'd grown up practically surrounded by soldiers and their silly attempts at seduction. Why, then, did having the Duke of Melbourne look at her make her knees weak?

> *"I do not know, my lord, what I should think."*

She could tell herself it was because she needed to secure his cooperation and his influence, but no business she'd ever engaged in made her feel like this. "What are you waiting for? We haven't much time."

"Do you know who John Rice-Able is?" he finally uttered.

"What? I'm not here to be quizzed about acquaintances." She ran a finger along his lapel. "Kiss me, or go away so I can return to the play."

"Is that a yes?"

This close she had to look up at him to meet his gaze. That dark hair with the upturn at his collar, that mouth— if he ever relaxed from the hard place he held himself, she didn't think she would ever want to leave his presence. If only those eyes of his didn't . . . trouble her soul, as well as arouse her body.

"I do know
When the blood burns, how prodigal the soul
Lends the tongue vow."

"No, I don't know him. Why? Is he an investor?"

"He's an author. I thought you might have been introduced."

Josefina brushed his black sleeve with her fingers. Not
touching him seemed absurdly difficult. "No. Are you
jealous of him?"

"Not if you've never met." Finally lifting one of his
hands, he touched her chin, lowering his face toward hers.
When only a breath separated them, he stopped again.
"Say my name," he murmured.

"Melbourne."

"No." His gaze lowered to her mouth. "Say my Christian
name."

"In few, Ophelia,
Do not believe his vows, for they are brokers . . ."

"Sebastian," she breathed.

He kissed her. Josefina wrapped her arms behind his
neck, breathing him in. Silently he pushed her against
the side wall, his mouth hot and hungry as it sought and
captured hers again and again. His hands brushed her
hips, and then his grip firmed, holding her hard against
him.

"I want more," she rasped, clinging against him and not
having to fake the sincerity and urgency in her voice. "I
want you, Sebastian."

Again silently, he slid a hand up from her waist to her
shoulders, the pressure of his fingers against the outside
of her right breast making her gasp. With those clever

fingers he lowered the shoulder of her burgundy gown, his lips following the trail of his hand.

> *". . . Breathing like sanctified and pious bonds,*
> *The better to beguile."*

He lowered the strap to her elbow, freeing her breast. For a heartbeat he gazed at the flesh he'd exposed, then lifted his gray eyes to her face. "It's been a very long time for me," he said, his voice shaking.

The loneliness and longing in his tone seared straight through to her heart. This was what she'd worried about, that he would want more of her than she even possessed. She'd already leapt into the fire, though, and her skin burned. "It's been a lifetime for me," she returned.

He kissed her again, those same clever fingers drawing feather-light, breath-stealing circles closer and closer around her breast until his short nails flicked across her nipple. She felt it all the way down between her thighs, and gasped again.

"Tell me where you'll live in San Saturus," he ordered, his mouth trailing down her shoulder and then clamping over her breast.

"Good . . . God," she managed, digging her fingers into his dark hair. "Why?"

"I want to hear you talk about it."

"I've only seen it . . . ah, once," she said in a shaking whisper. Her knees wanted to give way as he peeled the cloth from her left shoulder and began caressing her other breast, as well.

"What color is it?"

"White . . . white stone, with tall . . . mm*mmm* . . . windows to let in the ocean breeze."

"How many rooms?"

Was he thinking of moving in? Oh, God, she hoped so, if only so he would do this to her every night. "Hundreds. Enough for the royal guard and every cabinet minister."

He straightened, taking her lips again. "Do you want to know something?" he whispered against her mouth, his fingers still caressing her breasts.

"Tell me," she panted, pressing against his hands.

"I think you're lying." With another rough kiss he returned her sleeves to her shoulders and stepped back.

Josefina's mind was a puddle of lust and surprise and dawning frustration. "What? What are you talking about?"

"I don't know what it is, exactly," he continued, his voice still not quite steady, "but something's going on."

"The air bites shrowdly, it is very cold."

"The only thing that's going on, you bastard," she snapped, adjusting the front of her gown, "is that you've proven that you're not good enough for me." She pushed past him and grabbed the curtain.

Melbourne clamped a hand on her shoulder, his grip like iron. "We're not finished," he rumbled, turning her to face him. "How do you do it?"

Half panicked, she jerked free. "Do what? I have no idea what you're—"

"How do you make me . . . want you like this? Is it your perfume, or some drug on your skin? What—"

"So you think you must be drugged to feel attracted to me? We are finished here, sir." She yanked the curtain aside and stepped through, into the hallway.

Conchita immediately hurried forward. "Your Highness? Are you—"

Josefina brushed her away. With every fiber of her being she wanted to flee the building, flee London, flee her own skin, which was still hot and sensitive from his touch. So he thought he was being used, or seduced, that she was lying. But didn't everyone lie and seduce to get that what they wanted or needed? Oh, she hated Melbourne right now—and she still wanted him, damn it all. And damn him.

Chapter 9

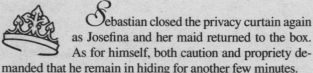Sebastian closed the privacy curtain again as Josefina and her maid returned to the box. As for himself, both caution and propriety demanded that he remain in hiding for another few minutes.

God, she aroused him, and though his logical, practical mind had determined to put a stop to their encounter before any lasting and provable damage could be done, his body—his cock—wanted badly to continue.

Initially he *had* meant to continue, to go as far as was necessary to discover what it was about her and about Costa Habichuela that troubled him so. But immediately—too immediately, as far as his body was concerned—she had struck a note that rang false.

Why would San Saturus—by all of her and her father's accounts a small, picturesque town made up mostly of natives and English ex-patriots—boast a white-stoned behemoth of a palace consisting of hundreds of rooms? The Mosquito King didn't reside there, or he wouldn't have given it away. And if the Spanish knew of a manor of that size overlooking a well-protected ocean harbor, they would have sent troops after it.

But perhaps she'd exaggerated in order to impress him. Perhaps the huge palace was a small villa with tens of rooms. Perhaps the ocean breeze was as pleasant and beckoning as she and the prospectus claimed. And perhaps he was an idiot looking for reasons to distrust a woman toward whom he otherwise felt a great deal of interest and attraction.

"Damnation," he muttered, and pulled open the curtain. As he did so, a gleam on the carpeted floor caught his eye. Josefina's pearl necklace lay there in a forgotten heap. Sebastian picked it up, placed it in his pocket, and went to find a footman and some glasses of port.

When he returned to his box, Josefina was seated beside the still-snoring Harek. Even with her back turned he could feel her hostility. That could be useful, as well. She would have to decide whether her anger outweighed whatever it was she needed from him. He handed one of the glasses to Shay and sat.

"What took you so long?" his brother whispered. "I was ready to begin poking Harek just so I could be certain he wasn't dead and the lot of you hadn't completely deserted me."

"I had them fetch me a better bottle," Sebastian lied. "I refuse to drink the watered down tripe they generally offer. But here, hold this a moment." He handed over his own glass before he reached into his pocket. As he produced the pearl necklace, his brother's eyes widened.

"What—"

"Shh." Leaning forward, he brushed his lips against Josefina's left ear. "I believe this is yours," he murmured, sliding his hand along the arm of her chair to place the necklace in her palm. "Put it in your reticule. It won't do for anyone to see you dressing in public."

"Thank you, Your Grace," she said audibly, her voice rich and easy as always. If not for the shaking of her fingers he would have thought her perfectly composed.

As he sat back and recaptured his drink, Shay continued to eye him. "She dropped it," he said matter-of-factly. "I saw it on the floor just outside."

"Mm-hm."

"Do you think I ran out and bought it just now? Watch the bloody play."

"I am."

During intermission Josefina smiled and chatted with their rapt fellow theater guests as though he hadn't rendered her moaning and half naked earlier, but he noticed that she had either Harek's arm or Shay's, and kept at least one of them between herself and him.

He wondered whether she was more angry that he hadn't completed the seduction, or that he'd caught her in what was most probably a lie. Whatever the answer was to that question, he meant to find out.

In the morning he stifled a yawn as he took his seat in the House of Lords. Four hours of Denmarkian tragedy followed by another six of sleeplessness had soured his mood beyond what even he could call reasonable. As soon as the morning's arguments began over Prinny's newest round of debts, he leaned forward to tap the shoulder of the gentleman seated below him.

The fellow turned around. "Melbourne."

"Lord Beltram. I was wondering if you'd received my inquiry."

"I did. In fact," and he patted his left breast pocket, then pulled a folded piece of paper from it, "I found your fellow. He resides in Eton. Teaches there, actually."

Sebastian took the paper from the minister. "My thanks,"

he said, opening it to read the address. "You've saved me a great deal of effort."

"Then perhaps you won't mind introducing me to those South American royals when they all return to London. At ninety pounds a bond, I'm pulling out of the Italian loans and buying stock in Costa Habichuela. How much have you purchased? Half the country, I'll wager, since you've got the rey practically in your pocket."

"Certainly I'll introduce you, William," he said carefully. If his suspicions were unfounded, he was not going to be the one to cause all of the infant country's much-needed investors to flee. England could use the alliance. "Though you know Harek's taken over the liaison position. I have too many of my own candles burning as it is."

"No doubt," Beltram said, chuckling. He looked past Sebastian. "Lord Deverill."

A hand clapped Sebastian on the shoulder. "Beltram, Melbourne," the marquis said with a short smile.

"Valentine," Sebastian returned. "This is a bit early in the day for you, isn't it?"

His brother-in-law sank into his seat. "You have no idea. Rose has decided she must have teeth, and Eleanor's decided that baths in lavender water will soothe the infant, so I've decided that at the moment Corbett House is the loudest, smelliest location in Britain."

Sebastian laughed. "You were warned that domesticity has its perils."

"Yes, I know. For the most part I actually adore it. To think that Nell and I made that small, squawking, giggling bundle—it's . . . humbling."

For a moment Sebastian gazed at his closest friend. "I know what you mean," he finally said, waiting for the pang in his chest he always felt when he thought of what he'd planned with Charlotte, and what they hadn't had time to do. The pain was still there, but it felt older, like a regret rather than a fresh wound.

"Speaking of idiots," Valentine said, breaking into his reverie, "apparently Harek's taking the princess to Tattersall's today."

"Were we speaking of idiots?"

"Maybe that was just me. I'm trying to figure out why a king looking for investors and contacts leaves his business liaison with his daughter while he rides off to Scotland."

"Because the best way to legitimize a new regime is to marry it with an old, established one."

Valentine looked across the crowded chamber. "You knew that from the beginning, didn't you? That you were being maneuvered toward the altar?"

"It wasn't exactly subtle."

"Then I understand why you resigned your post with them. What baffles me, though, is why you're still waltzing with the chit and taking her to the theater."

The question sounded so simple; it *was* simple. Something about the circumstances of Costa Habichuela troubled him, and he wanted his questions answered. To do that, however, he might just as easily have pursued a friendship with the rey and thereby spared himself any entanglements with the daughter. "Whatever my personal reservations," he said in a low voice, "I have no reason to discourage investors. If I cut ties without explanation, that would likely result."

"I'm glad to hear you say that," the marquis returned. "After Parliament I'm sending my accountant out to purchase a hundred bonds. With a family to think of now, I'm looking for a solid, long-term investment."

Bloody hell. "Hold off on that, will you?" he muttered.

"Aha! I knew it. What the devil's going on?"

Sebastian scowled at his hands. "Maybe nothing. I don't

know. It's just that I've conducted enough business to know that very few things have no downside to them. I'm still trying to determine what the underbelly of Costa Habichuela looks like."

"Fair enough."

It sounded that way, thankfully, but they both knew that he hadn't explained why he continued to focus his attention on Princess Josefina, and why even when he suspected that all was not precisely as she claimed, the most pressing matter seemed to be finding another opportunity to see her.

Harek had found a bench several yards from the main auction pen at Tattersalls, and as Josefina sat and greeted and chatted with everyone from viscounts to grooms, she felt as though she was holding court. The duke stood at her elbow, acting every inch the host, while Lieutenant May served as a visible, black-garbed bodyguard.

"I bought two bonds yesterday," a well-dressed young man was saying as he all but knelt at her feet. "Do you have plans to sell plots of land? I've read the prospectus, and I have to say that I'd rather take my chances owning land in Costa Habichuela than in relying on the charity of my father and older brother."

"He is the youngest son to the Marquis of Bronshire," Harek whispered, leaning over her shoulder. "Five older siblings."

"That isn't something the rey had planned for this visit," she returned with a smile, "but I will let him know that we have at least one interested party."

"And me, Your Highness!" someone further back in the crowd yelled.

"Aye!"

"Aye! I'd trade shoveling horse shit for sea breezes and good land any day!"

Everyone laughed. Goodness. She herself found London enchanting. It had never really occurred to her that anyone would be willing—much less eager—to trade a familiar life for an unknown one in an untamed, unseen land.

"Perhaps once we've had time to utilize the bank's generous loan, we might be able to formalize some sort of immigration agreement with England."

"Why wait?" someone else called. "I'd go in a fast tick!"

She laughed the comment off again. "I shall tell the rey," she repeated. As she spied a trio of ladies approaching, two of them familiar, she stood. "Lady Caroline, Lady Sarala," she said, inclining her head. "And this must be your sister, Lady Deverill."

The brunette marchioness curtsied, a shallow but respectful gesture that reminded Josefina of the woman's eldest brother. "I'm pleased to finally meet you, Your Highness," she said with a smile. "I feel as if I'm the last person in London to do so."

"Harek informs me that he's never seen the auctions this well attended before."

"Perhaps Your Highness would care to refresh yourself by joining us for luncheon?" Lady Deverill returned.

Thank heavens. "That would be acceptable," she said, trying not to sound too eager to escape. "Your Grace, I give you leave to see to that pair of bays you wanted to purchase."

Harek bowed. "My barouche is at your disposal, ladies."

"Thank you," the marchioness said with a smile that didn't meet her eyes, "but we have our own transportation. Your Highness, this way."

As they walked through the boisterous crowd, Conchita and Lieutenant May fell in behind them. In the company of the other three ladies, the addition of a maid and a guard seemed a bit gauche, and Josefina signaled Conchita to approach her.

"You and the lieutenant should return to Branbury House," she said.

"But Your High—"

"I'll be fine." She raised her voice. "Certainly one of these gracious ladies will be kind enough to return me home after our luncheon."

"Of course, Your Highness."

Conchita bobbed, her expression still dubious. "Very well. Lieutenant?"

With her servants gone, Josefina concentrated her attention on her companions. "Did Melbourne ask you to come by?" she asked, unable to keep her voice from sticking on his name. She hated the blasted man, and she hated the way she'd dreamed all night of his hands and his mouth caressing her. He thought he was so clever, to excite her and then accuse her of lying when she couldn't even remember what she'd said.

"Heavens no," Lady Deverill returned, stopping beside a large barouche with the yellow Deverill crest painted on the door panel. "Caro and Sarala have been talking about you, and I wanted to meet you."

"I'm pleased for that," Josefina returned, allowing the groomsman to hand her into the carriage, "because though my country can use the publicity of my presence, I have to admit that having so many people hanging on my every word is a bit . . . disconcerting."

"They all adore you," Lady Sarala commented with a warm smile, the trace of a foreign accent in her words.

"If I may ask, my lady, you're not from here, are you? London, I mean."

"I grew up in India," Lord Charlemagne's wife said. "And I must say, you've done a much better job at facing the *ton* of London than I did."

"My country's good will depends on it."

Lady Sarala nodded again. "Shay tells me that you had a sea of admirers at the theater last evening."

And only one with his mouth on her breasts. Josefina shook herself. These ladies were Griffins either by birth or by marriage, and last night Sebastian Griffin had called her a liar. It would be foolish to assume she'd been asked to luncheon purely out of friendship. "Everyone has been very gracious," she commented. "Our visit here has been fortuitous. And my father is so hopeful now for the future of Costa Habichuela."

"Do you mean to reside in Costa Habichuela yourself?" Lady Caroline sat beside her, while the other two ladies took the back-facing seat opposite.

"It is my home. Of course I mean to live there."

"Of course," Lady Deverill agreed hurriedly. "I think Caro only wondered if the rey might have you stay on in London to continue your efforts to raise funds and support for your country."

"My father spent so much time away from my mother and me that he has vowed we should never be separated again. He wanted me to travel to Scotland with him, but I insisted that I would be more useful here."

"Does he mean to secure additional loans there?"

"That is his intention, yes." She'd initially been against the attempt, but now she had to agree with his assessment that no time could be better for stirring up interest than the days immediately following a monarch's ceremonial arrival in a friendly country.

"I have to say," Lady Sarala added, "Shay has been fascinated by the prospectus you gave Melbourne. I can scarcely get him to put it aside each evening."

"I'm gratified that he finds it interesting. Costa Habichuela is a remarkable place."

"From what I heard a few minutes ago, a great many

Britons are anxious to experience it firsthand." Lady Deverill gazed at her with eyes the same color as her brother's, though the marchioness's were much warmer and more friendly than those of Melbourne. "Have you considered opening Costa Habichuela to immigration?"

"I believe the rey wants to assess the economic impact of additional citizens and farmed land before he makes a decision."

"A very sound approach," Lady Sarala agreed. "Economics is a bit of a hobby of mine."

Wonderful. All she needed today were more questions she didn't feel prepared to answer.

"I have to ask," Lady Deverill put in with the timing of a clock, "why in the world did you slap Melbourne? I don't think anyone's ever had the courage to do that before."

"He sent a coach for me when he'd promised to appear and escort me himself. It might have tarnished everyone's first impression of me, and thereby of my country."

"So it was only because of the possible harm to your country?"

Josefina grimaced. The truth didn't seem as though it could cause any damage. "Well, I think any woman would be hurt upon realizing that a very handsome man who'd offered an escort hadn't bothered to appear. And I have to say, he continues to be quite arrogant and speak very rudely to me. I don't understand why, when he seems to be unfailingly polite to everyone else who crosses his path."

Eleanor gazed at their new companion for a moment. She'd been about to say that the three of them had also experienced Sebastian's foul temper, but stopped herself. "Melbourne is rather famous for being inscrutable," she said instead.

In fact, her oldest brother was only less than polite to a very small and select group of people—the ones who engaged his emotions. If he was rude to Princess Josefina, and continued to be so, then it meant something.

" 'Inscrutable'?" The princess smiled, though the expression seemed a bit forced. "Since you're his family, I won't embellish the description."

"You are a true diplomat, Your Highness," Caro observed, and they all laughed.

Something large moved up beside the barouche. Eleanor glanced sideways. A large, gleaming black coach loomed there, a scarlet griffin on the door. *Blast it all*.

She raised her eyes to the massive coach's window. With the curtains pulled aside, Sebastian was easy to make out. He looked straight back at her, his usually inscrutable expression highly annoyed. Inwardly she cringed.

Yes, she'd decided to become acquainted with Princess Josefina Embry. And yes, that did most likely qualify as meddling. After the way he'd attempted to manipulate the lives of herself and her brothers, Sebastian deserved to be meddled with. What she absolutely hadn't counted on, however, was being found out so soon.

"Oh, dear," Caroline whispered. "He does not look happy."

Though she held her breath herself, Eleanor offered a reassuring smile. "He can be annoyed as he pleases. The Duke of Melbourne is not going to force us off the street." Not with witnesses about, anyway. She waved her fingers at her eldest brother.

"Nell, don't make him any angrier," Sarala cautioned in a hushed voice.

After another moment driving parallel with them, Sebastian rapped on the roof of the coach. Immediately the vehicle turned away down the next cross street. Eleanor let out her breath. *Thank goodness*.

"I apologize if my being here has caused you some

difficulty," Her Highness contributed abruptly. "I know Melbourne is not fond of me."

"Nonsense. He's not fond of anyone. Don't take it to heart."

The princess smiled. "Thank you, Lady Deverill."

"Call me Eleanor."

For a moment Princess Josefina looked as though she wanted to say something more, but instead turned the conversation to the weather. Eleanor studied her face, her expression. Her brother was infamously difficult to decipher, and this woman didn't look to be much easier. Unless she was greatly mistaken, though, Princess Josefina found Sebastian at least as interesting as he found her.

Sebastian looked up from the newspaper after his fourth attempt to read the same sentence. "What are you doing?"

At his elbow Peep sat in front of her own large plate of breakfast. She wasn't eating, however. Rather, she adjusted a spoon across a knife and aimed it toward her cup of tea. A large sugar lump sat in the bowl of the spoon.

"Watch. I think I have it this time." With her curled fist she smacked down the raised end of the spoon. The lump of sugar catapulted into the air past her cup and thudded into the back of his newspaper. Again. "Drat."

"Don't hit it so hard," he advised, and went back to reading.

According to the *London Times*, yesterday Princess Josefina Embry of Costa Habichuela had graced Carlton House with her presence, sharing luncheon with Prinny and the Duke of Harek. The day before she'd journeyed to Greenwich for a tour of a Royal Navy ship. Londoners of all stations were mad for her, with girls throwing rose petals at her feet, and men handing her letters proposing marriage. Every citizen with a spare shilling seemed to be rushing to invest in "Englandshire," as the public had begun referring to Costa Habichuela.

"Balderdash," he muttered under his breath.

"What, Papa?"

"Nothing, sweetling. I was just reading about Princess Josefina."

"The Aunties took her to luncheon a few days ago," his daughter commented, as another object hit the back of his newspaper. "They didn't invite me."

He wished they hadn't invited Josefina. All he had against Costa Habichuela, though, were some unverified suspicions, a nagging sense of wrongness, and a feeling of frustration so great it was very likely the cause of the other difficulties. "Perhaps next time," he said.

"I certainly hope so."

Sebastian lowered the paper again. "You know that your Aunt Caroline's family is arriving in London tomorrow. You'll want to spend time with them."

"Yes, but they aren't princesses."

"I'm sorry, Penelope, but there's nothing I can do about that."

"You didn't have to resign your post."

"Yes, I did."

"Why, because you're too busy? You haven't even gone out for the past two nights. You stayed here and played pick-up-sticks with me, and you've been in a very bad mood."

"I have not. And you're the one who said you wanted me about more."

"Mary Haley says you asked the princess to marry you, and she said no because you're only a duke, and that's why you had to resign."

He folded the paper and set it aside. "Does she now? I'm beginning to think that Mary Haley is a gossiping busybody, and that you spend entirely too much time in her com—"

The breakfast room door swung open. "I hoped you'd still be here," Shay said, a stack of books gathered in his arms.

Peep stood. "Mary Haley is not a gossip. She's my friend, and that's why she tells me things I should know. Now if you'll excuse me, I'm going to go feed the ducks in the park." She stomped out the door.

He could hear her clomping all the way upstairs and then the slam of her bed chamber door. "Blast it."

"Did I interrupt something?" Shay dumped his load of books on the breakfast table.

"Just a difference of opinion." He gestured at one of the footmen who stood in the room. "Tom, go make certain Mrs. Beacham is accompanying Lady Penelope when she leaves the house."

"Right away, Your Grace." The servant hurried out of the room.

"All right, what is it, Shay?"

Without asking whether he'd finished eating or not, Charlemagne pushed all of the dishes away from the head of the table and seated himself opposite where Peep had been. That done, his younger brother dragged the half dozen books within reach.

"Take a look at this," he said.

"It's the Costa Habichuela prospectus."

"Yes, and no."

Sebastian sat up straighter. "What do you mean?"

Shay flipped the book open and turned pages until he found the one he wanted. "Read that aloud," he said, opening one of the other books for himself.

"'While one would think its proximity to the equator would render the climate disagreeably hot and stifling all the year round, Costa Habichuela is blessed with a large expanse of—'"

"'—of coastline which each afternoon delivers a soft,

cooling breeze straight off the Atlantic Ocean,'" Shay took over. "'This breeze has the effect of both renewing and rejuvenating the populace, and also of bringing trade from distant shores, a topic which will be discussed in depth later herein.'"

"And?" Sebastian prompted.

Shay lifted an eyebrow. "What do you mean, 'and'?"

"You got hold of another prospectus. I don't need a lesson in oral recitation."

"Yes, I did get hold of another prospectus. Or rather, I already had one."

"Shay, I know you're brilliant, but I do have Parliam—"

"Take a look." Closing the book from which he'd been reading, Shay slid it over.

For a moment Sebastian looked at the title impressed into the leather on the book's front cover. "This . . ." He cleared his throat, the ramifications of what he was seeing beginning to dawn on him. "This is a survey of Jamaica."

"Dating from seventy-five years ago, and commissioned by King George the Second." He took the Costa Habichuela prospectus back and turned another few pages. "I kept thinking that some of this sounded familiar."

"In all fairness," Sebastian heard himself saying, "perhaps the rey doesn't have the gift for putting pen to paper. Borrowing a few—"

"It's whole chapters, Seb. All of the wests are changed to easts, the river and town names are altered, but everything else is identical. It even has the trade winds blowing in the wrong direction to accommodate the country's location on the coast." He grabbed another book. "And do you want to read about the populace? It's all in this one— *A Cultural Study of the West Indies.* And the—"

"That's enough, Shay."

"But—"

"I understand what you're telling me. There's not an original word in here."

"It does make one wonder what Costa Habichuela is really like," his brother commented.

Sebastian stood. "I think I'll go ask. Excuse me."

"The rey's not back from Scotland yet." Shay pushed to his feet as well, gathering books up in his arms as he went.

"Prince Josefina's here." He glanced at Charlemagne as his brother fell into step behind him. "I'm going alone."

Shay gave him an exasperated look, but nodded. "I suppose then that I'm to keep this to myself."

"Until you hear otherwise from me, yes."

"You're going to miss Parliament if you go now."

He grabbed his hat and gloves from Stanton and headed down the front steps toward the stable. No coach today; he wanted to ride. "To the devil with Parliament," he snapped.

Chapter 10

Josefina signaled Colonel Branbury's butler. "Grimm, please turn any additional callers away," she said as he reached her side. "Have them come back tomorrow."

He bowed. "Very good, Your Highness. And shall I send to the kitchen for more tea and pastries?"

"Yes, thank you." At least if the hordes of visitors were eating, they couldn't be talking. That might leave just enough air in the modest-sized drawing room for her to keep breathing. If she fainted in there, she would probably be trampled to death before anyone noticed her on the floor.

"Your Highness," Lord Ausbey said, bowing so reverently that the top of his curly blond head nearly brushed the pale blue carpet, "thank you so much for agreeing to receive me this morning. I am one of your most ardent admirers. In fact, I've written you a poem stating the depth of my feelings." He pulled a piece of paper from the inside pocket of his dark green jacket—apparently worn in honor of the green cross of the Costa Habichuela flag.

"I would love to hear it, Lord Ausbey," she said with a smile, putting a hand on his arm to keep him from unfolding the thing, "but I have—"

"Please, Your Highness, you must call me Adam. I long to hear my name on your lips."

Yes, men did seem to enjoy that sort of thing, she recalled, telling herself that the sudden tightness in her chest was cynical anger and not heated memory. She chuckled, pushing his arm down as she released him. Unfortunately he kept hold of the poem. "You flatter me, Lord Ausbey. Now excuse me while I see to my other guests."

Without waiting for a reply she turned away, wading further into the sea of admirers and would-be hangers-on. Conchita intercepted her, surreptitiously fluffing the cream-colored sleeves that had drooped amid the press of people.

"Your father would be ecstatic to see all this interest," the maid whispered.

"At the moment, I wish he were here to deal with it," Josefina returned in the same low tone. "Welcoming them and being charming is one thing, but how does one get rid of them?"

"Perhaps you should ask the duke," Conchita suggested, slipping into the background again as Lady Holliwell approached, a prospectus clasped in her arms.

They'd been printing the things as swiftly as they could. It had become a noticeable expense, but she supposed that spending a few shillings was a fair exchange for encouraging an investment of thousands of pounds. And the more interest they stirred, the better.

"Ah, there you are, Your Highness," the Duke of Harek said, stepping in front of the countess to offer his arm.

"You seem to have some admirers," she noted, indicating the group of women with whom he'd been chatting.

"They are here to see you." He covered her hand with his as she took his arm. "As am I."

"So much flattery today. My head is spinning." She forced her aching cheek muscles into another smile. "In fact, I'm feeling a bit fatigued at the moment."

"I believe I can manage our guests if you want to go freshen up."

"*'Our* guests'?"

"I speak in the sense of my being your host here in England," he said smoothly, his charming smile bright enough to leave shadows.

She glanced about at the crowded drawing room again. Her father would be kissing knuckles and shaking hands, each gesture and word bringing more wealth and support to Costa Habichuela. The rey, however, wouldn't be back in London until tomorrow. And her ears were ringing from all the noise.

"Then do please host for a few minutes," she said, pulling her hand free. "I'll just go upstairs to fix my hair."

"Have no worries." His smile deepened. "A princess is supposed to be delicate."

She nearly asked if he would prefer that she titter and faint, but that would have required staying in the middle of the madhouse and talking. As quickly as she could Josefina made her way into the hallway, where even more guests overflowed, and up the stairs to her private rooms.

"Your Highness," Conchita puffed from behind her, topping the stairs. "Is everything well?"

"I just need to catch my breath. Keep an eye on Harek, will you? I don't want him to declare himself rey while I'm pinning my hair."

The maid gave a quick curtsy, flashing an even briefer

smile. "If I sense trouble I will kick him. In this crowd he won't know who to blame."

Josefina pushed open the door. "An excellent idea."

Stepping inside, she closed it again, resting her forehead against the cool oak. She hadn't realized that being gracious and charming could be so taxing.

"Don't tell me you've run out of pretty stories to tell."

At the deep, familiar drawl she froze. *Melbourne*. She whipped around. "What the devil are you doing here?"

He leaned a haunch against her writing desk. From the chaos of the papers there, he'd been rifling through them. "I had a question," he said easily, not moving.

"Get out of my bedchamber. If you're here to call on me, then go downstairs with my other guests."

Melbourne straightened, seeming abruptly to fill the room. "One of the sycophantic horde?" he asked, moving past her as she edged around toward her bed and the pistol she kept in the bed stand there.

"I suppose so, since you can't seem to stay away from me."

He stopped at the door. "I can't, can I?" he mused, almost to himself. Slowly he reached out and secured the lock.

She heard the click from halfway across the room. Alarm ran down her spine. As mightily attracted to him as she felt, she was not a fool. Whatever he was up to would serve his purposes rather than hers. Josefina drew a breath.

"Since you won't leave, what is your question?"

"Who authored your prospectus?"

The question surprised her. "*That* is what you wish to know? I thought perhaps you wanted your old liaison position back."

"Who wrote it?" he repeated.

"Are you looking for someone to assist you with your

memoirs? I can give you a title—*A Very Unpleasant Man, or the Memoirs of Someone You Don't Wish to Know.*"

For a second he looked at her. "Are you afraid of anything?"

Only of how she felt in his presence. "I'm certainly not afraid of you, Sebastian," she said, deliberately using his Christian name. "You did give me leave to call you Sebastian, didn't you?"

"Yes, I did. And you gave me leave to remove that gown and strip you naked."

Her skin heated. "No," she returned, holding onto her scattering wits with all her strength, "that was a different gown. This one stays where it is, because you called me a liar."

Melbourne walked toward her. "You *are* a liar. Who wrote the damned prospectus?"

He knew. Somehow, he'd figured it out. Panic twisted through her. Her father should never have given Sebastian Griffin more information than strictly required. He was far too clever, and far too dangerous.

"Don't waste your time trying to think up something plausible," he snapped, stopping close enough to touch. "Tell me the truth."

Josefina took a deep breath, looking up to meet his gaze. "The truth," she said, her mind racing. "Very well. *I* wrote it."

"Ah." His eyes glinted. "You're very knowledgeable about a country you saw for a total of two days."

"I wrote it before I ever saw it." She frowned. "Father wrote me letter after letter describing Costa Habichuela. He needed money to carry out his dream, and in order to get money, he needed investors. To get them, he needed something official and in writing. We didn't have time to commission a complete, formal survey—that would have taken too much time with Spain pushing back against the rebels. So I studied other volumes to which I had access, and I . . . adapted them to fit what my father had described."

"So the natives of Costa Habichuela resemble those of the West Indies?"

"You *have* done some checking," she said, with grudging admiration. "No one cares about the history of the natives. They're there, and most of them speak at least some English. The rest is just . . . theatrical decoration."

"And San Saturus?"

"A little smaller than described, but it is pretty, and it does overlook an easily defended harbor."

"You have the trade winds blowing the wrong way."

She flushed. Lies were one thing, but she hated making stupid mistakes. "I didn't realize that until after copies had already been printed."

His gaze lowered to her mouth, then swiftly lifted again, as though he couldn't quite control his reaction to her. "What you've done," he said, "aside from the theft of someone else's research, is exceedingly . . . bold. Did you think no one would notice?"

"There's no harm in it." She lifted her hand toward him, running her fingers along the line of his jaw. Warm skin, and a barely discernable stubble of beard. Against all of her better thoughts and wishes, he fascinated her.

His muscles shuddered. "A seduction might distract me, Josefina," he said quietly, "but it won't make me forget what I know."

A seduction, though, might give her enough time to tell her father that Melbourne knew about the prospectus, and enough time to figure out if he meant to tell Sir Henry Sparks or anyone else and endanger the loan money that was already being issued to them.

"Weighing your options?" he murmured.

Damn it, he couldn't read minds. No one could do that. "And if you thought I was standing here to gain a favor or influence, what would *you* do?"

"Try me."

They stood halfway between the door and the bed, a breath from touching, for several hard beats of her heart. Lofty as he was in England, Melbourne probably had no idea the things she had to contemplate, the benefits of his favor against what either rejection or exposure could do to her. "I'm remembering a few nights ago," she said, managing somehow to keep her voice steady, "when you put your hands on me and then pushed me away."

He moved a feather's width closer. "And?"

"And so I think you should leave." She backed up, then deliberately turned away. "Whatever insult or accusation you level against me, what you did that night at the theater was worse."

"Get back here."

"No." Facing him again, Josefina stopped beside the bed stand, her hand on its dark, polished surface. "Go away."

She swore that he growled then, a low, primitive rumble that raised goose bumps on her arms. "I am not someone to be trifled with," he uttered.

"Neither am I." But before she had time to do anything more than pull the drawer open, his hands clamped down on her shoulders. Melbourne yanked her around, the ease of the motion leaving her no doubt that he was far stronger than she.

"I will stop your mouth," he muttered tightly, and kissed her.

Oh, God. He'd been teasing her at the theater, and the other times he'd kissed her. Pure arousal slammed down her backbone, potent and not at all subtle. His lips, his tongue, pushed and teased at her until she opened her mouth to him.

Abruptly he broke away. Breathing hard, his gray eyes glittering, he looked from her to the drawer before he pulled the pistol free. "Is this what you were after? Do you want to shoot me, Josefina?"

"No," she blurted, knocking the pistol aside and grabbing his hair to yank his face down to her mouth again.

She heard the weapon hit the floor, but she no longer cared. She wanted to crawl inside him, inside his mind, his body, his heart. Moaning as his hands swept down to her hips, pulling her still closer, Josefina fumbled with the knot of his cravat.

Melbourne pushed, throwing her onto the bed with him on top of her, kissing everywhere he bared her skin. She felt electric, as though bolts of lightning were running through her veins. "Sebastian," she moaned, giving up on the cravat and tearing at his waistcoat buttons. "I want to touch you."

Without answering he yanked down the front of her dress, sinking lower to take her left breast in his mouth, his tongue rasping across her nipple. Pure fire seared through her. He was *not* going to stop this seduction here, as he had done before. Her hands shaking, she pushed his jacket and waistcoat off his shoulders. He shrugged them off one arm at a time, the other hand still running crazily along her skin.

Sebastian lifted away from her just enough to pull the white linen shirt off over his head, the cravat following it to the floor. *Finally.* Josefina skimmed her fingers along the warm skin of his chest, through the light dusting of dark hair there, down to where his trousers banded his hips. His skin was soft, but she could feel the hard muscles beneath; muscles that jumped at her touch.

He gathered her skirts in his hands, kneeling as he lifted

them above her ankles, drawing them past her knees, her thighs, and baring her finally to the waist. For a moment he gazed in hard-breathing silence.

"Sit up," he finally ordered.

As soon as she complied, he moved into her again, one knee on either side of her bare left thigh. As they kissed, he reached around to undo the fastenings at the back of her gown. She felt it loosen, and the soft material puddled around her waist.

"Lift your arms."

"Stop ordering me about," she returned, though she did as he said. "I'm not a thing, you know."

He raised up to pull the dress off over her head, slowing and being more careful as it came over her hair. He'd been married, though; he would know that a female did not want her hair mussed when she had to go back out in public.

"I know you're not a thing," he murmured as her arms came free. "You are Josefina Embry, Princess of Costa Habichuela, which may or may not have a climate like that of Jamaica."

"I told you that the—"

"Unfasten my trousers," he interrupted.

She lowered her eyes to them, to the bulge at the apex of his thighs. "You want me," she muttered, swallowing as another wave of pure, shivering lust ran through her.

"I've wanted you from the moment I set eyes on you." Sebastian reached for her hands and drew them to his waist. "Unbutton me," he repeated, releasing her hands to run his fingers across her nipples.

Josefina gasped, feeling them tighten and harden. She would allow him to guide her in this. Otherwise he would probably leave again, and then her body would combust from heated frustration, and she would die. And he knew that, blast him.

"One day I'll give you an order, and you will follow it," she managed, though with her shaking voice and gasps of pleasure she likely didn't sound terribly forceful or convincing.

"Doubtful," he said, twisting his torso to replace his fingers with his mouth, sucking and licking.

If she didn't do as he said, he could probably torture her to death with just this. Hands unsteady, she tugged at the first button until it came open. As she lowered her fingers to the next button, he groaned.

So he liked her hands there, did he? Moving deliberately, very aware that she was completely naked while he was not, Josefina drew her hands downward, running them over the tented material at his crotch.

His entire body jerked. She did it again. Ah, so now who was in control?

"Bloody minx," he muttered, shifting to kiss the base of her throat.

A moment later one of his hands slid down her stomach, tickled through her dark curls, and brushed her most sensitive place. With a surprised shriek she barely remembered to muffle, she grabbed his shoulders to keep from collapsing on the bed.

He shifted against her, darting his tongue along the rim of her ear. "I know what feels good," he murmured, pressing his fingers deeper inside her, moving and caressing.

"Oh, heavens." Obviously he spoke the truth. And if there was more of that yet to come, she didn't want to miss it. As swiftly as she could, she finished unfastening his trousers and shoved them down to his thighs. "Goodness," she breathed as he came free.

"Goodness has nothing to do with it, Princess." In a moment he had her on her back again.

She'd had no idea what a mouth could do until he trailed his lips and agile tongue down from her throat, lingering again at her breasts, then continued on past her belly. Softly he kissed the backs of her knees, bending her legs and parting her thighs to do so. Then he turned his attention to the insides of her thighs.

Josefina writhed, tension and arousal flowing from her core all the way out to the tips of her fingers and toes. When his tongue darted against her folds, she thought she would explode. He pressed further with his mouth and his fingers, and she bucked.

"Stop! Stop. It's too much."

Sebastian raised his head to look at her. "Say what you mean," he hissed, his voice shaking a little. "If you ask me to leave now, I will." Slowly his mouth curved into that heart-stopping smile. "And then you'll miss what comes next."

She shut her eyes for a heartbeat, trying to regain some control over her thoughts and her spread, wanton body. "What comes next?"

"You do." He lowered his head again.

His fingers moved deeper, in and out, and an exquisite tightness began at the base of her spine. She heard herself moaning and mewling, but all she could do was grab handfuls of the bed coverlet and hold on. Abruptly the tightness gave way, and she felt . . . heaven. "God," she blurted, arching her back. "Good God."

He continued his assault, and it took all her remaining willpower not to scream. Finally as her muscles began to relax again, he moved back over her. "In the future," he murmured, "you and I may experience that together. But this was your first time, and I wanted to be sure you knew how good I can make you feel."

His rock-hard manhood pressed against her thigh. "But you're still . . . You know."

"Aroused. For God knows what reason I'm giving you a last chance to escape me, Princess."

Josefina tangled her fingers into his hair, pulling him down for another rough kiss. "I *am* a princess," she said unsteadily. "I may do as I please. Continue."

"With pleasure." He shifted, lowering his body against hers. Slowly he pushed his hips forward, entering her with a warm, indescribable slide. "It will hurt," he said a second later, his jaw tight and clenched.

She couldn't breathe, her heart beating madly at the sensation of him. "I'm not afraid of anything."

"I've noticed." He resumed his motion and the pressure increased, followed by a sharp pain as he buried himself deep inside her. She gasped, grabbing his shoulders again. "Apologies," he grunted. "It won't hurt again."

Sebastian began to move, a little at first, and then as her pain faded, he pumped his hips against her more strongly. The sensation of him inside her, the proof that he desired her, was exquisite.

His eyes closed. What was he thinking? Anything? About her? Or about the last woman he'd had? Josefina hit him on the shoulder, and his eyes flew open again.

"I won't be a memory," she managed, moaning in time with his deep strokes. "And I won't be a substitute for someone else."

"You're not," he rumbled, gently biting her ear as he thrust.

Ah. That tightness began inside her again. "Then you say *my* name, Sebastian."

His pace increased, deeper and harder. She could barely breathe as he rocked both her and the bed. "Josefina," he growled. "Jo . . . se . . . fi . . . na."

She shattered again, clinging to him. With a deep shudder he removed himself, holding hard to her as he climaxed along with her. For a second as she realized what he'd just done, she felt . . . disappointed. He'd protected her from becoming pregnant, yes, but if they *had* made a child, he would have to marry her. One did not father a bastard on a princess. *He* wouldn't.

Today answered one thing—she wanted Sebastian Griffin for herself, wanted him to gaze only at her, to spend his nights and his days with her, regardless of anything or anyone else in the world.

All of that, even though under the circumstances she would have been wiser to give her virginity to the Duke of Harek. *He* didn't ask questions.

For a long moment Sebastian lay with Josefina close in his arms and tried to regain his breath and his sanity. He nearly hadn't pulled away, nearly hadn't been able to make himself do it, and the ramifications were staggering.

Even though he had, and at the very last moment, the fact that he was there with her at all attested to his abject stupidity. For God's sake, the moment she and her father had given that prospectus to Prinny and said it was a true representation of Costa Habichuela, they'd committed a fraud against England.

And whether that text was in fact accurate or not—and he now had serious doubts about that—he had no business entangling himself, literally and figuratively, with this woman. Insanity.

Yes, it had been four years since he'd been with a woman, and yes, at one time he'd never wanted to touch another female. What the hell had she done to him? And why, even after he'd bedded her, relieved himself of the gnawing ache to be inside her, did he already want her again?

Get hold of yourself, Melbourne. He sat up, reluctantly releasing her. "You should get back to your guests," he muttered, sliding off the bed and retrieving a washing cloth from the dressing table.

She sat up, taking the cloth as he finished with it and

handed it to her. "And that's all you have to say? 'Get back to your guests'?"

"I may not at the moment be able to control the . . . lust I feel toward you," he returned crisply, yanking up his trousers, "but I don't—"

"You don't what?" she broke in, climbing off the bed and grabbing up her shift. "You don't like me? You don't—"

"I do like you. I'm not an animal, rutting just because it's the season to do so."

"Then what? Because I like you, as well."

He pretended for the moment that he wasn't flattered by that. No simpering or bemoaning her lost maidenhead for Josefina. She wanted to know where she stood, how circumstances had changed. "I don't trust you."

"Hm." She pulled on her shift, being careful of her hair, then stepped into her dress. "That's a rather risky thing to say, considering that all I have to do is open that door and scream, and we would be married by Sunday. And even if your almightiness could prevent that, you would still face a scandal." She turned her back on him, glancing over her shoulder. "Fasten my dress. I can't reach."

Sebastian stifled an unexpected smile. "I take this to mean you won't be screaming," he said, stepping over to tug her dress up and fasten the buttons running along her spine. As he finished, he leaned down and kissed the nape of her neck. Obviously having sex with her hadn't worked; his desire for her had not been purged from his system.

He heard her sigh, and responding heat tugged at his gut again. Moving around in front of her, he tilted her chin up with his fingers and kissed her. Josefina twined her fingers into his hair, leaning her slim body along his. Physically, despite the slapping and other acts of bravado, she was no match for him. Mentally and emotionally, the ground seemed much less certain. She certainly spun him about and stood up to him as no one else—including the members of his own family—did.

"No screaming," she whispered against his mouth, "if you'll join our party at Vauxhall the night after next."

Sebastian set her away from him again. "No." He picked up his shirt and pulled it on over his head.

"But I thought—"

"I want you. As I said, though, I don't trust you. You've answered some of my questions about Costa Habichuela, but not all of them." Squatting, he retrieved his waistcoat and jacket. "Until they are all answered to my satisfaction, I will not be put in the position of appearing to endorse your efforts."

Josefina put her hands on her hips, her lips pursed as she regarded him. "You're a very righteous gentleman, aren't you? Except where bedding a woman just because you happen to want her is concerned. I find it all a bit hypocritical of you, Melbourne." She walked over to the dressing mirror to check her hair.

Why had he expected that she would melt, become sweet and demure, just because he'd made love to her? In fact, he'd begun to wonder whether he hadn't been more affected than she had. And she had a point. True, the Griffin name and how it was perceived meant everything, but being a boor in private and a saint in public didn't sit well, either.

On the other hand, there was more to consider than how he felt. For God's sake, there had been a Grifanus standing for England since before the time of Christ. "No. Somewhere less well attended, perhaps. I won't be your trained monkey, Josefina."

"Say what you like, Sebastian," she returned. "I always get my way. Did you consider whether you're here because you wanted me, or because I wanted you?"

"We'll have to pursue that in depth later." If there was a later. Because he had the feeling that once he did have all of the answers he required and decided what action he needed to take, Princess Josefina would have reason not to wish to be with him any longer.

Chapter 11

"*I* assume you'll be sneaking out the window or something," Josefina said flippantly, making a last check of her attire and then walking past Sebastian to unlock the bedchamber door. "Don't fall on the roses. My father said Colonel Branbury's always been very particular about his roses."

"Thanks for your concern."

She wished he were easier to decipher, though she supposed that if he was, she wouldn't find him nearly so fascinating. "Send over a note inviting us to a box in Vauxhall. I imagine you will have a better location than Harek."

"No, and I won't say it again."

Josefina stuck her tongue out at him. Without giving him a chance to reply to that, she strolled out of the room and closed the door behind her. Thankfully the hallway was empty.

"Oh, heavens," she whispered, collapsing back against the door and fanning herself with both hands.

She'd done it. Irretrievably her virginity was lost. And

it had been deliriously exciting and arousing. To think, she'd waited until her twenty-fifth year for the experience, when she'd had an abundance of invitations starting before she'd turned sixteen. *Glorious.*

However much trouble he was, she was still glad that Sebastian Griffin had been the one to introduce her to sex. He'd wanted her, after what was apparently several years of not wanting anyone. There was power in that realization, and she reveled in it. He'd wanted *her.*

Harek seemed to, as well, but she had a difficult time imagining that he would bring as much . . . intensity to the experience as Sebastian had. Certainly he would focus more on his enjoyment than on hers. She ran a hand down her body, sighing. That had been an experience worth repeating. If he had agreed to blasted Vauxhall, at least she would have an indication that he felt the same.

Well, she still had two days to convince him. With a smile that probably looked as satisfied as it felt, Josefina descended the stairs to the drawing room again.

"There you are, Your Highness," Lord Ausbey said, blocking her way. "I must read my poem to you now."

Drat. At least it would give her an additional moment to compose herself. "If you want to recite it to me, I'm afraid you'll have to do so in front of an audience." She gestured at the chatty crowd. "I can't desert my guests."

The viscount cleared his throat. "Very well. Then everyone may see my devotion to you."

That had probably been his intention all along. "Proceed, my lord," she said, resisting the urge to sigh.

"I call it *The Tropical Flower,*" he said, unfolding the paper.

> *"Fair winds, calm seas, you shelter her,*
> *The enchanted maiden from far away.*
> *Bright sun, you cannot darken*

The fair skin of the glorious, heaven-sent angel.
We of the cold, fog-ridden land worship you
   from afar.
I, cursed with an earth-bound body and
   star-gazing eyes,
Look upon you in wonder, and weep that
   you are not mine."

He bowed to a scattering of applause, some admiring female-toned acclamation, and a few lower-voiced mutterings of ridicule. Josefina smiled, adding her applause to the general cacophony. "Very nice, my lord. Thank you."

"It is all sincere, Your Highness," he said, his hand covering his heart. "And if you would but . . ." His gaze focused behind her, and he trailed off. "Your Grace," he said, bowing and backing away simultaneously.

Had Harek pointed a pistol at the poor fellow? The poem hadn't been *that* awful. Josefina turned around, ready to scold the high-handed duke, but the words stopped in her throat.

Melbourne stood a few feet from her, his steely gaze on the boy. It was a wonder Ausbey hadn't swallowed his own tongue. *Jealousy?* The duke's gaze moved to her, and her skin heated. "Your Grace," she said belatedly, giving a curtsy as she remembered that as far as anyone else knew, he'd only just arrived.

"Your Highness," he returned, with the usual dip of his dark head. "I hadn't realized you were holding court this morning. A word, if you please?" He gestured her toward the doorway.

He managed to make even that mild request sound like an order. With a lift of her chin she followed him toward the open door, but stopped short of the entry. If she vanished again this morning, people would begin to wonder what she was up to. She turned around. "I cannot leave my guests," she said. "What do you require?"

Brief annoyance crossed his face, then vanished again. The gray-eyed glance touched her nearest guests, and they immediately found acquaintances or conversations elsewhere. "I have a bit more advice for you," he said in a low, intimate voice than sent damp warmth between her legs.

"More? Heavens. And stop frightening my guests away with those black looks of yours."

"I'm not playing, Josefina. Keep some distance between yourself and Harek and poetry-spewing pups. If they were to learn anything about your literary efforts, I doubt they would be as discreet as I."

"Are you jealous, Melbourne?"

He smiled, the expression not touching his eyes. Slowly he reached out for her hand and brought it to his lips. "Don't test me, Josefina," he said even more quietly.

She smiled right back at him, quickly withdrawing her hand before he could feel it tremble. "Truly, Your Grace?" she exclaimed loudly. "Lord Harek and my family and I would be pleased to share your box at Vauxhall! How delightful."

Without the slightest hesitation he nodded again. "My pleasure. Now if you'll excuse me, I have meetings." As he moved past her to the door he slowed, brushing her ear with his mouth. "Well played, Princess. Next comes my turn."

Before she could conjure a reply, he was gone. Damn it all, who did he think he was, anyway? The Duke of Melbourne, of course. Her lover. The most powerful, influential man in England. And her very large problem.

Sebastian rode home, handing Merlin over to Green at the stable and striding into the house. At Stanton's greeting he managed a grunt, grabbed the stack of personal correspondence awaiting his attention, and went into his office.

The bloody chit had managed to outmancuver him with alarming ease. The price he had to pay for losing control, he supposed. "Stanton!"

The butler opened the office door. "Yes, Your Grace?"

"I'll be hosting a small party at Vauxhall the night after next," he said crisply. "See to it that all the appropriate arrangements are made."

"Of course, Your Grace."

Once the door closed again, Sebastian sat forward to sift through the piles of letters and calling cards. All the usual, plus Rivers had set aside the weekly report from Whitlock, his Melbourne Park estate manager, and updates from three of his other properties.

Zachary had left a card with a note scrawled on the back that he'd absconded with Peep to see the menagerie at the Tower. That boy clearly needed offspring of his own. He hoped Caroline had by now begun to realize that as a Griffin she could have both her painting and a family. Perhaps Eleanor would know their sister-in-law's mind on the matter.

The next letter in the stack stopped him. It was from Eton. His heart rate accelerating, he broke the wax seal and unfolded it.

A moment later he shot to his feet. "Stanton!"

The butler reappeared in the doorway. "Yes, Your Gr—"

"When did this letter arrive?"

"With the post, Your Grace, some forty minutes ago. Is something amiss?"

"No. Send for Shay, and inform him that he and I are leaving for Eton within the hour."

"Right away, Your Grace."

On the butler's heels he left the office and pounded up

the stairs to his private rooms. It seemed that John Rice-Able was teaching at Eton, and would be happy to share his knowledge of the geography and societies of Central America. Finally he would get some damned definitive answers about the kingdom and country of Costa Habichuela.

"I know you told me to be quiet and let you think," Charlemagne said as the coach finally rocked to a halt and they stepped to the ground, "but you seem a bit . . . preoccupied with this."

Sebastian grabbed one of the lanterns off a coach post and strode toward the hall where the professors lodged. Dimly to the south he could make out the lines of Windsor Castle looming above them. "Why shouldn't I be?" he asked, lifting the light to read the name of the building and then moving through the main courtyard.

"Because you resigned your post and you've been avoiding contact with Princess Josefina and her parents. Costa Habichuela and its royalty aren't your concern any longer."

"They are my concern." He glanced sideways at his brother. "And you're the one who stormed into my house this morning, all aflutter about some plagiarisms."

"Some extensive plagiarisms. I didn't say we should flee London to go track down a professor who would probably be pleased as petunias to call on you at Griffin House."

Shay had a point. "I have my reasons," Sebastian grumbled. "And I don't necessarily want our professor to be seen in London at this moment."

"Why not? I mean of course it's Eton we're talking about rather than Oxford, but it's not as though being seen with him will ruin you. Not entirely."

"Very amusing. As I said, I have—"

"—your reasons. I accept that. But what do you think this Rice-Able fellow knows?"

Sebastian lifted the lamp again to look at the apartment numbers. *Ah.* "Let's find out." He rapped on the oak door.

"Who is it?"

"He's not expecting us," Shay muttered, "is he?"

"Not precisely," Sebastian answered. "Melbourne," he said more loudly. "I wrote you, and you said—"

The door rattled and opened. "Your Grace." A thin, well-featured man two or three years younger than himself gazed at him over a pair of reading spectacles. "I'm honored. I didn't expect—"

"I know," Sebastian interrupted. "Might we come in?"

"Yes. Yes, of course." The professor stepped away from the door, and Sebastian followed him inside, having to duck a little to pass through the low doorway.

The dormitory room was tiny and dark but for the small fire in the fireplace and a pair of tallow candles sitting on a cluttered table. Clutter, in fact, seemed the main theme of decoration. A separate door at the back stood open to reveal a small, rumpled bed surrounded by still more haphazard stacks of papers and books, maps and trinkets.

In the main room John Rice-Able grabbed a stack of books off a chair and carried them out to pile them on the bed. "Did you receive my note?" he asked, emptying a second chair. "I was surprised to hear from you. I didn't think anyone but my students had read my *History*."

"I did receive your note, Professor. This afternoon. I apologize for not sending word that I was coming, but this seemed more expedient." Belatedly he gestured at Shay, who stood close by the door and looked on with a bemused expression on his face. His brother no doubt recognized the lair of a fellow scholar when he stumbled into one. "This is my brother, Charlemagne."

The professor looked up, belatedly removing his spectacles. "Charlemagne? After the ruler of—"

"Yes," Shay interrupted.

"Apologies, Lord Charlemagne." The professor flushed. "It's just that, well, you have to admit that Charlemagne is an unusual name."

"Oh, I'm aware of that." Shay flashed his charming smile. "Why is an explorer teaching at Eton?"

"Teaching pays a better salary," Master Rice-Able returned. "And since my last book was published six years ago, I think I made a wise decision." He sighed. "My explorations will have to be done between terms."

If this fellow was helpful enough, Sebastian might be able to do something about supporting his exploration efforts. It would all depend on their chat tonight.

"Please Your Grace, my lord, sit. I have some water on for tea, if you'd care to join me."

Sebastian sat in one of the vacated chairs. "Thank you. Tea would be welcome." In his life of political and social maneuvering and alliance-making, he'd learned to assess a man's character quickly. He liked Rice-Able. The professor had an unassuming honesty about him that spoke well for the man—and it could turn out to be useful, later.

"If I may say," Rice-Able commented, digging through his cupboard for teacups and saucers, "to be here now you must have left London shortly after receiving my note. Why the urgency to make my acquaintance?"

"A matter of geographical curiosity. What is the degree of your familiarity with the Mosquito Coast?"

"I know it as well as any non-native can, I suppose, though it's been three years since I last set foot in the region."

Three years. Before the Mosquito King granted Costa Habichuela to Stephen Embry, but recently enough that he should have a fair grasp of the geography and climate.

"I suppose you would have visited some of the villages and towns along the coast?"

"I have." Rice-Able passed out his mismatched collection of cups and saucers, then went to the fireplace to get the teapot. "I assume you came all this way because you have specific questions you want answered. If you could tell me directly what it is you require, I could probably provide you with better information."

Sebastian sat forward as the professor returned to the table. "The difficulty, sir, is that I don't wish to guide your answers. Nor do I want you to tell me what you think I want to hear."

"I see." Rice-Able seated himself in the third chair, the only spot in the room that had been empty upon their arrival. "Ask your questions, then. I assure you that my answers will be honest. If I provide you with an assumption, I will disclose it as such."

"Thank you. Firstly, then, do you read the London newspapers?" If the professor did, he would know that the Embrys were in England, and he would probably be able to surmise the rest.

"Only when forced to, and under protest. And not in the past few weeks, if that was to be your next question."

Sebastian smiled. "I think we understand one another." He lifted his teacup and took a swallow. It was awful, something bitter and tasting like old sticks, but he didn't allow his distaste to show on his face. "Does anyone have governorship over the Mosquito Coast in general?"

"A few tribal leaders, I suppose. According to Spain it's a fellow named Qental, but that's probably just for ease of reference. It's a fairly wide-open, rambling area. Boundaries change with every rainy season as the swamps overflow and the course of the rivers alter."

"Is any of it liveable?"

"Certainly. The natives have managed a fair existence, living on fruits and fish and the occasional wild pig."

"Is there any trade?"

"Not particularly. The native groups tend to avoid one another and be very suspicious of outsiders. If I hadn't managed to secure a guide who spoke several of the local dialects, I doubt I would have survived to be chatting here with you."

"Do any of the . . . tribes speak Spanish, or English?"

"Some of them know a smattering of Spanish, but Spain hasn't made much of an effort to control the region. No profit to be made there. You can't dig for gold in a swamp."

"And English?"

"Belize is mostly English, but technically it's several hundred miles north of the Mosquito Coast region. You'll find a few tiny settlements of trappers and miners, but they're not pleasant places."

Sebastian realized he was clenching his hands so hard that his fingers were growing numb. He shook them out beneath the cover of the tabletop. "Why are they unpleasant?"

"Ah." Rice-Able cleared his throat and drank half the tea in his cup. "My views on this tend to make me a bit unpopular."

"I'm here because I wish to know your views."

Quizzical hazel eyes met direct gray ones. "The English are masters of settling places that can be forced to resemble England. Large quantities of clean, running water, open fields, and a mild climate. In general, while I believe anyone *could* adapt to practically any conditions, most Englishmen seem to expect the conditions to adapt to them. Refusing to acknowledge that a place is humid and insect-ridden is a very sure way to become sickly and ultimately, dead."

"You adapted," Shay commented.

"I prefer to remain alive to tell my tales rather than to die by my pride. When the natives recommend covering one's skin with putrid-smelling plant secretions to protect from insect bites, I do so."

"Have you heard of a town called San Saturus there?"

The professor's brow furrowed. "San Saturus. No. I don't recall anything large enough to be considered a town at all."

"Anything smaller than that with a similar name?"

"I drew up some maps. Just a moment, and I'll fetch them."

As the professor left the table to hunt through his papers, Sebastian took another drink of the awful tea. He knew what he hoped for—some indication that Josefina hadn't been lying. *Please, God, let there be a San Saturus.* And let it be where she claimed.

"How stupid of me," Rice-Able exclaimed, his gaze on a large, half-unrolled piece of parchment. "San Saturus. There it is."

Thank God. "Is it on the coast, between the Wawa and Grande de Matagalpa Rivers, by any chance?"

"That's a large area, but yes." The professor picked his way back to the table.

Sebastian and Shay cleared off the rest of the clutter to accommodate the map, placing their tea apparatus at the four corners to hold it open. The map was remarkable; far more detailed than any official document he'd ever seen for that region. "You should have been a cartographer," Sebastian commented, running his gaze up the coast in search of the contours depicted in the Costa Habichuela prospectus.

"Half the fun is denoting the plant and animal life in each area, and the elevation variations." Rice-Able placed an ink-stained finger on the map. "There's your San Saturus. I should have remembered. It certainly made an impression at the time."

"Why is that?" Sebastian pursued, sternly resisting the urge to influence Rice-Able's recollection by mentioning deep bays and white stone buildings. It had to be the absolute truth that he learned tonight, not the truth as he wanted it to be.

"It was the bodies. A trio of them. Laid out neat as you please, shirts, trousers, boots, hats all in place, but nothing inside them except for white-as-snow bones. I surmised at the time that they all must have been overcome by the sun, or more likely by swamp gas. Then ants devoured the flesh. I've seen ants reduce a full-grown boar to bones in twenty-four hours. That was a large colony, of course."

"What makes you think three dead men equals a town called San Saturus?" Sebastian knew he sounded curt; both the story and its ramifications horrified him.

"Close by the bodies we found several huts and some mining equipment. On one of the planks someone had burned the letters 'San Saturus' into the wood. This is probably the only map on which it appears." Rice-Able took another sip of tea. "I remember thinking the name was ironic, since Saint Saturus is the patron saint against poverty. I suppose the poor wretches were hopeful, anyway."

His heart and his head pounding, Sebastian pushed to his feet. *Damnation. Bloody, bloody hell.* She said she'd seen the palace, said she'd spent two days there. Jaw clenched and aching, he faced the door. "Are there any other villages of any size in that immediate area?"

"Not along the coast. That part of the territory floods every year. As you can see, even San Saturus was a mile or so inland."

"Seb," Shay said quietly. "You were right."

But he hadn't wanted to be. Not now. Not after this morning, when he'd taken Josefina naked in his arms. "Master Rice-Able, would you be willing to come to London and retell this story if required?"

"Yes, I suppose so. What precisely is going on?"

"A lie. A very large lie."

"Do you have anything else," Shay queried, "in addition to your map, that can be used to substantiate what you've told us?"

"My notes for two books. They are only as believable as I am, however."

"You have no reason to lie," Sebastian grunted. "You didn't know what I was looking to find."

"I still don't, though I intend to begin reading the London newspapers in the morning."

Sebastian could forbid that, he supposed, but there would be no way to enforce it. He reached for the door, then stilled. "Sir, have you ever heard of a country anywhere called Costa Habichuela?"

"No. Bean Coast? If you're still referring to the Mosquito Coast, no one could possibly grow enough beans to name an area that, unless it's meant as a jest."

A jest. If only it were that simple. Sebastian wanted to slam his fist hard into something. No capital city, no fertile coast, no English-speaking natives, no country, and therefore no rey. And no Princess Josefina.

"Thank you, Master Rice-Able. We'll send word to you if we require your presence in London." Badly in need of fresh air, Sebastian pulled open the door. "In the meantime, I would appreciate your discretion."

"Certainly. Good evening, Your Grace, my lord."

Shay at his heels and holding their carriage lamp, Sebastian strode back to the coach. So many thoughts roiled and pounded in his head that he couldn't seize on any one, couldn't make sense of anything. The only clear image in his mind was of Josefina clinging to him and gasping in pleasure.

"Home," he barked at Timmons, and climbed inside the coach.

Shay had barely taken his own seat when the carriage lurched into motion. "Sebastian, I know you're angry," his brother said, his voice and his expression, his entire body, reeking of caution, "but we have to be careful."

"Rice-Able was there three years ago," he heard himself say unsteadily. "According to Embry, Costa Habichuela was granted him two years ago. There's still a chance that—"

"Be serious," Shay retorted. "I know you're only rarely fooled, but it *can* happen. If it's any comfort, Embry's got Prinny wearing that absurd green cross everywhere, and he's cheated the bank and bond investors out of a hundred thousand pounds. You're the one who suspected him in the first place. Why did you, anyway?"

Sebastian drew a tight breath. Every inch of him wanted to explode into motion and anger and frustration and a thousand other things he didn't care to put a name to. What was he supposed to tell Shay? That he'd suspected everyone, and Josefina especially, because he liked her? That for the first time in four years he'd desired a woman, wanted to be in her company, and that he'd made a choice so abysmally wrong that he'd endangered the standing of his family and of his country? And deepest down, of his heart?

"Melbourne?"

He shook himself. "No particular reason," he lied. "And yes, I'll proceed with caution. I know what's at stake. No one else can know, Shay. No one. Not until I decide how to proceed."

"You don't have to stand alone."

"I appreciate that."

Except that he was alone. Again. And he had only himself to blame for it. Well, that wasn't entirely true. Josefina Embry owed him some damned answers. And she would bloody well provide them, at the time and place of his choosing.

Chapter 12

osefina hurried downstairs as the pair of muddy coaches stopped at the front of the house. Her parents had made good time.

Her mother emerged first. "Josefina, *mi vida*," she exclaimed with a wide smile, holding her arms open for a hug.

It felt good to be back in a safe, unquestioning embrace. So much had happened in ten days' time that she could scarcely believe it. "Welcome back, Mama. I missed you."

"We missed you as well, Josefina," her father boomed, grinning as he hugged both her and her mother. "You'll never guess the progress we've made. Another fifty thousand pounds for Costa Habichuela."

"That's fantastic! Did you receive my letter?" Josefina asked, trailing him into the house as the queen took charge of the unloading of what looked to be a considerable number of purchases.

"I did. Magnificent work. As we left Edinburgh the

bond sales there were even brisker than what you reported here. The Scots can always smell a good investment."

He looked so pleased with himself that she hated to break his mood. But he needed to know that Melbourne had discovered the origins of the prospectus. Whatever the duke's interest in her, she didn't know how long he would remain silent.

"I arranged for a half dozen ships to be at our disposal in Edinburgh," he went on, sending one of the maids for coffee and settling himself behind his borrowed desk. "They'll be provisioned and ready to sail within the month."

"A half dozen ships? What do we need with—"

"Settlers will need supplies when they arrive." He pulled out a cigar and lit it on the desk lamp. "I want to meet the Duke of Harek," he went on. "Have you sent for him?"

"He should be here within the hour." A tremor of uneasiness ran through her as she took a seat opposite her father. "What settlers?"

"Your letter said people were practically begging to emigrate to Costa Habichuela. It's the same in Scotland. I had Halloway print up some land sale forms."

Josefina frowned. "Beg pardon?"

"With a million acres of fertile land at our disposal, why not give every Englishman the opportunity to own some of it, at three shillings an acre? In perpetuity, just like noblemen here."

Her heart stopped. "What? But—"

"And with ships already hired, we can grant passage at a reasonable price, plus an additional amount per pound of their belongings. And of course some of them will want to transport livestock." He scowled thoughtfully. "I'll have Orrin make up a list with the individual expenses printed out, to go with the land sale certificates. Oh, and we're selling hundred-acre lots, if anyone asks."

"You aren't—"

"If pressed, our land office can break some of the lots into ten-acre parcels."

Josefina began to feel light-headed. "What land office?"

"I opened one in Edinburgh. And the one here opens tomorrow. Orrin hired a solicitor's office to take care of the details while we were up north." Finally he looked at her. "What are you frowning at?"

"Papa—father—there are things we're never to speak about, even in private," she said in a low voice, cautious despite the closed door. Colonel Branbury's servants didn't know anything more than the rest of London, and they meant to keep it that way.

"Then don't speak of them. I'm also compiling a list of citizens we badly need to run the government and a rapidly expanding township. Bankers, blacksmiths, physicians, solicitors, map-makers, teachers—" He scooted a piece of paper over to her. "You probably know better than I. See if you can finish it in the next day or two, and we'll post it in the *London Times* and at the land office."

She looked from the long list of occupations back to her father as he sat at his ease, puffing on the cigar. "If this is a jest, it's not amusing."

"It's not a jest."

"But you can't—"

He leaned forward. "Don't you think it's unfair that we would come asking for money and then refuse to allow anyone to join us in sharing the bounty of our new paradise? They'll come anyway, rest assured. It's in our own best interest to keep the influx orderly. It's the opportunity of a lifetime, at a price far better than they'll find elsewhere." The rey grinned again. "And the Costa Habichuela natives are friendly, and speak English, unlike those savages in the United States."

"I know it would look odd if we didn't offer people a chance to immigrate," she hedged, fiddling with the corner of the paper he'd given her, "but isn't that something we should do closer to the time of our departure?"

"Now is the time to strike. You should have seen the reception we received in Scotland. They covered the streets with rose petals. Interest in Costa Habichuela will never be greater than it is at this moment."

Josefina took a shallow breath. "But settlers weren't part of the plan."

"They are now. Go put on your tiara before Harek arrives. I hope you've been wearing it to receive guests. We are royalty, and we need to act like it at all times." He pushed to his feet, hands flat on the desk as he leaned forward to look down at her. "At *all* times."

"Of course, Your Majesty." She stood, gave him a curtsy, and left the room.

Her throat constricted. Why had she never thought of this? Of course when people heard about a paradise some of them would wish a chance to reside there. Logically they had to be allowed to do so. *Damnation.* She had had such thoughts—worries—before, but now they felt . . . real. Mentally debating theories and letting her mind wander to pick apart cracks—if there were cracks—was one thing, but now it wasn't a theory any longer. People would be sailing to Costa Habichuela.

She went to her bed chamber and found the tiara where Conchita kept it. As she sat at the dressing table and frowned into the mirror, her door opened.

"Here, let me," her mother said with a smile, closing the door again and approaching to take the tiara from her.

"Did father tell you he opened a land office in Scotland, and that he's opening another one here tomorrow?"

"Yes. I attended the first one, and we're all to attend the second." Carefully her mother set the crown into Josefina's hair, then picked up the ivory comb to rearrange a few straying locks.

"Did you try to talk him out of it?"

"He didn't consult me, *mi ángel bonita*. You know how he is."

"But he's going to send people to Costa Habichuela."

"With supplies. Even if San Saturus isn't precisely what they expect, they can turn it into a beautiful capital city."

"The money is one thing, but why press our luck?" Josefina countered at a whisper. Her father would be furious if he knew they were having this conversation, even just the two of them, and even in absolute privacy. "We've never seen Costa Habichuela, Mama."

"You and your father have been working on this project for the past two years without rest. You know by now that he does nothing without good reason. Trust him, as he trusts you." Her mother kissed Josefina's cheek.

"I don't doubt that he'll be successful in finding settlers. It's what happens afterward that . . . troubles me," she returned.

"To others, we may exaggerate," her mother said, straightening. "Among ourselves, we always speak the truth. If he says everything will be well, believe it." She held out her hand. "Now tell me about the Duke of Harek. Is he as handsome as Lord Melbourne?"

Josefina followed her mother out the door. "He's quite pleasant-looking."

No man was as handsome as Melbourne. And her mother was wrong about one thing. Among themselves, they *did* lie. Because she knew that Sebastian Griffin knew the prospectus was fake, and that he suspected something more was afoot. And she'd told no one. And now abruptly she herself had a few questions about the wisdom of her father's newest plans.

An hour later Josefina met Harek at the morning room doorway. "Your Grace, may I introduce you to His

Majesty, Stephen Embry, Rey of Costa Habichuela, and Her Majesty, Queen Maria? Mother, Father, His Grace the Duke of Harck."

Harek smiled his most charming smile, the expression lighting his green eyes. "I have several times asked Her Highness to call me Charles, and I request the same of Your Majesties." He bowed. "I am very pleased finally to meet you."

Her father stood. "Likewise, Charles." They shook hands. "Thank you for coming to our assistance on such short notice. I have to admit, I was rather taken aback at Melbourne's desertion."

The duke's smile faltered a little. "Ah. I don't know Melbourne well, but he has been helpful in easing the transition. He offered us seats at the theater the other evening, and has invited all of us to join him at Vauxhall Gardens tomorrow night."

"He said he simply had too many other duties to give us the amount of attention the liaison position required," Josefina offered, somewhat surprised to hear herself lying yet again to her parents, and again on Melbourne's behalf. In all likelihood *he* had some of the answers she wanted, though, and it wouldn't do if she was forbidden to speak with him. Besides, she wanted to have sex with him again.

"Well, he handled his departure as a gentleman then, I suppose." The rey put an arm across Harek's shoulders. "Join me in the billiards room, Charles, and tell me about yourself."

Harek glanced over his shoulder as he left the room. "My apologies, Queen Maria, Princess Josefina. Duty and billiards call."

"He is pleasant to the eyes, Josefina," her mother agreed as the two men headed up the stairs. "And on the ears. Well mannered, with a sense of humor, and a duke. Better for you perhaps than stone-faced Melbourne."

"Perhaps," Josefina agreed, picking out the most non-committal word she could.

"Do you like Charles?"

She shrugged. "Well enough. He's already made mention that he has no qualms about foreign travel. He's only just returned from Canada, in fact."

"Your father will convince him to offer for you, you know, if our duke hasn't already decided to do so."

"I know."

And if she'd met Harek first, and Melbourne not at all, she would be perfectly content. And the order and circumstances of acquaintance didn't actually matter, anyway, because Melbourne would never leave England. Her father had made a mistake, encouraging Prinny to select Sebastian as his representative. And for the first time she began to wonder whether her father wasn't making several mistakes, now.

Sebastian sat up. He felt thick and groggy, and as he looked at the clock on the fireplace mantel in his bedchamber, it took a moment for the time to register. Twenty-one minutes past five. That didn't make any sense, because they hadn't arrived home until past three, and he knew he hadn't fallen asleep until well after that.

Which would make it nearly half past five in the evening. *Damnation.* "Bailey!" he yelled.

The door lurched open and his valet half-stumbled into the room. "I'm here, Your Grace."

Sebastian flung the sheets aside and stood. "Why the bloody hell didn't you wake me?"

"Your brother, Lord Shay, said not to." Bailey hurried to the wardrobe and returned with a shirt and trousers.

"This is not Shay's house. It is my house."

A small fist banged on his door. "Papa, are you decent?"

Rarely, it seemed. Stifling the thought, he finished

buttoning his trousers. "Come in, Peep," he called, pulling his shirt on over his head.

His daughter, in a lovely yellow silk gown that deepened the gray of her eyes, pranced into the room. "Did you sleep well?"

"Too well," Sebastian replied, sending another glare in Bailey's direction. "What have you done with yourself today, my angel?"

"I studied French, and I had to miss my pianoforte lessons because you were asleep, and Mrs. Beacham took me to the park, and Stanton asked if I knew the dinner menu because you were still asleep, and I didn't, so I told him summer pease soup and rabbit fricassée because I like that, and so does Uncle Zachary."

"Zachary likes any food that's not moving," Sebastian commented, allowing Bailey to help him with his waistcoat and cravat. "Is he eating with us?"

"Everyone is. Did you forget? You said it was because Aunt Caroline's family is here, and if you got one dinner out of the way, perhaps they would leave you alone."

"That's not to be repeated, Penelope."

"I know that," she returned, disgust in her voice. "I have your confidence."

"Yes, you do."

"I have everyone's confidence. I know so many things, it makes my head spin."

And thankfully there were quite a few things she didn't know. "I appreciate all of your efforts today as the lady of the house," he said aloud, sitting at his dressing table to shave.

"I know you do. I'm going to make certain Cook has baked something chocolate for dessert."

"A splendid idea. Will you send Stanton up here on your way?"

"Certainly."

It was probably a good thing that Peep had come in and interrupted what would have become a furious rampage at being coddled. He'd lost most of a day on Josefina and whatever she was up to. In addition, the so-called rey was due back from Scotland today, and God knew what he'd been up to there.

"Your Grace, shall I send down for tea, or coffee?" Bailey asked, holding the bowl of shaving soap.

"No. I'm—"

Stanton scratched at the door and pushed it open. "Your Grace?"

"Have Merlin saddled. I'm going out for a short time."

"Your guests will be arriving shortly."

"I won't be long."

The butler bowed, pulling the door closed as he left the room. "I'll see to it immediately."

As soon as he finished shaving he headed downstairs. His stomach rumbled, but he ignored it. At the moment, hunger was the least of his worries. In the foyer Stanton handed over his riding gloves and hat and offered a great-coat, which he declined.

"I'll be back within the hour," he decided. That would give him enough time to confront her, and not enough time for her to spin his anger into lust and arousal, which, damn it all, he was already thinking about.

"Your Grace, you should have Green accompany you," Stanton said as he strode down the front step.

"I don't need a wet-nurse," Sebastian shot back, swinging into the saddle.

"Of course not. But . . . a great many people rely on you, and you're obviously angry, and you haven't said where you're going."

Sebastian pulled Merlin to a stop. He couldn't recall Stanton ever expressing his opinion so directly. And the butler had a point. Having a witness to a meeting with

Josefina, though, even a discreet one, seemed at the moment both foolhardy and potentially dangerous. "I'll be at Colonel Branbury's house," he said curtly. "Have Shay host if the guests arrive before I return."

"Very good, Your Grace."

Twenty minutes later he dismounted, handing Merlin off to a groom. "Leave him standing," he said brusquely. "I won't be long."

As he reached the front door the butler pulled it open. "Good evening, Your Grace," he intoned.

"I require a word with Princess Josefina," Sebastian said crisply, stripping off his gloves.

"Her Highness isn't in. If you would leave your card, I will inform her of your visit when she returns."

Damnation. "The rey and Queen Maria, have they returned from Scotland?"

"They arrived this morning, Your Grace, but they've all gone for an early dinner with His Grace, Lord Harek."

"And where might they be?"

"I wasn't informed, Your Grace."

"And after? Where will they be going after dinner?"

"I am not at liberty to discuss the royal family's schedule, Your Grace."

Sebastian eyed the butler. He could break the man and get the information he wanted within a minute, but the ramifications would be more harmful than the information helpful. It was one of the few times that being no one of consequence would have been useful.

"Very well," he said curtly. "Please inform Her Highness that I called. I will wait to speak to her at Vauxhall tomorrow night." He turned on his heel.

Not many people dared rebuff him, and he had to give a point or two to Branbury's man for his loyalty. He didn't appreciate being thwarted under any circumstances, and he badly wanted to track Josefina down. But the questions he had for her and her parents needed to be kept private until he had proof.

Proof. Proof of what? He returned to Merlin and headed back to Griffin House. Proof that a supposedly fertile country was nothing but swampland? Proof that Costa Habichuela in its entirely probably wasn't worth the hundred thousand pounds they'd been loaned?

Was that all of it? Embry had taken possession of a plot of mud and borrowed money against it. In itself the action seemed minor, until one took into account all of the Englishmen buying bonds to cover the loan. Their sure investment—the one he'd helped to arrange—was likely to lose them every penny they'd put into it. Banks had been forced to close over less.

As for him personally—well, he'd never trusted Josefina, and his suspicions had proven to be precisely on the mark. That fact did not make him feel any better, however. In fact, the only positive factor in all of this was that she probably had no intention of actually settling in Costa Habichuela.

He pulled Merlin to a stop. She could remain in England. He could . . .

"Stop it," he muttered, and Merlin flicked his ears backward.

He could what? Continue to see her? At best she and her parents had fraudulently applied for a loan. At worst, they were stealing outright from the Bank of England and the citizens of London. In no way could he or would he associate the Griffin name with that kind of debacle. The loan disaster itself could do the family more harm than he cared to contemplate.

As he reached Griffin House again, light streamed from every window. A herd of carriages and horses cluttered the drive and the stable yard, his grooms shouting at one another as they attempted to manage the chaos.

Sebastian sighed as he dismounted and tossed the reins to Green. What he truly wanted tonight was some quiet and a snifter of brandy so he could puzzle the mess out—though what he hoped to discover at the bottom of a bottle, he had no idea.

He desperately needed someone else who could corroborate John Rice-Able's claims. At the moment it was the Embrys' word against the professor's. And people wanted to believe that the charming princess they celebrated was exactly what she claimed to be. Hell, he wanted that, and he knew better.

"Your Grace," one of the house's footmen said, pulling open the front door for him, "your guests have all arrived, and have gathered in the drawing room."

He could hear the noise they were making from outside. "Thank you, Tom. See to your post."

The footman bowed. "Your Grace." He raced off in the direction of the pantry—hopefully not to hide, though that seemed a fair idea.

"There you are," Valentine said, looking down at him from the balcony. "Damn."

"Why are you cursing?" Sebastian queried, squaring his shoulders and climbing the stairs toward his brother-in-law. "Are you that unhappy to see me?"

"In a word, yes. Because if you're here, I can't escape to go looking for you. Remind me again why I'm a part of this lunacy?"

"Because you married my sister, which makes you part of the family, and Caroline married my brother, which makes her part of the family, which means we both have to spend the evening with Caroline's other family."

"And again, damn." Valentine put an arm across his shoulders, steering them toward the drawing room. "They're all here, you know."

"I know."

"I mean all of the Witfelds. Even the married ones. And their husbands."

"Damn," Sebastian muttered.

"My thoughts exactly."

Caroline had six younger sisters. At last count three of them were married, and one more engaged. Including Caroline, he probably had a baker's dozen worth of Witfeld clan members in the drawing room—and that didn't count their offspring. But since he couldn't avoid them all, at least he could use them to distract himself, to keep himself from wondering where Josefina might be tonight. She and Harek were no doubt chatting and laughing while she plotted how next to bring more trouble to the Griffin doorstep.

With a slight grin Valentine pushed open the drawing room doors and stepped back to allow him unobstructed entry. Every face in the room turned in his direction. Good Lord, Valentine hadn't been joking. Every Witfeld he'd ever met—and he was certain a few he hadn't—stood in his drawing room.

"Good evening," he intoned, pasting on a mild expression. Tonight he would play the amiable host, even if it killed him. He was accustomed to the role, after all, though it felt more difficult than usual this evening—all because at the moment he would much rather be chasing through London after a chit he simultaneously wanted to strangle and to kiss senseless.

The Witfeld herd bowed in an undulating wave. "Your Grace," everyone breathed, as though he'd just descended from the heavens to share a meal with the mortals.

Taking a breath, he moved in to find the head of the Witfeld household. "Edmund," he said, shaking the patriarch's hand. "I hope you had a pleasant trip down to London."

"It was noisy, but no other complaints." Witfeld moved

closer. "I apologize for the size of the horde. With the cattle breeding doing so well, Sally decided all of our girls should get to see London. That meant we had to bring along three husbands and a fiancé, plus Susan's two boys and Grace's daughter."

"The more the merrier," Sebastian returned. "If you have need of anything while you're here, please let me know."

"I'm just hoping I don't misplace any of them."

"I've debated having bells sewn into Peep's gowns. You might consider that."

Edmund chuckled. "Don't tempt me."

For the next twenty minutes he waded through Witfelds and their in-laws. They'd wintered together the year before last at Melbourne Park, but he hadn't seen any of them but Edmund since then. The main area of interest tonight centered around the youngsters, with Peep appointing herself her young cousin Rose's guardian.

"Are you avoiding me, Your Grace?" a sweet feminine voice cooed from behind him.

He turned around. "Miss Anne," he said with a smile, nodding at the petite young lady with honey-blonde hair and gray-green eyes. As far as he was concerned, the nearly nineteen-year-old was the only Witfeld chit aside from Caroline with anything resembling brains in her head. "I know your sister invited you to London a month ago. Why the delay?"

"Joanna threatened to follow me, as she's also unattached. I didn't think it would be wise to unleash her on the Town for the entire Season."

Considering that Joanna two years ago had attempted to compromise herself in Zach's presence and thereby trap him into marriage, Sebastian wasn't about to argue the point. "Thank you," he said.

"You know," Anne continued, looping her arm around

his, "there are those who think you and I would be a good match."

He lifted an eyebrow. "Who are these people?"

Anne lowered her head, looking up at him through her long eyelashes. "My mama."

"Ah. Well, my dear, if you weren't sixteen years my junior, and if you didn't terrify me no end, then perhaps."

She laughed. "I told her that you're no match for me. But watch yourself with Joanna. She refuses to be the last of us to marry."

Sebastian glanced in Joanna's direction, to find the silly girl looking in his direction. *Bloody wonderful.* "Thank you for the warning."

She patted his arm. "I like having you in my debt."

Sebastian chuckled. "Did I mention that you terrify me?"

"Yes."

On the surface, Anne Witfeld and Josefina Embry were very much alike—confident, intelligent, and outspoken. Deeper inside, however, they couldn't have been more different. Anne was what she presented to the world. Josefina, though, was a tumult of contradictory stories, emotions, feelings, and moods. All in all, in fact, Anne would probably have been a more manageable companion. But he looked upon Anne as a much younger sister with some disturbing tendencies toward being too clever for her own good. No, Josefina was the woman he wanted.

Sebastian blinked. He wanted her in his bed, that was. She was far too dangerous to his equilibrium and his peace of mind for anything more than that. And that didn't even take into account the fact that she was very likely involved with breaking the law.

"Your Grace?"

Stanton stood at his elbow, but Sebastian had no idea whether it was the first or the fifth time he'd spoken. "Yes, Stanton?"

"Shall I call for dinner?"

"By all means."

The butler moved to the front of the room. "Dinner is served," he announced, and pulled open the double doors of the formal dining room. As he stepped aside, the members of the Griffin and Witfeld families began a loud and laughing stampede to the doorway.

"Sebastian," Nell's low voice came, as she took his arm.

He leaned sideways, kissing her hair. "Thank you for coming tonight and helping to level the numbers."

Surprise crossed her sensitive face. "You're welcome."

"Just please keep Joanna away from me," he continued.

"I shall do my utmost." His sister cleared her throat. "I came to see you yesterday afternoon. Stanton said you had urgent business at Eton."

"I did."

"You took Shay with you."

Sebastian lowered his brow. "I frequently have Shay join me for business expeditions. What's amiss, Nell?"

"Nothing, if all you went to see to was business."

"Then nothing is amiss," he lied smoothly. As far as the rest of the world was concerned, that would be true, and no one would discover otherwise until and unless he decided that he had proof, and that it was time for them to know. "Are you doubting my leadership of this family?"

She freed her arm. "You know, I thought something might be troubling you, and that you could use a friendly ear. But keep your mask on, Melbourne. Eventually when you wish to take it off you'll find that there's nothing beneath it."

Sebastian inclined his head. "Thank you, my dear. It's always nice to know where one stands."

He supposed he could argue that the family didn't want a patriarch who bent and broke with every breeze, that though they might complain about his rigidity they actually relied on it. Any such conversation, though, would be a waste of breath. He knew what his family required to remain safe and secure, and he provided that regardless of the cost to himself.

And that was why the only thoughts he should be having about Josefina Embry were how best to distance the Griffins from any possible scandal. Under no circumstances should he be thinking about her smooth skin and her soft mouth and the fascination he found in never knowing what she might say or do next.

"—for luncheon tomorrow," Eleanor was saying. "I think she might enjoy it, since she's always talking about becoming a pirate and traveling the world."

Penelope. That had to be whom Nell was discussing. "That's fine," he improvised. "I'll be in Parliament most of the day."

His sister looked at him for the space of several seconds. "I know you're human," she finally said. "I've seen it."

"Well, by all means continue your observation. I have a dinner to host." He handed her to her seat and made his way to the head of the table. Yes, he was human. And where Princess Josefina was concerned, he needed to become less so. Immediately.

Chapter 13

Josefina stood on the front steps of Branbury House and waved as Harek's coach rolled off into the night. Pleasant as both he and the evening had been, she was glad he was gone; all she'd wanted for the past few hours was the chance to retire to her bed chamber alone and think.

The rey stood in the foyer behind her as she turned around. "I think Melbourne may have done us a favor in withdrawing," he commented, removing his gloves and handing them over to Grimm. "What an amiable fellow Charles is."

She smiled. "He is that."

"He wants to marry you."

Josefina stopped halfway to the stairs. *Don't be disappointed*, she told herself. Melbourne would never make such an offer, regardless. "I thought he might," she said aloud.

"I haven't given my definitive approval yet," her father continued, "since for one thing I only met him this morning, and for another I have to consider timing. With the land office opening tomorrow, interest will already be high. In a fortnight or so, when our celebrity has begun to recede a bit, that will be the time to make the announcement, I think."

"You might ask me if I like him," she countered.

He waved a hand at her. "Your mother said you liked him. We already discussed it. It's more important, though, that he understand our goals."

"I believe you can convince anyone of anything." *Well, nearly anyone.* She drew a breath. "And now I shall say goodnight, because I am quite tired."

The rey smiled. "Yes, get a good night's sleep. The people will want to see you looking radiant tomorrow."

She watched him down the hall in the direction of his office before she climbed the stairs. Once Conchita had helped her into her night rail and left, she sat in bed for a long moment, looking into the darkness and listening.

As the house settled into its night quiet she rose again and lit the candle on her bed stand. The prospectus she'd authored sat on her writing table. The other book, the one she'd borrowed this morning from Lord Allendale's library, lay at the back of her wardrobe behind a stack of hat boxes.

She knew of a handful of people who'd seen Costa Habichuela with their own eyes—her father and his military colleagues, all of whom were presently in his service and shared his vision, and this John Rice-Able, whose book Melbourne had been reading when she'd found him in the library. Perhaps Mr. Rice-Able could answer a few of the questions that had very recently begun troubling her.

Silently she sat at the writing table and opened the book to the section on Central America.

An hour later the candle had burned down to a nub, and she'd read the entire section twice. Josefina sat back, rubbing her eyes. It might not be true, she told herself, turning to her prospectus and flipping through it, re-reading some of her pasted-together phrases. Of course she hadn't believed that her father had been gifted with a paradise, despite what he boasted, but Rice-Able described Costa Habichuela as hell.

"His book could be a lie," she muttered, standing to return the book to its hiding place. Who was to say whether his book had any more credibility than hers? Simply because she'd never seen Costa Habichuela with her own eyes didn't mean everything she'd put together had been false. Previously, though, she hadn't cared. Her father's letters emphasized what he wanted her to present in the prospectus, and she'd done so. It had been enough to secure their loans. But perhaps she'd done her job too well.

When something seemed too good to be true, a man was supposed to pause for a second to wonder whether that might be the case. If people invested in bonds without first doing research, they were foolish. Perhaps they shouldn't have made Costa Habichuela so . . . perfect. But as of her father's return from Scotland this had become more than a bank swindle. He was either selling poor, hopeful people plots of land that could be settled and made profitable, or he was tricking them into buying their own graves. And with Mr. Rice-Able's written accounts, she had reason to doubt that her father's descriptions resembled Costa Habichuela at all. And now it mattered; she might be a thief, but she wasn't a murderer.

What was she supposed to do, though? Tell the authorities? Tell Sebastian? She might as well throw herself into the Thames. The safer alternative, then, was to do nothing. To allow her father to load his ships with immigrants and sail them across the Atlantic. If Melbourne and Mr. Rice-Able were correct, in all likelihood no one would ever hear from the settlers again, and if any did survive then she and her parents would be long gone before anyone heard the tale—and with countless hundreds of thousands of pounds to secure their continued freedom and well-being.

Just do nothing. It would be simple. And she had more than a suspicion that even if the worst were true, and even if amiable Lord Harek were to find out about it, the wealth they would receive in exchange would be more than enough to compensate him for any blows to his conscience. With a duke along, their next money-raising effort would have much more respectability.

But then, what if the worst was true, and she did go along with it, and the authorities found out before they could flee? They wouldn't just be imprisoned or transported for this. They could well be executed.

An icy shaft of fear ran through her. Even doing nothing might not be an option, if Melbourne went to anyone with his suspicions. And why wouldn't he? He was a Griffin, a paragon of virtue, a legendary defender of England. They might have had sex, but according to him, that had been practically in defiance of his own best interest. So even if she might dream of being with him again, why should she believe for one second that he would choose protecting her over the welfare of what were essentially his citizens?

She'd nearly chosen him over her *own* welfare, and that was more and more clearly insanity. Being a good lover did not make him a good protector. And the fact that she believed Melbourne to be a good man made the circumstances even more perilous for her and her family, now that her father had decided that one hundred and fifty thousand pounds wasn't enough.

She needed to talk to someone. She needed to tell her father about Sebastian, and hope that he would either be able to tell her that Costa Habichuela was close enough to a paradise that they had nothing to fear, or that he had a plan to protect them. To protect her. As if he could possibly have a plan to protect her heart.

She went downstairs early to find both of her parents already eating breakfast. Another flutter of nerves twisted through her gut. First some answers about the true nature of Costa Habichuela, she told herself. Determine how much difficulty she—they—might be in. Only then could and would she decide what to do with what she knew.

"Good morning," she began, smiling, and headed for the sideboard, though the thought of eating anything at all made her stomach roil. As Grimm held her chair for her, she nodded her thanks and sat opposite her mother, with the rey at the head of the table. "Grimm, please give us some privacy," she continued.

"Of course, Your Highness." The butler snapped his fingers. He and the two hovering footmen in the room vacated, closing the doors behind them, and in a moment she and her parents were alone.

"What's this?" her father asked. "Charles will be here within the hour. We have a very important appearance to make this morning."

"I'm aware of that." Josefina sat for a moment, gathering herself. "Father, I have some concerns about this next step we're taking. I think we need to discuss them."

He lifted a light eyebrow. "We discussed this already."

"Yes, but where are you sending these settlers?"

"Are you jesting?"

"I'm quite serious. I would like to hear exactly what your plans are."

He set down his fork with a clatter. "I will not be interrogated by you. This project has been our sole concern for the past two years. Why are you questioning it now?"

"Because I think you left out some details," she returned.

"I thought this was about loan money. And perhaps marrying me off to a peer. Nothing more."

"That was the original idea."

"Then why alter our plans?"

"Did you have any idea that we would be handed one hundred and fifty thousand pounds within a fortnight of our arrival in London?"

"No. Our reception here has been astounding."

"Yes, it has been. We've been presented with the opportunity to double that. Perhaps triple it. We'll never have to worry about money again. We can live like royalty." He laughed. "What am I saying? We *are* royalty."

"I have no difficulty with that," she returned. "As of this moment, we're only hurting the banks. They'll have to refund that bond money to the investors or face riots. The citizens won't lose anything but hopefully some of their naivete."

"And?"

"And that changes once you begin selling land. These people are buying a dream, Father. A hope for the future. What are they going to find when they get to Costa Habichuela?"

"Paradise."

She drew a breath. "That's what we've told everyone else. What's the truth?"

The rey frowned. "It is not your place to question me, Josefina. You will play your part with a smile. Because if you don't, we'll all swing for this. Do you understand that?"

Josefina swallowed. "I understand." It was the closest he'd ever come to admitting anything, even about the loan money. The secret of their success, he always said, was to treat what they did as real, even among themselves. "Just tell me if there will be trouble when the ships and settlers arrive at Costa Habichuela."

"I imagine there will be." Stephen Embry leaned forward, grabbing her hand. "But we shall be gone from England by then. And Josefina, this is the last time we will speak of this." He released her again.

Oh, dear. She'd been right. Melbourne had been right. And once he heard about the land sales—if she'd been uneasy about it, she couldn't imagine how he might react. Or rather, she could imagine it. "There's one more thing," she said quietly, misery rising in her heart.

"Make it quick. We can't afford to make the household staff suspicious."

"I know. It's just that . . ." God, she didn't want to say it. "Melbourne has been asking some very pointed questions about the conditions in Costa Habichuela. I don't think he believes the prospectus. In fact, I know he doesn't. He knows we took the information from other reports."

Slowly her father pushed to his feet. "Did you tell him anything?"

"No! Of course not. But I don't know what he'll do when he learns that you're—we're—encouraging people to sail off and settle there."

The rey strode to the sideboard and back. "Damnation," he muttered, chewing on his moustache as he paced. "I should never have suggested his involvement. I was thinking of the benefit of having the Griffin name attached to ours, not that the self-righteous fool would delve into our affairs. This is my fault."

Melbourne was a great many things, but she would never consider him a fool. "We should cancel our engagement with him at Vauxhall."

"That won't do any good. As you said, once he hears about the land sales he's bound to do something. No, we'll meet him as intended. I'll take care of matters."

The way he said it sounded ominous. "How?"

"Don't worry yourself over it." He snapped his fingers several times. "Just avoid him until tonight."

"I'm going to luncheon with his sisters and his daughter."

"Would he confide in them?"

Would he? He seemed so private, even to those he knew well. "I don't think so."

"Then go to luncheon." He crossed around the table again to kiss his wife. "I'll meet you both in the foyer in forty minutes. I need to talk to Captain Milton. Vauxhall is a very crowded place, after all. Anyone can get in if they have the entrance fee. And a man like Melbourne has enemies. A number of them, I'm sure."

As he left the room, Josefina looked at her mother. Nagging horror touched her as she considered her father's words. "He wouldn't," she whispered.

"He's angry," Maria Embry soothed. "He'll find a way through this. Your father is a very clever man. And I know he's grateful that you told him of Lord Melbourne's concerns."

"Yes, but this isn't about tricking someone into paying plantation rental to us or buying livestock that doesn't exist, Mama. This—"

Grimm and the footmen returned to the breakfast room, and Queen Maria resumed her breakfast. Josefina tried to, but what little appetite she'd had was now gone completely.

She'd done her duty to her family, and told them about a very likely and serious threat. Her father had said he would deal with it. Therefore, everything was back where it belonged, proceeding exactly according to the plan the rey had begun mapping out two years earlier—except for the settlement of Costa Habichuela.

Why, then, did she feel sick with dread? If something happened now to Sebastian, it would be her fault. They had no agreement between them, and she'd certainly never promised him anything, but this felt like a betrayal. Not just of him, but of her heart.

"Thank you for seeing me, Admiral," Sebastian said, offering his hand to the uniformed man standing behind the large mahogany desk.

Admiral Mattingly had a warm, hard grip, and a reputation much the same. "It's a pleasure, Your Grace," he rasped, "though an unexpected one, to be sure. What may I do for you?"

At the admiral's gesture, Sebastian took a seat, declining the offer of a cigar. "I have an odd request," he began, wondering what the rest of his family would think if they learned that he'd left London and Parliament for the second time in three days, this time for Dover. "I'm looking for anyone who might have sailed along the eastern coast of Central America. I've been offered some timber at a very good price, but I would like an outside opinion of the quality before I agree to anything."

"Most of our fleet's either in the Mediterranean or along the western coast of Spain at the moment."

"Yes, I know my odds aren't very favorable, but I wanted to try."

"All the way from London on horseback for a question about timber quality?"

Sebastian nodded.

"It must be a great quantity of timber." The admiral regarded him for a moment, then pulled a piece of paper from a drawer and scrawled something on it. "Lieutenant Calder!"

The young man who'd shown Sebastian in to the admiral pushed open the door, stepped into the room, and clicked his heels together. "Yes, sir!"

"Take this down to the *Endeavor* and deliver it to Captain Jerrod."

"Yes, sir!" The lieutenant took the note, saluted, and vanished again.

"He's a good lad, very efficient," the admiral said, indicating the door, "but can't set foot on a deck without casting up his accounts. Have some tea, Your Grace. We should have a reply in twenty minutes or so."

"Thank you, Admiral."

"Jerrod sails tomorrow. He may not be able to help, but it's a shame to see you come all this way for nothing. England needs its timber."

Sebastian smiled. Admiral Mattingly knew he frequently carried out directives for Prinny. This one might be a bit self-serving, but depending on whether he could find someone who knew the Mosquito Coast area and whether they could corroborate John Rice-Able's stories or not, the result could have a national impact.

In just under twenty minutes Lieutenant Calder rapped on the door and entered the office again. "Admiral, Captain Jerrod sends his regrets that he cannot assist you personally, but he has put one of his lieutenants at your disposal."

"Well, send him in, Calder."

"Yes, sir!" Calder left again. A moment later a tall, handsome young man with black hair and merry green eyes entered the office. "Lieutenant Bradshaw Carroway at your service, Admiral," he said, saluting.

"Carroway, this is His Grace, the Duke of Melbourne. Assist him in any way you can."

Sebastian stood. "Might we take a walk?"

The lieutenant inclined his head. "After you, Your Grace."

They left the office and headed along the harbor battery.

"I apologize for taking you from your duties, Lieutenant. Admiral Mattingly says that your ship leaves tomorrow."

The young man nodded. He had to be several years younger than Zachary, barely out of his teens. "You got me out of counting sacks of oranges, Your Grace. I am extremely grateful." With a grin, he gave Sebastian a sideways glance. "You don't remember me, do you?"

"Should I?"

"We met two years ago, very briefly. My older brother brought me along to a soiree you attended."

"Who is your brother?"

"Tristan Carroway, Viscount Dare."

It was Sebastian's turn to smile. "Of course. I should have remembered."

"I danced with your sister, Lady Eleanor. Your brother Charlemagne practically demanded my entire family history before he'd let me on the dance floor." Carroway chuckled again. "But what may I do for you today, Your Grace? Captain Jerrod said someone had a query about South America."

"Central America, actually. The Mosquito Coast. Are you familiar with it?"

"I was on the *Triumph* last year. We chased an American frigate up and down that coast for two months before we got word of a cessation of hostilities."

Last year. Sebastian took a slow breath, covering his abrupt excitement. "Have you heard of a King Qental there?"

"Yes. Shifty fellow. Sold us the services of two guides to see us safely along the coast, and they nearly had us stranded on a sandbar two days later."

"Is the area habitable?"

"In certain places. The higher the ground the more likely it is to last from one rainy season to the next. But there's not a great deal of high ground along the coast."

"Do you know of a place called Black Diamond Bay?"

Carroway considered for a moment. "No."

"How about a small settlement called San Saturus?"

"No. There were a few mining and trapping encampments, and I suppose one of them could have been called that, but I don't recall it."

"Are you familiar with an Englishman named Stephen Embry?"

"Embry. Tall fellow, big blonde moustache?"

Good God. "Yes, that's him. How do you know him?"

"As a favor to the governor of Belize we ferried a group of Englishmen from there to Jamaica. Mostly soldiers hiring out to the Spanish rebels. Or leaving their service, rather, since they were headed for Jamaica."

"Why do you remember Embry?"

"He was calling himself a colonel in the *Army Nationale*, some sort of personal friend of Bolivar. From listening to him, he was leading the rebellion himself. All of his men wore some very sharp-looking black uniforms with green crosses on the breast. I remember thinking they must have been hotter than Hades wearing black wool in the jungle. Of course every one of them looked spotless—but on the Mosquito Coast they wouldn't have seen much action against the Spanish regulars, anyway."

"Lieutenant, would you be willing to swear to all of this in a court of law?"

Carroway frowned. "They're just my observations."

"They're good enough."

"I would be happy to, then, but—"

"But you're sailing tomorrow. Damn."

"I'll write out a statement, if you think that will help you."

"It would help immensely. Thank you."

"Anything to keep me from counting potatoes. They were next on the inventory list."

It was exactly the information he wanted, and needed, but Sebastian couldn't help wishing for a single heartbeat that Bradshaw Carroway had been a guest of the rey of Costa Habichuela and had stayed in a splendid bedchamber in the rey's royal palace in San Saturus. "One last question. Do you know of a country in that region called Costa Habichuela?"

"The Bean Coast? No. If we'd known of any such place, we would have stopped there to resupply instead of having to sail all the way back to Belize."

They turned back toward the admiral's office. "Thank you, Lieutenant Carroway."

"Please, call me Shaw. I might have married your sister if your brother hadn't threatened to spread my innards in the garden for fertilizer if I asked her to dance with me again."

Sebastian chuckled, grateful for even a minute's distraction.

They returned to Admiral Mattingly's office, and the lieutenant wrote out a statement of his recollections concerning the Mosquito Coast, Colonel Stephen Embry, and the nonexistent San Saturus and Costa Habichuela. With the paper secured in his coat pocket, Sebastian thanked Carroway, the admiral, and His Majesty's Navy. Then he retrieved Merlin and headed back to London. He had a party to attend at Vauxhall, and some answers to wring out of a pretty young lady who was apparently not at all what she claimed to be.

Chapter 14

 The hordes that surrounded the small building, hastily labeled *Costa Habichuela Land Office*, actually cheered as Josefina and her parents disembarked from their coach. And she'd thought the crowd at the bank had been large.

"Magnificent, isn't it?" the rey said, waving. "Hello, friends, and welcome!"

"How did so many people know about this?" Josefina asked in a hushed voice as she took her father's arm. "You only told me yesterday."

"I arranged for the newspapers to place ads beginning yesterday morning," he returned, falling in behind Captain Milton as the soldier led the way to the closed office doors. "Ah, there you are, Mr. Halloway, Mr. Orrin. Let's open these doors, shall we?" The rey faced the crowd. "Thank you all for your support and your enthusiasm. I want to be the first to welcome you as new citizens of Costa Habichuela!"

The crowd roared. So many people, the majority of

them from the lower classes—clerks and farmers, rag and bone men, servants, street sweepers, miners, and bakers. They wanted new lives in paradise, and would spend every penny they owned to purchase one. It was an odd, miserable feeling to see their happy, hopeful faces and to know in a month or so every one of them would hate the idea of Costa Habichuela and everyone who represented it. They would hate her. And she would deserve it.

"Smile," her mother whispered, taking the arm her father had released.

"How can I?" she returned.

"Because we have no alternative, *chica*."

The Duke of Harek swept up to them. "Join the rey, Your Majesty," he said to her mother, smiling. "I'll keep our princess from being carried aloft on the grateful shoulders of the people."

"That's a bit melodramatic, don't you think?" Josefina commented, accepting a rose from a young girl.

"Nonsense. They worship you. *I* worship you."

She eyed him, wishing he were Melbourne. "Do you now?"

"I do. I've spoken with His Majesty, in fact. And though nothing's been formalized, I want you to know that I intend to ask for your hand." Light green eyes assessed her. "You're not surprised."

"Should I be?"

His smile deepened. "I suppose not. My only concern actually, is whether you might decline in hopes of receiving a similar offer from Melbourne."

Her heart wobbled. "Melbourne? I can barely tolerate the man."

"You don't have to pretend, Your Highness. His wealth and power are unmatched. But we all know he won't marry when he'd be expected to leave England, even if he did ever decide to remarry at all."

"You're quite the Melbourne scholar," she said, trying to keep her voice from tightening. Of course by now she knew what Sebastian would and wouldn't do, but that didn't mean she wanted to hear it said aloud. How could her father have miscalculated so?

"In some ways I am," Harek returned in a lower voice. "For instance, I know you've shared a bed."

The blood fled her face. "What? Why—"

"I don't mind. Truly. Raising a child with Griffin blood, especially if it has enough of his looks to make its parentage apparent, could be very beneficial to us. Income-wise, I mean. So continue as you will."

For a moment her mind refused to accept what she'd just heard. "I—I have no idea what you're talking about, sir, and even if I did, I would not—"

"I'm not some monster, Your Highness. I did not say what I did to offend or threaten you. You are pleasing to me, and I think we will be a good match. Many marriages are made merely for political or monetary gain. That may be the case here as well, but at least we like one another. And as long as we're in London, yes, please continue to encourage Melbourne. I see no downside to any such arrangement."

"The . . ." She paused, clearing her throat and trying to gather her thoughts. "I admit," she finally ventured, "that *now* you surprise me."

He inclined his head. "You are a princess, and I am a duke. We are above most of the nonsense that concerns other people."

"Thank you, Lord Harek."

"Please call me Charles."

"Charles, then."

Lieutenant May approached, bowing with his hand across his breast. "Your Highness, His Majesty requests that you join him and the queen."

"Thank you, Lieutenant."

So that was the life she should expect. Before she'd arrived in London, when she and her father had studied the registry looking for unmarried aristocrats with whom they might form an alliance, she'd been looking at wealth, and the age and elevation of the title. And then she'd set eyes on Sebastian Griffin, and even with her requirements satisfied, her expectations had heightened.

As she'd already realized, Harek was a much better match for her than Melbourne. Charles didn't ask questions, and he kept quiet about what he knew.

Harek was the match she needed to make. But the part of her that was simply Josefina Embry, without the tangles and webs and complications, didn't want a husband who approved of her having affairs, who would just stand by and let anything happen because it either didn't affect him, or it happened to be to his benefit.

And yet a choice in such matters belonged to someone who hadn't trodden the path she'd taken. Besides, her father was taking care of the problem the Duke of Melbourne posed. A shiver ran through her again.

Was she that person? Someone like Harek who allowed the wrong things to happen? She had been, before. She'd helped them along. It shouldn't have been a difficult question now—if she did nothing, she remained wealthy and safe and free. If she acted to help Melbourne, she and her parents would probably hang.

Unless there was a third alternative. She had approximately ten hours to come up with one. And a luncheon with Sebastian's sisters and his delightfully imaginative daughter to further complicate matters.

For the first time she wondered if she could do this. But the consequences if she failed were too horrific to contemplate. And so were the ones if she succeeded.

*   *   *

"Do you actually know any pirates?"

Josefina smiled as Sebastian's daughter buttered a thick slice of bread. "Well, if they admitted to piracy they could be arrested, but I had my suspicions. There was one fellow who wore an eyepatch and always had a green parrot on his shoulder. I'm fairly certain he was a pirate."

The little girl bounced in her seat, her eyes widening. "What was his name? I have several lists I've made of known pirates."

"He called himself Dread Ned."

"Oh," Lady Penelope breathed. "A new one. Did he have all his arms and legs?"

"Peep," Eleanor Lady Deverill said, grinning behind her napkin, "you must let Princess Josefina eat. You'll starve her to death."

"But I have to add Dread Ned to my list."

"I don't mind," Josefina put in. "Truthfully, it's fun to discuss something other than Costa Habichuela."

The girl shifted sideways in her chair at the outdoor café where they sat, then leaned against Josefina's right arm. "I'm glad we could have luncheon today," she said happily, devouring her bread. "I like you very much, Princess Josefina."

Heavens. Such a small gesture, leaning on her arm, but it said so much. It spoke of trust, of reliance—not traits with which she had much experience. Today, it warmed her insides as few other things ever had. "I like you very much, too, Lady Penelope. Call me Josefina."

"Josefina. And you may call me Peep. Could you describe Dread Ned in detail, so I may do a sketch of him?"

"Of course, Peep. Anything to help your research."

From the pleased, amused expressions of Peep's aunts, she'd said the right thing. Peep had done her share of being charming as well. The girl was delightful, and from her easy confidence was clearly her father's darling.

For a moment she allowed herself to think that she and young Peep could easily be fast friends—until she considered tonight. If anything happened to Sebastian it would be her fault, and then Peep would hate her. And she would hate herself. Five hours. She had five hours remaining to think of something that could protect both the Duke of Melbourne and herself—and Peep—from harm.

Valentine Corbett met the coach as Eleanor stepped back onto her drive. "Hello, my love," he drawled, kissing her in the way that still made her toes curl.

"Not in front of the servants," she muttered, pushing at his shoulder.

"Anywhere we bloody well please," he rumbled back, sweeping her into his arms and carrying her up the steps and into the house.

Eleanor yelped. "Valentine!"

"How was your luncheon with Her Highness?" He sat on the couch in the morning room, settling her comfortably across his lap.

"Peep adores her. She's already making plans to steal a ship and sail to Costa Habichuela for a visit. They would have spent the day sketching pirates if we'd had enough time."

"And what about the chit herself?"

Eleanor ran a finger along his chin. "Why so curious, Deverill?"

He took her finger into his mouth, gazing at her as he sucked.

Her heart accelerated. "I know how naughty you are, but I won't let you distract me."

"From what, my heart?"

"Valen—"

The morning room door opened as her husband kissed

her again, slow and soft. "Go away, Hobbes," Valentine ordered, otherwise ignoring the intrusion.

"Get your hands off my sister, you blackguard," Shay's mild voice came.

"My apologies," Valentine countered, emerald eyes twinkling as he gazed at Eleanor. "Go away, *Charlemagne*." He kissed her again.

"Have either of you seen Sebastian?"

Valentine straightened. Her heart pounding now for another reason entirely, Eleanor stood. "What do you mean, have we seen him?" she snapped. "That's a rather alarming question."

"Melbourne can take care of himself," Valentine commented, stretching out his long legs. "I think the question is, what's happened to make you need to find him so urgently, Shay?"

It continued to amaze Eleanor the way her husband could find the exact heart of a matter. "Yes, Shay, why do you want to find him so badly?"

Her brother's face folded into a frown. "I can't say."

"You can't, or you won't?" she pressed.

"I'll assume all of this means you haven't seen him." Shay turned for the door. "As you were, then."

"Shay, what's going on?"

"Nothing."

"Valentine, don't let him leave."

With a sigh her husband pushed to his feet. "Save both of us from a messy bout of fisticuffs and unbutton, Charlemagne," he muttered, walking toward the doorway.

"Damnation. Look. I know we all feel justified in meddling in Melbourne's . . . dealings with the princess, but there are some things we—he—have uncovered that tell me this is more serious than we thought."

"More serious?" Eleanor repeated, closing on her brother and grabbing his arm. "You mean between them?"

"No. I mean . . ." He looked from one of them to the other, swearing under his breath. "I promised him."

"So you and Melbourne know something, and as usual he makes a sweeping pronouncement that no one else is permitted to learn anything."

"Nell, don't make more of this than—"

"We had luncheon today with Princess Josefina, you know," she interrupted. "Sarala, Caro, and I. And I brought Peep along, because she's been begging to see the princess again. And I've invited her family to our next Griffin dinner."

"Don't," he said abruptly.

"Why not?"

He blew out his breath. "Fine. I took a look at the Costa Habichuela prospectus," he grumbled, sitting beside the fireplace. "It seemed familiar, so I did some comparisons. It's stolen from several other works, including an old survey done of Jamaica. Seb confronted the princess about it, and apparently didn't like the answers he got."

" 'Apparently'?" Valentine repeated.

"He did some more research and found an explorer who's teaching at Eton. We met with him the day before yesterday. He confirmed that there is nowhere on the Mosquito Coast that resembles a paradise, that he's never heard of Costa Habichuela, and that the city of San Saturus is an old prospector's camp where the last three occupants apparently died from swamp gas poisoning and had their bones picked clean by ants."

"No." Eleanor blanched. "He has to be mistaken. That would mean—"

"It would mean that Melbourne's princess has been telling some untruths," her husband took up. "How convinced is Sebastian that something nefarious is going on?"

"Fairly. I have some new information for him, but he's not in Parliament, and he's not at home. Merlin's gone, as well." Shay ground his fist into his thigh. "I had the feeling—a very strong feeling, actually—that Seb liked Princess Josefina."

"We all did. That's why we've been meddling." *Blast.* How often had all of them heard Melbourne's speech about proceeding with caution, about not making a decisive move without having all of the facts to hand? And Peep had already practically added Josefina to the family. Damnation. "If he had told us what his suspicions were instead of behaving in his usual high-handed manner, I . . . well, I certainly wouldn't have invited her anywhere, blast it all."

"Beg off," Shay said. "We have four days. Who's hosting our dinner this week?"

"Zach and Caro. All the Witfelds will be there, as well."

Valentine snorted. "An hour with Mrs. Witfeld might drive the entire royal family back to South America."

"If only we could rely on that happening." Biting her lip, Eleanor faced her brother again. "We can't beg off without arousing suspicion. What we need to do is find out what Melbourne's plans are."

"Hence my coming here to find him. And since you know this business now, we need to inform Zach, too."

"I'll do that," she said. "You and Valentine keep looking for Sebastian."

Her husband kissed her softly on the mouth. "Time to be heroes," he drawled, and motioned Shay toward the door.

As soon as the men were gone, Eleanor sent word for the coach to be readied again. This was awful. She'd liked Josefina Embry. They all had. Including Sebastian. She wanted to ride to that woman's house and demand to know exactly what was going on.

If Shay was right, and she had no reason to doubt him, this was more than just a betrayal of friendship. The Costa

Habichuela contingent, and Josefina in particular, had put the Griffin reputation at risk. And she had the continuing suspicion that Sebastian had more at risk than his good name.

They all needed some answers. And the sooner, the better.

"Where the devil have you been?"

Sebastian looked away from his dressing mirror as Shay, Valentine at his heels, strode into the bedchamber. "I had some business."

"Business that's left Merlin looking as though you've galloped him from here to the Channel and back?"

"That's a damn good guess." He stood, and Bailey helped him on with his dark gray coat. "Thank you, Bailey. I can manage from here."

"Very good, Your Grace." With a bow the valet left the room, closing the door behind him.

"What do you mean, it's a good guess?" Shay demanded, his expression angry and concerned.

"I went to Dover. I thought—"

"Dover? Without telling anyone?"

"I haven't required a wet nurse in some time, Shay. Now are you going to let me finish?"

His brother frowned. "Apologies. Continue."

"Admiral Mattingly is in Dover. I thought he might be able to point me to someone who'd sailed along the Mosquito Coast." Sebastian eyed his brother long enough to remind him whose concern this really was. "Now you may ask your next question."

"Wasn't what John Rice-Able told us enough?"

"Not for me. That made it one opinion against another, one book against another."

"Did you find someone?" Valentine asked, arms crossed as he leaned against a bed post.

"I did." Sebastian lifted Carroway's statement from the dressing table. "A promising young lieutenant named Bradshaw Carroway. Apparently you once threatened to gut him, Charlemagne, for dancing with Nell."

"My thanks for that, Shay," Nell's husband commented.

"Let's take a look," Shay returned ignoring the commentary as he held out his hand. Sebastian gave him the paper.

"I assume you've broken my confidence and told Valentine all about the Costa Habichuela problem?" Sebastian tucked his watch into his pocket and headed for the door. "Anyone else?"

"By now the whole family knows. Except for Peep and the Witfelds, of course."

"Remind me not to bring you into my confidence any longer," Sebastian returned curtly, pulling open the door.

"Melbourne, wait a moment."

"I have an appointment this evening. Give me back the statement. I may need it." What he wanted to do was burn the thing, but that would mean giving up and letting the farce play out as it would. As a member of the House of Lords he couldn't do that, though, even if his status as a Griffin would have allowed such a thing.

"If you've been gone all day, you probably haven't heard the latest," Shay said to his back.

Sebastian paused, stifling the retort he'd been about to make concerning the spread of gossip. Shay didn't pass on idle rumors, however angry he wished to be with his brother for telling the rest of the family about his conundrum. "What is it, then?"

"This morning in Piccadilly the Embrys attended the opening of the Costa Habichuela land office. They're selling ten- to hundred-acre lots of land at three shillings an acre. Stories put the queue at a quarter mile long."

"They're looking for settlers to that godforsaken place?" Sebastian couldn't keep the incredulity out of his voice.

"They're finding them. By the hundreds. Apparently the rey opened another land office while he was in Edinburgh." His brother cleared his throat. "I'm sorry, Seb."

Turning around, Sebastian pinned him with a glare. "What the devil are you sorry for, Shay? I'd certainly rather know than remain ignorant."

"Where are you off to?" Valentine asked.

"I'm hosting a box at Vauxhall."

"Nell didn't tell me anything about it."

With a slow breath that did nothing to steady him or halt the fresh anger coursing beneath his skin, Sebastian left the room and headed downstairs, the two men behind him. "You're not invited. I'm hosting the rey and his family."

"What? Why, when you know—"

"Enough. I'll see you tomorrow."

Not giving them time to protest that, he strode into the playroom to give Peep a kiss and tell her not to wait up, then trotted downstairs to the foyer. Stanton held his black greatcoat while he slipped into it.

"You shouldn't go alone," Shay said in a low voice.

"I'll be perfectly fine, unless you've wagged your tongue to the rest of London."

His brother squared his shoulders. "I've done no such thing, and you know that."

"Fine. This is my concern, and I'll resolve it. Good evening."

"We know you're angry, Melbourne," Valentine put in, "but confronting them on your own is pure pride and stupidity."

He rounded on his brother-in-law and closest friend. "And what would you do, Valentine? Go home. Good night."

Valentine watched as Sebastian climbed into his coach and it rolled off into the twilight. "Damn," he muttered.

"What do we do now? The mighty Melbourne has spoken," Charlemagne commented from beside him on the front portico.

"Well," Valentine returned, collecting his coat and gloves from the butler, "I'm going home, col—"

"You do that, then."

"Let me finish, nitwit. I'm going home, collecting Eleanor, and then we're driving to Vauxhall and renting the nearest box to Melbourne's I can get my hands on. And you?"

Shay flashed him a grim smile. "Sarala and I will meet you there. And I'm not a nitwit."

"Right. I was thinking of Zachary. We'd best inform him, as well."

Valentine pulled on his gloves and headed out to his horse. It appeared the Griffin clan, of which he proudly considered himself a part whatever he might say aloud, was going to war. Heaven help Costa Habichuela.

Chapter 15

$\mathcal{S}$ebastian stood in the downstairs sitting room at Colonel Branbury's house and refused to pace. Probably no one would ever appreciate how much self-control it took to keep him there, when all he wanted to do was find Josefina and shake her until she told him the damned truth.

At the moment he had to doubt that any conversation he'd ever had with her was sincere. And that meant everything he felt for her, everything he'd done with her, had been part of some kind of plan, a manipulation, to keep him quiet while she and the rey stole funds from England and prepared to send any citizen gullible enough to wish for a new life into a hellhole.

He clenched his fists, wishing for a moment that he could be someone other than the Duke of Melbourne, someone who could put his fist through a wall and beat the rey to a bloody pulp without sacrificing his and his family's reputation.

The door opened. "Your Grace," the rey said with a

smile, coming forward to offer his hand. "Thank you for inviting us to join you tonight, and for your continued support."

Putting a matching smile on his face, Sebastian shook hands. "I'm glad you were able to find new assistance so readily."

"Yes, Charles has been a blessing. He should be here at any moment." The rey walked to the liquor tantalus and unlocked it. "A port while we wait?"

"Certainly." Reminding himself that patience would serve him better than violence, Sebastian accepted the glass Embry handed him. If Prinny hadn't made his preference for the rey and his family so public, stopping this nonsense would have been much simpler.

"Did you know that we've decided to sell lots of land now? There's been so much interest that I reckon we'll have people coming regardless. This should help keep things more orderly."

"Oh, Father, can't we limit our conversation to social events for one evening?" Josefina entered the sitting room, her breathing fast and her face flushed. "No business tonight, if you please."

The hairs on his arm lifted as she brushed by him to join her father. Belatedly Sebastian realized he was staring. He sketched a bow as she faced him again, offering her hand. "Your Highness," he murmured, gripping her fingers hard as he kissed her knuckles. If the chit had any sense of self-preservation she would immediately distance herself from her father and then throw herself on the nearest duke—him—and beg for forgiveness and protection.

At the thought arousal stirred through him, as if separate from all common sense and better judgment. It *was* separate, he supposed. It was the only way he could explain being furious with her and wanting to protect her at the same time. It was why he still looked for ways to justify or excuse what she was doing.

Later, Melbourne, he ordered silently. She knew he had his suspicions, and he didn't know how much she might have told her father about their conversations. And so he was in this up to his neck—which meant that Prinny and England were, as well.

"Aren't you going to tell me how lovely I look this evening?" Josefina asked, tilting her head to look at him coyly.

St. George's buttonholes. "You look beautiful tonight, Your Highness."

She was exquisite, in a low-cut silk gown of deep blue, with fine lace at her sleeves. Blue ribbons wound through her hair like velvet rivers in blackness, with her silver tiara glinting in the candlelight. If he could trust her, if he could believe anything that came out of those soft red lips, he wouldn't have been able to resist her. Even now, warm desire pulled at him, urged him to forget, just for a little while, how dangerous she was to his equilibrium, to his heart.

"Apologies for my tardiness," the Duke of Harek's voice came from the doorway.

Blinking, Sebastian forced his gaze from Josefina and faced him. "Good evening, Harek."

"Melbourne. Your Majesty, Your Highness." The duke bowed. "I have a good excuse for being late. I just purchased two hundred-acre lots of prime Costa Habichuela pastureland."

"Did you now?" The rey clapped. "That's splendid."

"I wanted to show that my support for your cause is more than mere lip service."

Wonderful. All Sebastian needed was for Harek to attack the rey or Josefina when the truth came out. He sent a look at the princess, to find her gaze on her father. Before she noticed his attention and smiled, he would have sworn that she looked displeased. Was that because of the land sale, or because of Harek's obvious interest? It shouldn't have mattered, but it did. He was a male, after all, and she was the first woman he'd wanted in four years.

Harek approached Josefina, taking her proffered hand. "You are the loveliest flower of your country, Your Highness," he intoned, keeping her fingers gripped much longer than propriety demanded.

"Thank you, Charles," Josefina returned with a warm smile.

Sebastian shifted, hiding his jealousy behind his glass of port. *The loveliest flower, ha.* It was entirely likely that she was the *only* flower of Costa Habichuela.

"So, Melbourne," Harek continued, finally relinquishing Josefina's hand, "you've an unmatched eye for fine investment opportunities. How much Costa Habichuela land do you own?"

"None, yet," Sebastian said carefully. "I spent the day in Dover, I'm afraid, and wasn't aware that the rey had opened a land office until an hour ago."

"Dover?" Josefina repeated. "What sent you to Dover?"

Wouldn't you like to know? "One of my old friends is in His Majesty's Navy. He ships out tomorrow, and I didn't want to miss seeing him off."

"Very patriotic of you," she noted.

"Good evening, Lord Melbourne, Lord Harek," Queen Maria said from just inside the door, cutting off his reply.

He wondered for a moment whether Embry's wife knew what the devil her husband was up to. She had a stateliness about her that Embry lacked, and that Josefina had inherited. But an aristocratic air didn't make her any less a conspirator. For now he would assume everyone to be guilty of something.

"Shall we be off?" he asked, setting his port aside. "I

have my coach, but I didn't know how many members of your entourage would be accompanying us."

"Just Captain Milton and Lieutenant May. They will serve as outriders and will accompany us on horseback."

With a nod Sebastian motioned for the ladies to lead the way outside. He wasn't accustomed to sitting back and watching events unfold, but waiting and observing would have to be his strategy—at least until he knew where Harek stood. Even so, Bradshaw Carroway's statement burned in his pocket, and he longed to fling it in Josefina's face.

Instead he took her hand and helped her into the coach. "Still angry with me?" she whispered as she leaned into him.

"You have no idea," he returned.

He stepped inside last. The rey and Queen Maria sat together facing forward, while he and Harek faced them, Josefina between them. "You know," the princess said conversationally, facing him, "Charles has told me about all of the animals he hunted in Canada. Quite an extraordinary variety. Do you hunt?"

"I've brought down my share of pheasant and grouse, I suppose," Sebastian returned, "and the occasional fish from the pond at Melbourne Park. My duties tend to keep me out of the field."

"I always said a hunt is good for the soul," Embry contributed. "Since my time as a soldier, though, I've rather lost my taste for killing."

That was an odd thing for him to say, considering how many people he was luring to their probable deaths. "Is there any good hunting in Costa Habichuela?"

"Certainly," the rey answered without hesitation. "Deer, wild pigs, alligators, and monkeys. The Moskito Indians make a delectable monkey stew."

"I look forward to partaking of it," Harek said with a smile aimed at Josefina.

So the bastard planned to marry into royalty. It made sense—or it would have, if these people were actually who they claimed to be. As to that, Sebastian still had no real idea. For all he knew, King Qental *had* given a portion of land to Stephen Embry, and the local people *had* named him their rey. It was the quality of the land he disputed at the moment—not its existence. That question would have to be answered before he could inform Prinny of all this, though. It could take weeks for the governor of Belize to answer the letter he'd sent, however, and he wasn't certain he had that long.

"When are your first new settlers sailing to Costa Habichuela?" he asked offhandedly.

"In three weeks, if the outfitting of our ships proceeds as planned, and if the weather holds."

Three weeks. Damnation. He had even less time than he'd thought. "Do you sail with them?"

"I'd like to be there to greet them when they come ashore, and there are some preparations to make. My plan is to leave in a fortnight."

"I daresay you'll be glad to see us gone, Melbourne," Josefina said in her rich, nuanced voice. "Even having resigned your liaison post, you seem to spend more time with us than not." She smiled at him, her brown eyes daring him to make further comment about the time they'd spent together.

His gaze lowered to her soft mouth. With all the lies she spewed, she shouldn't have been so delicious to kiss. He clenched his fist, digging his short nails into his palms to keep himself motionless and not take her sweet mouth right there in front of her parents.

"Any time spent with you has been my pleasure," he returned, trying not to let the words sounds as intimate as he meant them and realizing that he spoke the absolute truth.

Abruptly she turned away from him to face Harek. "And you, Charles, will you be sorry to see us gone?"

"I'm not certain I shall—see you gone, I mean. You know I love to travel."

The rey chuckled. "You do have a stake in Costa Habichuela now, and may have a greater one."

"I can only hope, Your Majesty."

The cadence of the coach's wheels changed as they crossed the last bridge and entered Vauxhall Gardens. "I've always wanted to visit here," Josefina said, leaning across Sebastian to peer out through the curtained windows.

She might just as easily have pressed her bosom against Harek's arm, but hadn't done so. Whether it was attraction or another manipulation, he had no idea. "There are no special events tonight," he said, breathing in the lilac scent of her hair, "but we can expect jugglers and acrobats, and a fair crowd. And pickpockets, so I advise you to keep your valuables close to hand."

"It all sounds so exciting," Josefina breathed. "Promise you'll show me about."

Again him, and not Harek. *Good.* "I shall be happy to, Your Highness."

The coach stopped, and Green hopped down from his seat beside Tollins to flip down the steps and open the door. Sebastian emerged first, to the usual choruses of "Melbourne, look, it's the duke himself," and other admiring comments. He ignored them, as he always did, and held out a hand for the princess.

She grasped his fingers as she descended the steps to the ground. "Is it true that anyone at all may enter Vauxhall, as long as they have the entrance fee?"

"It is. Hence the proliferation of pickpockets and lightskirts and others involved in criminal activity."

Josefina gave him a sharp look. "Doesn't that include just about everyone at some time or another?"

"You're too cynical, Your Highness," he murmured, ignoring Harek as the duke emerged.

"You're too naive, Melbourne," she returned, her warm breath caressing his cheek.

"Apparently I am, because I still desire you." Before she could respond to that, he released her to assist her mother. "I've arranged for dinner to be served in my box," he said, offering Queen Maria his arm and then taking the lead as they made their way through the crowd.

Embry's two officers, unmistakable in their black uniforms with the green crosses, positioned themselves to either side of their group. Merely for show or not, they did have the crowd falling aside more readily than even he could manage. All around him now, amid the laughter and loud chatter, he could make out his own name, and theirs. Everyone seemed to know who the rey and the queen of Costa Habichuela were, and that they and Princess Josefina were in attendance tonight.

He wondered what the admiring crowd would be saying if they realized that the Embrys were frauds and thieves, and quite possibly as common as the baker who stood by the path selling biscuits. Given the mercurial quality of London crowds, especially when one put on airs far above oneself, he wouldn't have been willing to wager a shilling that they would survive the night.

Was that Josefina, some self-deluded soldier's daughter? Looking at her, the way she carried herself, it didn't seem possible. And royal or common, deluded or thief, his blood still hummed at the thought of having her again.

"Look, Mama," her excited voice came from directly behind him, "that man is breathing fire!"

"And there's Melbourne's box, I believe," Harek said from beside her, "so we should have a good view of the disaster if the fellow inhales by accident."

"Oh, that's awful," she returned. "Don't say such things."

Sebastian looked over his shoulder at her. "Say it or not, when someone partakes in a dangerous venture, they shouldn't be surprised at catastrophic results." He led the way up the shallow trio of wooden steps. Within the roomy, elevated rectangle a handful of Vauxhall footmen stood guarding platters of food. A dozen chairs stood ranged beneath the angled canopy, and a fair handful of onlookers already stood ranged around the box. Obviously when they'd seen the food they'd realized that someone would be in attendance.

"Splendid location, Melbourne," the rey complimented, showing the queen to one of the chairs. "You can see the main pavilion from here. Will Prinny be in attendance tonight?"

"I don't believe so." And thank God for that; tonight would be trying enough without adding the temperamental Regent to the festivities.

"I would like a tour of the gardens," Josefina announced. Harek immediately took a step forward, but she faced Sebastian as she spoke. "Show me about, will you, Melbourne?"

He inclined his head. "Certainly, Your Highness. We will need a chaperone for you, however."

She narrowed her eyes for the briefest of seconds, clearly annoyed at the suggestion. "Lieutenant May will accompany us, then. Though I hardly think either of us could be accused of an impropriety in so public a setting."

"Melbourne is right, my dear," Embry said. "One can never be too cautious. Lieutenant, please accompany my daughter."

The young man saluted. "Of course, Your Majesty."

Sebastian offered his arm, and she wrapped her warm fingers around his sleeve. They descended from the box again, May on their heels. "Shall we head for the lake?"

"That is acceptable."

They passed two boxes before the occupants of the third one caught his attention. Stiffening, he stopped. "And what are you doing here tonight?" he asked in the coolest voice he could manage.

Valentine raised a glass of wine in his direction. "You know how Eleanor loves acrobats," he said with a jaunty grin.

If they'd been alone, Sebastian would have told him precisely what he thought of this damned poor excuse for a spying expedition. On the other hand, their presence was partly his fault for mentioning where he was going. "Sarala, Nell, Shay," he said curtly. "Where are Zach and Caroline, then?"

"In the midst of Witfelds," Shay answered, his gaze on Josefina and her bodyguard. "We thought it best not to risk Mrs. Witfeld's health by keeping her out-of-doors at night." He bowed. "Good evening, Your Highness."

"Lord Charlemagne, Lord Deverill." She smiled, her eyes lighting. "Hello again, Eleanor, Sarala. And thank you again for asking me to luncheon. I miss having female friends to chat with."

Eleanor smiled back, though Sebastian knew her well enough to see that the expression didn't go past skin deep. "You have friends here now."

"Excuse us," Sebastian broke in before fists began flying, "we're touring."

"Shall we join—"

"No." He looked directly at Shay. "Enjoy your dinner."

As they walked on, Josefina glanced back over her shoulder. "Your family seems very close. To one another, I mean."

"We are friends as well as siblings," Sebastian agreed.

"And you like that. I can see it in your eyes."

"Their presence is precious to me," he admitted, telling himself that if he spoke candidly, she might be convinced to do the same. "I don't rely on many people, but I know I can rely on them—that they'll help me even when I can't admit that I need it."

She gazed at him. "You're talking about when you lost your wife, aren't you?"

He couldn't quite hide his flinch. "Yes."

Josefina cleared her throat. "It must be . . . comforting, to know you always have someone you can go to, talk to, when you need a sympathetic ear."

Was she just commiserating? Or was she hinting that she wanted to talk to him? "I have a pair of ears," he said slowly.

"Yes, but will they listen?"

"I suppose that depends on what you wish to say to them."

"Nothing in a third or fourth's company. With only two, who knows?"

Sebastian turned to greet an acquaintance, at the same time sending a glance at Lieutenant May, a dozen feet behind them. "If you're up to something, Josefina," he said in a low voice, "I will wring your neck. I swear it. I am through with games."

"No games," she whispered back, waving at someone and half-facing away, "I need to speak with you in private."

"We have to make it look like an accidental separation. Do you see that archway ahead and to the right?"

"Yes. And may I point out that this would have been easier if you hadn't insisted on a chaperone?"

"No, you may not." Considering the level of mistrust he felt toward her, she should be thankful he'd chosen a chaperone over a pistol. Of course he also carried one of those. "Meet me on the other side of the arch." As he spoke, he unclipped his pocket watch and placed it in another pocket, letting the chain hang free. "You!" he roared at no one in particular. "Stop, thief!"

Josefina slipped backward into the surging crowd as Melbourne grabbed Lieutenant May by the elbow and snapped something at him about doing his job. With a gesture toward his absent watch, he sent May in one direction, while he disappeared in another.

That was well and efficiently done. Her own heart pounding at the enormity of what *she* was about to do, Josefina made her way in the general direction of the archway, moved past it, then slipped into the middle of a group of revelers and out again as they passed the rose-covered arbor.

Ducking beneath it, she found a dimly lit path beyond. She felt far too exposed there, and stepped behind the hanging, twining branches of a huge wisteria. Every logical, self-concerned bit of her mind screamed at her to go back to the box and keep her blasted mouth closed. With only a fortnight remaining in London, she and her parents had a very good chance of getting away completely unscathed. Especially when her father declared that he would take care of the difficulty the Duke of Melbourne represented.

And that declaration was why every bit of bone and muscle and blood demanded that she stay exactly where she was until she could warn Sebastian. Whatever might be at stake, she would not allow him to be harmed. And she would not allow those people who were happily and hopefully buying up acres of Costa Habichuela to be harmed, either. She couldn't.

A large man in the garb of a gentleman entered the path beyond the archway and turned around. Just after him a thin woman with scarlet red hair pounced forward, wrapping her arms and legs around him. They kissed noisily, and the man yanked the tight bodice of the woman's dress down to expose her breasts.

As Josefina watched, fascinated, a hand swept around

her mouth from behind. "Lord Castleton and his latest purchase," Sebastian's low murmur came against her ear.

He shifted his hand to her shoulder, turning her to face him. Finally they were alone again, as briefly and precariously as it might be. And he was angry with her, she knew—and he had a good reason to be. Still . . .

She put her hands against his chest to steady herself. "So, Seb—"

His mouth closed over hers, hungry and hot and tasting of port. Barely remembering to be silent, Josefina wrapped her arms hard around his neck, holding herself against him as desire speared through her.

When he backed an inch away from her, she licked his jaw. "Do those two arouse you?" she whispered unsteadily.

"You arouse me. You're a witch, aren't you? This is a bloody spell." He kissed her again, plundering and breathless. His left hand cupped her breast, his touch burning through the thin silk of her gown.

"St-stop," she managed, pushing him back.

"Right." He wiped his mouth with the back of his hand. "We don't have much time. This way." Turning, he vanished between the wisteria and an oak tree.

Barely able to make out his dark form in the night shadows and thick foliage, she followed as silently as she could. Finally they reached a tiny clearing and he faced her again, his eyes silvery orbs beneath the faint sliver of moon. "You wanted to talk to me, I believe?"

And the passionate, arousing Sebastian of a moment ago was vanished, replaced by the hard, unyielding Duke of Melbourne. They *were* almost like two different entities sharing the same body, she realized, and she wasn't certain whether it was the private or the public persona she needed tonight.

"Thank you for trusting me this much," she said, matching his hushed voice.

"I don't trust you at all," he returned. "But apparently I continue to hold out a hope that you may have some small bit of decency left to you."

It was the worst thing anyone had ever said to her. And she couldn't even dispute it. "There are two things I wish you to know." She kept her chin up, meeting his gaze. "And they're both the truth."

"Why don't you tell me, and I'll decide whether to believe you or not?"

"Very well. I . . . I had no idea my father meant to sell property to anyone."

"Why is this fraud worse than taking the bank's money and encouraging sales of bonds to finance the theft?"

God, he did know everything. "Because only the bank is harmed. It would have to buy back the bonds. The land sale is different. It's more than a . . . theft," she answered, surprised that she was willing to say the word aloud. It was one her father never, ever allowed to be spoken. "He actually means to have settlers go there. People could die, Sebastian. Families."

"What do you actually know of Costa Habichuela?"

"I knew it wasn't Eden, but I didn't actually care about the weather or the terrain. Now, it matters."

"So you are completely innocent of any wrongdoing, and have only been led astray by your dear papa?" The cynical skepticism in his voice hurt more than a slap to her face would have.

"Obviously you don't care about what I did or didn't know, and if it comes to saving my neck from the gallows I'd rather you not be able to use my own words against me. All I'm telling you is that no one can be allowed to sail to Costa Habichuela thinking of it as they do now."

He gazed at her, his expression undecipherable in the darkness. "What was your second truth, Your Highness?"

"I told my father that you knew the prospectus was a fiction. He—"

"Ah. And what sense of honor bade you do that?"

"Because I was frightened," she snapped. "When we first began this, the state of Costa Habichuela didn't signify. But with the land sales . . . I borrowed that book you were looking at in the Allendales' library. I hoped he might have been telling the truth about San Saturus and Black Diamond Bay."

Melbourne nodded coolly. "So now you've told me, and your so-called conscience is clear. Let's go back before they come looking for us."

She put a hand on his shoulder before he could turn away. The muscles beneath her fingers jumped. She *did* affect him, whether he liked it or not. Just as he affected her. "There's more," she muttered.

"What?"

"When I told my father about you, he said he would take care of it, and he said that Vauxhall Gardens was crowded."

"Very well," he said a moment later. "You've warned me, and you've threatened me. I suggest that—"

"I'm not threatening you, Sebastian. I'm worried."

"Then you shouldn't have become involved. I am going to put a stop to this, Josefina. The penalties will be severe. If you want to avoid the gallows, I suggest that you tell me everything you know and pray that I can protect you."

"You're the one who needs protection, you fool," she countered. "Being a duke doesn't make you immune to injury. And I'm not telling you anything that would harm my father. This is not about betrayal. It's about my conscience, whether you happen to believe that I have one or not."

She turned around, but this time he grabbed her elbow. "Eventually, my dear, you're going to find that you can't remain neutral. You will have to choose a side."

Josefina pulled her arm free. "Don't expect that I will choose yours."

Obviously Sebastian either didn't believe that he might be in danger, or he thought that being a Griffin constituted enough protection. Either way, when he set off into the gloom Josefina had no choice but to follow him.

Just inside the archway he stopped again. "We are finished, you and I," he said, his back to her and his words like a knife blade. "I appreciate that you've told me of your disapproval of your father's actions, but your information is nothing I didn't already know."

"Well, aren't you wise," she retorted to his broad shoulders.

"Not wise enough, evidently. At the conclusion of tonight, don't expect to have contact with me again except in a court of law. No more of your little games, whoever you are."

"I know who *you* are, Melbourne," she snapped, fighting unaccustomed tears. "You are a heartless, soulless man. And I want nothing further to do with you."

"Then we're agreed." He gestured her to precede him. "You go first. I'll find my watch and join you in a moment."

"Of course," she returned stiffly, brushing past him. "We wouldn't want you to have to put your courage or your heart where your body has been."

Before he could return the insult she moved back into the Vauxhall crowd. She didn't know why they called it the Pleasure Gardens, because to her it was the worst place on Earth. Oh, she'd been so stupid. Warning him, telling him what she could without absolutely condemning her father—it had seemed so important.

Sebastian neither needed nor wanted her help; apparently he'd already had all he wanted of her. So now he would see her in prison and hanged, because she'd committed a fraud and her father had turned it into worse. At least Melbourne would be able to prevent an exodus to Costa Habichuela.

"Your Highness," Lieutenant May panted, trotting up to her. "I couldn't find the cutpurse. And I apologize for leaving you unattended. Your father will have my head. But when His Grace sent me to—"

"No harm has been done," she said easily, knowing how difficult it was to refuse Melbourne when he gave an order. "My father doesn't need to know anything. I only hope the duke has had better luck, so that we won't need to even mention it."

"I have, and we won't." Melbourne materialized at her shoulder, his watch in his hand. "I ran the rapscallion down halfway across the gardens."

"And did you have him arrested for daring to cross you?" Josefina asked, taking May's arm when the duke offered his.

"No. He was just a boy, probably doing as he was bid. I expect an adult to know right from wrong, but I make an exception for children."

"I only hope whoever put him up to stealing doesn't carry a grudge, Your Grace," May said with a rare smile.

Josefina's insides jolted. Whether he chose to believe it or not, Melbourne might just have laid out the plot for his own murder. And she was supposed to sit idly by, his own story at hand to provide proof of who'd done the deed. Of course according to him, she was already guilty of everything, so one more murder wouldn't matter. With him gone, he would only be the first of many, anyway, because no one else would be able to stop her father. Stupid man. He had more than his own arrogance to consider tonight.

May and Milton were both seasoned soldiers who'd served with her father on dozens of campaigns. They had both killed, and knew how to do it well and efficiently. And both had fortunes resting on the rey's success. Her breath quickened, and she worked to slow and steady it.

As they made their way back to the box, the pathways and clearings seemed even more crowded, the visitors more raucous. A juggler strolled by, half a dozen apples in the air and a loose mob following behind him to wager loudly on when and how many pieces of fruit he would drop. She edged closer to May.

"Too much liquor flowing tonight, I think," the lieutenant said, giving her a reassuring glance. "We're nearly back to safety."

Her heart thudded again. She couldn't even see if Melbourne still walked behind them. What if Captain Milton had killed him already? Gasping, she turned around so quickly that May stumbled.

The duke walked calmly a pace or two behind them, his expression cool and aloof, still convinced of his own invulnerability. "Is something amiss, Your Highness?" he asked.

"No. I thought you might have toddled off somewhere to neglect your duty to me again."

"I never forget my duty, Your Highness."

Yes, and everyone knew that. He couldn't be bribed, and he wouldn't be coerced, the fool.

"Here we are. You go on ahead, Your Highness."

At May's instruction she lifted her gaze. The rey sat in the box beside her mother, both of them looking in her direction. Harek stood a little to one side gazing at the fireworks, a glass of something red in his hand. She didn't see Milton anywhere, though in the jostling, jovial crowd that wouldn't have been easy had he been standing in plain sight.

"How was your tour, daughter?" her father asked, gesturing for her to approach.

"Very enlightening," she returned, trying to keep from shaking as she released Lieutenant May's arm.

When she glanced back at Melbourne to thank him for his services as guide, she caught sight of Milton beyond, closing on them quickly. Steel flashed in his hand. *Oh, God.*

Without thinking she threw herself on Melbourne, wrapping her hands into his lapels and twisting him around with all her strength. She kissed him hard as they half-stumbled away from Milton, in the direction of the box. His arms reflexively closed around her, but she scarcely noticed as she put herself between him and the captain.

"Melbourne's asked me to marry him," she said in her loudest voice, praying both Milton and her father would hear, "and I've said yes!"

Chapter 16

Sebastian scarcely heard what Josefina was shrieking, but the kiss registered, along with the very public setting. He grabbed her shoulders to shove her as far away from him as he could. *Damn her. Damn her to h*—

Then just beyond her shoulder he saw the knife, saw the soldier, Milton, hurriedly ducking away into the crowd, and a thousand things exploded into his brain. She'd been right. Embry had meant to kill him tonight. At that moment, Josefina Embry had just saved his life.

In that instant, his world shifted. Swallowing, he pulled her hard against his side. "I meant to ask your permission first, Your Majesty," he ground out. "My feelings overcame me."

"They overcame both of us," she joined in, her voice shaking. He risked a glance at her. Her face was as white as his felt, her expression verging on hysteria.

Strangely enough, that calmed him. He needed to take charge. Milton was still somewhere with the knife, and

Josefina might well have just placed herself in danger, as well. Whatever else had just happened—he would deal with the ramifications later. Now he needed to take responsibility for the action itself, settle as much of the outside chaos as he could.

"I hope you will forgive our ham-fistedness and give us your blessing," he continued, guiding her toward the box.

Embry had shot to his feet at Josefina's announcement, his face nearly as pale as hers. So he'd been taken off guard, too. By now everyone in the gardens would be hearing the news—the Duke of Melbourne had just announced his marriage to Princess Josefina of Costa Habichuela.

"Let go of me," Josefina muttered through clenched teeth.

"Shut up," he breathed back, stopping in front of her parents. "Your Majesties—"

"Welcome to the family, Melbourne!" Embry bellowed, thereby informing anyone who might have missed Josefina's shrieking that there had just been a betrothal. "Or I must call you Sebastian now, I reckon."

Sebastian tightened his jaw. "Yes, please do."

The Duke of Harek, whom he'd nearly forgotten, abruptly shoved a chair aside so hard that it cracked the box's railing. "Just a damned minute," the duke snarled. "You and I have an agreement, Your Majesty. I will not—"

"We talked, Charles," Embry interrupted. "We did not and do not have an agreement. Now please desist, and we shall discuss it in private later."

"We certainly will." With a furious glare at Sebastian, Harek pushed past the lot of them and strode into the crowd.

"Perhaps we should go, as well," Queen Maria said unexpectedly. "We've created quite a stir, and with only two guards—"

"You're right as always, my dear. Lieutenant, lead the way back to the coach."

Sebastian didn't correct the queen by pointing out that only one guard seemed to be present at the moment. There were far too many people about, and if Captain Milton still intended on killing him, he didn't want to inform anyone else that he was suspicious.

"Melbourne!"

He flinched at the stunned tone of Shay's voice. Drawing himself in more tightly, he faced his approaching brother. "We'll discuss this later, Charlemagne. I need to see my betrothed and her parents to my coach."

Shay visibly shook himself, obviously realizing that a public outburst from another member of the Griffin family would only make matters worse. "Of course," his brother said, moving aside as the lieutenant, Embry and his wife close behind him, left the box.

His hand still wrapped hard around Josefina's arm, Sebastian pulled her down the steps with him. "You are hurting me," Josefina hissed, pulling against him.

"I don't particularly care," he returned, shifting his grip a little but keeping her close beside him.

"I saved your life."

"Thank you. Though yelling 'assassin' might have been at least as effective, and fewer people would be staring at us and gossiping right now."

"As if I *want* to marry you," she retorted. "I only had a second. It was all I could think to do."

Rather, he imagined it was all she could think to do without exposing her family for the frauds they were. "You and I are going to have a very serious, very private little chat," he breathed. "And you are going to tell me every bloody thing you know, so I can hopefully find a way to extract us from this disaster."

"That's well and good for you," she whispered back, "but I *am* the disaster."

And ten minutes earlier he'd sworn to cut all ties with her. Shakespeare's "tangled web" didn't even begin to describe the mess he'd fallen into.

Captain Milton emerged from the crowd ahead of them. He muttered something at the rey, who shook his head. Sebastian narrowed his eyes. Tightly as he'd been holding himself in over the past days, his control was beginning to fray. It was bad enough that he had to smile at the man who'd most likely ordered his murder. With the would-be assassin rejoining the party, the response he should make and the one he wanted to make were miles apart.

"Sebastian," Josefina said, her voice low and urgent, "don't do anything to reveal that you knew about—"

"Your Majesty," he interrupted, as they reached the coach, "I have to apologize again for not broaching the subject of marriage with you first. I beg your understanding, and ask that you take my coach home and allow me a few hours to consult with my staff so I may present you with a proper assessment of what I can do for Costa Habichuela in exchange for Josefina's hand."

The rey's expression shifted from guarded to self-satisfied, the pompous oaf. "That's very gentlemanly of you, Sebastian. We shall see you in the morning, then." He offered his hand.

Finally and reluctantly releasing his grip on Josefina's arm, Sebastian shook the rey's hand. If he'd had only himself to consider, he would have flattened the bastard. He forced a smile. "Until tomorrow."

Green closed the coach door and stepped back. The groom and Tollins exchanged a glance that Sebastian couldn't read, and then Tollins clucked at the team and they were off.

"Where to, Your Grace?" the groom asked, as Lieutenant May and Captain Milton fell in behind the coach, leaving the two of them in the darkness.

"I don't recall asking you to remain behind," Sebastian stated, facing the servant.

"Begging your pardon, Your Grace, but coach tiger ain't my usual position. I reckon that you brought me along to keep an eye on things, and so I am."

"Hm." Sebastian looked around at the crowd of horses, grooms, and vehicles. Overhead, a burst of fireworks winked white into the sky. "I need to get home," he said, heading for the bridge. It was still early, and Peep was probably still awake. He did not want her to hear this particular news from anyone but him.

"I'll hire us a hack," Green said, matching his pace.

He needed to think, and what he wanted was a few moments in private. At the same time, he knew that Embry had other soldiers, and he couldn't guarantee that Josefina's stunt had caused them all to withdraw. If he'd been the rey, he wasn't certain how he would proceed—a chance at additional riches versus permanently closing the mouth of someone who might expose him.

From the manner in which she'd acted, Josefina clearly thought that Embry would choose the riches. With her one loud statement she—and her father—most likely thought they'd silenced him, and gained his cooperation. Well, he'd allow them to think that. For the moment.

"How did you manage it, Josefina?" her father chortled in between bouts of outright laughter. "You said he was suspicious of us!" He put a hand over his chest, as if he couldn't contain his amusement. "I nearly removed him from the equation. Good Lord. You should have said something!"

Josefina sat in the opposite corner of the coach and rubbed her arm. Sebastian's grip would leave a bruise. "I suppose everyone has their price," she improvised. "When he realized that Harek was on the verge of proposing, I think he understood what an opportunity was about to pass him by."

"Excellent, excellent, excellent. I've always said if there's one constant in the hearts of all men, it's greed. Our entire endeavor works because of that principle."

"Are you happy with the match, *mi querida*?" her mother asked.

The future groom wasn't. He was furious at the idea of having to marry her. No doubt he would find a way to escape it and to see her hanged at the same time. Once she'd made the announcement, extricating himself from it had been the only thing he'd even mentioned. But if the alternative to her declaration was seeing him stabbed in the back, she would accept his anger. "We will be wealthy beyond our wildest dreams," she said aloud.

"But are you happy to marry him?" Maria Embry pressed.

"Of course she's happy, my love," her father broke in. "We've won. Still a few details to work out and all that, and I want the wedding to take place as soon as possible, but with Melbourne in the fold and under control, we can do as we please."

She wished she could be so certain of that. A wedding would secure her family's future, and Melbourne's options were limited. His anger and disgust, though, troubled her heart.

"I'm glad he gave us until tomorrow," her father was saying. "We need to draw up some papers, something to make certain he has to keep quiet about what he knows or incriminate himself. Oh, and I should give him a title."

"He's already a duke, Father."

"What did we give Prinny?" he went on, as though she hadn't spoken. "It can't be as high as that—perhaps I'll make him a regular Knight of the Green Cross. You know, with the Duke of Melbourne involved now, we should have a loftier name the next time. Costa del Oro, perhaps. We would have to alter the prospectus and the bond and land sale documents, but we can certainly afford the expense now."

Josefina sat silently, trying not to let her mouth gape open as her father happily plotted the formation of a new and improved country on the Mosquito Coast. He truly didn't care what might become of any settlers who would arrive to find no gleaming capital city, no sparkling harbor, no Costa Habichuela at all. And no princess.

Once Sebastian discovered that an ex-patriot soldier's daughter had publicly trapped him into marriage, she would likely be thankful that she could only be hanged the one time. Why hadn't her father bothered to tell her that he meant to expand their scheme? He expected her to take the risks.

A soldier's daughter. She'd slapped Sebastian. She'd put on airs. She'd given the impression that she barely considered him elevated enough even to speak with her. She'd taken him to her bed. He would never forgive her.

Josefina shook herself. What was wrong with her, pining over losing something she'd never had? It wasn't as though they cared for one another. Their attraction was simply a mutual lust. Everything, everyone, was just a means to an end, and she'd played the last and best trick. And now more than ever she needed to keep Sebastian close by in order to keep herself safe, because he would never just let this go. *Never.*

A low stir of . . . something went through her. If the only way to save herself and Sebastian, save her family, save the other people who relied on her father's wits, was to go forward with a wedding, then she would do it. And even if Sebastian hated her for it, he would marry her as long as it appeared to be the right thing to do. Perhaps eventually he would even forgive her.

Stanton pulled open the front door as Sebastian reached it. "You've returned early, Your Grace. I hope—"

"Where's my daughter?" Sebastian barked, heading for the stairs without bothering to shed his gloves or coat.

"I believe her to be in the billiards room with Mrs. Beacham, Your Grace. Is something amiss?"

Sebastian raced up the stairs. "The family will be arriving shortly," he said over his shoulder as he ascended. "Show them to the morning room. If you see any Witfelds other than Caroline, send them away." He frowned as he topped the stairs. This nonsense wasn't their fault. "No. Send any extraneous Witfelds to the breakfast room. Have Cook make them sandwiches or something."

"I'll see to it, Your Grace."

He reached the billiards room and pushed open the door. "Mrs. Beacham, please excuse us," he said, keeping his voice low and even. "Lady Penelope will see you in her bedchamber shortly."

The red-haired governess curtsied. "Good evening then, Your Grace. I shall be waiting, Lady Peep."

"Very well, Mrs. B."

The governess left the room, closing the door softly behind her. When Sebastian turned back to the room Peep was eyeing him, a too-large billiards cue in her small hands. He paced to the window and back, but the drive below remained empty.

Now that he'd gotten to her, he didn't know what to say. In addition, he couldn't stand still—with time to think, he would have to acknowledge what had taken place tonight and how he'd been so off-balance that he hadn't been able to prevent it.

"Did you shoot someone?" Peep asked, leaning on the cue in a petite imitation of her uncles.

"No."

"You're making me very uneasy, Papa. I think you should tell me what's happened."

Bright as Peep was, she was still a little girl. His little girl. And there were some things about people and their machinations that he didn't care to educate her about. Not yet. "Come here," he said, taking a seat on one of the chairs lining the wall. "We need to talk."

She laid the cue across the table and climbed onto the arm of the chair. "Is everyone well?" she asked, a quaver in her voice.

"Everyone's perfectly fine." *Wonderful.* Sending his daughter into a panic would complete the evening. "A very complicated thing has happened. The circumstances of it could change at any moment, and probably will, but I thought you should know how things stand."

"Very well, as long as no one is hurt."

Sebastian cleared his throat. How the devil was he supposed to begin this particular tale? "I kissed Princess Josefina," he proffered.

Penelope narrowed her eyes. "You didn't ruin her like Uncle Shay ruined Aunt Sarala, did you?"

"How the devil do you know about that?"

She sighed. "Papa, really. I keep abreast of everything. Did you ruin her?"

"No. But at the moment she and I are . . ." He closed his eyes for a heartbeat. "We've told people that we're going to be married."

"Married?" his daughter repeated, looking as shocked as he'd ever seen her.

"That is the present situation, yes."

"And you told other people before you told me? Who?"

"Telling anyone was something of an accident, my

heart. As soon as it happened I came home straightaway to tell you."

She folded her arms across her chest. "Where is Josefina? I would like to speak with her."

"She went home. I'll see her tomorrow."

"Will this make me a princess?"

The first glimmer of humor he'd felt all evening touched him. "I'm afraid not. You've always been *my* princess, if that helps."

Twisting, she hugged him, resting her cheek against his. "I like her," she stated. "She knows pirates and soldiers. But when you got mad at me for inviting her into the house, I thought you didn't like her. That made it very hard on me. You should have told me that you were falling in love. I gave Uncle Shay some very good advice when he was courting Aunt Sarala. I'm helpful."

Love. According to the rest of his family, he was no longer capable of the emotion. In love with Josefina? At the moment he wasn't certain whether he wanted to kiss her or strangle her. He knew quite well what he wanted to do to her father. "As I said, Peep, this is only the situation at this moment. We made the decision for . . . business reasons, and it will undoubtedly change."

She lifted her head to look at him, her gray eyes serious. "Papa, I can't help being troubled to hear you say this is all business. You're a very wealthy duke, you know, and you don't *have* to marry anyone."

Sebastian lifted an eyebrow. "Thank you for reminding me." Down below a carriage turned up the drive. "So if I did love her, you wouldn't mind if I married her?"

Even as he spoke, he regretted the question. For one thing, he shouldn't have been putting such thoughts in Peep's head. For another, he certainly had other, more pressing things to worry about at the moment.

"Because of Mama, you mean?" she asked.

"Yes. Because of Mama."

She pursed her lips, obviously considering. "Would you still love Mama?"

"Always." His heart lurched, as it always did when they talked about Charlotte.

"Well, I love Buttercup, and I love you, and I love Aunt Nell and Uncle Valentine and Uncle Shay and Aunt Saral—"

"Your point being?" He curled one of the dark ringlets of her hair around his finger.

"My point is that you and I both love several people, and I don't think adding one more will hurt anything."

Except perhaps the future of the entire Griffin clan. He took his daughter's hand and stood. "You are very wise, my lady."

"I know. Who's coming to visit us? Are you certain it's not Josefina?"

"No, it's your aunts and uncles. There's likely to be some arguing, so I'll need you to go up to bed."

"Very well. This news has worn me out." She tugged his sleeve down to kiss him on the cheek. "Don't yell at them too much."

"I won't." In fact, it was far more likely they would all yell at him—and with good reason.

As Penelope went upstairs, he headed down. "Who's here?" he asked Stanton, then remembered the length of Peep's litany of close relations. "No, tell me who's not here. That will be simpler."

"No Witfelds are here, Your Grace," the butler answered. "Shall I send the sandwiches into the morning room?"

"Yes. We may be there for quite some time."

Chapter 17

achary wolfed down his seventh cucumber sandwich. "A knife?" he mumbled around it. "You're absolutely certain?"

Sebastian paced to the hearth and back. "For the third bloody time, yes, I'm certain," he snapped. These people might be precious to him, but he did not under any circumstances enjoy being called to task. "Why, do you think it might have been a spoon?"

"No. I'm just trying to grasp the—"

"She clearly saved your life," Nell interrupted. "I was set to hate her, but Sebastian, if she hadn't—"

"If she hadn't been a part of this to begin with, no one would have been trying to kill our brother." Shay sat where he'd been for the past three-quarters of an hour, his fists still clenched and his expression the most grim Sebastian had seen in four years. Since the last family tragedy.

"You can't say that for certain," Valentine countered, twining and untwining his fingers with Eleanor's. "Whether or not Melbourne became involved directly, the rey would still be here plotting, and I'd wager pounds to pence that this family would have been the first to uncover the fraud."

"And then who would have stopped the assassination?" Eleanor seconded.

"By announcing a wedding?" Shay snorted. "Come now, Nell. She planned this all along."

"I don't think so." Sebastian wasn't even certain he'd spoken aloud until he caught the quizzical gazes aimed in his direction. "She did try to warn me that I might be in danger. I didn't listen."

"I've been part of this family for only a year," Sarala said abruptly, the remains of her India-raised accent still in her words, "so please tell me if I'm overstepping."

"You're not," he said shortly. As a member of the family she had as much right to grind at him as anyone else in the room, though if he clenched his jaw any harder he would break some teeth.

She nodded. "Then with the limited amount of time you have before meeting with the Embrys, perhaps we should be considering where things stand now, as opposed to how or why they came to be this way."

He drew a breath. "Very well. Josefina told her father that I suspected something. With a public announcement bringing me into the family, Embry will consider me both silenced and an ally, reluctant or not. He's probably already counting the additional money I'll provide them."

"I love greed." Valentine leaned forward to pull the tray of sandwiches away from Zachary. "It's easy to play on, and easy to predict."

"So how can we use it to get Seb out of this mess?" Zachary sent a glare at Valentine. "Giving Embry money will only encourage him." Surreptitiously he slid the sandwiches back in front of him and took another.

"Whose side is Princess Josefina on?" Caroline asked,

speaking for the first time since she and Zachary had entered the room.

"Her father's, obviously."

Eleanor shook her head. "I don't think so, Zach. She gave Sebastian some very confidential information. And while bringing a wealthy ally into the fold does help her father's cause, Embry's first choice in dealing with Melbourne was to see him dead. Whatever happened after, she went against her father then."

It would have been better if she'd never sided with the rey at all. "Much as you must all be enjoying seeing me make mistakes and squirm because of them, the real issue is not what happens between Josefina and myself. It's how to correct my—our family's—association with Embry."

"Bugger that," Shay retorted bluntly. "Whatever we might have said about your interference in our lives, no one in this room wishes you pain."

Seeing their serious, concerned faces, he would accept that statement as the truth. "Very well. To buy us some time, tomorrow I will play the son-in-law-to-be," he decided. "Embry may think that including me in his plans helps him, but it also helps me. I still have questions, and he's the best one to answer them."

"What about the—"

"Shay, go back to Eton and get John Rice-Able. Hide him somewhere, but I want him available in the event that we need someone's word to counter Embry's. As for the rest, I think we'll have to wait until after my meeting. I can prepare, but he still has to make the next move."

"I don't like it," Zach protested anyway. "One of us should go with you tomorrow."

"Not if I want him to say anything helpful. Go home. We'll meet back here for dinner."

In pairs his siblings and in-laws bade him good night and left. His head ached. What the devil was he supposed to do between now and the morning? Sleep was out of the question. Riddles and knots twisted his insides until he could barely breathe, much less think straight. There had to be something he'd missed, something he could do that would make a difference. What that something might be, though, continued to elude him. The rest of the family might enjoy seeing his human side, but he took absolutely no pleasure in revealing his own bloody mistakes.

The last to leave were Nell and Valentine. The marquis handed his wife into their coach, then leaned in and said something to her. As Sebastian watched from the portico, his closest friend turned around again and approached him.

"Let's take a stroll through the garden, Melbourne," Valentine said, gesturing.

"No. I don't need any advice on extricating myself from female entanglements. Go home."

Valentine sighed. "Tell me this, then—at the moment your plan is to gain all the information you can and then present it to Prinny and the authorities in order to prevent innocent citizens from sailing off to their doom, yes?"

"A bit long-winded, but yes."

The marquis looked him straight in the eye. "They'll hang her, you know. The princess."

Sebastian flinched, and he knew Valentine saw it. "If she is on our side, then I'll do what I can to protect her from that."

"Ah. *What you can.* Within the bounds of propriety, I suppose. You'll have quite the task making yourself look heroic and avoiding a scandal, as it is."

"That's enough, Deverill."

"Just pointing out the obvious," Valentine returned easily. "Everyone knows you'll do anything to avoid a scandal. That was why you publicly begged for her father's permission to marry her once she threw herself on you, wasn't it? Because declaring the lot of them thieves and frauds right then would have been what—completely reasonable and believable?"

"Just say what's on your bloody mind and leave," Sebastian ground out, his fists clenching again. Yes, he'd been asking himself those same damned questions, and no, he didn't know what the answer might be.

"I *will* say it, then, since you're too damned stubborn. You like Josefina. My guess is that you like her more than you probably even realize."

"That's enough."

"One scandal over four hundred years of Dukes of Melbourne," Valentine pressed, "and two thousand years of Griffins and Grifani and whatever else there was—I think your family name can stand up to it. Don't blame your cowardice about following your heart on anything but yourself."

Sebastian hit him. He'd wanted to hit someone all evening—anything to focus his frustration. Deverill had just made himself the best target.

Valentine staggered, sweeping his leg around as he went down. Caught behind the knees, Sebastian fell backward. In a second he and Valentine were rolling on the sharp gravel of the drive.

An elbow slammed across his chin, and he tasted blood. Good. Fury, frustration, closed over him. His fist connected hard with Valentine's ribcage, and the marquis grunted.

"Stop it!" Eleanor's voice came. They both ignored it.

He couldn't remember the last time he'd been in a physical fight; most, all, of his battles were verbal, wits and politics. This felt deeper, and far more satisfying.

"Stanton! Assistance!"

Deverill's sleeve tore off in his hand, and Sebastian threw it aside. Shoving hard, he got a knee underneath him and started to push to his feet. Abruptly cold water drenched his head and shoulders.

Sputtering, he released Valentine and rolled sideways. "Who the devil did that?" he roared, staggering to his feet.

Eleanor gripped a large bucket in both hands, Stanton beside her with another. Deverill stood and shook water out of his hair. "Damnation, Nell," he grumbled.

"And just what did that solve, you two?" Eleanor retorted, her expression cold but her hands shaking. "You said you were going to have a *word* with him, Valentine! For heaven's sake!" She slammed down the bucket and stalked back to the coach.

Valentine rubbed his jaw, eyeing Sebastian. "Feel better?"

Drawing a deep breath, Sebastian motioned for Stanton to go back to the house. "Actually, yes," he said reluctantly. The fury that had boiled in his chest all night at least felt manageable, now.

"Good. I was running out of barbs to hurl at you." Squatting, the marquis retrieved his coat sleeve, then straightened again. "I'll see you tomorrow."

"Bastard."

"Fop."

Sebastian wiped his chin. "Blackguard."

"Nocky boy."

"Rakeshame."

"Stiff rump." With a quick grin Valentine returned to his coach and climbed in. A moment later the vehicle rumbled onto the street and turned for Corbett House.

Sebastian wrung out his coattails. Whatever his intention, Deverill had brought up several very good points. And he had something he needed to see to.

He returned to the house. "Stanton, have Green saddle Merlin. I need to change clothes, and then I'll be going out. Don't wait up." He passed the butler, then stopped again. "And the next time you break into a fight of mine, I expect you to take my side, not try to stop it."

The butler softly closed the front door. "Yes, Your Grace."

He headed upstairs, shedding his coat as he went. Yes, Valentine had made a great deal of sense. The Griffin name *could* withstand a little out-and-out scandal. When it came down to it, could he? It seemed that over the next few days he would find out. Starting with tonight.

Josefina sat up in her large bed, a spread of correspondence around her. As she carefully reread all of the letters her father had ever sent her, it began to make sense. What she'd done was wrong; it always had been. But even when she knew they were scheming about something, even when she knew she was spinning untruths into even prettier lies, she enjoyed the way they immersed themselves in the fiction until it felt and looked real. And her father was so confident in his superiority that he could make it seem as though whoever fell for their plays deserved to be taken advantage of.

Her mother had always called him a dreamer, taking on one campaign, one war after another looking for fame or glory. As she read now, she could see the growing edge of desperation in his depiction of himself and his situation, the envy toward first Wellesley and then Bolivar and Rivera. Even toward her mother's father, with his high position in the Spanish colonial government.

Was that what drove him? Envy? Or arrogance? She supposed it didn't matter, and the thing she'd truly wanted to find somewhere in his correspondence—a conscience, a concern for anyone but himself—simply wasn't there. Considering the various schemes with which she'd helped him over the years, she supposed she didn't have a conscience, either. Or she'd thought not, anyway.

Two things had changed that. Previously their plans had been about money. Now, though, he wanted other people to risk their lives, and that was far different than encouraging them to part with a few quid. And then she'd met Sebastian Harold Griffin.

She should have hated him, she supposed. He was arrogant, and confident, and ridiculously mindful of propriety and the way his peers perceived him. But he'd also been lonely, and enticing, and he'd gotten angry when he'd suspected lies—not because they affected him, but because they affected the people of his country. *His* people, he'd said, and she understood that he felt a genuine responsibility toward them and for them.

Josefina took a slow breath. So now she knew. And tonight she had saved Sebastian's life, not to protect her father's plans, but for herself. It was fitting, she supposed, that however it turned out, neither man would ever forgive her for choosing that particular route. She didn't know why she had, except that it seemed the one declaration sure to give her father pause. And maybe she'd done it because ten minutes earlier Sebastian had said he never wanted to set eyes on her again, and now he had do.

Her half-open window slid up. She gasped, diving off the far side of the bed and scrambling for the pistol in the bed stand. Letters went flying everywhere. Fumbling, her legs tangling in sheets and her night rail, she yanked open the drawer. "Go away," she hissed, "or I will shoot."

"I'm not going away," Sebastian's low voice came, "so either shoot me or put that blasted thing away."

She gripped the pistol as he climbed with absurd grace over the window sill and into the room. Brushing off his coat, he closed the window again before he looked at her.

"I never imagined you as the climbing the trellis sort," she said.

"That was my second one," he returned. "And hopefully the last. Since you did go to the trouble of saving my life earlier, I would hope that you don't actually intend to use that." He gestured at the pistol.

"That depends on why you're here. We didn't part on the best of terms."

"I'm here to talk. I need some answers before tomorrow." He tilted his head, his gaze in the candlelight taking in her bare feet and arms, and lingering at the purple mark above her right elbow. "I apologize for that," he said in a low voice. "I have no excuse."

Josefina wasn't so certain about that. Still, if he'd given her the advantage, she meant to keep it. "I accept your apology," she said in her most regal voice. "What happened to your lip?"

"A disagreement," he returned, touching the bruise that overran the left corner of his mouth.

Swallowing, she placed the pistol back in the drawer and closed it away. "This has become complicated, hasn't it?" Keeping her gaze and all her attention on him, she bent sideways to finish untangling her right foot from the bed sheets.

"Yes, it has."

"I hope—did you talk to Peep? I don't want her to be hurt by all of this." Lady Penelope Griffin was such a sweet girl; it didn't seem like more than a day or two ago that Josefina had felt that confident about her own place in the world.

Sebastian nodded. "I don't think she quite understands it, but then neither do I."

"How will you get out of it? Marrying me, I mean." It would probably include her arrest and hanging, but she wanted to hear him say it. Hearing him condemn her would make her own decisions easier.

Steely gray eyes met hers. "I don't know yet. My actions will depend on yours, I suppose."

She glanced at the empty bed between them, and lust

swept through her like a warm breeze. "I assume that means you want something of me. I may be a bit mercenary, Melbourne, but there are some things I won't do."

"I'm reassured to hear that. Come here."

"No. You come here."

He regarded her in silence. Low heat spread through her, catching her breath and making her heart skitter. In brief moments of insanity she could imagine what it would be like to be married to this man—to be a princess, a real princess, every day for the rest of her life, to walk into a room on his arm, to always have that look he gave her now, only for her. She shivered.

"My question to you," he said finally, "is where you stand in this. And I'm sorry, but you do have to choose."

"Between you and my father?" she countered. "That's not much of a choice, Melbourne, to either betray him or be used and abandoned by you. Or is your plan to whisk me away from danger, to find me employment somewhere in the country, perhaps as a governess? I should make a splendid governess, don't you think?"

"I can protect you, Josefina."

"Once the people who've dance with me, invited me to their homes, flattered me, courted me—once they learn what's happened, who I really am, they will never speak to me again. I'm destroyed either way, Sebastian. And no, I'm not blaming you. I went along with this, and it's on my head. But I do know where reality lies."

Sebastian walked around the foot of the disheveled bed and stopped just in front of her. "You do know where reality lies," he agreed quietly, touching her chin with his fingers and tilting her head up to look her in the eye. "Are you going to help me put a stop to the fiction?"

"I will not help see my father hanged." A tear ran down her face. He wiped it away with his thumb. "I can't do that."

He leaned down and kissed her. Sebastian told himself he'd gone to see her tonight because he wanted answers; the truth was, he wanted her even more. Every bit of her aroused him. Even the way she refused to cooperate and make the situation easier for him. Everyone else cooperated with him—it was in their best interest to do so. It could be in hers, as well—enough people owed him favors or money that he could keep her from prison. She was right about one thing, though; Society would never forgive being made to look foolish. *Later,* he told himself. He would make things right later.

"This won't change anything," Josefina breathed as she pushed the coat from his shoulders.

"It's already changed everything." Sebastian slipped his fingers beneath the thin straps of material at her shoulders and drew them down her arms. Even her skin intoxicated him; smooth, soft, and warm, remembered and new at the same time. Her scent was different than Charlotte's, lilac rather than summer roses. He was glad of that, though it didn't take perfume to make him aware of the differences between Charlotte and Josefina.

He kissed her again, trailing his hands down her bare back to her hips and pulling her closer against him. Josefina was a trickster, an actress, and only in the past few days had he begun to realize that she had a conscience, and a heart. She'd risked a great deal, telling him what she had. And she was the key to the rest of it, if he could discover a way to resolve this without forcing her to do what she would otherwise refuse. It had recently become essential not to lose her. How long would he have been able to keep his vow of being rid of her? A day? A week? He'd lasted four hours.

"Sebastian," she moaned, pushing at him.

He took a half step back, and she reached between them to unbutton his waistcoat. It followed his coat to the floor, his cravat going after. When he ran his fingers lightly across her breasts, her nipples pebbled. Taking a shuddering breath, he bent down, replacing his fingers with his tongue.

Josefina reached down his back and tugged his shirt free of his trousers. He broke contact with her breasts only long enough to pull the shirt off over his head. The last time he'd been in this room with her, he'd ended with his boots on and his trousers around his knees. Tonight they had hours, and he intended to use them.

At the back of his mind he could acknowledge that this could be his last night with her, his last time to touch her, kiss her, take her. What he wanted was to give her so much pleasure, make her desire for him so overpowering, that he would finally be able to sway her to listen to his logic.

He teased at her with his tongue, with gentle nips of his teeth, and she gave a shuddering moan in response. Arousal tugged hard at him, but he resisted the urge to simply push her down on the bed and mount her like an animal. After four years of abstinence, by choice or not, being with Josefina made him feel as though he'd come to life again.

Releasing her, he sat on the edge of the bed to pull off his boots. Josefina swept around behind him, her breasts pressing against his back as she slid her arms down his shoulders and kissed the nape of his neck. Briefly he reflected that if they could simply remain in bed, they would have no problems whatsoever.

The logical, reserved part of himself began to submerge into the bliss of pure sensation. It was more than that, though. If all he'd required was an offer of sex, there were myriad women who wouldn't have hesitated to climb into his bed.

"You know," she murmured, "being with you is bad for me."

He looked over his shoulder at her. "Is it?"

"Oh, yes. I would be risking much less if you were a shopkeeper or a banker." She pulled on his shoulders, putting him flat on his back to look up at her. "And I imagine I am equally bad for you."

"In all the time you've been privy to your father's . . . plans," he whispered, pulling her down over him to kiss her again, "how is it that until a few days ago you remained a virgin?"

Her lips smiled against his. "Perhaps I was waiting for you."

Frowning, Sebastian rolled onto his stomach, ignoring the discomfort to his cock. "I'm already here, Josefina. And for God's sake, I hear enough empty flattery every time I set foot out-of-doors to last me a lifetime. I asked a question. Pray either answer it truthfully, or decline to answer it at all."

Deep brown eyes assessed him. "My father has always had a very high opinion of himself," she said, sliding down on her hands and knees until she lay on her stomach facing him, just inches away. "Because of that, he insisted that everyone else also have a high opinion of him, and of his family. I had very good tutors and governesses, and an exceptional education. And since you want honesty, I wasn't about to risk throwing away my . . . potential by falling into bed with a soldier or a tobacco farmer."

"But I was worth the risk?" he countered, pulling her hand to him and sliding her forefinger into his mouth.

He felt her responding shiver. "That remains to be seen," she returned. "But I do enjoy being in your company more than anyone else's I can recall."

Sebastian was not going to logic himself out of having her. Swiftly he sat up again to remove his second boot and unfasten his trousers. Pushing them down, he kicked out of them. "I didn't think I liked surprises any longer," he said, putting a hand on the small of her back when she would have turned over. "You have proven me wrong."

Slowly he ran his palms from her shoulders down her back, pausing at her round bottom, and then down her thighs and past her knees to the soles of her feet. Whatever it was about her that drew him, he liked it. He liked thinking as a man rather than as a duke with a world of duties and responsibilities. He liked the challenge of deciphering the twists and turns of her mind, and sinking into the soft curves of her body.

As he ran his mouth back up in the same manner she squirmed, moaning again. "Sebastian, stop teasing."

"Does it feel good?"

"Yes. Oh, yes."

"Then it's not teasing."

"But I want—"

He grabbed a pillow from the head of the bed. "However, if you insist," he murmured. "Lift up."

She rose to her hands and knees, and he slid the pillow beneath her hips. Her bottom tilted into the air as she sank back down again at the pressure from his hand. Hard and throbbing, he moved over her, placing his hands on either side of her shoulders, nudging her legs farther apart with his knee.

"Tell me that you want me," he said, unable to keep the words from ending in a growl.

"I want you," she gasped.

"Describe it," he ordered, trying to slow his breathing and the hard pounding of his heart.

"I want you inside me," Josefina said, arching her bottom against his aching, sensitive cock.

Adjusting himself, he pushed slowly forward, burying himself in her from behind. Tight, and hot, and exquisitely his. No other man had ever had her, and he vowed at that moment that no other man ever would. "Like this?" he managed.

"Oh, yes," she groaned as he began slowly pumping his hips. "Yes."

Only now could he ask himself what the devil he was doing in this woman's house and in her bed, because now he didn't care what the answer might be. All that mattered at that moment was the sound of her rhythmic, barely stifled moans, and the indescribable feeling of their joined flesh. If the rest of their lives outside this room could promise half as much, he would never be able to part from her.

He didn't want to, as it was. Sebastian kissed her shoulders, felt her shake and quiver and come. Slowing his pace, he drew it out for her as long as he could, until she gave a muffled cry into her bed sheets. "Want to try something else now?" he whispered into her ear.

She nodded, her fingers still clutched into the sheets. Pulling away, breathing hard, Sebastian turned onto his back and drew her over his chest. Josefina kissed him hungrily as he pulled her left leg across him so she straddled his hips. Immediately understanding, she sank down onto his length, her satisfied groan nearly sending him past his slipping control.

With his hand on her hips, he showed her how to move. A moan broke from his own lips as she caught on and began lifting up and down on him. "You're a quick study," he said, cupping her breasts in his hands.

Josefina leaned forward and kissed him again. "I want to see you lose yourself like I did," she panted, riding him harder.

"I can't," he grunted, trying to keep his eyes from rolling back in his head. "It could mean even more trouble for you."

"Sebastian, you don't, ah, have to be in control every moment. Oh, my. Sometimes you're not supposed to be."

"With you, you mean? My lack of . . . control where you're . . . concerned is what got us into this mess to begin with."

"Good."

He moaned again. "Good?"

"Yes. Good."

He would have questioned her further, but he lost the power of speech. Trying to push her off him, he fought her for another few seconds, then exploded, shuddering.

"Damnation, Josefina," he growled when he could speak again. "Don't you realize what might have just happened?"

She draped herself across his chest, her black hair curtaining her face from him. "Why, do you think things could get worse?"

He brushed the midnight waves back so he could see her eyes. "Yes, now they can."

Josefina lifted her face, looking at him from inches away. "Now we're as tangled together in here as we are out there." She flipped a finger toward the window and London beyond.

He frowned, more angry that she'd fought him than dismayed at what might have come of her—their—actions. "And you consider that a good thing?"

Her expression sobered. "Just think of it this way. The court won't execute a woman who's bearing a child." Her voice caught.

For the first time he realized how frightened she must be by what he threatened. He'd been so concerned with his own righteous indignation that he hadn't delved into her feelings. "If you'll trust me, I promise you that no harm will come to you."

Josefina held his gaze for a long moment. "You don't know everything I've done. And not just in England."

"When I climbed through your window," he murmured, "I didn't expect to find you lying here wearing a halo and angel's wings, Josefina. My only question is whether you'll make the right decision this time."

"I don't think I have much choice," she finally said.

"Then tell me what you know."

Chapter 18

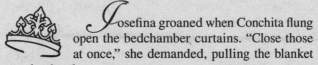osefina groaned when Conchita flung open the bedchamber curtains. "Close those at once," she demanded, pulling the blanket over her head.

"His Majesty says you must come downstairs. The Duke of Melbourne is here."

But he'd just left. Josefina sat up, her heart hammering madly. "What do you mean, he's here?"

Conchita smiled. "He must be anxious to marry you, Your Highness."

Good heavens. *They were engaged.* In the deliriousness of last night and earlier this morning, she'd forgotten. If they were married, they could spend every night like that. *Goodness.*

She scrambled out of bed, grabbing her shift off a chair and pulling it on while Conchita stood up to her elbows in the wardrobe. Considering that she had no explanation for why she'd shed her nightrail and crawled back into bed naked, avoiding the question altogether seemed the wisest course of action.

"What time is it, anyway?" she asked, frowning as Conchita held up an ornate blue gown. "Simpler. This is a morning visit; not a coronation."

"It's half ten," the maid replied. "You must have been done in; I've never known you to sleep so late, Your Highness."

Done in, and awake until nearly five o'clock, when Sebastian had finally climbed back out her window and slipped away. She felt sated, like a cat after a bowl full of cream. "I had a restless night," she offered, going to the dressing table for her hairbrush.

"I think the rey did, as well. The green one?"

"Yes, that's fine." Josefina paused in her brushing, her heart skipping a beat. "What makes you think His Majesty also slept poorly?"

"He had Tomas up and attending him before first light, and then he spent near three hours closeted with Halloway and Orrin." The maid sent her a sly sideways glance. "Considering who's about to join the family, I imagine there's a great deal of preparation to make."

So he'd met with his cohorts about strategy, and she'd slept through it. Under the circumstances she felt grateful he hadn't tried to wake her up to participate. She hadn't told Sebastian everything last night, but she'd done enough—enough to enable him to stop her father or to throw the lot of them into prison.

She dressed and finished her toilette as swiftly as she could, then threw open her door and hurried downstairs to the morning room. In the open doorway she paused, relishing in the abrupt delight that coursed through her as she saw the man standing inside.

Sebastian lounged by the fireplace, a cup of tea and saucer in his hands and his gaze on her father seated beneath the window. The duke had worn brown and gray, his cravat starched and white and not a fold out of place. Even if she'd never set eyes on him before she would know that this tall, lean man with the deep gray eyes and that sensuous mouth was someone to be reckoned with.

As though sensing her in the doorway, he turned and faced her. Her heart skipped again, for an entirely different reason this time. He was glorious. And that look in his eyes, the possessiveness and the desire, that was for her.

"Good morning, Your Highness," he said, setting his tea on the mantel and sketching a deep, formal bow. "I hope you slept well."

Josefina held out her hand to him, hoping her father couldn't see her fingers shaking. "Good morning, Melbourne. And yes, I slept quite well, thank you."

He strode forward to take her fingers, bringing them to his lips. At his touch, warm desire flew just under her skin. "Good," he murmured.

"Now that the greetings are finished with," the rey said from his chair, "let's settle matters, shall we?"

Sebastian turned again to face her father. "Before I set pen to paper about anything," he said, his voice cooling, "I have several matters I want clarified."

Her father stood. "Until you put pen to paper and sign your agreement to marry Princess Josefina, lad, I simply don't feel comfortable discussing anything else. A monarch's, and a father's, prerogative, I suppose."

"I go into nothing blind." Before her eyes the gentle, passionate Sebastian vanished, replaced in the same instant by the implacable Duke of Melbourne. "That is my prerogative."

"Then I will leave it to you to explain why you proposed to my daughter as a jest. Are you so mighty you think to toy with royalty and escape unscathed?"

For a moment the duke stayed silent. "The advantage

I provide to your . . . mission *is* my respectability and my status," he said quietly. "Putting me in a position where either is compromised would undo whatever it is you hope to accomplish by adding me to the equation in the first place."

"What I hope to accomplish," her father retorted, his tone less even than the duke's, "is secure loans to aid my country, and settlers to do the same. That is how we arrived in England, and that is how we shall leave." He narrowed his light blue eyes. "Anything that counters my statements is merely jealous rumor and speculation."

"If you expect me to throw my lot in with you, you're going to have to do better than make pronouncements."

Her father drew himself up straighter. "You seem to be assuming, Your Grace, that I am perpetrating some sort of fraud. While I admit that our prospectus was partially . . . borrowed from other sources, that was only done in the interest of saving time better spent setting up a government."

Heavens. He seemed so sure of himself that she could almost believe it. Did *he*? Had his wish to be someone important become so all-consuming that he now believed his own fantasies? Was he mad?

"I see," Sebastian said slowly. "Perhaps I have sped to conclusions I should not have. You must tell me what I would be signing, though. I don't think that's an unreasonable request."

"All I wish you to put in writing is that you will marry my daughter, making her your wife and duchess, and that you will contribute to the betterment of Costa Habichuela in your speech and writing, and by pledging us a sum of say, twenty-five thousand pounds annually."

Josefina blinked. "Twenty-five thousand?" she gasped. "Father, that's outrageous! It's far too much."

"I won't debate Josefina's value, but only my willingness to part with sums I could better use to support her. Five thousand a year." Sebastian *hadn't* blinked.

"Twenty."

"Ten, or I might as well purchase my own country."

The rey's jaw twitched. "Ten, then."

"And your daughter would not become a duchess," Sebastian went on, his fingers brushing hers as he spoke. "She has a higher title, and would retain that."

"The . . ." For the first time her father hesitated.

Of course he would want his daughter to have a legitimate title over a lofty invented one. Sebastian was brilliant—and yet he hadn't wavered about the marriage, itself. Surely he knew he couldn't marry a soldier's daughter who routinely tricked people out of their money, even if the betrothal hadn't been just a ruse invented to save his life.

"I was the only one declared a ruler," the rey said a moment later, pacing to the window and back, knotting his fingers together as she'd seen him do on countless occasions when he was working through some plan or other. "Maria and Josefina's titles are honorary. She would of course assume the title of Duchess of Melbourne upon her marriage to you."

It sounded like complete nonsense, but Sebastian merely nodded. "Josefina's children, then, would be noble, and not royal."

"Yes. Correct."

"Who will inherit your kingdom, then?"

She expected that to stump her father, but he smiled. "You will. And then *you* will be Sebastian Griffin, rey of Costa Habichuela. And still the Duke of Melbourne, naturally."

"Naturally." Sebastian regarded the rey. "I think the chasm of our differences is narrowing."

"I'm gratified to hear that. This is a situation where all of us can do quite well for ourselves if we proceed wisely.

Mine is a new monarchy. I won't deny that of course your alliance with Josefina lends more respectability to my cause."

"I don't join enterprises that don't make me money," Sebastian returned in such a matter-of-fact tone that Josefina looked at him. "Particularly when I have concerns over the fate of British citizens. To satisfy me, you will give me both your written assurance that I will be made rey upon your death, and a guarantee that this will be profitable beyond the pittance of loan money designated, I assume, for you."

"I can't guarantee that," her father retorted.

"I can, if you would allow me to advise your investments."

"Why should I trust you to do that?"

Sebastian smiled, charming and cold at the same time. No wonder most people feared to cross him. "Because I will be a member of your family, Your Majesty. What affects you, affects me, and vice versa."

That hit on her father's main point in encouraging the marriage. Josefina watched him, waiting to see whether he would accept Sebastian's offer, or whether the duke had put too neat a ribbon on the package.

"You have the reputation for being a man of honor and principle, Your Grace," the rey said, taking a seat once more. "Pray excuse me if I find your conversion somewhat . . . convenient."

The duke snorted. "'Convenient'? It's anything but." He lifted an eyebrow. "It was your initial plan to involve me, was it not? Prinny said you requested that I be the one to assist you."

"Perhaps."

"Then I suggest you take advantage of my participation."

Josefina held her breath. Whatever Sebastian was doing,

obviously her father needed to cooperate in order for it to succeed. But was she at this moment standing by and letting Melbourne set a trap for her father that could end in his incarceration and death?

The rey held out his hand. "Agreed. With reservations."

Sebastian shook the proffered hand. "I believe I can set your mind at ease."

"What will set my mind at ease is seeing you standing in a church beside my daughter."

"I require one month to make the arrangements," Sebastian said calmly. "A duke and a princess cannot marry without ceremony. We can do without the reading of the banns, but I will have to get dispensation from Canterbury. We will have to hold an engagement ball. And as the wedding will take place at St. Paul's, there are a limited number of dates from which to choose."

"St. Paul's," her father repeated reverently. "Why not Westminster?"

Sebastian's face stilled. "My first marriage took place at Westminster," he said tightly, the first real emotion she'd heard from him all morning touching his voice. "This one will be at St. Paul's, or not at all. I will not negotiate that point."

"St. Paul's will be lovely," Josefina said firmly, then faced her father. "And a month between the engagement and the wedding seems very short as it is. I don't want to give the appearance that we're rushing anything."

At Sebastian's sideways glance she had to fight off a blush. After the first time she'd refused to let him leave her as he'd climaxed, it had seemed pointless for him to do so the other four times. Obviously she—they—were tempting fate, but after this disaster with her father she would be parting company from his troupe, anyway. And she would end up ostracized from Society regardless.

"Yes, you're right, of course," the rey agreed with clear

reluctance. "I suppose I can delay everyone's departures by an additional fortnight."

"I believe we are in agreement, then. I'll have my solicitor draw up the papers, and we can sign them this afternoon."

"Very good." Her father walked to the door. "As you two are now betrothed, I'll leave you alone for a moment to talk."

Her heart began pounding all over again at just the thought of spending another few moments in privacy with Sebastian. He gripped her fingers, squeezing them, and met her gaze for the briefest of seconds. Then to her surprise he let her go and walked after her father.

"We'll have time to talk later," he said. "If I'm to return by . . ." he consulted his pocket watch ". . . four o'clock, say, I have a great deal to do."

The rey stood aside as Melbourne passed him, stopped in the foyer to collect his hat and gloves, and left the house. The warm parts of her chilled as the front door closed behind him. She shook herself, trying to be rid of the abrupt feeling of loneliness with which his departure had left her. He'd been trying to tell her something. What, she had no idea.

"A month before the wedding," her father grumbled. "I don't like it."

"A month is still pushing the boundaries of propriety," she said. "He couldn't make it sooner than that. And neither could we."

"Yes, yes, I know. But it gives him too much time."

"Time for what?" she asked, keeping her voice as calm as she could. "To change his mind? He's putting the agreement in writing. Melbourne would never risk crying off after that."

"That's not what troubles me. He's up to something. My guess is that he means to have me give over all of the loan money to him for investment, at which time he'll seize the funds and attempt to expose me." He smiled. "Well, I have a surprise for him. He's not getting a single penny."

Oh, dear. "If he's trying to trap you, he'll be suspicious if you don't go along with his plans."

Her father stroked his moustache. "Yes, he will be. Excuse me, Josefina. I have a few things to mull over."

"Of course, Father."

She sank into a chair as he left the room. A disaster. It was all a disaster, and she was directly in the middle of it. Sebastian suspected her father, her father suspected Sebastian, and each thought she was on his side. "Damnation," she muttered under her breath.

If she had someone to talk to, someone with whom she could reason things through, this would have been so much easier. But she knew of no one in whom she could confide. The only women she'd begun to consider friends were Sebastian's sisters, and they would be on his side. Her mother, or Conchita, even, would both side with their own survival, which meant they would support her father. As for the men in her life, they were even more polarized.

Sebastian had warned her this would happen. The middle ground was fast disappearing, and she needed to choose a side. Legally, morally, the Duke of Melbourne held the high ground. Siding with her father, though, gave her two things—a chance at escape from prosecution, and something that had become absurdly important over the past day: marriage to Sebastian.

Her happiness weighed against the safety of several hundred naive, gullible settlers. It hardly seemed fair. It wasn't fair. And yet she supposed she truly only had herself to blame for being in the position of having to choose.

Josefina drew in a ragged, shaking breath, then headed upstairs to change into something more appropriate for making social calls. Safety was the most she could hope

for, because people who'd made the choices that she had
didn't get to ask for or expect more. Even if that one thing
she truly, deeply, stupidly wanted was love.

As mercenary as she'd tried to be, this argument with
herself was obviously because she'd reached her limit.
And for God's sake, she needed to do the right thing.
Finally.

The largest problem would be getting away from the
house without arousing anyone's suspicions. For a few
moments she paced back and forth in her bedchamber,
wishing that Sebastian would climb back in through the
window. *Be practical*, she ordered herself. She had no
time for missish daydreams.

Very well. Her hands shook as she pulled paper, pen,
and ink from her writing desk. Mental resolve was one
thing, she supposed; physical fortitude was another altogether.

Now for the escape. *"Dearest Caroline,"* she wrote,
muttering the words as she put them to paper.

> *Thank you again for asking me to luncheon today.
> Given the chaos of this morning and what will fol-
> low this afternoon, an hour or two of calm and
> quiet will be <u>much</u> appreciated.*
>
> *My only request is that you come by for me at
> noon rather than one o'clock, as I shall need this
> afternoon free. I look forward to chatting with you
> again. Yours in gratitude, Josefina, Princess of
> Costa Habichuela.*

Folding the letter, she addressed it to Lady Caroline
Griffin and summoned Grimm. "Please see that this is
delivered to Lady Caroline right away," she instructed the
butler, "and ask whoever takes it to wait for a reply."

"I'll see to it immediately, Your Highness."

She shut her door, then quietly and carefully opened it again when she heard the butler's footsteps return downstairs. A moment later he rapped on a door. "It's Grimm, Your Majesty," he said, apparently in response to a query. "You wanted to review all outgoing correspondence."

Josefina closed the door again, sagging back against the solid barrier. Being part of a family comprised of frauds and tricksters did have its benefits. At least it made her cautious. She probably should have gone directly to Eleanor, but her father would think the same thing. Hopefully sending a letter to a Griffin sister-in-law would be less suspicious than directing it to Sebastian or one of his immediate siblings.

Now all she could do was wait and see if she received an answer other than bafflement or refusal, and if Lady Caroline's coach arrived at noon to allow her to flee the house with her news—that her father knew he was being plotted against. Then she would pray both that Sebastian had a secondary plan, and that she wasn't making the last and greatest mistake of her life in trusting him.

Chapter 19

"Ten thousand pounds, Your Grace?" his finance man stumbled. "Of course you have that amount at your discretion, but I'm not certain any of us would wish to be transporting that sum of ready cash through the streets of London."

Sebastian finished writing out his instructions to Sir Henry Sparks, folded and sealed the missive, and handed it to the younger man. "I need to have this money to hand, Rivers," he said curtly. "Take Tom and Green with you; arm them if you'd like. But get it back here."

Rivers stood, clearing his throat as he tucked the note into his breast pocket. "I shall see to it at once, Your Grace."

Pulling another piece of paper from his office desk, Sebastian glanced up. "Thank you."

Rivers backed out the office door. "Yes, Your Grace."

Sebastian scowled at the blank page before him. He could excuse Rivers's nerves; most of his business dealings were done by note rather than by a cash exchange.

But he didn't want to give Stephen Embry any excuse to balk. If the plan worked as he hoped, the rey would hand the cash back, along with any other funds at his disposal, for a quick, profitable investment.

Some of the half dozen solicitors he employed would be arriving momentarily, and then would be the difficult part—setting out in writing something that would incriminate Embry without appearing to do so, keep Josefina out of any legal entanglements, and allow him to maneuver without being implicated in any wrongdoing.

He wrote out those points. As he penned Josefina's name, he paused. If the world were a perfect place, where would he stand in regard to her? Sebastian sat back in his comfortable leather chair. If the world were a perfect place, Charlotte wouldn't have wasted away before his eyes and died after just under four years of marriage. Obviously he couldn't pin any of his hopes on perfection. But if Josefina had been what she claimed, if her father had for a moment told the truth . . .

Sebastian closed his eyes for a half dozen heartbeats, then went back to his list. Valentine had said the Griffin family could withstand a scandal. The difficulty was that Josefina was at least three scandals all wrapped into one hard-headed, quick-tempered, tale-spouting minx who twisted him into such knots he couldn't tell down from up. And he loved her because of that.

His breath caught. *Christ.* Sebastian shoved to his feet. Love was not a word he used lightly, even in thought. And he could easily admit that he frequently found Josefina and her lack of candor annoying beyond bearing. But she matched him. She stood up to him. She challenged him. And even with the chaos that accompanied her—or perhaps because of it—she made him feel . . . alive. Half insane, but alive.

Someone rapped at his door. "Enter," he said.

He expected the solicitors, but it was his sister-in-law who stepped into the room. "Sebastian, I need to speak with you."

"Caroline? We'll all be meeting tonight. Can it wait until—"

"I just received this," she interrupted, holding out a piece of paper.

Lifting an eyebrow, he took it from her fingers and unfolded it. After he read it, his eyes snapped up to hers again. "You asked her to luncheon today?"

"No, I didn't. In fact, I was on my way out the door to go shopping with Anne and Joanna when this arrived, along with a footman who'd been instructed to wait for an answer."

His mind began spinning. So Josefina had asked to meet with a member of his family before the afternoon's meeting. And in the company of a married female acquaintance she wouldn't require her maid as a chaperone. "How did you respond?"

"I said my sisters and I would be there at noon as she requested."

"Your sisters and—"

"The three of us were getting into the carriage when the footman arrived. I didn't know what else I could say without giving Joanna a reason to throw a tantrum. She's been livid that I know a princess and haven't introduced her, as it is." Zachary's wife frowned. "I assume this is about something she couldn't say to you during your meeting with her father this morning."

"That would be my guess, as well."

"Then do you wish me to bring her here?"

That would be the most convenient route, but if Josefina had resorted to sending covert communications, then he had to wonder whether someone might be following her. He'd already declined a moment of badly wanted privacy with her to keep her father from suspecting that she might have changed sides. Sebastian glanced at his pocket watch. Nearly noon. "Take her back to your home," he said slowly. "Is Zach there?"

"Yes. He's going over some of the cattle breeding reports with Papa."

"Good. Keep him there. I'll head over to speak with him. Can you get me a few moments alone with Josefina without everyone realizing?"

"I believe so." She pulled the door open again. "Do you trust her, Sebastian?"

He gave a brief smile. "That is a very good question. Thank you, Caro, for coming to me with this."

She smiled back at him. "None of us can predict where the heart will lead," she said. "I'm glad you realized that about Zachary and me. And I hope . . . Well, I'll leave it at that for now."

Stepping forward, he kissed her swiftly on the cheek. "Just try to keep Joanna away from Josefina. We don't need a bout of female fisticuffs."

With an amused nod, Caroline slipped out the door and back to the foyer, where he could hear Joanna complaining about being denied an audience with the duke, and Anne noting that she should be grateful. What had happened? When he'd seen Josefina earlier he hadn't sensed any new urgency about her, and certainly not anything that would cause her to set this particular play into motion.

He shoved the paper back into its drawer. A luncheon, he supposed, could be exactly that. Caroline had good instincts, however, and today he completely agreed with them. Something was afoot, and it centered around Josefina. As usual. Sebastian gave a quick, fond smile.

Trotting upstairs to change his coat, he paused to take the latest book assigned to him by Zachary from his bed stand. *A History of Cumberland Cattle* had served him well in assisting him to sleep, and with its title in large, gold print it also served as his excuse for calling on his brother.

As he reached the foot of the stairs, Stanton was pulling open the front door to admit Misters Harkley, Swenk, and Challington, his solicitors. *Damnation.* "Gentlemen," he said, taking his gloves and hat from the butler as he spoke, "I have two tasks for you, both of which need to be completed by four o'clock. The second one we will discuss when I return, but the first is for you to draw up an agreement between myself and Stephen Embry, the rey of Costa Habichuela, wherein I will make him an annual payment of ten thousand pounds."

Harkley, the most senior of the three, nodded. "We will begin at once, Your Grace. May I ask what this sum is paying for?"

"For Embry's daughter. My wife-to-be. Josefina Katarina Embry."

The gasps of the stolid, jaded trio made him smile as he left the house for the stable. If his marriage shocked those three, he could only imagine what must be going through Mayfair today. And even that would be nothing compared with the *ton*'s reaction when they discovered that her father was a thief and that the Duke of Melbourne was marrying someone he'd begun to realize was without a noble bloodline. Common, they would say, though he strongly disagreed. There was absolutely nothing common about Josefina Embry.

Unless he could come up with another way around this, the scandal would be monumental. No one would dare give either of them the cut direct, but there would be gatherings where invitations failed to arrive, and luncheons where the old wags would gossip and shake their heads. It would be worse for her, but better than if she remained in England unmarried.

So the question wasn't so much whether he had the courage to raise a tempest, but whether Josefina had the courage to ride one out. And whether letting her vanish back across the Atlantic might actually be better for her than any protection he could offer.

"Papa!"

One of the grooms brought Merlin out of the stable, but Sebastian turned around at the sound of Peep's voice. He frowned as he saw the direction she came from, with Mrs. Beacham nowhere in sight behind her. "Did you climb through the library windows again?"

"It was an emergency," she panted, grabbing his hand. "And Mrs. B dared me."

"What is it, then?"

"Not here, for heaven's sake." She tugged on his hand, pulling him away from the amused stableboys.

"Very well, Peep," he said when they had nearly reached the house again. Mrs. Beacham came hurrying around the corner, skirts flying in the breeze, but he waved her back. "I only have a moment."

"Mary Haley told me when we went riding this morning that when you marry Princess Josefina we have to leave England and live in Costa Habichuela. I don't want to go." Her gray eyes swam with tears.

He squatted down, and she flung herself into his arms. "I thought you wanted to travel," he said, removing his handkerchief and handing it to her.

"I do," she sniffed, "but Costa Habichuela is very far from our friends and family."

Especially since it didn't even exist. "We're not leaving England, sweetling."

She lifted her head. "You're not marrying Josefina now? You said everything might change."

"Nothing's changed." He hesitated. "You didn't mention that bit to Mary, did you?"

"Of course not. She's a terrible gossip."

"Good. And I am planning on marrying Princess Josefina. Does that trouble you?"

Peep shook her dark curls. "Not as long as we don't have to leave here."

"We don't. I promise."

"Very well. Because I've been thinking that when I do travel to Africa and to China, it would be nice if you had someone here to keep you company while I'm gone."

He hugged her again. "That is very thoughtful of you."

"Yes, I know."

Stifling a smile, he straightened. "Then go back to the house and apologize to Mrs. Beacham for fleeing. And no more climbing through windows." Considering he'd done that very thing last night, he'd withhold any further punishment.

With Penelope appeased, his only concern was Josefina. And stopping a fraud, and keeping settlers from dying. Sebastian sighed as he returned to Merlin and swung into the saddle. If he could figure out what to do with her, the rest would be easy.

After twenty minutes in Lady Caroline's home, Josefina began to question whether she'd gone to the correct Griffin family member for assistance. The coach had arrived at noon, but other than that Caroline gave no sign that she hadn't thought up the invitation all on her own. Her five hundred or so sisters and her mother certainly seemed to think this was a purely social occasion. That had been the reason she'd chosen Caroline rather than Eleanor, but good heavens.

"Your Highness," the unmarried of the twins, Joanna, she thought, was saying, "you must tell us how His Grace proposed to you. Was it romantic? Because I've been trying to attract his attention for two years, and nothing at all worked."

Sebastian would chew you up and spit you out as no meal at all, she thought, but smiled. "It happened very quickly," she said aloud. "More surprising than romantic, I suppose."

"But what was your secret?" Joanna persisted. "Everyone thought he would never remarry after his wife died."

"Joanna," the younger unmarried Witfeld, Anne, cut in, "that's quite enough. Aside from the silliness of asking a woman how you might pursue the man she's marrying, I would think a great deal of Princess Josefina's success came from the fact that, unlike you, she's not ridiculous."

"You're not married either, Anne!"

"I'm not asking how to pursue taken men, either. As it happens, I'm waiting for a man who considers travel to be more than a trip between Shropshire and London."

"Joanna! Anne! That's quite enough," Caroline thankfully interrupted as she reentered the room. "Your Highness, did you want to see those books we were discussing?"

Josefina stood up so quickly she nearly spilled her lemonade. "I would love to."

Joanna shot to her feet, as well. "I'll assist you, Your Highness."

Damnation. "Oh, the—"

"What you will do, Joanna, is give Princess Josefina a few minutes to breathe before you rattle her ears off. She came here for some peace. Stay here, for goodness' sake."

With a last stern look at her sister, Caroline led Josefina down a hallway and into a large, open room jumbled with books and comfortable-looking overstuffed furniture.

"Thank you for fetching me from Branbury House, Caroline," Josefina said in a low voice as soon as they were alone. "I have some urgent news for Sebastian. If I tell you, will you pass it to him without delay?"

Caroline's gaze refocused somewhere past Josefina's

shoulder. "I believe I can manage that, yes," she said, and backed out the door, closing it behind her.

The hair along Josefina's arms lifted, and she turned around. "Sebastian?"

"Caroline informed me that you'd invited yourself to luncheon," he said, not moving from where he leaned against the wall between the tall windows. "She reckoned you might want to speak with me."

"Oh, thank goodness," she breathed, striding up to him and tangling her fingers into his hair. She pulled his face down for a fierce kiss.

Sebstian slid warm hands around her waist, strong and possessive. His return kiss simply curled her toes, loosened the knots of tension in her shoulders, and created all new tensions elsewhere—tensions that also required his attention.

"So you did want to see me," he drawled, running a thumb across her lips.

She shook herself. "Yes. I'm so glad she told you what I'd done."

The way she'd . . . melted once she'd realized he was there—that was the other thing only he seemed to rouse in her. A complete and utter distraction. Under the circumstances it troubled her, both because she needed all of her wits, and because it made her wish to conjure all sorts of fantastical scenarios in which she and he could end up together. Fantasy, fairy-tale endings only happened for real princesses, and she was certainly not one of those.

"Are you in danger?" he asked, his fine brow lowering. "I won't allow you to return to Branbury House if there's any chance—"

"No," she interrupted, wishing she could tell whether he was concerned as a gentleman or as a man, "I'm not in danger. My father would never do anything to injure me."

"He did try to have *me* killed."

"You're not his daughter. And you may still be in danger."

"How so?"

"He knows you intend to tie up the stolen funds he gives you for investment. He won't hand them over to you."

Sebastian looked at her for a moment, then slowly walked to one of the chairs beneath the windows and seated himself. "Damnation," he muttered. "I thought I was being too direct, but I see only a limited number of ways to stop him without incriminating you."

Josefina's heart thudded. "I've been thinking about that," she said, moving to perch on the edge of the chair opposite him. "I'm certainly not innocent in this." She clenched her fist into her thigh. "And even without this . . . as you said, I'm not an angel."

When she looked up again, his gaze was not on her face, but on her hands. "So you wish me to see the lot of you thrown into prison? Or worse?"

"Of course I don't *wish* it; I'm not Joan of Arc. But I do understand the part I've played. If stopping him requires incriminating me, then—"

"No."

"Sebastian, you can't meld reality to fit your preferred fiction any more than my father can. And you know what his plan will be—invent some plausible reason he has to delay in giving you any funds until he's forced us to marry. And then your fortune, literally and figuratively, will be tied to his."

He opened his mouth, then closed it again. "I don't believe in losing," he finally ground out.

"Neither does my father. I know when we discussed this last night I thought the chance of a quick, profitable return on his so-called investment would be more than he could resist. But what I didn't tell you was that I spent two hours before you . . . joined me, rereading his letters. All of them."

"And?" he prompted.

"And I think he's always . . . I'm not certain how to say it." She took a breath. "He's always wanted to be someone important. First to be a valuable member of Wellington's staff, and when that failed, to be a valuable part of Bolivar's struggle against Spain. But he was a foreigner in South America, and he wasn't ever really accepted by Bolivar and his generals. The little schemes of ours provided him with blunt, but not with power. So then he came up with Costa Habichuela, where he could be a king. There's nothing greater than that, I suppose. Not where he's concerned. I went along with it, like I've always done, because I enjoy living comfortably."

"I understand his reasoning. And yours."

"No, I don't think you *can*. You were born to be the Duke of Melbourne. You've never stood at one side of the room and envied the power and privilege of someone else." She cleared her throat, willing her voice to remain steady and the tears pushing behind her eyes to go away. She certainly didn't need them now. "When you strip *your* dreams away, you're still Melbourne. Without his dreams, my father is a failed military officer who wouldn't serve in his own country's army when he didn't get his way. And I'm his daughter."

There. She'd said it as plainly as she could. Her father was common, and she was common.

"So to clarify," he said in his low, cultured voice, "you're not worthy of my protection or of my affection."

Josefina closed her eyes, hoping he couldn't see how much it hurt to hear him agree with her assessment of the circumstances. "Precisely," she whispered.

"Do I strike you as being cruel or deceitful?" he asked abruptly.

As she opened her eyes again he rose, stepping forward to kneel in front of her, his hands covering her clenched ones. "No, you do not," she returned.

"That's interesting, as on occasion my siblings have accused me of being both." He scowled briefly. "There's been a Griffin—or a Grifanus, rather—in England since the time of the Romans. My ancestors were among the first to be elevated to the nobility, and one of my forbears was, legend has it, the reason that the title of duke came into existence here. My point being, I suppose, that my family has a knack for doing the right thing at the right time, and for profiting from that bit of good fortune."

It was the most cynical she'd heard him be about his own family, and himself. Distracting as it was having him at her feet and touching her, the admission surprised her. "Sebastian, you don't have to make an excuse for doing the right thing. You're a good man; that is what good men do."

"You misunderstand me, Josefina. I know what I *want* to do, and that is what I intend *to* do. If it's the wrong thing, then so be it; I find that I'm willing to trade on the pristine reputation of my forefathers on this one occasion."

"But you can't let my father order those ships to sail," she protested.

His lips curved upward. "That's not exactly what I was referring to, but you're correct."

"Then what were you referring to?" She frowned down at him. "For heaven's sake, I'm surrounded by people who talk circles around the truth. Don't be an—"

"I want to marry you."

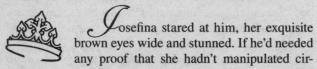osefina stared at him, her exquisite brown eyes wide and stunned. If he'd needed any proof that she hadn't manipulated circumstances to trick or trap him into a wedding, the expression on her face provided it clearly enough.

Sebastian waited another half minute, reluctant amusement warring with growing annoyance. For God's sake, every other female in London would be in raptures if he proposed to them. "You did hear me, I assume," he finally muttered, lifting an eyebrow.

"I heard you. I just don't know what to say."

"Ah." Releasing her hands, he pushed to his feet. "If you're looking for the greatest advantage to yourself, it lies in saying yes. If you're looking for a trap or a condition, there is none."

As he walked to the window, determined not to let her see that he felt far less composed than he pretended, he heard her rise. He half-expected her to slip out the door, and jumped when her hand touched his arm. He turned around.

"So you've made up your—"

Josefina kicked him in the shin. Hard.

"Ow, damn it all," he snapped, refusing to bend down and rub his injured limb. He didn't want her to aim a follow-up blow to his head.

"I did not come here to be proposed to," she said, folding her arms over her pert breasts.

"If you're attempting to shield your bosom from me, I've already tasted its delights," he countered. "Why the devil are you angry with me? Even if you don't care for me, I did just essentially offer to save your life."

"It took me a long time to decide to take a stand against my father," she retorted, her color rising further as his gaze dropped again to her chest, "when all he's ever wanted is what's best for me."

"Deciding you should be a princess of a make-believe country was not the wisest way to go about that." He knew he sounded cynical, but she had just cracked him in the knee.

"No, it wasn't. But regardless of his methods, my coming here means that I've betrayed him. And then you say you want to marry me, and now it feels as though I'm being . . . rewarded for siding against my father."

Rewarded. That sounded more promising than a kick in the leg. Sebastian allowed himself a second to dwell on that. "You are an uncommon woman, Josefina," he said, choosing his words deliberately. "And you're correct; I should have kept my attention on the larger issue. I withdraw my proposal."

"You—" She snapped her mouth closed. "Very well."

He hid the abrupt urge to smile. "Our task is to keep those ships from leaving. Since I won't be able to withhold his stolen money to convince him to do so, our options are limited."

"You need to have us arrested," she stated, her voice shaking.

"That is my very last choice."

"Well, unless you can alter the winds and blow the ships back to England when they sail, I don't see any other choice."

Alter the winds. She'd done so in the prospectus. But something in the way she said it this time gave him the inkling of an idea. *Alter the winds.*

"I need to get back to the others," she said into the silence. "What are we going to do?"

He looked at her. "This afternoon I'm going to sign all of the agreements, and be frustrated when your father won't hand over any funds for investment."

"But the agreements obligate you to marry me. And to give him ten thousand pounds. Annually."

"I know you rejected my proposal, my dear, but—"

"I did not," she countered indignantly. "I rejected having you propose when we have more pressing matters to deal with."

"I'll keep that in mind, then." She *did* want to marry him. His heart sped. "When you announced to the world that we were to be married, you essentially made it so. Signing a piece of paper is a mere formality." Taking her chin in his fingers, he tilted her face up and kissed her softly. "As for the rest," he murmured, "you'll have to trust me until I can speak with my family and put a few details into the equation."

"I'm not accustomed to trusting people, Sebastian." She kissed him back, sighing against his mouth in a way that threatened to steal not just his breath, but his soul. "But I trust you."

He took her arm and walked her to the library door.

"I mean to propose to you again, Josefina," he whispered. "And the next time you'd best not kick me."

"I've recently stopped making promises," she said unsteadily. "At least ones I can't keep."

"You did what?" Shay demanded, rising to his feet and anger obscuring the weariness in his face.

"I signed the agreements," Sebastian said again, filling his glass with port and resuming his seat by the Griffin House drawing room hearth. "If you're going to have me repeat everything I say, this is going to be a very long night. And Mr. Rice-Able looks as though he could use some sleep."

The explorer-cum-professor actually looked more stunned than tired, but Sebastian could certainly understand why. From what Shay had said, he'd practically dragged the poor man out of his classroom at Eton.

"Forgive us if we're lagging behind," Eleanor put in, "but I thought the goal was to separate yourself from the Embrys, not to become further entangled with them."

"I have to agree, Melbourne," Valentine added. "When you go to Prinny with this, telling him you've signed up to marry the chit stabs you a bit in your own foot, don't you think?"

"P . . . Prinny?" Rice-Able squeaked.

"I'm not going to Prinny," Sebastian countered, hoping the professor would refrain from fainting.

"You'll need to inform him before you call in Bow Street."

"I'm not calling in Bow Street either, Zach."

"What's up your sleeve then, Melbourne?" Valentine put an arm across his wife's shoulders when it looked as though Eleanor wanted to jump off the settee and strangle her oldest brother.

"I'm going to perpetrate a fraud of my own," Sebastian

said, taking a breath. "And I would appreciate if you would help me do it. All of you."

"Count me in," Valentine said immediately.

The others, though, his siblings especially, didn't look nearly as amenable. He couldn't fault them for hesitating, either. Since he'd been seventeen and inherited the dukedom and the responsibility for raising his sister and two brothers, he'd been handing down proclamations about the proper way to behave and what Griffins did and did not do.

"You?" Shay muttered. "You are going to go against . . . You're Melbourne. You can't."

"I have to do this *because* I'm Melbourne. But more because I'm also Sebastian Griffin. I need to do it this way." He cleared his throat. "You've all said you hoped that someday my . . . methods would come back to haunt me. Perhaps they have. Now please let me know whether you'll assist me or not."

"Um, perhaps I should wait out in the hallway," John Rice-Able muttered, starting to his feet.

Sebastian lifted a hand, motioning him hack to his seat. "Since I am asking for your help as well, I don't intend to keep any of this matter from you."

"If this 'fraud' of yours succeeds," Eleanor said stiffly, clearly not appreciating that he'd had their audience remain, "will it absolve you of your obligation to wed Princess—or whatever she actually is—Josefina?"

"No, it won't. I should say, in fact, that I intend to marry Josefina regardless of whatever else may happen."

"Isn't that taking your sense of duty too far?" Shay suggested.

Sebastian clenched his jaw. Discussing his feelings—he hadn't made a habit of that ever, and especially not over the past four years. And articulating something so . . . delicate-seeming felt careless. "Suffice it to say that my intentions regarding Josefina have little to do with obligation or duty."

"Oh." Eleanor sat forward. "*Oh.*"

"You mean to say that after all this time the chit you finally choose is—"

"Watch your next words very carefully, Zachary," Sebastian murmured, "or you and I will have a serious disagreement."

"Enough of this." Valentine rose and fetched himself a glass of claret. "Rice-Able?"

"No, thank you."

"I'll ignore that, because you look as though you could use it." The marquis filled a second glass with the red liquid and handed it to the professor before he reseated himself. "I want to know what the fraud is. A baby is well and good, but she's fairly easy to trick. I need a challenge."

"Very well. It occurred to me today. Though Josefina is willing to do whatever is necessary to stop the settlers from leaving England, even if it means seeing herself arrested along with her father, that is not an option I will pursue. So we have three goals: Stop the settlement of Costa Habichuela, get the investors and buyers their money back, and keep Josefina from serious trouble."

"Without going to Prinny or to Bow Street." Shay's angry expression grew more thoughtful; he had never been able to resist a good puzzle. "And by using John, here."

"It can't be announcing that Costa Habichuela doesn't exist," Sarala contributed, "because that would involve arrests and injury to Josefina's character."

"You're going to flood Costa Habichuela with Spanish soldiers, aren't you?" Valentine tipped his glass in a toast. "Rather ambitious, but I'm not certain it qualifies as fraudulent."

"Actually, you're quite close, Deverill. I am going to flood Costa Habichuela, but not with soldiers. With water.

A hundred-year flood that wipes out San Saturus and sends any surviving residents fleeing to Belize. All of the good pastureland will be washed into the Atlantic Ocean, the pristine harbor, destroyed."

Valentine laughed. "You are bloody brilliant, Melbourne. You've wasted your skills being benevolent."

"But there is no pastureland," Rice-Able noted, between gulps of claret.

"I absolutely believe your description of the Mosquito Coast, Master Rice-Able. In order to stop a disaster, I will ask you to say that any pastureland is gone. It's not an untruth."

"No, I suppose it's not. Having been there, I understand why it's important to prevent an influx of settlers arriving with the expectation of finding paradise. God, what a tragedy that would be. But inventing inclement weather— the idea does not make me comfortable."

"If Prinny—Prince George—learns that Stephen Embry has both presumed on his friendship and made him look foolish—to be blunt, with the war on the Peninsula, England can't afford to have its monarch look poorly. In addition, Embry will be imprisoned, and he'll have no incentive to reveal where his ill-gotten funds are." And his family would be blamed for any misdeeds, though Sebastian didn't include that in his argument; John Rice-Able didn't care for Embry's daughter.

"You'll be helping to set things right," Sarala said with a sweet smile. "The conditions you describe will be true. The only real falsehood will be the statement that the territory became unliveable recently, rather than informing anyone that it's been that way all along."

"How will I convey this information? I'm the author of a poorly received book. This Embry purports to be the rey of a country."

This would be the tricky part. "You're going to receive

a letter from a friend who witnesses the disaster," Sebastian said, "a friend who forwards his correspondence to the *London Times*. I will see that it's printed."

John Rice-Able actually gave a short chuckle. "I thought I'd lived all my adventures. London in the company of the celebrated Griffin family is the last place I would have expected to find another. Your cause is definitely a worthy one, Your Grace. I am at your service."

Sebastian clapped his hands together as keen relief flooded through him. "Excellent. Shay, Sarala, might I convince you to concoct the letter?"

Charlemagne nodded curtly. "Of course."

That didn't sound very enthusiastic. "Do we have a problem?"

"No, we do not." With a pointed glance at Rice-Able, his brother stood, offering a hand to his wife.

Later, then. "Make the damage apocalyptic."

"Angels will fear to tread on the ground of Costa Habichuela by the time we're finished."

Rice-Able stood, as well. "Perhaps I might be able to lend a hand."

"Shay, come by for breakfast with whatever you've composed," Sebastian called as the trio left the room.

"I'll check my calendar."

"That was a bit chilly," Valentine observed as the front door opened and closed.

"Nell, I need you and Caro to have invitations made for an engagement ball to be held here three nights from now."

"Three nights? That's barely enough time to get the invitations finished, much less distributed," Eleanor protested.

"Hire sufficient people to get it done."

"No."

Sebastian glared at her. "I'm not going to debate this.

I need a crowded gathering under my control where we can discover the news about Costa Habichuela. That is—"

"You control every gathering you attend, Sebastian. And I will not—*not*—allow you to tell yourself that being engaged and getting married is just part of your plan to stop Embry." A tear ran down her face, and she angrily brushed it away.

"Do you think you can keep me from marrying?" he asked, fury clipping his words.

"I only want you to do it for the right blasted reasons," she retorted, her voice shaking with emotion. "So no, I will not help you rush through an engagement ball. Choose another event."

He folded his arms over his chest. Had that been his plan? To make the entire engagement and wedding part of the plot to stop Embry? Josefina would certainly be more likely to go along with it that way. "Zachary, Caro, can we get Anne to pretend that she's being courted by John Rice-Able?"

"Yes," Caroline answered without hesitation.

"Good. That will give him a reason to attend the Tuffley soiree night after next." He faced his sister again. "Does that meet with your approval?"

She lifted her chin. "Does that mean there'll be no engagement ball?"

"There will be," he said, "once I convince Josefina to say yes."

"She turned you down?" Zachary asked skeptically.

"She kicked me, actually. My timing did leave something to be desired."

"Josefina kicked you," Eleanor repeated. At his nod, she pursed her lips. "Perhaps I do like her after all."

"What do we do for the next day and a half?" Valentine finished off his claret and stood. "Are we happy about the match, do we have reservations about the Costa

Habichuela settlement, or should I stay indoors and work on increasing the size of my brood with my wife?"

"Valentine," Nell muttered, shaking her head at him.

"Bringing up the chancy weather in Central America might be a good idea. But don't be too obvious."

"Please. I am a master of subtlety. Come, my dear."

"I'll keep you abreast of events," Sebastian said, handing Caroline to her feet and following the quartet to the door. "And Nell?"

The youngest Griffin sibling faced him, her expression wary. "Yes?"

"Josefina makes me happy."

Eleanor leaned up to kiss him on the cheek. "Then we'd best make your fraud a successful one."

As Josefina finished sewing the green cross on the sleeve of her newest gown, an emerald wonder in silk and lace, she could hear her father and Halloway in his office across the hallway. Both men were laughing, making alternating remarks about the stupid arrogance of the Duke of Melbourne and the rich scent of the ten thousand quid he'd handed over when he'd signed the marriage agreement.

To her father the money meant he'd won—not only had he managed to avoid parting company with any funds, but he'd also added more to his coffer from the very same fool trying to stop him. To her, though, the money meant that Sebastian was serious when he said he wanted to marry her.

"Is something troubling you, *hija*?" her mother asked from the neighboring chair.

"Isn't something troubling you?" she retorted, dropping her stitching onto her lap. "He's gone too far this time. People could die."

Maria Embry lifted a delicately arched eyebrow. "Have you ever lacked for food, or comfort, or an education?"

"No. Of course not." She frowned. "But this is different."

"Your father is a nobleman trapped in a commoner's body. He's only trying to be what he is. A king must have subjects."

"Dead ones?"

"They will have supplies. And you've never been to the Mosquito Coast. Don't be so sure this endeavor is doomed."

"But this . . ." Josefina lowered her voice even though she doubted her father could overhear her in the midst of all his self-congratulations. "He's not just taking money from a bank any longer; he's taking the life savings of families who have less than he began with. Supplies or not, what do you truly think will happen when they arrive at Costa Habichuela?"

"My point is that we can't know," her mother returned in the same cool tone she used for dinner conversation. "And it is your father's business, and none of mine." She looked down at her sewing again. "If you have questions, you should ask him."

"I have. I'm beginning to think he believes all the tales he's been telling. This must stop, Mama."

The older woman glanced toward the half open door. "I don't know how to stop it without destroying him utterly," she murmured. "It's not that I have no compassion for those *pobres desgraciados*; it's just that I have more compassion for my husband." Her fingers paused in their task. "Would you care to tell Melbourne the entire truth? He would look at you differently, and he would certainly find a way to avoid marrying you."

Melbourne knew, and he still looked at her the same way. He still wanted to marry her. While her mother had been wrong about him, however, she certainly spoke the truth where the rest of Society was concerned. They would all loathe her father, be disgusted at the idea that they'd willingly associated with him. Melbourne could keep some of it from touching her, but in return it would touch him.

"I'm going to bed," she said, gathering up her sewing kit and then ringing for Conchita. "And I still wish you would at least suggest that he buy back the land he's sold. No one needs to suffer or die because of his dreams. That is not anything I can be proud of."

She arrived at her bedchamber before Conchita, and deliberately walked over to unlatched the window and push it open. She could ask herself questions about her reasons for wanting to marry Sebastian, but she knew they'd never had much to do with his ability to protect her.

It was more troubling to consider whether she had the same illness as her father, that need to be more lofty than she was. Because she liked the way Sebastian made her feel—precious, valued, exalted.

"No," she muttered, sitting on the edge of the bed. With Harek she'd had much the same opportunity for a title and legitimate social elevation. She might have taken it, too, before Sebastian had surprised her in this very room. But the way she felt when she imagined a life with Harek—it was nothing close to the shivers of dread and delight just setting eyes on Sebastian gave her.

And he *needed* her, which left her not as uncomfortable as it had initially, but rather humbled. He found her necessary not because she was a princess or a great heiress or good at convincing people to part with their money, but for something she couldn't quite put words to. When they'd first met she'd seen his aloneness, heard it in his aloof, cool voice. Over the past days that loneliness seemed to have left him, and she thought she was the reason for it. It was a heady, powerful, joyous feeling—one she'd never thought to have in her life, and one she didn't want to give up. Ever.

She looked toward the window again, her heart twisting. She didn't want him to have to climb through windows and leave before dawn; she wanted him to be there, and to know that he was there forever. Not because of what she claimed to be, but because of who she was. And because in his company she liked who she was better than she ever had before.

A few more days. Just a few more days and she would know whether she had earned the life she wanted with Sebastian, or whether she needed to flee into the night, alone.

Chapter 21

"Good morning, Your Grace," Stanton said, as Sebastian came downstairs.

"Good morning. Is my daughter awake?"

"She is in the breakfast room."

"Thank you. I'm only in for family and the Costa Habichuela party." He turned down the hallway.

"Very good, Your Grace. Lord Charlemagne arrived five minutes ago. He is in with Lady Peep."

Ah, Shay. Sebastian took a breath. He hadn't wanted a fight this morning, feeling more inclined to smile idiotically for no reason at all, but he wouldn't back away from a quarrel, either. For a man of four-and-thirty who'd spent half his life governing the most powerful country in the world, the way he craved being around Josefina was just . . . pitiful. "We'll need some privacy."

"I shall see to it."

Sebastian pushed open the breakfast room door. "Good morning."

Peep ran forward, grabbing his hands to drag him

toward his seat at the head of the table. "You need to talk to Uncle Shay," she said, releasing him to pull out his heavy chair.

Charlemagne sat in his old place just on the right, while Penelope's half-consumed breakfast lay across from that. "Yes, I know I do," Sebastian answered. "I thought he and I might take a walk in the garden while you finish your break—"

"It can't wait that long," his daughter interrupted. "Uncle Shay, tell Papa what you told me."

Shay's dour expression tightened. "Peep, I wasn't—"

She held out her hand, gesturing for him to stop. "*I* will tell you. Uncle Shay says I *can* be a princess." The seven-year-old put a hand over her heart.

Sebastian lifted an eyebrow. "He does, does he?"

"Yes. He said that if you marry Princess Josefina, then I may be a princess if I want to, because everyone in her family can be whatever they want to be. And when you marry her, I will be part of her family!"

His amusement at Peep's conclusions vanishing as he heard the reason for it, Sebastian scarcely noted Stanton's brief appearance followed by the exit of Tom and Harry, the two footmen. "I don't believe that is precisely what your uncle meant, my dear," he said in the calmest voice he could muster.

She pinned Shay with a suspicious gaze. "Isn't it?" she demanded.

"In actuality," Sebastian cut in before his brother could make matters worse by trying to explain the fiasco logically, "I believe what Uncle Shay meant was that upon her marriage, Josefina will no longer use her honorary title of princess. She will be known as the Duchess of Melbourne."

"Like Mama."

A muscle in his cheek jumped. "Yes, like Mama."

Shay pushed to his feet. "Care to take that walk now?"

He resisted the urge to clear his throat. "Yes. We'll be back in a few minutes, Peep."

"Take your time. I'm enjoying this peach. Is Uncle Zach coming by, too? Because if he is, I'm going to hide the rest of the peaches."

"No, I'm not expecting him, my sweet. Your peaches are safe." With that, Sebastian strode down the hallway and out the front door, Shay on his heels. Halfway to the stables, his brother dropped back.

"I'm not going to make this a foot race, Melbourne," he said, stopping.

Sebastian turned on his heel. "Whatever your reservations about this situation with the Embrys, you are not to discuss it with my daughter. Is that clear?"

"I don't call it a 'situation,'" Charlemagne retorted. "I call it you going stark raving mad and ordering everyone to see nothing out of the ordinary about it. You are helping to perpetuate a fraud against England, dammit."

"Only so I can end it," Sebastian muttered tightly. "What precisely about this 'situation' makes me a lunatic?"

"You need me to tell you?"

"Yes, I do."

"Fine." Shay jabbed the toe of his boot into the gravel. "Aside from the insanity of thinking you can single-handedly manage to protect everyone from a fraud of this magnitude and save the chit from harm, you've spent four years mourning Charlotte."

Irritation bit into him. "I am *not* going to discuss—"

"You've known this woman for less than a month," Shay interrupted. "And you expect me to believe that your sudden desire to marry her has nothing to do with the circumstances of her father and this fiasco?"

Whether that had been true at the beginning or not, it was now. "Yes."

"I see. So when did you decide she was the one to re-place Charlotte?"

"She's not replacing anyone," Sebastian snapped. "Charlotte and I were cheated, and I mourn her. I will miss her for the rest of my life. I never looked for anyone else, and I certainly never expected to find anyone, but I did. The moment I set eyes on her."

"Sebast—"

"I'm not finished," he countered. "Would I be marrying her if she hadn't announced it first? I don't know. Probably not, mainly because of the reaction of people like you."

"That's a sharp knife you just stuck me with," Shay muttered, his eyes squinted against the midmorning sun. "My concern is your . . . heightened sense of honor, Sebastian. I don't want to see you trapped because of it."

"Actually, I feel . . . uncaged. Valentine says the family's racked up enough good credit that I can spend some of it if I like. And so I am." He gave a brief smile, then sobered again. "I suppose what I'm trying to say is that my heart didn't die with Charlotte, which is surprising to me, because I thought it had. And at the moment it seems to be directing the proceedings." Sebastian gazed steadily at his younger brother. "Do you have a problem with that?"

"I have reservations." Charlemagne frowned. "You didn't talk with Josefina about your plan to flood Costa Habi-chuela, did you?"

"No," he returned reluctantly.

"Strategy, or because you know she could still bring us down with one word of warning to the rey?"

"Strategy. I trust her." He probably shouldn't, and his belief in her was something he couldn't even articulate, but it was there, and he chose not to question it.

"Then I'll be worried enough for the both of us."

Slowly Sebastian nodded. "I'll accept that. Did you bring the letter?"

Shay pulled a folded piece of paper from his pocket. "I think we covered all the points. Rice-Able's quite a hand at this, I have to say. And now he's talking about taking a sabbatical and going exploring again."

"If this works, I'll fund his expeditions for the remainder of his life. Let's take a look."

"Look!" Stephen Embry ordered, a broad smile on his face. He shoved Josefina's breakfast plate aside and tossed down a newspaper in its place.

"What am I looking at?" she asked, gazing at the headlines. Tariffs, the number of dead in the latest battle on the Peninsula, grain riots in York—none of it affected her directly. Oddly, though, it felt like it did—because it affected Sebastian.

"Page three," he said, reaching over her shoulder to turn the page when she didn't react quickly enough. He jabbed his finger at the large square on the left. "There."

"Oh." Her heart stopped and then resumed in a flurry of rapid beats.

"That's all you have to say? 'Oh'? Read it aloud. I want to hear it."

She cleared her throat. " 'The Griffin family of Devonshire is pleased to announce the engagement of its patriarch, Sebastian, the Duke of Melbourne, to Josefina Embry, Royal Princess of Costa Habichuela. The lovely Josefina is the only child and heir of Stephen and Maria Embry, Rey and Queen of Costa Habichuela. The couple's engagement ball will be announced shortly.' "

"Ha, ha!" the rey laughed, snatching the newspaper back and rereading the announcement. "I would have put in a bit more about Costa Habichuela and how we're selling plots of land, but it is nicely set off by the border and the Griffin coat of arms. Not a bit shabby."

"You didn't place the announcement?" Josefina asked,

her voice not quite as even as she would have liked. Heavens, it was in *print*. For anyone to see.

"I would have, if it hadn't appeared today. You may have tricked Melbourne into this, but I have to say, I'm impressed. He'll make a good ally. And son-in-law."

Sebastian had placed the announcement. Of course propriety required that certain customs be observed, but propriety hadn't dictated that she be described as "the lovely" anything. Apparently he wanted the rest of London to know that this was not simply a politically or socially motivated alliance. He liked her.

And she liked him. *Oh, what was she doing?* Over her shoulder Grimm and one of the footmen were busily removing breakfast foods from the sideboard. "Grimm, that will be all for now, thank you."

The butler bowed. "Your Majesty, Your Highness." In a second she and her father were alone in the breakfast room.

The rey popped a grape into his mouth, his attention still on the newspaper. "Glorious. Glorious," he chuckled.

"Father—Papa—I need to ask you a question," Josefina said, keeping her voice low and mindful of his warnings about being overheard.

"What is it, my sweet?"

"As you said, Melbourne can make us a very good ally," she began, choosing her words and her tone with care. "We can be comfortable for life."

"We can and will be, you mean. I've left him no choice, and I'll never put myself in the position of being dictated to or controlled by him."

The smug superiority in his voice used to make her feel the same. Now it made her flinch. "Explain to me, then, why you have to intentionally anger him by sending off shiploads of people for whom he feels responsible. We don't need that income or that potential trouble any longer."

"I think *I* can decide what we do or don't need. And those shiploads of people have put sixty thousand quid into my pocket thus far. That's six years worth of Melbourne's charity."

"But he would give you more if he trusted you."

Slowly he folded the newspaper. "I've fought and scratched my entire life," he finally said. "Don't fling Melbourne in my face as some paragon of virtue. He was born into wealth and status. Do you think he's ever suffered so much as a poor night's sleep in his life?" He took a breath. "It's easy to have principles when nothing challenges them."

Actually she thought Sebastian had his share of sleepless nights, completely aside from the death of his wife. How could he not, when so many people relied on him and when he took so much of what happened to any of them so personally? She'd heard what he'd done for those people at the Abbey, feeding them and providing them with supplies to replant their blighted wheat, and they didn't even live on his land. "You're not the only one who's fought for everything you have."

"You, you mean?" He lifted an eyebrow, an imitation of what he'd seen Sebastian do. "You have no idea what—"

"Not me," she countered quickly. "I know how hard you've worked to see that I was given a privileged upbringing. I'm talking about all those people who've bought land and passage to Costa Habichuela. Most of them just want the opportunity for a new life—like you did."

"Not like me," he returned, a sneer entering his tone. "I never trusted anything but my own wits and other peoples' greed. If those fools choose to spend their last shilling on something that sounds far too good to be true, I can only hope they aren't overly surprised when it turns out to be exactly that."

"Papa, that's awful. We only used to take money from those who could afford the loss."

"Someone's bound to take advantage of such gullibility. It might as well be me." He sat forward, taking her hand. "And you. I couldn't have done this without you, Josefina. I'm just an old soldier at heart. You, you're a lady. A lady who will become a duchess in less than a month."

A tremble ran up her arms. She and Sebastian, together until death did them part. Rapture. Heaven and hell at the same time—the thought of them together was what made it so difficult to stand against her father. If she simply went along with his plan, she would gain precisely what she'd come to want most in the world.

"Tell me this, then," she forced herself to continue. "Eventually some kind of word will get back from Costa Habichuela that it's not a paradise, that it's not even habitable. Are we here in England when this happens? Because Melbourne *is* England, and I can't see him fleeing to reside in the Americas somewhere. He will anchor us here."

"Not if he's dead."

All of the blood left her face. "*What?*" she gasped, shooting to her feet.

He gave a laugh that sounded forced. "I'm just bamming you, darling. Of course Melbourne will travel with us, because it will be in his best interest to do so. After all, once the Embrys and the Griffins are united, our fate becomes his."

Josefina still couldn't breathe. For God's sake, he'd nearly killed Sebastian once for threatening to expose the fraud. She thought the marriage announcement had saved the duke, but apparently he'd only been granted a stay of execution. If Sebastian died—and her throat closed to think of it—she would still keep the title of Duchess of Melbourne. That might even work better for her father's schemes than having a troublesome and influential son-

in-law about. *Good God*. That had probably been his original plan, from the moment he'd asked Prinny to introduce
them to Melbourne.

"Josefina?"

She blinked, forcing air into her lungs. "You are not a
killer," she whispered.

He shrugged. "I've killed in the name of half a dozen
countries and causes. If it came to choosing between my
family and Melbourne, my duty falls to protecting my
family."

"No." Slowly she backed away from the table. "I am
grateful for all that you've given me, but once I marry Sebastian, we part company. I don't wish to be involved with
this fraud any longer."

The rey stood, his expression hardening and his hands
clenching. "You're an Embry, my dear. When people find
out about Costa Habichuela, as you've assumed they will,
do you think that being the Duchess of Melbourne will
protect you? That you can sit in your grand house and escape all the talk and accusations? You're part of this for as
long as I say you are. And Melbourne is, as well, until I
decide he's not." Abruptly his face relaxed and he smiled
again, the charming rey everyone wanted to invite into
their homes. "Go change into something appropriate for a
carriage ride. We're going to take a turn about Hyde Park
in Branbury's barouche. I want the bride-to-be seen."

Josefina fled the breakfast room, hurried up the stairs,
and ran to her bedchamber. With the sound of her slammed
door still echoing, she bent over her wash basin and vom-
ited up her breakfast.

"What have I done?" she muttered, sinking to the floor.
Tears ran down her face and splashed onto her arms.

If Sebastian hadn't tempted her so, if Harck had been
the one to stay about, she might have been able to do it.
She might have been able to remain the woman who was

only after what she thought she deserved. And Harek probably would have gone along with it, so long as he could live comfortably and shoot animals every so often.

But she wasn't that woman any longer. She didn't particularly like that woman. She liked the one she'd become since she'd kissed Sebastian, since she'd met someone who clearly valued her for who she was rather than what advantage she might bring him. And that had to be true, because being associated with her was to Sebastian's *dis*advantage in every way she could imagine.

And she was still so, so selfish, because she wanted him anyway. A sob broke from her chest, followed by another, and another. She curled up on the floor of her borrowed bedchamber and wept.

Whichever way she turned, she would bring Sebastian derision and ruin, and even death. If she called off the wedding there would be a huge scandal, and her father would have no reason to think that Sebastian would keep his silence about what he knew. If she married him, he would be forced into a life of fraud and deception, which would destroy him, or he would refuse to cooperate—and her father would kill him.

"Your Highness?" Conchita's voice came from the doorway as the door quietly closed behind her. "What's happened? Are you ill? Your Highness? Miss Josefina? What's wrong?" The maid knelt beside her.

Josefina lifted her head. "Conchita, please don't say anything about this," she managed, struggling to sit up. "I'm just . . . just overwhelmed."

"Of course you are. An engagement to a duke, a wedding, the people all wanting a send-off from their beloved princess before they sail to Costa Habichuela, all of the balls and parties spent getting support for your papa—this is a success because of you, Your Highness. The weight on your shoulders would crush most men, I think."

"Yes, yes, that's it," Josefina stammered, letting the servant help her to her feet. "Please say nothing; I don't want to worry my mother and father."

"I won't say a word. Let's get you pretty again for your drive."

"Yes," Josefina repeated absently, her mind beginning to race. Conchita was correct; *she* was the keystone to this plan of her father's. Remove the keystone and there would be no union between the Embrys and the Griffins. Sebastian knew to be wary of her father now, and if she simply . . . vanished rather than declaring that she wouldn't marry him, people might speculate, but it would be about her and not about him.

It could work. It would work. So she would go driving with her father as he planned, and then tomorrow she would be gone. Without the keystone, the building could collapse, and the bricks fall where they would. She would be miserable, but she deserved nothing less. And the Duke of Melbourne would be free to do whatever he needed to stop this disaster from happening.

Chapter 22

"Do you have any idea what time it is?" Valentine, the Marquis of Deverill, grunted as he half-stumbled down his stairs.

"Seven o'clock," Sebastian returned with a brief grin. "In the morning."

"And people used to say *I* was the devil himself. They had it wrong, obviously, because only Beelzebub would pull a contented husband and father out of his nice, warm bed at this bloody hour of the morning."

The Corbett House butler pulled open the front door as Valentine, still complaining about being forced to rise, reached the foyer. Sebastian waited, arms folded, while Valentine pulled on his greatcoat and gloves. Excitement and anticipation ran just beneath his skin, but he refused to pace. Whether he could remember the last time he'd felt . . . hope—not just for his daughter or his family, but for himself—or not, he had no intention of kicking up his heels and laughing. It wasn't dignified.

"I'll return Lord Deverill to the house in an hour or so,

Hobbes," he said, gesturing Valentine to lead the way outside, mostly because he wasn't certain the marquis would follow if given a choice.

"Very good, Your Grace." With a quickly stifled smile the butler closed the front door on them.

Green stood in the drive, holding the reins of his own horse as well as those of Merlin and Iago. "Good morning for a ride, my lord," he said, nodding at Deverill.

"Bastard," Valentine muttered. "Where the devil are we going?"

"For a ride. The morning air always helps me clear my head."

"It will probably kill me," his friend noted dourly. "You do this every morning?" he continued dubiously, as he swung up on his bad-tempered bay.

"Yes. And you'll be happy to know that I delayed an hour before coming to get you."

"We're not riding off to rescue villagers this morning, are we?"

"It's not on my calendar, but no promises."

They clattered down the drive, turning in the direction of Hyde Park. At after seven o'clock the streets were already filling with milk wagons and vendor carts, but the members of the nobility who wouldn't hesitate about approaching him were thankfully still mostly to bed. A certain young lady was probably still asleep as well, her thick black hair spread wildly across the pillows and her long lashes caressing her soft cheeks.

"What's wrong with you?" Valentine asked abruptly.

"Nothing. Why do you ask?"

"Because you're grinning like a lunatic. It frightens me."

Sebastian tamped down his expression. "As I told you, I like to ride in the mornings."

"That's not it." The marquis eyed him. "You're happy, aren't you?"

Valentine was exceptionally aware of his surroundings and the people in them, but even so Sebastian hadn't realized he was being that obvious. "Yes, you've guessed it," he countered, attempting to sound sarcastic. "With a nation to flood, a fraud to stop, and a wedding I never intended, why shouldn't I be ecstatic?"

The marquis narrowed his suspicious green eyes. "That's a cart of turnips," he stated. "You're ready to burst into song at any moment." His expression eased into the fond, amused one he generally reserved for Eleanor and their daughter, Rose. "Having been smacked squarely between the eyes by Cupid's arrow, myself, I recognize the symptoms, Seb. And I'm happy for you. Truly. I, ah, I'd actually begun to wonder what you would do with yourself after you finished seeing Nell and your brothers married off."

"Truthfully," Sebastian said slowly, aware that this was a conversation he wouldn't have tolerated a year ago, "I had no idea, myself. Running the estates and businesses and looking after my duties to the government—it's enough to fill a day." He cleared his throat. "Or so I told myself. I didn't expect this, you know."

"I know. I . . . You have to admire a chit who can set the Duke of Melbourne back on his heels." He looked around. "Speaking of whom, is it my imagination, or are we heading in her direction?"

Damnation. Perhaps Zachary would have been a better riding companion this morning. All he needed to do was mention cattle or biscuits, and they could ride all the way to Brighton without Zach noticing. "I thought to ride by and make certain everything looks in order. We have a play beginning this evening, and the king and his conscience have to be in attendance and unaware for it to succeed."

As they turned the corner, Sebastian pulled Merlin to

an abrupt halt. A lithe figure in a plain green walking dress darted across the street and into a waiting hack. The heavy-looking portmanteau in her hands bumped against the side of the coach as she hauled it inside with her.

"Was that—"

"Yes, it was."

He looked toward Colonel Branbury's house. The only movement came from an upstairs curtain lazily stirring in the morning breeze. She'd left her window open. Had that been meant for him last night, or had she climbed down the trellis this morning?

"What does this mean?"

"I don't know. She was alone." Up in front of them the hack turned right onto another street—in the opposite direction of Griffin House. She wasn't coming to see him.

"Green," he barked, turning in the saddle to face his groom, "stay here and watch the house. If you see any unusual activity, report it to Lord Deverill. He'll be back at Corbett House."

"And where will you be?" Valentine asked, lifting an eyebrow.

"Behind that hack."

"Seb—perhaps Green should do that."

"*I'm* doing that. You make certain everything's set for tonight. This play opens whether I'm in attendance for the premiere or not." Every muscle wanted to race after the vanished hack, but again there was more to consider than just him. "Tell me you'll see to it, Valentine."

"Yes, I will bloody see to it." The marquis cursed, Iago picking up his master's mood and fidgeting beneath him. "Are you armed?"

"I have a pistol."

Valentine pulled a weapon from his own pocket. "Take this one, too," he said, handing it over. "And be careful, Sebastian."

He tucked the second pistol into his other coat pocket. "I will be."

With a kick of his heels he sent Merlin galloping down the street after the hack. It could be nothing; perhaps she'd slipped out to purchase something for her wedding trousseau. But the knot in his gut said otherwise. Josefina had never to his knowledge done anything but the unexpected.

And if his bride-to-be was fleeing her home, luggage in hand, he meant to know why. And then he meant to stop her.

"And you just let him go?" Eleanor demanded, hands on her hips and her expression highly annoyed.

"What the devil was I supposed to do, throw him off his horse and sit on him? I came back here and I told you. I think that's very responsible of me." Valentine flung his gloves down on the breakfast table and walked over to pick Rose up from her little chair. That would keep Nell from punching him, at any rate. Chits and their protectiveness. He'd had no idea they could be so fierce, not just in defense of their children, but of their loved ones.

"Valentine."

"If I'd had my druthers I would have ridden off with Sebastian and sent Green back here to inform you, but I was asked to do otherwise."

"That's not the point."

"It *is* the point. I assume the rey will realize that his daughter is missing. It's not going to be easy to disguise the fact that Melbourne's gone, too, particularly when we need everyone to appear at the Tuffley soiree tonight at the right moment. If the Embrys suspect an elopement, they may ride for Scotland."

"If they weren't behind Josefina's flight in the first place." She scowled again. "Damnation. We don't even know if we should provide an excuse for her absence, or if we should remain ignorant of it."

"Hence my wanting to be elsewhere." While Rose pulled at the knot of his cravat, Valentine gazed at his wife. "Any ideas?"

"I suppose we wait to see how the Embrys react. In the meantime, we have a few things left to do for tonight. The letter needs to get to the newspaper, but I don't know who Sebastian's source might be. If it gets into the wrong hands, the news will spread before we're ready, or not at all."

"I can take care of that." Newspaper sources were, after all, some of the best to have when one enjoyed having advance knowledge of certain people and events. That hobby continued to serve him well, though now he found it more amusing than useful.

"I'll go to Griffin House and collect Peep. Since we don't know where her father's gone, it's probably better if no one's home at all." Eleanor held out her arms, and Valentine handed Rose over to her. "Will you inform my brothers?"

With a swift smile Valentine leaned down and gave her a soft, lingering kiss. "I don't know what I was thinking when I said I was glad not to have any family," he said quietly, kissing her again. "This is the most fun I've ever had."

She grabbed his lapel with her free hand before he could turn away. "You don't regret any of this, do you?" she whispered, her face concerned.

He faced her, gazing into her light gray eyes. "Eleanor, never ask me that again," he returned sharply. "You and Rose are the reason I breathe." He kissed her once more, feather-light. "I love you. And I love your damned family."

"I love you," she returned, smiling and a little teary-eyed.

"Go fetch Peep. I'll be back with reinforcements." He

brushed his fingers through Rose's silky dark hair. "And tonight I want to discuss making another one of these."

Her smile deepened, lighting her eyes. "I look forward to that conversation."

The hack was the worst sprung vehicle Josefina had ridden in since she'd become a princess. She wouldn't be surprised to find her bottom bruised before she even reached the inn where the mail coach stopped.

Finally they jolted to a halt and the driver leaned down to swing open the door. "The Bull and Mouth, Miss. That'll be three shillings."

She climbed out, dragging the heavy portmanteau with her. Pulling three shillings from her reticule, she handed them up. Without even bothering to tip his hat at her, the driver guided the hack back into the street.

The morning mail coach already stood in the crowded Bull and Mouth courtyard. Josefina tugged the brim of her bonnet forward to obscure her face, then squared her shoulders and walked up to the inn door.

"That's a heavy-looking bag there, my light o'love," one of a pair of rough-looking men there said with a grin. "Shall I hold it for you?"

"Thank you, no," she said firmly, shouldering past them.

"Ooh, 'thank you, no', she says," the second one chortled. "Like a real lady."

"Pardon me, Your Majesty," the first man took up, giving her a deep bow.

If she'd had her usual entourage of Conchita and Lieutenant May with her, she would have told the two men her opinion of their manners. As matters were, however, she needed to keep her mouth shut. It wouldn't do for anyone to go about referring to her as royalty, even in jest.

They allowed her through the door, and she made her way past the crowd inside the inn to the bar. She hoped all of the people there weren't looking for seats on the mail stage, or she would be stuck waiting for the next one.

"What can I get you, miss?" a young girl of fifteen or sixteen asked her.

"Where do I purchase a seat on the mail stage?" she asked.

"The fellow at the bar with the red neckcloth," the girl said, and moved on to the next arrival.

Sending up a swift prayer, Josefina found the tall, bony man who wore a blue coat and a red neckcloth that looked like it had seen better days. "Excuse me," she said.

He faced her, taking a blatant moment to look her over from head to toe. "What can Red Jim do for you, my pretty bird of paradise?"

He was the second man in a row to refer to her as a whore. She clenched her jaw. "I would like to purchase passage on the morning stage," she said.

"No room left," he returned, giving her another look before he resumed his conversation.

Flexing her fingers, she tapped him on the shoulder. "None at all? My aunt is very ill, and I need to get to York without delay."

"I'm sorry, miss, but the only seat left is up on top. Only men up there today. Rough sorts."

"I'll take it," she said, setting her portmanteau at her feet and opening her reticule. "How much to get me to York?"

"That's three quid, miss, and two days sitting out in the weather. It ain't a pleasant way to travel."

"I'll risk it." Beginning to wonder whether she should have taken more money from her father's funds, she counted out the fee and handed it over. She told herself that she'd borrowed part of the ten thousand pounds Sebastian had given in return for her hand. He could afford the loss.

As soon as she thought of him, she wanted to cry again. If she'd been able to leave him a note she would have done so, but she hadn't dared. She couldn't take the chance that her father would read it.

Red Jim opened up a ledger book and took a square piece of paper from his pocket. Scribbling something on it with a pencil stub that he tucked back behind his ear, he gave her the paper. "The stage boards in the courtyard, in fifteen minutes. No refunds."

"Thank you."

He ignored her, going back to his conversation once more. *Fifteen minutes.* It seemed like both far too long and far too short a time to wait. Conchita had been instructed not to wake her until ten o'clock this morning, so she should be better than two hours out of London before anyone realized she was missing. Even then, her father would have no idea what to do or where she might have gone.

If he told anyone she'd gone missing, the publicity could hurt his land sale efforts. More likely he would invent a reason that she had to sail home to Costa Habichuela, and he would have some of Captain Morton's men look for her in secret.

Sebastian could be a bigger problem. He wouldn't keep silent to help her father's cause, but he might choose to do so to minimize a scandal. She had intentionally left no clues, so he could proceed however he wished. If the wedding truly had been nothing more than the most efficient way to stop her father, then Sebastian could only be relieved. If he'd meant to marry her because he . . . because . . .

Stop it, she ordered herself. She could wallow in self-pity once she was seated on the coach headed north. Until then, she needed to pay attention to what she was doing and saying, even where she was looking.

She picked up the portmanteau and left the inn. The two men by the door were gone, but the courtyard still teemed with horses, passengers, and the people seeing them off and taking the delivered mail. Picking a spot along the wall where she could see the horses being harnessed and busy Aldersgate Street beyond, she adjusted her bonnet again and waited.

A few people looked at her, but from the comments she could overhear they seemed curious mostly because she was a young woman traveling alone. She had her story to explain that, and it didn't trouble her. As for those like the two men by the door, she had the loaded pistol she'd taken from her bed stand. She was after all a soldier's daughter. However refined her education, she knew how to take care of herself.

A tear ran unbidden down her left cheek, and she swiftly wiped it away. When she considered it, by leaving London she was actually doing nothing more than returning herself to the social position where she should have been all along. Her mother had been a lady of quality, a viceroy's daughter, and her father an officer. She was supposed to be a governess at worst, a parson's or minor landowner's wife at best. Marriage—that was not going to happen now, not ever. But a princess, a duchess? The Duchess of Melbourne, yet? Nonsense. Ridiculous, fairytale stupidity. From today on she would be real. Nothing more, and nothing less.

"Tickets, please!" Red Jim stood up on a wooden box in front of the mail coach's door and repeated his bellow. "Tickets!"

She joined the group who hurried forward. Two women and one man took seats inside the substantial vehicle while Red Jim took her ticket and made a note in his ledger book. "Samuel, help the girl aboard," he called. "First floor, if you please."

"Aye."

One of the grooms took her portmanteau and tied it with the others being loaded at the rear of the coach. The other, Samuel, she assumed, took her around the waist and lifted her skyward. She yelped as the driver grabbed her from above and perched her on one of the pair of thinly padded benches facing one another on the roof. Quickly she gathered her wits and moved to the forward-sitting seat. She had no desire to face backward for two days.

A scrawny man with a missing front tooth clambered up to sit beside her. "Mornin', love," he said with a broad smile. As he adjusted his coat she caught a whiff of sheep smell.

Below, Samuel helped an elderly woman and her younger female companion inside the coach, while the two men from the inn doorway climbed up the outside of the vehicle to sit opposite her. *Splendid.* "Well, we'll have a pretty view, won't we, Johnny?" the bulkier one drawled.

"Aye, Tim. Hello again, Your Majesty."

Swiftly she weighed her options before she responded. If they were journeying all the way to York they might better serve as allies. "I prefer Miss Grimm," she said with a shy nod. Colonel Branbury's butler would never know she'd borrowed his name. "I apologize if I was rude before; I'm hoping to take a governess position in York, where my aunt is convalescing, and I suppose I'm a bit . . . nervous about it."

"No worries, love. We'll put in a good word for ya, eh, Tim?"

"That's right, Johnny."

The sheep-smelling man didn't offer his name, but grinned in apparent agreement. Well, it could be worse, she supposed. She charmed people for her father all the time. And with two days to sit together, by the time they reached York there was no telling how much helpful information she might learn.

The coach lurched into motion and rolled out of the courtyard. The sheep man waved at someone, but she and apparently Johnny and Tim had no one to bid farewell to. In twenty minutes they'd reached the outskirts of London, and travel along the crowded road became a shade easier.

As they rolled northward she slowly began to relax. She'd made it. No one would guess where she'd gone. Without a note to go by, her parents would probably think she'd returned to Jamaica and the few friends she had there. Sebastian—what would he think? She had no idea. Chances were that he wouldn't look for her at all.

"You been to York before, Miss Grimm?" sheep man asked after better than an hour on the road.

"No. My aunt works for a family that took a house up there. Until now we've been corresponding."

Tim and Johnny had been muttering to each other for the past several miles. Since it didn't seem to be about her, she didn't pay them much attention. Instead she let her mind wander to what plan she would have to conjure if it turned out that she was carrying Sebastian's child. No one would hire an unmarried woman with a baby; she would have to be a widow, she supposed. The alternative would be to give the infant up, and she would never, ever do that. It would be all she ever had of Sebastian.

"—telling you, Tim, I've seen him before. He's a lord or something."

"Oh, aye, Johnny. A lord riding along in the dust behind the mail coach."

"Maybe he forgot to frank a letter."

Both men laughed. Suddenly alert, Josefina watched them. Their gaze was past her, looking back along the road in the direction of London. Every fiber of her wanted to turn around and see what they were talking about—who they were talking about. But neither could she afford to raise any unnecessary suspicion. No one—including her—had any reason to connect a lone, apparently well-dressed man with her.

"I'm just saying," Johnny continued, "he looks familiar. Like one of them cabinet ministers of Prinny's or something."

"Where've you seen a cabinet minister?"

"I took a horse down to Tattersall's last year for Sir William. All the dashers was there. Him, too, I think."

Josefina clenched her hands into her dress. Oh, for heaven's sake, one look and she could relax again. But if it *was* some cabinet minister, he might recognize her. She closed her eyes, trying to steady her breathing. No cabinet minister, no nobleman, would expect to see Princess Josefina Embry riding on the top of the north-bound mail stage.

With a last deep breath she turned her head and looked over her shoulder. Fifty yards behind the coach and easily keeping pace with the lumbering vehicle rode a lean, dark-haired man. Her heart stopped.

It wasn't a cabinet minister. It was the Duke of Melbourne. And he looked right back at her.

"Oh, dear."

Chapter 23

"You know who that fellow is, Miss Grimm?" Tim asked.

Swiftly Josefina faced forward again. What had she done wrong? How had she given her plan away? She hadn't told a soul, for heaven's sake. And why the devil was he just following her, instead of storming the coach? All three men seated with her were looking from her to Sebastian in a blatantly curious fashion, and she gulped a breath. "What is our next stop?" she asked, her voice wobbling.

"Biggleswade," sheep man answered promptly. "Near an hour from here."

"You think that bloke means to follow the coach all the way to Biggleswade?" Johnny gazed at their pursuer again.

She couldn't see Sebastian giving up and turning around, when he'd clearly been behind them since London. "I think he might," she conceded.

"So who is he?"

"He make some sort of trouble for you, Miss Grimm?"

Apparently the two men who'd been ready to steal her luggage earlier were now her staunch defenders. For a brief moment she considered it. But even if they did manage to stop Melbourne's pursuit, he now knew she was heading north. For a shilling or two Red Jim would undoubtedly be happy to reveal that she'd purchased passage to York. Chances were, he already had. Aside from that, she had no wish to see Sebastian pummeled.

"I don't suppose one of you would be willing to marry me," she muttered, twisting to look behind her again. He hadn't fallen back, nor had he moved any closer. He was torturing her, damn it all, trying to force her to make the next move.

"I already have a wife, miss," sheep man offered. "Bess has a temper, but she's a good lass for all that."

"He wants to marry you?"

"It's very complicated, Johnny, but yes, he says he wants to marry me."

"He done you poorly, then?"

"No. I'm afraid I'll do him poorly." She already had. "As I said, it's very complicated."

"Aye, it sounds a mess." Johnny elbowed Tim in the ribs, and the two of them began muttering to one another again.

Josefina sank lower onto the hard seat. And she'd thought the hack had been a rough ride. So much for her grand plan. All she could hope for now was that if given enough time to follow her, Sebastian would realize how much easier it would make everything if he simply turned around. Failing that, she supposed she could wait until they reached Biggleswade and attempt to explain it to him—though the thought of speaking with him again made her tremble. And then there was the third alternative, that he would tire of playing his waiting game and stop the stage.

"You know how to darn stockings and such?" Tim

asked abruptly, eyeing her hands as though looking for callouses or something.

"What? Of course I know how."

"Then I reckon I'll take you. I could stand to have a hot meal waiting for me when I come home. And you're pretty enough."

Oh, good God. "Tim, I'm grateful for your kindness, but—"

"Willie, lad," Tim interrupted, turning to nudge the driver in the back, "stop this hack."

"I ain't stoppin' every time you need to take a piss."

"I'm gettin' married. Just need to tell the lady's other fella to get himself back to London before he gets hurt."

Willie guffawed, then turned around to see the rider behind them. "Hell, I can't miss this," he said, and hauled on the reins. "Whoa, lads. Whoa, there."

Blast it all. "Perhaps we should continue on," Josefina urged, her voice squeaking.

"Na. I know his kind. Soft-handed dandy. I'll bloody 'is nose a bit, and he'll turn tail. So what's your given name, girl?"

Josefina flung up her hands. "Mabel."

The coach rolled to a halt, and Sebastian drew even with them. He was surprised; he could have ridden them down an hour ago, or stopped her before she ever climbed aboard. It seemed more important to discover what she intended to do rather than to impose his own will on events. Hopefully the stop signaled that Josefina had come to her senses and realized that whatever she was up to wouldn't succeed.

"Hello," he said, looking up at her.

"Hello yourself, mate." one of the large men seated opposite her returned. "You got no business following us, so go on home."

Sebastian kept his gaze on Josefina. "A friend of yours?" he asked her.

"Me and Mabel is to be married. So you get yourself back to London, old rip."

She rolled her eyes, giving a slight shake of her head. *Mabel.* Not Princess Josefina. "Mabel can't be marrying you, because she's marrying me," he stated, crossing his wrists over the pommel of the saddle.

"Sebastian, go home," she finally said, her voice unsteady. "I know what I'm doing."

"Marrying . . . What's your name, my good man?"

"Tim. Timothy Boots."

"Marrying Mr. Boots is your solution to our dilemma?" he continued.

"That's right, me rum cove. Me and Mabel Grimm. Don't make me come down there and wallop you."

"Well, sir, I think you will have to come down here and wallop me, because otherwise Miss . . . Grimm is leaving with me."

"Sebastian, don't. This is ridiculous."

"I agree." In the coach everyone was hanging out the window, listening to every word being spoken. Whatever happened, people would hear of it. Everyone would hear of it. And he didn't give a damn. "Why don't you explain to me what you're doing sitting on the roof of the mail coach bound for York?"

"I'm removing myself from the equation," she returned. "No one will have me to use for leverage. I won't need protecting from anything, because I won't be there."

Mr. Boots climbed over the edge of the roof, balanced on one of the wheels, and then dropped to the ground. "That's right. She won't be there."

Blowing out his breath, Sebastian dismounted and led Merlin to the coach, where he looped the reins through the left front wheel spokes. "I told you I had a plan," he said, shedding his coat and dumping it across the saddle.

"Now you don't need a plan. Tell the truth."

"I like my plan better. It leaves me with more options. Come down here, and I'll tell you about it."

"You stay up there, Mabel. I'll be done with this jack-a-dandy in a minute."

Evidently they were going to fight. Timothy Boots had probably two stone on him, but he looked like a brawler rather than a fighter. "I'm not leaving without you, Mabel," Sebastian said, his attention shifting to the circling Mr. Boots.

"Can't you understand that this is best?" she countered. "I'm setting my life, my place in the world, to where it belongs."

"Where you belong," he retorted, "is with me."

"You're just . . . you're just lonely. You'll find someone else. Someone who doesn't surround herself with chaos and misery."

Boots lunged at him, but Sebastian sidestepped and the blow missed him. "You hear what you're getting, Mr. Boots? Chaos and misery. Now me, I like chaos. And the misery is a matter of opinion." He risked a glance up at Josefina. She'd crawled across her bench mate to peer over the edge at him. "And yes, I am lonely. Every time I say goodbye to you."

"That doesn't make sense."

"Of course it does." Boots swung at him again, and he blocked the blow with his forearm, twisted, and tripped the man. "Before I met you, I wasn't lonely. I was alone. And content with that. You woke me up, Jo . . . Mabel. I'm alive again. And now, without you, yes, I'm lonely. Aren't you?"

Timothy Boots pushed to his feet and came at Sebastian

again with a roar. Taking the hit in the chest, Sebastian winced as they thudded into the side of the coach. For God's sake, it was difficult enough to declare his feelings in private. Doing so in front of strangers, and while keeping a giant from smashing his head in, was insanity. And fitting, he supposed.

"I don't understand," Josefina wailed.

Growling, Sebastian threw Boots off and turned to look up at her. "It's not complicated, Mabel. I love you. Do you understand that?"

A hard blow thudded into his chin, and he buckled. Scrambling forward, he crawled under the coach and stood up on the far side. Boots came charging around from the rear. This time Sebastian met him with a hard punch to the face. He followed that with a jab into Boots's gut, and the fellow collapsed.

"Get me down, help me down!" he heard coming from the left side of the coach.

Staggering and shaking the cobwebs from his head, he made his way back just in time to see Josefina jumping down from the rear wheel and landing in a rather ungainly sprawl. He took her arm and helped her to her feet, and she thudded into his chest, grabbing onto the back of his waistcoat and holding him tightly.

He closed his eyes, hugging her hard. More than her actual flight, the desperate way she held onto him told him how close he'd come to losing her. If he'd missed seeing her climb into that hack, he would have had no idea where to find her—and clearly she hadn't intended to return.

"You love me?" she whispered brokenly, running a shaking hand along his cheek.

She sounded so surprised. When they'd first met, he'd thought her so sure of herself. Sebastian looked hard into her deep brown eyes. "I love you," he repeated. "Nothing in heaven or on earth could convince me to marry you if I didn't." With that, he kissed her.

The crowd in the coach gasped. So the fight was perfectly acceptable, but the show of affection was scandalous. And even if these people knew what the two of them had gone through, their reaction probably wouldn't change. He kissed her again.

Mr. Boots stumbled around the back of the coach. *Damnation.* Sebastian turned, putting Josefina behind him, but she pushed back in front. "Tim, Mr. Boots," she said, "I sincerely apologize, and I thank you for standing by me. But I made a mistake. I love this man, and if he still wants me, then I will marry him."

A slow, satisfied smile curved Sebastian's mouth. He couldn't help it. "You love *me*," he whispered into her hair, sliding an arm around her waist and tugging her back against his chest.

He knew women wanted him, wanted his name and his power and his money. Josefina found those things about him difficult, and she loved him. He'd never thought, hoped, or wanted a woman to say that to him ever again. Hearing her say it, he felt . . . content. And more happy than he'd ever expected to be again. The idea that he could remain that way stunned him.

"I got me nose bloodied for you," Boots growled at her. "That's hardly a fair return for a promise of marriage."

In his arms, Josefina stiffened. "I did not—"

"Perhaps I could pay your passage north," Sebastian interrupted. "I can't have you luring Mabel away from me again."

"Take it, Tim," the other large fellow on the roof urged, "before he beats you all the way to Sunday."

"Ah, it ain't natural," Boots said, spitting into the dirt. "You've had training."

Sebastian nodded. "Yes, I have. What is the price of a seat these days?"

"Three quid."

That sounded fair. Boots hadn't even exaggerated the amount. "I'll give you five pounds, if you give me your word not to try to find Mabel Grimm ever again."

The big man stuck out his hand. "You have my word."

Sebastian shook hands with him, then gave over five pounds. With a last, jaunty grin at Josefina, Boots circled to the back of the coach to untie her portmanteau and toss it at her feet. As he climbed back up to the roof, Sebastian freed Merlin, and they backed away from the coach.

With a whistle the coachman sent the horses forward again. In a moment the vehicle was out of sight behind a row of oak trees, as if it had never been there at all. If he'd arrived at Branbury's house a minute later than he had, she would still be on it.

"Sebastian Griffin," she said, dusting dirt from his sleeves and his hair, "why did you follow all this way instead of stopping the coach back in London?"

"Because half the fun is seeing what you'll do next."

"But how did you know I was on the coach at all?"

"Well, Mabel Grimm," he returned, taking her hand, "four years ago I cursed God, and told him to leave me be. I think this morning he gave me a last chance to change my mind. I went riding, and decided I wanted to go by Branbury House. You were climbing into a hack."

"You loved your wife very much," she stated, turning her back to pet Merlin.

"I did, and I still do." He started to pull his coat back on, then changed his mind and led her and Merlin off the road, past a pretty stand of elm trees, and into a meadow full of yellow and purple wildflowers. "I need you to know something."

"After what I've put you through—am still putting you

through, I don't know why you . . ." A tear ran down her face, and she brushed it away. "I don't want to share you, but I certainly can't resent—"

"Stop it."

"But I—"

"No, Josefina. With your help, I discovered something about myself. I'm trying to explain it." At the creek which ran through the meadow, he pulled off Merlin's bridle and let the bay drink. They had a long ride back, and the fellow could use a rest. As for him, he wanted Josefina. Badly. "I thought I'd finished with it. With love, marriage, all of that. Charlotte was quiet, and thoughtful, and very witty. She filled my heart. And when she died, my heart . . . froze. All of me froze. Then I met you, and I feel warm again. My heart grew again, like a tree, I suppose. I don't think she has to leave it for you to have the new parts. All of them. Does that make sense?"

"Yes." Josefina tangled her fingers into his dark hair and kissed him again and again.

She still couldn't quite believe it. He'd followed her and demanded that she return. And he wanted her whether they resolved all of this trouble or not.

"It'll cause such a scandal if I marry you," she breathed, as he sat in the grass and pulled her down across his lap.

"*When* I marry you," he corrected, "the scandal will be much harder on you."

"And rightly so." The thought of the looks she would get, the whispers behind her back, made her want to be ill, but she'd certainly earned them all.

"I think I can help with that." Sebastian untied her bonnet and set it aside. "If you're willing to continue to be a princess for a time."

"But I'm not a princess. You know that. I never was one."

Slowly he gathered her skirts in his hands, pushing them

up past her bare thighs to her waist. "You're *my* princess," he rumbled, kissing her throat as his fingers roved along her skin.

As he dipped between her legs, she moaned. "I think you should tell me your plan," she gasped, fumbling at the fastenings of his trousers.

"In a minute." .

She pulled open his trousers, and he came free, hard and erect and aroused—all for her. Sebastian kissed her again, dragging her right leg around his hip so that she straddled him. He grasped her bottom and slowly pulled her forward, both of them watching as he disappeared tightly inside her.

Josefina flung her arms around his shoulders and tilted her head back, the sensation of him moving inside her still new and terribly vital to her all at the same time. How could she want someone so much when she still considered the wisest thing to do would be running as far from him as she was able? Whatever his new plan was, it had best be miraculous, because she didn't think she could make herself run from him again. Not for anything—not even for his sake.

"Come here," he murmured roughly. "Kiss me, Josefina."

Immediately she straightened, tightening inside as she kissed him, their tongues dancing in the same rhythm as their bodies. She moaned again, then cried out as she pulsed and shattered. "Oh, God," she breathed. "Oh, God, Sebastian. Tell me everything will be well. Just lie to me."

"I'll never lie to you," he said with a hard, breathless groan of his own. He lay back, pulling her with him to drape across his chest. "And everything will be well."

While her own breath returned to normal, she lay with her head on his chest, listening to his heartbeat. "Conchita was supposed to wake me at ten o'clock. They'll know I'm missing by now."

"Did you leave a letter?"

"No. I didn't want my father to have any idea where I might be or why I'd gone."

"You think he might realize that you've been unhappy with his plotting?"

She lifted her head to look at him. "My father is very good at convincing people of things, and I think it's because he half believes them, himself. So no, I don't think he's realized anything he doesn't wish to."

He kissed her on the chin. "Then we'll have to invent a reason plausible to him for your temporary disappearance. Because I'm sorry, but I badly need you to return home."

"He means to kill you after the wedding, Sebastian. Whatever you're planning, he's willing to murder you if you get in the way."

"I won't give him the chance."

"How are you going to accomplish that?"

"I have a surprise planned during the Tuffley soiree. We all need to be there. At least your father and my brother-in-law do. I left Valentine in command of my troops. And if you're missing, your father may not attend."

That made sense. Stephen Embry would stay where he felt the safest until he'd determined exactly what had happened with her. "I'm sorry," she said, lowering her head again. Damnation. Even when she tried to improve matters, she threatened to destroy them. "I'm so stupid."

"No, you're not. This brilliant plan of mine may just crumble into dust. At the moment, however, I consider it our best hope." She felt his chest rise and fall as he sighed. "I've recently become a believer in hope."

She considered her escape from her father's point of view. "I'll tell him I went to see Harek," she said finally. "As far as my father knows, I'm more comfortable with the idea of marrying someone less . . . diligent about the truth."

"Should we include Harek in this, then? I've always seen him as a bit of a square toes, but more ambitious than willing to work for his blessings."

After all this, he continued to ask her opinion. She smiled. "I would agree with that. He . . . When he thought he would be the one to marry me, he encouraged me to continue an intimate relationship with you. His thinking, I believe, was that if I bore your child, you would see that the family lived in comfort."

"The muckworm. No. We're not using him. Think of something else."

"You disagree with his assessment?"

"My disagreement is with the idea that he could marry you and let another man touch you." He sat up, setting her back a little from him so he could look her in the eye, the stern, unyielding Melbourne in his gaze. "That will never happen."

She shivered deliciously. "I have no argument with that, Sebastian. Where shall I have gone this morning, though?" She frowned. "Perhaps we should stay close to the truth. That's always easier."

"Which truth?"

"I'll tell him that this has been overwhelming, and I nearly fled back to Jamaica. Then I realized that I couldn't fail him, and I returned."

Sebastian kissed her again. "Perfect." With a slow smile that made her insides melt, he helped her to her feet and refastened his trousers. "Let's get back. I'll tell you the plan along the way. Just promise me, Josefina, or Mabel, or whomever you wish to be, that whatever happens, you won't run again."

"You would trust my word?"

"I would trust your word."

"Then I promise."

Chapter 24

$\mathcal{S}$ebastian handed Josefina to the ground one street away from Branbury House, then dismounted. For the story she'd conjured to have the most plausibility he should have hired a hack for her the moment they'd reached the outskirts of Town, but he remained reluctant to let her out of his sight.

Even back in the heart of Mayfair he couldn't stop touching her shoulder and smelling the lilac scent of her hair as she sat sidesaddle in front of him. His sister, especially, could attest to his tendency to be overprotective, but this was beyond that. The sight of her disappearing around the corner in that hack was still too fresh to dismiss.

"I'll see you tonight." He brought her knuckles to his lips. "I love you, Josefina."

"I still think you're making a very large mistake, Sebastian, but I love you, too."

The statement didn't reassure him overly much, but he left it at that. He untied her bag from Merlin's saddle and handed it to her. "I'm a powerful man," he said quietly, swinging back onto the bay. "People fear me, what I can do if they cross me. You, Josefina, terrify me. Be careful."

"You, too."

He watched her down the street, keeping a stand of trees between himself and the house. When the front door opened and her mother came rushing out, he turned Merlin for Corbett House.

He'd said he would never lie to her, and he'd been serious. But when he'd told her that she terrified him, he hadn't quite meant it that way. It wasn't so much her, as it was how fiercely he'd come to care for her, and what losing her could do to him. He'd lost Charlotte from something completely beyond his control. He would allow nothing within his control to keep him from Josefina.

The front drive of Corbett House was liberally cluttered with carriages. Apparently Valentine had notified the entire family of this morning's events. As he dismounted from the weary Merlin, one of Valentine's grooms met him. "I'll stable Merlin here tonight," he said, patting the bay on the withers. "See that he gets a nice ration of oats and an apple."

The groom rubbed Merlin on the nose. "I'll see to it, Your Grace."

He felt ready for rest and an apple, himself, but his day was barely half over. Rolling his shoulders, he headed to the house.

"Papa!" Penelope scampered out the front door and flew into his arms. He lifted her, ignoring the sore muscles low in his back. At four-and-thirty, fisticuffs took a bit more effort than it used to.

"What have you been up to today?" he asked her.

"I've been very worried about you," she said, hugging him tightly. "You smell like lilacs."

"Do I?"

"Yes. Lilacs and dust."

Shay stood in the doorway as he climbed the shallow steps, but evidently he realized the wisdom of not questioning his older brother's scent. "Any trouble?" he asked instead.

"No. She's back at home." He set Peep down with a kiss on her forehead. "I apologize for worrying you, my dove."

"Are you still getting married?"

"That is my plan, yes."

"I would like to wear a tiara to the ceremony."

He grinned. In all of this, his staunchest supporter had been his daughter, the one he'd thought might resent Josefina the most. "I think you should wear one. You and Josefina are my two princesses, after all."

"Yes, I know." She looked at Shay, who'd been joined by Sarala and Eleanor, and frowned. "Do I have to go back to the nursery now? I'd really like to know what's going on."

"I'll tell you what I can, as soon as I can," Sebastian answered. "I'm afraid that will have to do."

She sighed. "Very well. I'll finish teaching Rose how to talk."

When she'd thudded up the stairs, Sebastian raised an eyebrow at his brother. "Where's everyone else, then? I'm not telling my tale more than once."

Eleanor touched his arm. "Just tell me whether you and Josefina are . . . of the same mind about this, then."

"We are."

His sister pulled his shoulder down to kiss him on the cheek. "Good."

Silently echoing that sentiment, he followed the lot of them into the downstairs sitting room. Their troop had two new members, John Rice-Able and Anne Witfeld. "Welcome to the game," he said, nodding at his sister-in-law.

"Thank you for trusting me. Now could we go over this once more? I've just discovered that I'm being courted." The petite blonde grinned at the explorer-cum-professor.

He smiled back at her, color reddening his cheeks. "All for a good cause," he returned.

Sebastian sat in a chair near the fire. They always saved one for him there, though he wasn't certain whether it was in deference to his position as head of the family, or whether they were indicating that he was old and took a chill easily. "Very well. I'll tell you of my day's adventures, and we'll rehearse one more time."

"We should stay in tonight," Maria Embry said, as she fiddled with the lace on Josefina's sleeve.

"No one but the members of this household know that anything unusual happened today," Josefina reminded her. "And since we said we would be there, and since my betrothed will be there, we need to attend."

Her father straightened the sash over his left shoulder. "I agree." He pinned Josefina with annoyed blue eyes. "I'm grateful you decided to return," he continued stiffly, "and I'm thankful that Melbourne has no idea you tried to flee the country. But that was damned selfish, Josefina. You might have ruined this for all of us."

He'd done that to himself. "That's why I returned, Father."

"Let us speak no more of it." Her mother gestured them toward the foyer. "You look very beautiful tonight, *querida*."

"*Gracias, Mama*." She felt beautiful, not so much because of the splendid lavender gown and silver tiara she wore, but because she knew Sebastian cared for her. And because even with the heart-stopping guilt she felt at standing against her father, she'd made the right choice— quite possibly for the first time in her life.

Sitting opposite her parents in the coach, she gazed out at the deepening twilight. Nervousness rattled through her muscles, but she knew how to conceal that, even from the man who'd taught her how. She wondered whether her father would ever realize how lucky he was that Sebastian had chosen to be merciful.

"You're quiet this evening," her mother commented.

"My life is changing," she returned with a small smile. "It's a great deal to think about."

"You do like Melbourne, do you not?"

Josefina nodded. "I do." She refrained from commenting that her feelings didn't much signify one way or the other, since the rey had already stated that he would have Sebastian killed once the duke had outlived his usefulness.

For the first time, though, she wondered whether her mother knew that. How much of any of this did she realize? Always she deferred to her husband in matters of family and income, but was she ignorant about the worst of them? Josefina had allowed herself to be fooled about how far her father would go. She preferred to think that her mother was the same, but she wondered if she would ever know for certain.

"Look at that," her father said, peering out the coach window. "Half the peerage must be in attendance tonight." He grinned at Josefina. "It's because of you, you know. It's your first public appearance with Melbourne since the announcement of your engagement appeared."

Apparently her short-lived flight had been forgiven and forgotten. Josefina took a deep breath, then another. It didn't help. Whatever the Griffins planned for the evening was a surprise; these people were here to see her with Sebastian. *Goodness.*

"Melbourne should have escorted us." The rey frowned. "Then you could have walked in together."

"I think he's probably still annoyed that you didn't give him any funds to invest."

"Yes, well, he's simply going to have to learn that he can't best me."

"He's beginning to realize that, no doubt. And I think it'll be very eye-catching when he greets all of us in the middle of the room."

He chuckled. "It will be that."

"I still would like to leave early," her mother said. "If Josefina has been overwhelmed by events, we need to make it otherwise."

"She can rest after the wedding."

The coach stopped, and two liveried footmen appeared to hand them to the ground. Josefina wanted to look for Sebastian's coach, but neither did she want to appear too eager to see him. Aside from that, with so many vehicles lining the drive and the surrounding streets, she would probably never be able to pick out a Griffin coach, anyway.

Lord and Lady Tuffley bowed as the butler announced the Costa Habichuela contingent and they entered the upstairs ballroom. "Good evening, Your Majesties, Your Highness. Thank you so much for gracing us with your presence."

"The pleasure is ours," her father returned, seeming to expand as his social superiors fawned over him. "Your house is splendid, Tuffley."

The viscount chuckled. "Thank you, but I give that compliment over to my wife." He leaned closer. "Prinny is to be here tonight, you know," he said in a conspiratorial tone, rocking back on his heels. "Quite the coup for us."

"Indeed. I shall raise a glass to him, myself. Without his kind assistance, my dreams for Costa Habichuela would never have been realized."

Josefina could barely breathe. She had no idea whether Sebastian's plan tonight would work. Adding the Prince Regent to the roster of players—oh, goodness. She'd never fainted in her life, but she was ready to do so now.

Lady Tuffley left her hostess duties at the door to personally guide them to the refreshment tables. "The sugared berries are especially tasty tonight," she said. "Do enjoy yourselves. And Your Highness, I would be honored if you would join me for luncheon on Friday. Several of we high-ranking ladies meet weekly to discuss our charitable activities."

"Thank you, Lady Tuffley. I need to confer with Lady Deverill about my schedule—I know the Griffins have several events they wish me to attend—but I will let you know as soon as I can."

The viscountess smiled. "Of course. Thank you."

As she walked away, her father sampled a berry. "These *are* delicious," he muttered. "And why in the world didn't you accept her invitation? You heard her—a group of high-ranking ladies."

"Because I don't know her politics," Josefina whispered back. "I prefer to discuss this with Eleanor before I accidently ally with the wrong party, or support a cause the Griffins oppose."

"I don't think we'll be remaining in London long enough for that to matter."

"I prefer to be cautious." Oh, she hoped Sebastian would arrive soon. It felt as though every conversation tonight had two meanings, two reasons behind it.

It only got worse. Everyone had to come by to talk with her. She smiled and chatted about nonsense, reminding herself every few seconds that Costa Habichuela was a paradise, that she was anxious to see the new settlers arrive and take possession of the land they'd purchased, and yes, she looked forward to joining the mighty Griffin family.

"Have you had a chance to see Queen Charlotte's garden yet?" Lady Jane Lyon asked. "The roses are—oh, they're here. He's here. It's Melbourne."

The murmur seemed to reverberate around the large ballroom. The hair on Josefina's arms lifted. With a shallow, shaky breath she turned around.

As they usually seemed to, the Griffins had arrived together. Melbourne himself greeted Lord and Lady Tuffley, brothers and sister and their spouses directly around him. Just behind them Caroline's family stood, most of them doing their best not to look awestruck.

Sebastian wore all black again tonight, the close-fitting coat and trousers emphasizing his tall, lean, handsome build. He seemed to emanate power. From the reaction of the other party guests, she wasn't the only one to think so. But when those gray eyes lifted and searched the room, he wasn't looking for any of them. He was looking for her.

The moment their gazes met he left the Tuffleys and strode across the room to her. Everyone else simply stepped back, out of his way. Not even her supremely confident father dared put himself between the two of them.

Sebastian took both of her hands in his, bringing them to his lips and looking down at her over them. "Good evening, Your Highness," he murmured, the low, intimate tone rumbling through her.

"Your Grace," she returned, knowing she must be blushing. It wasn't that his presence made her feel weak or twittery; rather, with him she felt more confident and strong than she ever had before. With Sebastian, she didn't need to daydream or prevaricate—and for her, that realization was a heady, exciting, arousing one. She wanted to throw herself into his arms and kiss him right there in front of everyone.

She heard the mutterings around them—the chorus of "Look, it's a love match," "Who would have thought?" and "If it smells of power, Melbourne must have it." They didn't seem to trouble Sebastian as he finally released her to greet her parents, so she ignored them, as well.

"Did you hear that Prinny's to attend tonight?" she asked, working to keep her voice smugly happy rather than nervous and anxious.

"I had not," he said with an easy smile that elicited still more commentary. "I imagine he'll want to dance with you to celebrate our engagement."

He was warning her, then. She would have to continue the farce with Prinny, himself. Thank goodness she had time to prepare for that bit of torture. "As long as His Highness knows that the first waltz of the evening is taken."

"By me, I would hope."

The crowd laughed as he grinned. The rest of the Griffins surrounded them, offering her and her parents public greetings and congratulations, and more private kisses to her cheek and touches to her hand to show their support. And this family was to be her family. Then and there she vowed to be worthy of their confidence.

"Tuffley!" Melbourne called, looking over his shoulder at their hosts. "How about that waltz?"

Chapter 25

 Sebastian glanced at his pocket watch as their waltz ended and he escorted Josefina back to her parents. Last year, when Shay had been courting Sarala, the family had united in defense of her and to thwart a man who would have done harm to her reputation. Tonight, though, they weren't attempting to fool one self-serving, ambitious half-wit. Tonight they needed to fool everyone—his own sovereign, all of his peers, every man and woman in the country.

With Josefina's hand over his arm and the Embrys beside them, he gave a slight nod to Caroline. His sister-in-law strolled forward to where her mother and two unmarried sisters stood watching, and at least in Joanna's case, lamenting the scarcity of dance partners.

"Anne, are you ever going to tell Mama about John?"

"John?" Joanna repeated, her face reddening. "Who is John?"

Anne fanned her face. "He's a professor at Eton," she

returned, doing a fair impression of shyness, considering that she didn't have an ounce of that to her name. "I met him at the British Museum."

"Mama, that is not fair!" Joanna stomped her foot, garnering them the attention he'd been counting on. Considering that Joanna's man-hungry demeanor had once prompted her to attempt to trap Zach into marriage, he didn't have much sympathy for her. "Now even Anne has a beau?" she continued plaintively.

"He's an explorer," Anne continued brightly, "or he used to be, before he accepted the teaching position. I asked him to come here tonight, so you and Papa can meet him."

Sally Witfeld clapped her hands together. "Another daughter with a beau. We are truly blessed."

"I knew I should have gone to the museum," Joanna snapped. "You said it would be dull."

"I said that *you* would find it dull," Anne countered. "I rather enjoyed it." She laughed.

The rey chuckled. "Ah, to be young again."

Good. He was listening. "I've met the fellow," Sebastian commented. "He seems a good sort. A bit earnest, but that makes him a good counter for Anne's high spirits." Actually, it did.

He glanced from his quarry to his young sister-in-law. She made a good actress, but even with that in mind her color was high. Hm. Interesting. She'd been after a man who liked to travel. Perhaps in John Rice-Able she'd found him.

"Ladies and gentlemen," the Tuffley's butler enunciated, "His Highness, the Prince Regent."

The crowd bowed in an undulating wave spreading out from the doorway. Prinny strolled into the room, thankfully without one of his ubiquitous mistresses. Even so half a dozen footmen and retainers accompanied his rotund, sapphire-colored Eminence, like planets around their sun.

Embry was probably taking mental notes on how to make a royal entrance.

"Melbourne," the Regent called, gesturing him over.

Keeping Josefina with him, Sebastian approached. "Your Highness," he said, "if you mean to chastise me for not coming to you first with my news, pray do so quickly so we may drink a toast in honor of my wife-to-be."

Prinny clapped him on the shoulder, offering a pleased grin. "There's no amusement in chastising the contrite, my boy. Tuffley, let's have some champagne!"

"Right away, Your Highness."

In a remarkably short time everyone in the room had been armed with glasses of champagne. Hopefully Tuffley had been prepared for the extravagance; later Sebastian would take him aside and offer him a replacement case of the stuff. Prinny lifted his glass, angling it at Josefina. "Ladies and gentlemen, to Josefina, Princess of Costa Habichuela, and soon I hear, to be the Duchess of Melbourne."

"To Josefina."

Her hand trembled a little on his arm as everyone drank to her health, but that was the only outward sign she gave that she was anything but exactly who Prinny proclaimed her. She truly was a princess at heart.

"To Josefina," he echoed in a whisper.

"Now let's have a waltz!" Prinny continued, finishing off his glass and tossing it to a waiting footman. "We Highnesses must dance a waltz!"

A second waltz so close to the first bordered on scandal, but no one in attendance so much as batted an eye. With a squeeze of her fingers he released her to Prinny.

For God's sake, this plan had to work. If it didn't, Prinny would never forgive that he'd made a very public display of support for Costa Habichuela and its monarchs. Christ, the Regent was still wearing that damned green cross.

Sebastian took a quick breath as Shay glanced up from his pocket watch. It was time.

A moment later John Rice-Able rushed through the ballroom doors, brushing aside the butler as he searched the room. Anne Witfeld had positioned herself close to the entrance, and after a few deliberate, dramatic seconds the professor hurried up to her.

"Ah, there he is," Sebastian said from his place beside the Embrys. "That's Anne's beau."

"He is a bit earnest-seeming, isn't he?" the rey noted politely, then took Sebastian's arm to turn him away. "We need to discuss something."

"I'm not renegotiating my payments to you, Embry. Ten thousand a year and my silence is quite enough, I think."

"It's not about money," Josefina's father returned in a low voice. "It's about your residence."

"My resi—"

"In the next few weeks we might find it judicious to do a bit of traveling. I suggest that you join us."

"I am not—"

"Your Grace," Anne's voice interrupted, her tone serious. "Melbourne? John needs to speak with you."

"We'll discuss this later, Embry," Sebastian hissed, facing his sister-in-law. "Can't this wait, Anne?"

John Rice-Able pushed in front of her. "I don't mean to overstep, Your Grace," he said in a rushed, urgent tone that caught the attention of everyone around them, "but my friend Mayhew Crane is first mate on the *Barnaby*— it's a frigate that traverses the Southern Atlantic. He—"

"I am at a soiree, John," Sebastian interrupted, feeling Embry's attention abruptly sharpen.

"Yes, I know. And—" John seemed to notice the rey for the first time. "Oh. Your Majesty. I beg your pardon. I'm so sorry to be the one to deliver the news."

Hiding his growing admiration for the professor behind a frown, Sebastian took Rice-Able's arm. "What are you talking about? And keep your bloody voice down."

As soon as he said that, everything around them quieted. He'd learned long ago that the best way to spread a rumor was to publicly ask that it be halted. On his other side, Embry took a step closer.

"That's what I'm attempting to tell you, Your Grace. Mayhew wrote me from Belize. It's all gone."

"Belize is gone? What—"

"No! Costa Habichuela. The rains, a terrible flood. It's all been washed away!" He produced a letter from his pocket, and Sebastian snatched it a second before Embry could.

"This is not amusing, John. In case you've forgotten, I'm marrying Princess Josefina of Costa Habichuela."

"Yes, Your Grace. I know. That's why I had to tell you. When . . . when I traveled through Costa Habichuela a few years ago, I noticed that the land was very fertile, but I also saw that the reason for its richness was that most of the country sits on an ancient river mouth. A flood plain. And with the awful rain and the storm off the coast, it's—"

"Wait a moment," Embry broke in, glaring at the clearly upset gentleman. "What the devil do you think you're—"

"Listen to this, Your Majesty," Sebastian broke in.

"John, knowing your attachment to the Witfeld and Griffin families, I have some desperate, terrible news for you. On our way west, the Barnaby *passed through the worst gale I can remember. Our mast cracked in two, and we nearly lost everything, including our lives. That though, I only tell you to set the awful scene for you, to prepare you for worse."*

The music trailed raggedly to a stop, and Prinny, Josefina on his arm, approached them. "What's this news, Melbourne?"

"We're just discovering, Your Highness." He gestured at the letter. "If you'll allow me?"

"Yes, continue."

He sent Josefina a quick glance, then looked down again.

"We limped into the harbor at San Saturus for repairs, to find the splendid breakwater crumbled into the sea. This was our warning of the devastation we would find. We next discovered that the town had been entirely washed away."

"Oh, no," Josefina choked, putting a hand across her mouth.

"The handful of survivors we found had only remained behind to look for relatives and belongings. We gave them what food and water we had to spare, and in return they told us that the entire area had suffered under a fortnight straight of heavy rains and winds. Following that, the sea became increasingly rough, and then for several hours waves washed over the land up to the foothills to the west. All buildings, trees, and even soil were swept out into the ocean, leaving nothing behind but a black, stinking morass of swampland and dead animals. I fear disease is not far behind."

"Stephen," Prinny said, his face contorting in sorrow. "You have England's deepest sympathy."

"There is some good news," Sebastian noted, turning the letter over. "It seems that Belize has opened its arms to the survivors."

Shay moved up to join their enlarging circle. "Thank God for that."

"We have to do something." Slowly Sebastian handed the letter over to Embry.

"We have to accept that it's over," Josefina said firmly, in a sad, carrying voice.

Her father whipped his head around to face her. "You," he snapped, white-faced. "How could you—"

"We must accept that our place is now in Belize," Queen Maria interrupted. Sebastian looked at her in surprise as she took her husband's hand in hers. "I can only be thankful that those who purchased land in Costa Habichuela have not yet sailed."

"Yes," Josefina echoed. "The people must come first. We must return their money. With no land at all, we have no need of it."

"We can rebuild," Embry said stridently, pulling his hand free.

"With what, Father? You heard what the letter said. Costa Habichuela has returned to what it was so many years ago—a swampland. There's no foundation we can build on."

John Rice-Able cleared his throat. "It says in the post-script that Mayhew sent a copy of my letter to our mutual friend, Robert Lumley. He is on the writing staff of the *London Times*. Mayhew was very anxious that no one set sail for Costa Habichuela without knowing the present conditions."

"The lad deserves a medal," Prinny commented, his sentiment echoed by the nods of their audience.

That would be troublesome, considering that there was no such man, and no such ship. "Josefina," Sebastian said, reaching for her hand. Slowly he drew her closer, enfolding her in a hug. "I'm so sorry."

"Yes, I suppose we're finished here now," Embry

grunted, his muscles still rigid with fury. "We'll leave for Costa Habichuela tomorrow. Come Maria, Josefina. We have packing to do."

Sebastian's heart stopped. "I understand where your duty lies, Your Majesty," he said, "and the urgency of your departure. But I also know where my heart lies. If Josefina will stay, I have no wish to postpone our wedding. As you said, you have no country to rebuild. Your daughter, though, has a new life to begin."

Embry stared at him. Clearly the man had no idea that the duke he'd thought he owned had been anything but tricked into a union. The idea that genuine feelings might be involved, and that they might be significant, had probably never occurred to him. His gaze flicked over to his daughter. "Josefina?"

Her gaze, though, was on Sebastian. "You said you would ask me again," she breathed.

His nerves skittered as he silently sank onto one knee, taking her hands in his. "Josefina," he said, "I don't care whether you are the princess of a paradise, or a soldier's daughter whose house has been washed out to sea. You challenge me, you amaze me, and you showed me that a place I thought had vanished, was only misplaced." His voice shook, and he cleared his throat. "You helped me find it again. I love you, Josefina, with every ounce of warmth you've reawakened in my heart. Will you marry me?"

Tears ran unchecked down her cheeks, but she was smiling. "I'm very glad I slapped you that night," she quavered. "I love you, too, Sebastian. Very much. Yes, I want to marry you."

Blowing out his breath, he removed the Melbourne signet ring from his finger and placed it on hers. It was far too large, but she and everyone else understood the significance of the gesture. Applause erupted, deafening, and at least in the case of his own family and friends, sincere.

Sebastian stood up again and swept her into his arms. "Then nothing else matters," he whispered softly in her ear. "Nothing."

Prinny himself walked them downstairs and onto the front drive. That in itself was the best assurance they could ask for that Sebastian's plan had been successful. Josefina sighed again. Everyone had believed the story. And after tomorrow, when the same letter appeared on the front page of the *London Times*, no one would be setting sail for Costa Habichuela.

In one evening they'd unraveled two years' worth of her father's plans. She glanced at him again, walking up to their borrowed coach and being consoled by the Regent. She couldn't imagine how he must feel, how angry he must be with her.

"You're not going home with him," Sebastian said in a low voice, her own apprehension echoing in his deep voice. He hadn't released her hand since he'd stood to hug her.

"I'm not going home with *you*," she countered in the same tone, then tried a smile. "I'd ruin your reputation."

"Very amusing. I know you're anxious. So am I."

"Don't expect me to say farewell forever to my parents with three minutes of warning." Her voice caught. Not everything had been set back the way it was before.

"I'm not expecting that," he shot back. "But your father was willing to risk other lives. I'm not willing to risk yours."

While she truly didn't think that her father would harm her, she also understood quite clearly that Sebastian had lost his first wife and that he would do anything to protect her. "What do you suggest, then?" she asked, conceding to his worry.

"Nell," he called, and his sister approached. He whispered something to her, and a moment later she nodded.

"Josefina," she said, "I would love if you could stay at Corbett House while your parents make arrangements to return home."

Her father immediately turned around, his eyes narrowing. "I don't—"

"A splendid idea, Lady Deverill," her mother broke in, nodding. "And a good opportunity for you to become better acquainted with your new position, *hija*."

Gruffly her father nodded. "Yes, of course."

"We'll come and see you in the morning, Your Majesties," Sebastian said. "I'll have my solicitors assist you in expediting the return of the land sale funds. And the loan money, I suppose. No need for improvements to San Saturus, now."

"Indeed." Prinny offered his hand, and her father shook it. "I will see to it that the bank forgives any interest due."

With a last glare at her, the rey climbed into the coach. Her mother kissed Josefina on the cheek. "I will send Conchita to Corbett House with some of your things. Please do come by in the morning." Surprisingly, she took Sebastian's free hand between hers. "Both of you."

"We will, Mama. *Yo te amo.*"

"*Te amo, querida.*"

When they arrived at Branbury House in the morning, Sebastian half expected to see all the doors and windows opened and the house completely gutted. Instead, servants scampered about like ants, carrying obscene amounts of luggage into several leased coaches. Briefly he wondered how much of England's money Embry had spent.

Keeping silent about that, he helped Josefina down from the coach. He'd been tempted to spend the night at Corbett House, himself, but refused to confuse his desire to be protective with the perils of stifling and overwhelming her. "Ready?" he asked, kissing her fingers.

Squaring her shoulders, she nodded. "If I can convince them to stay, at least until the wedding, would that still be acceptable?"

"It would—"

"No, don't say it," she cut him off. "They can't stay. There's been a flood; they need to hurry back to Costa Habichuela or face too many questions."

"I'm sorry for that." Sebastian nodded as the butler pushed aside a stack of hat boxes to allow them entry. "If there was a way, I'd like them to stay. For you."

"Curious way to go about it."

He looked up. Embry stood at the top of the stairs, gazing down at them. "Your Majesty," he said for the benefit of the servants, trying to keep the sarcasm from his voice and unsure whether he'd succeeded. "I trust my solicitors have been of help?"

"Oh, yes. Hardly a need for me to do anything but produce the currency and sign my name several hundred times." He backed away from the railing. "Join me in the office. Both of you. I wouldn't dream of separating you."

Good thing, that, because at the moment he had no intention of letting Josefina out of his sight. "Certainly."

"Where's Mama?" she asked, as they climbed the stairs.

Embry made a dismissive sound and gestured somewhere into the depths of the house. "Packing. Your things, probably. I told her you were the one in no hurry, but my word doesn't seem to count for much, these days."

Sebastian closed the door behind them as they entered the office. "I might have let you get away with it, if it had only been the bank's funds you liberated," he said.

"Arrogant bastard. Yes, you outmaneuvered me. Congratulations. It's not just me you've destroyed, though; two dozen people rely on me for their livelihoods." He faced his daughter. "Did you ever consider them, Josefina?"

"You didn't," she retorted, then bit her lip. "I asked

you, over and over, not to put people's lives at risk. Did you ever consider them? And their families? Their children?"

He slammed his fist into the desk top. "I was considering *my* child. *You* were my priority."

"Then congratulations to you, Embry." Sebastian took a half step forward, putting himself between Josefina and any route her father would have to take to get to her. "She'll be a duchess within a month. And I promise you that I will spend the rest of my life giving your daughter the life you always wanted her to have." He glanced at the paperwork still cluttering the desk. "If you haven't noticed, there's one piece of paper that hasn't been revised. Ten thousand pounds a year will enable you to live very comfortably anywhere. Even with two dozen people relying on your . . . skills."

Embry eyed him. "Ten thousand a year, eh? Is that the going price for a duchess-to-be? What if I cancel this deal and take her with me when we go?"

"I'm not going with you, Father. Papa. You've given me a wonderful life, and wonderful opportunities. I will never dispute that. But I'm grown, now. I don't want to travel with you any longer. I want . . . I want Sebastian."

A muscle beneath Embry's eye twitched. "Will you give my daughter and me a moment alone, Your Grace?" he asked.

"No."

"Please do, Sebastian. I would like to say goodbye."

He nodded stiffly. "I'll be close by."

Josefina watched him out the door. At least he closed it behind him, though she wouldn't be surprised if he had his ear pressed to the other side.

"He's a bit possessive, isn't he?" her father commented. "I should have noticed that."

"He knows that I nearly left London yesterday," she

offered, deciding that didn't jeopardize any of the story they'd concocted. "I appreciate someone ranking me above anything else in the world."

"That's easy to do when the 'someone' is the most powerful man in England and has an income of over a hundred thousand quid a year. Some of us have to work for what we have."

"That's not fair." She drew a breath. "I don't want to fight, Papa. I want to wish you well. Where will you and Mama go?"

"Prussia, I think. They'll appreciate a friendly colony in Central America." He studied her for a moment. "It would be helpful if you were along to wed a Prussian lord."

"You're actually going to attempt this again?"

"It nearly worked." He offered a brief smile. "This time I'll stop at the loan and the stocks, I think. You could be a princess again, sweetling."

"Papa, you might have been arrested. And hanged. You were very lucky this time. Why take the risk?"

"I learn from my mistakes. I won't make any the next time."

"But you have ten thousand a year. You could buy land, or begin a trading company."

"I'm not ready to sit in a chair and count my coins. Ten thousand is a good beginning, but I can do better. I could do even better with you there."

"No. If you truly want what's best for me, then be happy for me. You were the one who selected Melbourne for me in the first place."

"I was, wasn't I?" He grimaced. "Come and give your old papa a hug, then. We have to be off to Brighton before nightfall."

She put her arms around his shoulders. "Promise that you'll write to me, like you did when I was younger." She wouldn't believe half of it, but it would still be good to see that he hadn't abandoned his . . . dreams, she supposed they were.

"I will." He set her back away from him. "Go see your mother and tell her goodbye."

Tears gathered in her eyes, and she sternly ordered them gone. He didn't appreciate weakness, and she would show none. "Please take care of yourself."

She headed out the door as he sat down to gather his paperwork. He would have to recalculate his approach without her there, and that was probably what he was doing already—making plans for his next attempt at greatness. He would still be a rey here in England, but a poor and pitied one. He would never accept that.

The farewells to her mother were more difficult, and by the end both of them were crying. Through the window of the morning room she could see Sebastian pacing in the garden, and she sighed. When it had happened, she didn't know, but at some point in her life she must have done something good—very good—to be allowed the rest of her life with him.

"You chose well, *chica*," her mother said, joining her at the window. "I think he loves you very much."

"I love him very much. Thank you for helping us last night."

"I don't think your father realizes yet how very lucky he was. Anyone else, under any other circumstances, would have been happy to see him in prison."

"I tried to tell him that. He won't listen."

"He hears you. Acknowledging it, though, is a different matter. Hopefully this lesson will make him a bit more cautious in the future."

"So you knew how far he was overreaching."

Her mother smiled. "I know I love Stephen Embry. He tries so hard to do great things that he's never stopped to realize what he's already accomplished."

Josefina could dispute that he'd accomplished much of anything but a very long string of lies and thefts, but she let it go. Instead she gave her mother a last, tight hug. "Let me know where you'll be so I can write you."

"I shall. We will come see you as often as we can. I want my grandchildren to know their *abuela*."

"So do I." Straightening, she cleared her throat. "We should go, so you can finish packing."

"Send Melbourne in for a moment before you leave, will you?"

Josefina nodded. "Of course."

Sebastian looked up from contemplating a beetle as Josefina left the house. "Are you well?"

"Yes. A bit sad, but also hopeful." She shook her head. "It's very strange."

He drew a breath. "I am sorry that you have to be separated from them."

"I know. It's important that I am, though, at least for a time. I learned some fairly awful habits."

"You learned to survive. Don't expect me to fault that." He took her hand, drawing it to his lips. "I don't expect you to be someone different now, either. This," and he shook her fingers, "is you. I love you."

She smiled. "You're a very nice man."

He chuckled back at her. "Not until recently. Shall we go?"

"My mother asked to see you. She's in the morning room."

Inwardly stifling a cringe, he nodded. "Very well."

He saw her to the coach, then went back inside the house. Maria Embry stood beside the small writing desk, her gaze on him as he entered the room. "You wanted to see me?"

"Yes. I wanted to give you something." She held out a piece of paper.

Frowning, he took it. "What's this?"

"Read it."

Half his attention still on Josefina's mother, he unfolded the thing and perused it. Then he read through it again. And once more, just to be certain. His heart shuddering, he shot his gaze up to hers again. "Is this legitimate?"

"Yes." She smiled, a kind, wise expression that reminded him of her daughter. "It's the only thing that is, I suppose. Two of them exist. That one is for you."

"Does Josefina know?"

"She's known all along. She just doesn't believe it, any longer." Maria leaned up and kissed him on the cheek. "It's certainly not a secret, but I thought she might want to hear it from you."

"Thank you."

"Thank *you*. You're giving her the life I always wanted her to have."

A little dazed, Sebastian went outside and climbed into the coach. "Take us back to Corbett House," he instructed Tollins as he closed the door and sat.

Josefina's maid, Conchita, sat in the far corner, but he ignored her as he faced her mistress. "What do you say to an engagement ball within the fortnight, and the wedding a week after that?"

"I say it's not soon enough, but I shall tolerate it." She touched his cheek. "Are you well? My mother didn't slap you, did she?"

"Not physically."

She furrowed her fine brow, her beautiful brown eyes concerned. "What do you mean?"

"She gave me a piece of paper." He patted his breast pocket, but didn't remove the thing. It was going somewhere very safe at the first opportunity.

"And?" she prompted.

"Apparently your father did meet Qental, King of the

Mosquito Coast. And Qental did grant him a million acres of coastal land there. And the king personally granted Stephen Embry the title of rey of said land."

Her face went white. "What?"

"So, my love, you *are* a princess." He leaned over and tilted her chin up, kissing her softly. God, he could spend his days doing that. He *would* spend his days doing that.

"*What?*"

"It's verified and witnessed by the Governor of Belize. I've seen his seal, and this letter bears it."

Her mouth opened, then snapped shut again. "Goodness," she breathed, then abruptly sat straighter to kiss him back, sweeping her hands into his hair as though she wanted to climb inside him. "And I thought I would be a plain, ordinary duchess." She backed off a little to gaze into his eyes. "I want to be a plain, ordinary duchess. No one else in your family needs to know, do they?"

Sebastian laughed. "No. You shall be a duchess. My duchess. As for being plain and ordinary, I don't think even you could manage that."

She grinned back at him. "Then I shan't try."

Author's Note

One of my old college professors used to say that reality was no excuse for fiction. What I think he meant was that just because something actually happened, that doesn't mean it necessarily sounds plausible in writing. Sometimes, though, actual events seem to be made for fiction. It's in that category I have to place the true exploits of Sir Gregor MacGregor.

In 1823, a group of English settlers landed along the Mosquito Coast, believing that a rich, wealthy, newly formed country called Poyais lay there, and having already purchased land or accepted government positions from Poyais's "cazique," Sir Gregor MacGregor. A great many of these people perished from dysentery, malaria, and the heat before their rescue, when it was discovered that there was no land of Poyais, and that their maps and extensive guide books were fictional.

It had all been masterminded by MacGregor, who went on to try his schemes throughout Europe, spent time in prison for it, and ultimately upon his death in 1845 was honored by the President of Venezuela, who marched behind his coffin while newspapers in Caracas celebrated him as a war hero.

If you'd like more information on Sir Gregor, I highly recommend the book *The Land That Never Was: Sir Gregor MacGregor and the Most Audacious Fraud in History* by David Sinclair. Apparently Sir Gregor was also indirectly responsible for the United States's acquisition of Florida, but that's another story.

～ ～

*A*h, summertime. The kids are off from school and underfoot, the temperature may rise to an uncomfortable level, and your body can't believe it's already swimsuit season . . . but fortunately Avon Books has just the solution for the dog days of summer—escape into a sweeping, passion-filled romance.

Embrace the heat with these sizzling Romance Superleaders—so captivating they come with their own warning: You won't be satisfied until you read all four books.

Enjoy!

～ ～

Not Quite A Lady
LORETTA CHASE

Darius Carsington is the youngest of the Carsington brothers and divides his life into two parts: 1) studying animal behavior, especially mating habits, and 2) imitating these habits. His father challenges him to either bring one of their dilapidated estates back into shape within a year or get married. Having no interest in marriage, Darius moves to the country and—much to his father's despair—quickly begins to put things to rights. But his lifestyle is challenged when he meets the intriguing Lady Charlotte Hayward, a seemingly perfect lady with a past of her own.

"You put your hands on me." Charlotte's face was quite rosy now.

"I may have to do it again," Darius said, "if you continue to blunder about the place, alarming the wildlife."

He had not thought her blue eyes could open any wider but they did. *"Blunder about?"*

"I fear you have disturbed the dragonflies during an extremely delicate process," he said. "They were mating, poor things, and you frightened them out of their wits."

She stared at him. Her mouth opened, but nothing came out.

"Now I understand why none but the hardiest of the livestock remain," he said. "You must have either frightened them all away or permanently impaired their reproductive functions."

"Impaired their— I did *not*. I was . . ." Her gaze fell to the hat he still held. "Give me my hat."

He turned it in his hands and studied it. "This is the most frivolous hat I've ever seen." Perhaps it was and perhaps it wasn't. He had no idea. He never noticed women's clothes except as obstacles to be got out of the way as quickly as possible.

Still, he could see that the thing he held was an absurd bit of froth: a scrap of straw, scraps of lace, ribbons. "What does it do? It cannot keep off the sun or the rain."

"It's a *hat*," she said. "It isn't supposed to do anything."

"Then what do you wear it for?"

"For?" she said. "*For?* It's . . . It's . . ." Her brow knit.

He waited.

She bit her lip and thought hard. "Decoration. Give it back. I must go now."

"What, no 'please'?"

The blue eyes flashed up at him. "No," she said.

"I see I must set the example of manners," he said.

"Give me my hat." She reached for it.

He put the nonsensical headwear behind his back.

"I am Darius Carsington," he said. He bowed.

"I don't care," she said.

"Beechwood has been turned over to me," he said.

She turned away. "Never mind. Keep the hat if you want it so much. I've others."

She started to walk away.

That would not do. She was exceedingly pretty.

He followed her. "I collect you live nearby," he said.

"Apparently I do not live far enough away," she said.

"This place has been deserted for years," he said. "Perhaps you were unaware of the recent change."

"Papa told me. I . . . forgot."

"Papa," he said, and his good humor began to fade. "That would be . . . ?"

"Lord Lithby," she said tautly. "We came from London yesterday. The stream is our western border. I was always used to come here and . . . But it does not matter."

No, it didn't, not anymore.

Her accents, her dress, her manner, all told Darius this was a lady. He had no objections to ladies. Unlike some, he was not drawn exclusively to women of the lower orders. She seemed a trifle slow-witted and appeared to possess no sense of humor whatsoever, but this didn't signify. Women's brains or lack thereof had never mattered to him. What he wanted from them had nothing to do with their intellect or sense of humor.

What did matter was that the lady had referred to her *father's* property bordering Darius's. Not her husband's.

Ergo, she must be an unmarried daughter of the Marquess of Lithby.

It was odd—not to mention extremely annoying— that Darius had mistaken her. Usually he could spot a virgin at fifty paces. Had he realized this was a maiden, not a matron, he would have set her on her feet and sent her packing immediately. Though he had little use for Society's illogical rules, he drew the line at seducing innocents.

Since seduction was out of the question, he saw no reason to continue the conversation. He had wasted far too much time on her already.

He held out the hat.

With a wary look, she took it.

"I apologize for startling you or getting in your way or whatever I did," he said dismissively. "Certainly you are welcome to traipse about the property as you've always done. It is of no consequence to me. Good day."

Sins of a Duke
SUZANNE ENOCH

*Sebastian Griffin, Duke of Melbourne, is not pleased
when the Prince Regent appoints him as cultural liaison to a tiny new kingdom. Sebastian is not entirely
convinced that this kingdom is as great as its ruler
claims it is—or if the kingdom actually exists! And
the fact that Princess Josefina intrigues him far more
than he wishes, makes the situation all the more complicated. Reluctant to lose Prinny's favor, but unwill-
ing to allow England to be taken in, Sebastian settles
on the only plan that makes sense: He will play pretty
with "the princess" until he discovers the truth.*

Princess Josefina, a maid and one of the black-
uniformed men flanking her, faced him as he approached. Tonight she wore a rich yellow gown, low
cut enough that the creamy mounds of her breasts
heaved as she drew a breath. God, she was spectacular. Of course that didn't signify anyth—

She slapped him.

Sebastian blinked, clenching his rising hands
against the immediate instinct to retaliate. The blow
stung, but of more concern was the responding
roar from the onlookers in the Elkins ballroom. He

looked directly into her dark brown eyes. "Never do that again," he murmured, curving his lips in a smile that felt more like a snarl.

"My father and your Regent made a very simple request of you," she snapped, no trace of the soft-spoken flirt of this afternoon in either her voice or her expression. "If you are incapable of meeting even such low expectations, I will see you relieved of your duties to Costa Habichuela immediately, before you can do any harm with your incompetence."

It took every ounce of his hard-earned self-control to remain standing there, unmoving. No one—*no one*—had ever spoken to him like that. As for hitting him . . . He clenched his jaw. "If you would care to accompany me off the dance floor," he said in a low voice, unable to stop the slight shake of his words, "I believe I can correct your misapprehension."

"*My* misapprehension? I, sir, am a royal princess. You are only a duke. And I am most displeased."

The circle of the audience that surrounded them drew closer, the ranks swelling until it seemed that now people were coming in off the streets to gawk. Sebastian drew a deep breath in through his nose. "Come with me," he repeated, no longer requesting, "and we will resolve our differences in a civilized manner."

"First you will apologize to me," the princess retorted, her chin lifting further.

All he needed to do was turn his back and walk away. The crowd would speculate, rumors would spread, but in the end his reputation and power would win the argument for him. As far as he was concerned, though, that would be cheating. And he wanted the victory here. He wanted *her* apology, *her* surrender, her mouth, her body. Slowly he straightened his fingers. "I apologize for upsetting you, Your Highness. Please join me in the library so we may converse." He reached for her wrist.

The princess drew back, turning her shoulder to him. "I did not give you permission to touch me."

At the moment he wanted to do so much more than touch her wrist. God. It was as though when she hit him, she'd seared his flesh down to the bone. "Then we are at an impasse," he returned, still keeping his voice low and even, not letting anyone see what coursed beneath his skin, "because I am not going to continue this conversation in the middle of a ballroom."

She looked directly into his eyes. Despite his anger, the analytical part of him noted that very few people ever met him straight on. Whatever she saw there, her expression eased a little. "Perhaps then instead of conversing, we should dance."

Dance. He wanted to strangle her, and she wanted to dance. It did admittedly provide the best way out of this with the fewest rumors flying. The rumors it *would* begin, though, he didn't like. Was she aware that she was making this look like some sort of lover's quarrel? He couldn't very well ask her. Instead he turned his head to find Lord Elkins.

"Could you manage us a waltz, Thomas?" he

asked, giving an indulgent smile. "Princess Josefina would like to dance."

"Of course, Your Grace." The viscount waved at the orchestra hanging over the balcony to gawk at the scene below. "Play a waltz!"

Stumbling over one another, the players sat and after one false start, struck up a waltz.

That would solve the yelling, but not the spectacle. "May I?" Sebastian intoned, holding out his hand again.

After a deliberate hesitation, the princess reached out and placed her gloved fingers into his bare ones. "For this dance only."

With her now in his grasp, the urge to show her just who was in command nearly overpowered him. Mentally steeling himself, he slid a hand around her waist, in the same moment sending a glance over his shoulder at Shay. "Dance," he mouthed. Not for all of heaven and earth would he prance about the floor alone.

"Are you going to explain to me why you sent a carriage without bothering to attend me yourself?" Princess Josefina asked.

"Your English is surprisingly good for a foreigner," he said deliberately. "As a native, allow me to give you a little advice. No matter who—"

"I will not—"

"—you may be elsewhere," he continued in a low voice, tightening his grip on her as she tried to pull away, "you should consider that in England you do not strike a nobleman in public."

"For *your* information," she returned in the same

tone, "my English is perfect because until two years ago I *was* English, raised mostly in Jamaica. And I will strike anyone who insults me."

That settled it. She was a lunatic. "You're mad," he said aloud. "I can conceive of no other explanation as to why you would speak to me in such a manner."

She lifted an elegant eyebrow. "If I am the only one who tells you the truth, that does not make me mad. It makes everyone else around you cowards."

The muscles of his jaw were clenched so tightly they ached. "I should—"

"You should what, Melbourne?" she cut in, her gaze unexpectedly lowering to his mouth. "Arguing with me excites you, doesn't it?" She drew a breath closer in his arms. "And there is nothing you can do about it, is there?" she whispered.

Sleepless at Midnight
JACQUIE D'ALESSANDRO

Lady Sarah Moorehouse belongs to the Ladies Liter-
ary Society of London, a group of young ladies who,
rather than read proper novels by Jane Austen, would
much rather read books they're not supposed to . . .
Mary Shelley's Frankenstein, *for example. During*
a discussion, the women decide that they, too, would
create the perfect man—figuratively, of course. Each
is assigned a task, and Sarah's assignment is to pilfer
clothing from the host of a country party, the very at-
tractive and very broad-chested Matthew Devonport,
Viscount Langston, who catches Lady Sarah in his
bedchamber, his shirt in her hands.

"Daffodil," Matthew murmured. "Very nice. You're
as talented with watercolors as you are at drawing."

"Thank you." Again she seemed surprised by his
compliment and he wondered why. Surely anyone
who looked at these pictures could see they were
excellent. "I've painted sketches of several hundred
different species."

"Another passion of yours?"
She smiled. "I'm afraid so."

"And what do you do with your sketches? Frame them for display in your home?"

"Oh, no. I keep them in their sketch pads while I add to my collection. Someday I intend to organize the group and see them published into a book on horticulture."

"Indeed? A lofty goal."

"I see no point in aspiring to any other sort."

He shifted his gaze from the sketch and their eyes met. "Why aim for the ground when you can shoot for the stars?" he murmured.

She blinked, then her smile bloomed again. "Exactly," she agreed.

Aware that he was once again staring, he forced his attention back to the sketch pad. He flipped through more pages, studying sketches of unfamiliar plants with unpronounceable Latin titles, along with several flowers he didn't recall the names of, but which he recognized thanks to his hours spent digging holes all around the grounds. One bloom he did recognize was the rose, and he forced himself not to shudder. For some reason the damn things made him sneeze. He avoided them whenever possible.

He flipped another page. And stared. At the detailed sketch of a man. A very naked man. A man who was . . . not ungenerously formed. A man, who based on the letters printed along the bottom of the page, was named Franklin N. St.—

She gasped and snatched the sketch pad from his hands and closed it. The sound of the pages snapping together seemed to echo in the air between them.

Matthew couldn't decide if he was more amused, surprised, or intrigued. Certainly he wouldn't have suspected such a drawing from this mousy woman. Clearly there was more to her than met the eye. Could *this* have been what she'd been up to last evening—drawing erotic sketches? Bloody hell, could this Franklin person who'd modeled for her sketch be someone from his own household? There *was* a young man named Frank on the grounds keeping staff . . .

Yet surely not. She'd only just arrived! Still, in the past he'd made his way into the bedchamber of a willing woman the first night of a house party. . . . He tried to recall the man's features, but as best he could remember from his brief look, his was shadowed and indistinct—the only part of which was.

"Friend of yours?" he drawled.

She drew what appeared to be a bracing breath, then hoisted up her chin. "And if he is?"

Well, he had to give her points for standing her ground. "I'd say you'd captured him quite well. Although I'm certain your mama would be shocked."

"On the contrary, I'm certain she'd take no notice at all." She stepped away from him, then glanced in a pointed fashion at the opening in the hedges. "It was lovely chatting with you, my lord, but please don't let me keep you any longer from your morning walk."

"My walk, yes," he murmured, feeling an inexplicable urge to delay his departure. To look at more of her sketches to see if he could discover yet another layer of this woman whose personality, in such a short period of time, had presented such contrasts.

Ridiculous. It was time to leave, to continue with his mind-clearing walk. "Enjoy your morning, Miss Moorehouse," he said. "I shall see you at dinner this evening." He made a formal bow, a gesture she responded to with a brief curtsy. Then, with a soft whistle to Danforth, Matthew departed the small clearing, with Danforth at his heels, and headed down the path leading toward the stables. Perhaps a ride would help clear his head.

Walking a brisk pace, he reflected on his meeting with Miss Moorehouse and two things occurred to him: First, the woman's in-depth knowledge of horticulture might be of use to him, provided he could glean the information he wanted from her without her realizing his reasons for wanting it—a challenge, given her nosey nature. He'd attempted to get such information from Paul, but while his head gardener knew a great deal about plants, he did not possess a formal education such as Miss Moorehouse clearly did. In having her as a guest, he might have stumbled quite inadvertently upon the key to finding the missing piece to his quest.

And second, the woman very effectively, albeit very politely, dismissed him from his own bloody garden! As if she was a princess and he a lowly footman. He'd not made an issue of it as departing was precisely what he'd wanted to do. Bloody hell. He still couldn't decide if he was more annoyed or intrigued.

Both, he decided. Miss Sarah Moorehouse was one of those annoying spinster women who peered out windows when they should be sleeping, always turned up in spots where you didn't wish them to be, and tended to see and hear things they shouldn't. Yet the dichotomy of her bookish, plain appearance and her erotic nude sketch fascinated him. As did her knowledge of plants. If she could prove to be of some use to him in his quest, well, he'd simply find a way to suffer her company.

For he'd do anything to end his mission and get his life back.

And if, by some chance, she'd followed him into the garden last night, he intended to see to it that she did not do so again.

Twice the Temptation
SUZANNE ENOCH

*In two connected novellas, Suzanne Enoch will cap-
tivate her historical readers with a sparkling romance
and mystery about a cursed diamond necklace set in
Regency England, then catapult them to contempo-
rary times, where billionaire Richard Addison and re-
formed thief Samantha Jellicoe will solve the case.*

"It occurs to me, Miss Munroe," Connoll said, taking a half step after her, "that you might wish to give
me your Christian name."

She paused, looking over her shoulder at him.
"And why is that?"

"We have kissed, after all." And he abruptly desired to kiss her again. The rest of his recollections
had been accurate; he wanted to know whether his
impression of her mouth was, as well. Soft lips and
a sharp tongue. Fascinating. He wondered whether
she knew how few women ever spoke frankly to
him.

With what might have been a curse, she reached
out to close the morning room door. "We did not
kiss, my lord," she returned, her voice clipped as
she faced him directly again. "You fell on me, and

then you mistakenly mauled me. Do not pretend there was anything mutual about it."

This time he couldn't keep his lips from curving, watching as her gaze dropped to his mouth in response. "So you say. I myself don't entire recollect."

"I recollect quite clearly. Pray do not mention your . . . error in judgment again, for both of our sakes."

"I'm not convinced it was an error, but very well." He rocked back on his heels. "*If* you tell me your given name."

He couldn't read the expression that crossed her face, but he thought it might be surprise. Men probably threw themselves at her feet and worshipped the hems of her gowns.

"Oh, for heaven's . . ." she sputtered. "Fine. Evangeline."

"Evangeline," he repeated. "Very nice."

"Thank you. I'll tell my mother that you approve of her choice."

Connoll lifted an eyebrow. "You're not precisely a shrinking lily, are you?"

"You accosted me," she retorted, putting her hands on her hips. "I feel no desire to play pretty with you."

"But I like to play."

Her cheeks darkened. "No doubt. I suggest that next time you find someone more willing to reciprocate."

Connoll reached out to fluff the sleeve of her cream-colored muslin with his fingers. "You know,

I find myself rather relieved," he said, wondering how close he was to treading to the edge of disaster and still willing to career along at full speed. "There are women of my acquaintance who would use my . . . misstep of earlier to gain a husband and a title. You only seem to wish to be rid of me."

Evangeline Munroe pursed her lips, an expression he found both amusing and attractive. "You were blind drunk at nearly ten o'clock in the morning. In all honesty, my lord, I do not find that behavior . . . admirable, nor do I wish to associate myself with it on a permanent basis."

"Well, that stung," he admitted, not overly offended. "Suffice it to say that I am not generally tight at mid-morning. Say you'll dance with me tonight at the Graviston soiree, Evangeline. I assume you'll be attending."

"Are you mad? I have no intention of dancing with you." She took a step closer, lifting up on her toes to bring herself nearer to his height. "I have been attempting to convince you to leave since the moment you arrived. Why in God's name would that make you think me willing to dance with you? And I gave you no leave to call me by my given name. I only told you what it was under duress."

"I'll leave, but not until you say you'll dance with me tonight. Or kiss me again, immediately. I leave the choice up to you."

She sputtered. "If I were a man, I would call you out, sir."

"If I were a woman, I would kiss me again."

* * *

"What do you have there?"

"I don't know," Samantha said absently, brushing dust off the top of the box and stepping to the ground. Mahogany, polished and inlaid—and old. Not some child's treasure box.

"Goodness," Montgomery said, looking over her shoulder. "Open it."

She wanted to. Badly. She was in charge of security for this building, after all, so technically she needed to know about everything inside it. Even old, hidden things. Even when they were inside the stable walls of Rick's ancestral property.

And a closed box of all things—she'd spent the last ten months resisting temptation, but nobody could expect her to ignore a box that had literally fallen into her hands. Rick wouldn't.

Taking a deep breath, she opened the lid. A blue diamond the size of a walnut winked at her. Gasping, she snapped the box closed again. *Christ*.

Montgomery gaped. "That—"

"Excuse me for a minute, will you," she stammered, and headed for the door.

The box gripped hard in her hands, she crossed the temporary parking lot they'd put in for the exhibition, opened the low garden gate with her hip, and strode up to the massive house.

A diamond. A *fucking* diamond. That sneak. They'd been dating—hell, living together—since three days after they'd met, and he'd made it clear that he wanted her in his life for the rest of his life. But he also knew that she had an abysmal track record for staying in one place for very long and that she didn't work with partners.

If this was his way of giving her a gift without sending her running for the hills, well, it was pretty clever, really. He knew she liked puzzles—and a hidden box in a secret hole in a wall was a puzzle. But a diamond wasn't just a gift. Diamonds meant something.

"Rick!" she yelled as she reached the main foyer.

"What?" He leaned over the balcony above and behind her. "You didn't kill Montgomery, did you?"

"I like Montgomery."

For a heartbeat she just looked at him. Black hair, deep blue eyes, a professional soccer player's body—and all hers. The smart-ass remark she'd been ready to make about the diamond stuck in her throat.

"What is it?" he repeated in his deep, slightly faded British accent, and descended the stairs. He wore a loose gray T-shirt, and his feet were bare. Mmm, salty goodness.

Still clutching the box in one hand, she walked to the base of the stairs, grabbed his shoulder, and kissed him.

Rick slid his hands around her hips and pulled her closer. She sighed, leaning along his lean, muscular body. Out of the corner of her eye she saw Sykes the butler start through the foyer, see them, and turn around to head back out the way he'd come in.

Pulling away from her an inch or two, Rick tucked a piece of her hair back behind her ear. "What exactly were you and Mr. Montgomery discussing?" he asked. "Not that I'm going to complain about it."

She took another breath, her heart pounding all over again. "I found it, Brit. It's . . . Thank you, but . . . it's too much."

His brow furrowed. "What are you talking about, Yank?"

Samantha moved the box around between them. "This. When did you put it—"

Rick took it from her hands, glanced at her face, then opened it. "Good God," he breathed, lifting the sparkling orb out of the box by its silver chain. "Where did this come fr—"

"You didn't put it there?"

Of course he hadn't. She was an idiot. Did that mean she's been hoping for a diamond? So much for independent Sam Elizabeth Jellicoe. Great.

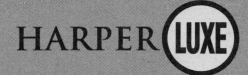